A Factory *of* Cunning

Also by Philippa Stockley

The Edge of Pleasure

A Factory *of* Cunning

PHILIPPA STOCKLEY

HARCOURT, INC.
Orlando Austin New York San Diego Toronto London

www.HarcourtBooks.com

First published in Great Britain by Little, Brown

Library of Congress Cataloging-in-Publication Data
Stockley, Philippa.
A factory of cunning/Philippa Stockley.—1st U.S. ed.
p. cm.
ISBN 0-15-101172-9
1. London (England)—History—18th century—Fiction.
2. Aristocracy (Social class)—Fiction. 3. Women immigrants—Fiction.
4. Scandals—Fiction. 5. Revenge—Fiction. I. Title.
PR6119.T65F33 2005
823'.92—dc22 2004025589
ISBN-13: 978-0151-01172-8
ISBN-10: 0-15-101172-9

Text set in Centaur
Designed by Cathy Riggs

Printed in the United States of America
First edition

A C E G I K J H F D B

A Factory *of* Cunning

Prologue

Scribbled at the quayside, London.
UNDATED
To Doctor Hubert van Essel, Amsterdam

Dear Hubert,

Hounded out of Holland with hardly a moment to bid farewell, I now face destitution in this foreign place: stripped of everything before reaching land! I beseech you to send a letter of credit to the lawyers you once spoke of, at the part of town called Hol-born. Fear of what I escaped; despair at what lies ahead . . . I trust no one and so dare not write more, obliged to give this hasty note to a stranger, with the scant hope that it reaches you.

Does all mankind wish me harm?

When we have found lodgings I shall write more.

With the greatest urgency—

Journal

May 3, 1784
Two Gentlewomen from La Manche

If I ever travel to a strange country again it will in a straight-sided box. Not tossed up and down in a hold full of nutmegs, trapped with a Flemish Harlot and a pinchbeck Lutheran—and the fear of capture, which has a stronger stink.

It had been bad enough beforehand, grinding along in the stage from Amsterdam to Rotterdam, avoiding the curiosity of such unchosen chaff, diverting their attention from me to their stomachs and a growing interest in the ungodly welfare each to the other. Money laid out to keep them fed and sleepy was worth spending many times over. All to be crammed afterwards into the gut of a leaking tub, with shouts of "no room on deck, whores and godsods below the waterline!" lumping us together. We were bullied through a hatch so steep-stepped that the red-haired whore fell on top, tumbling us into a sump of stinking water.

She helped me up, professing to wonder if anything was broken while having a good grab at what was not, until my maid came between us. The priest was making flourishes with his stick, prodding at the sacks whilst trying to smooth his crust of a wig, as if he had been bred on *this fine ship that will have us safe to London in no time.*

Ship? Bitch. Water leaking in where the tar was peeled, the stink of piss to make the strongest sick which, with a clogging dose of damp spices, increased at every shuddering roll.

We were so troubled with discomfort, banged from one side to the other while ropes slapped at our heads, that we were at each other's throats. I was hard put not to grab one of the cloth-wrapped bottles the priest had wedged between two bales (for him and the woman from the Low Countries, though we had paid) to pacify them. After several expeditions behind the nearest bale to unflap himself and leak out against a sodden bulkwark what the sea oozed back, he lolled placidly against his *Friesian cow,* his hand no longer on his Bible.

There is nothing squares the sexes in stupidity so much as a constant need to vomit. I do not know how long the journey lasted; limping in endless dark through the weft of spit-coloured water, grunting forwards, to be pushed back by currents as strong as they were sluggish. Towards the end of a cold, flat night, shouts from above told us we must be near landing.

My maid and I, not willing to witness a renewed twining of our companions, made quietly on deck, pulling our dismal clothes close and shrinking to the side, so shrouded that it was a wonder the captain had taken our word for our sex, when the Harlot must give us the lie. Yet we seemed luminous as Spanish Fly. Hands better put to hauling ropes were everywhere, instead of keeping us clear of the scum of craft ramming our overladen coffin that the merest tap would set flying to a colander.

Bellowed at to make shift, the sailors left off. We crouched to one side, rounding the great bend that a leering hand called Cuckold's Point, where the sky lost its cloud. I huddled against Victoire, watching the dank air throw out a few stars. Paler than the glitter that once lit my native *Place Royale,* these feeble planets pricked at mean buildings cringing from the water like muddled pigs. No wonder England's famous captain, Cook, took murder over such a homecoming. It may be that he sent back a fiction of death, to stay basking with the great winged dolphins of the *Hawaiian Islands.*

Already disheartened by such ugliness, commotion drove us back from the side: an East Indiaman set to nudge us under with its towering walls; merchant ships knit with dots and dashes in the rigging; sloops; fishing boats; coal-ships from Newcastle, so loaded that each swell must drown them; row-boats; skiffs, and sailboats hooped with canvas over brazier and meagre cargo. In every cross-hatched snatch of waves lightermen darted, pitch torches breathing and sucking fire, hustling reckless between merchantman and frigate for an illicit bargain. A hundred ships, if one.

Languages pelted from each side as if the world wove the wet air: shuttles of every tongue flinging laughter and curses, crossed with the shriek and crack of tarred rope and sail. Shouts of sailors clipped our low-slung sea-horse, close enough to smack spray up our sides. Accustomed to it at last, we dozed, until far-off thunder woke me. A bright-grey sky held no rain, only frost and dawn. Someone shoved us. Roused up like rolls of Holland, we were manhandled to where the captain and first mate talked to a man in a short brown coat, who broke off, to offer to help us over the side.

"We are in deep water, would you kill us?" I gestured towards the far-distant bank. The pilot made me lean over and see where a row-boat grated on the broken river, lit by a hooked lamp whose flickering threw the water into sharp flakes like flashes of a giant fish bursting the surface. In such a perilous spot, hemmed by masts and sails, so tiny a craft would be sucked back and crushed beneath our ship's belly.

With our passage in his pocket, imagining what pleasures he would get in Redriff, or along Wapping High Street, the captain was keen for new cargo and men. "I unlade you here," he said in Dutch English, with neither warmth nor interest, as if we were baggage. "Here, you see for yourselves. You are lucky we don't drop you over, and you swim."

"Barbarous—," I began in lively expostulation, when the trollope's face, dabbed with drunken red, popped up from the lip of the hold, as if a whiff of Wapping had got her by the nostrils. That devil's face made me uneasy; her paramour most likely knocked senseless, pockets empty. If the captain and his crew didn't get a lick of what they were longing for, they were cheated. Skirts round her knees, breasts dangling, she laboured out. A squeal from Victoire impressed the captain that, in contrast, we promised neither ingress, nor income. He did us the brisk honour of helping us on to the ladder himself.

"Keep your wits, ladies. There are plenty here who will have your money and anything else they fancy. Nor pay a penny on the steps, or they may throw you back in; no, not till your feet are high and dry. I have seen these ugly men before, and they know it. May God go with you."

Journal continued

Morning of May 3, 1784

That slippery slattern from the *Lightning Bolt* got my pocket book and bills of lading, not to mention other papers. After stamping on my skirts going down into the hold, she had it feeling me for injuries. My pocket slit had seemed too narrow for such common hands—which mistake many women make.

With just the small gold Victoire has knotted in a thin silk tied about her waist, and various items around mine, we are in a bad way until Hubert sends fresh supplies. I can remember only two of the addresses on the list that I had brought for introduction, out of seven that all smelled of money. God willing the harpy can't read French; not so much for those, but for what else was concealed in the purse besides.

I discovered the theft the moment the lightermen set us down on the steps, checking that we were secure against any harm they might propose. Too late! Sneering, not offering to take us back to challenge that grease-handed doxy, they asked if we would like to lose what else we had.

We were at Iron Gate Stairs, they said—tho' one slimy stair is like another—and if we wanted a bed, a kiss gave the address of a

Jewess in the Minories who would *look after us properly*—making me certain we must quit that neighbourhood as seemly as our legs would carry us. I charged the quietest among them to carry a note to the ship's captain, with another inside, for Hubert. Which transaction cost dear.

Above, the Tower rang five. The Harlot had called it *a fine spot to live; a Lady* would want for nothing, she said, and have *the High Life.* This was at odds with what I knew: too many heads had been sliced there for comfort—my own, after our recent loss, felt likely to slip free of my shoulders at the barest touch.

I thought of our precarious state; of the Harlot's way of staring rudely in my face, however close-pulled my veils, as if to mark me, which boldness should have been warning enough. I recalled the notice she took when I paid for provisions—not to see how much money, but where it went after.

Parts of her loose conversation came back: her boasting, with a pretended fineness, to the clergyman (in which he had no interest, consumed by his own bluntness). He had let her run, whetting her with the fascination of her tongue. She spoke of having an important relation (procuress or fellow criminal, most like) an hour and a half's walk from the quayside, and gave the name of this place as Spittle Field, or Fields, exactly like spittle; of which, along with hot air and other queasy humours, she was full. Her distant *Cousin* was Irish, and she claimed some of that romantic blood herself.

Nevertheless I noted the name, *Spittle Field,* in case it was countryside, like my once-familiar *Bois de Boulogne,* where we could look about and find our bearings. But as the lovers talked on, it grew clear that Spittle Field was a bustling part of the town, favouring silk-weaving and finishing; mantua-making, and the arts that go with it. Then I pricked my ears, since she said there were many French *as had escaped persication* in the last century—*Huge-Nots*—to make fortunes in all parts of Commerce. She scorned them as *Catholics,* showing off her ignorance and bigotry. Given her head, there should soon be murderous tales of Blackamoors, Musselmen, and Jews.

I flattered her that she must live in a grand house, although she was the commonest sort of two-penny standup—if she could keep to her hind legs long enough. Baited, she fell to preening, arranging her neck-handkerchief in a disgusting manner for her neighbour's benefit.

There were mansions of many storeys where master-weavers lived, she went on, while God's handservant drooled down her, in Church Street and Princes Street and Browns Lane. Repeating those names soft under my breath I gave a rousing kick to Victoire who, long inured to the discomforts of coach travel with vermin for company, has the art of dropping off so gently you would think *Mrs Agnostic* at prayer.

Even with the sun only half up, the quays were bursting. Voices bounced off the cobbles in slangs and shorthands that could have been Mandarin, which hubbub confused us. The women of the town, uncorseted cocked pistols, were so flagrant they made the ship's whore look convent-bred. Brisk trade was conducting in open view, while others dragged hiccuping culls to get poxed and robbed in a nearby tavern. Packets flew hand to hand quick as eye-bats, to thunder from barrels and carts. Had we not been robbed already we should have been then: turned, trimmed and tossed aside.

We had one bundle apiece, poorly tied in a shawl at which, compounded by our water-draggled clothes, chairmen took one glance and did not uncross their legs where they lounged against a wall drinking, or rested, curled up inside their boxes.

After seeking directions, we took the road alongside the Tower, having been told to continue until we reached White Chapel, a part of the city named after a church so white it could blind. From there, we learned we might ask our way to Spittle Fields.

Trudging along the Minories, watching out for a constant stream of wagons, persistent rain began. Our clothes dragged in the wet, making every step two or three. This stretch of highway left me uneasy, with its ugly, poor houses, some with overhanging floors on the brink of descending to the lower, others that looked thrown up on a whim that might as easily have them down again; a street uncertain of coming or going, murky and dangerous, the air itself festooned with bad intentions. Who would stay except felons and sharpsters, jacks and jades, in the hope that the Light of Law might lose them up an alley?

In passageways so narrow the occupants could touch across the casements, we glimpsed men in layered garments, Turk or Levantine, that I had thought left behind in Amsterdam. Others, more rat than human, watched from the shadows in hand-me-down waistcoats prinked with blackened tinsel and overcoats thirty years old, the skirts sticking out and blades shining out too.

Lingering in a place that recognises refinement as a purse tempts tragedy. Appraised from every side, only exhaustion stopped us breaking into the trot that would be our undoing.

There was not one trace of powder in this unending hell-hole except on the head of a black man with a tanner's apron and fearful knife, who bowed as he passed, from whom we shrank for fear of skinning.

The stink of tanning blowing in from one direction and yeast from the other, with only rain and wind to wash away their cling, defeated us. Poverty soured a running gully and the mud beneath our feet.

Finally, too worn out to care if we sat down and died, we stopped at a cross-roads, until a passing carter offered to drive us. Our protector, John Settle, said he would take us to Browns Lane, not far off, where there were houses with rooms.

"You are certain," I demanded, since by his voice he too was a stranger to London.

Settle said he had once lodged there—in a big house, he added.

He was just arrived from Sussex, *having dropped off a load of earth to the place that made the bells.* This explained traces of soil and a damp shovel in the back, where Victoire was now jouncing, swearing quietly. At other times, he said, since that trade (of providing dirt for bell-making) was irregular, he was a common carter, bringing hay to the Hay Market, or droving.

He wanted compliments for his industry. I stayed silent.

"You are not from England, Madam?"

We were not going along quick enough.

He tried a few countries—Peking and the Ivory Coast—before landing, by some calculation of his own, on Holland. He would not go unsatisfied. No, I lied, I was English, but had long lived in Holland, which had flavoured my voice, *as he so cleverly understood.*

He beamed. "Then you will be content that it is an English house you are coming to. There's plenty of damn Frenchies round these parts, as have lived here so long they don't think we can send 'em back, about which they are grievous mistook. You might wonder sometimes that you aren't in *Paree* itself."

The mere word lifted my heart, while his sad horse stumbled on. Settle was in a mood to talk to anything that did not eat grass.

"The houses where we are going," he continued, giving the bay a tap, "*Frenchy* all through, you can smell 'em. It's a funny froggy scent they give out, just walking past, I have never tried it but my horse likes it. Worse than that, there's women as gives out a funny scent, too. But you wouldn't want to know, being *ladies.*"

"The whole street?"

He saw my expression.

"Don't be alarmed. Only here and there. You'll know the bad ones straight off, they have a very high colour, and a very high—."

"*Thank you.*" I said.

"Fear not, Madam, they won't bother you, they've got other game—although watch out for the old ones."

We had slowed down; he was looking for the turn.

"There are evil places near by here, Warp Lane and Frying Pan Alley. Never set foot there if you want to keep your honesty."

Beneath my skirts, my sopping petticoat-skirts were brown to the knee.

"Perhaps, sir, you also mistake us for *ladies* of that other kind?"

Settle backed against his nag and set off, with an aside to Victoire that if *she* was in need, to send word at the Bell Foundry. *All sorts of bells;* church bells, *wedding bells.* He had a taste for her. Not surprising in a man of earthen compass, who had never set eyes on the genuine French article.

"Warp Lane and Frying Pan Alley," I repeated carefully under my breath, tasting the names and feeling, for the first time, that our feet were about to touch dry land.

We had arrived.

Journal continued

Afternoon of May 3, 1784

As soon as Victoire's languishing lover and toe-rag horse disappeared, we turned on our heels. Settle had driven us along the very Warp Lane that was to be avoided like the plague. It was only a short walk back.

Within the half hour we were in possession of two rooms and a washstand, on the first floor of the largest house on the north side. That is, half the first floor, front-to-back, less the space taken by the stairs. The house was, as I have noted, large; yet otherwise unremarkable, with grey ground-floor shutters nailed shut from outside and a landlady who asked nothing but a week's money on the stoop.

I could not have been more pleased—only dissatisfied not to have taken a look at Frying Pan Alley, which was evidently tailor-made for our particular trade. I sent Victoire to reconnoitre and buy supplies, ignoring her wimpering. The carter had mentioned shops and the market of Spittle Field itself. If Victoire had lungs to make such a noise, she had legs to discover our breakfast.

While she was out, I wrote letters to the only two introductions I could remember, and one other name Hubert had spoken of, as well as continued these notes in a plain book for a journal. When I required writing paper from the lady of the house, Mrs Sorrell, she stared lengthily sideways, before hauling the scullery maid in from the yard pump. Young *Betty,* who looked as though pumping was the most exalted of her talents, was sent off to a nearby print shop. Though comely, Betty was surely simple—unlike her mistress, the frowsiest thing ever seen in possession of property.

I was putting the last fold in my letters when scuffling and a series of barks, or yelps, started up from below. Straight after, feet raced up the stairs. Not women's. Women's feet, when entitled to be described as racing, scamper or dance. Soft leather and the small weight held aloft, the wish to be dainty and the more frequent need to be secretive, lends our sex its lightness of touch, whereas this clopping could only be a frisky colt, or a pair of young men.

At which, two fops flew into the room where I sat rooted by the window. There was just time to pull my cloak round me as they burst in.

"Where have you hidden her?" exclaimed one, advancing so boldly that I began to mistake my possession of the chamber. Despite the early hour both were frizzed, crimped and powdered, with hair near as wide as their shoulders. One wore a blue military-cut and white kid breeches, while the other affected to look pensive, snuff-coloured from his soft long boots to his dusted hair, with negligent linen and a face peaky from powder.

"Hidden whom, gentlemen?"

"Martha, the Deuce! Here the day before yesterday, bright as day—all her things, where are they?" This Poet spoke helter-skelter, as if his verse might be lost if he didn't hurry it along, although the words were so vapid they were already gone from me. Whipping out a lace-edged handkerchief, he dabbed gingerly at his eyes, glaring through its delicate perimeter, first at me and then the bare rooms, searching for something.

They had a point. The room wore an air of having being stripped. Excepting the chairs they sat on—quite at home—and the old writing table, there was a post-bed with a poor mattress on ropes, a carved black *cassone* at its foot, a large corner cupboard, and a stand with a ewer. These fineries constituted the whole. I had not yet stepped in the second room but invited them to do so, and search moreover in the chest and beneath the mattress, in case the missing lady had been overtaken by shyness.

"Dam'me," said Snuff-coat, hurling his skull-bobbed cane on the floor so hard it bounced, "the peculiarest thing, very odd; we were all the best of friends, by God."

"'Specially you, Dads," cut in his blue friend, as the other jumped up and strode off, barged into the small room, barged out again, and crouched on the bed in a pathetic posture.

"Joshua Coats." Blue introduced himself with a bow, hinting that *he* did not bang about as he pleased. "This sad specimen is Dadson Darley, professional fool and Romantic, cousin of the York Darleys, knows a filly that'll go, loses his head at the sight of a lace and proposes at the first flounce. Father in despair. Ought to have been a bonnet-trimmer."

"And Martha?" I gestured to the chair, since Mister Coats would not—unlike his friend—again sit, unless the offer was very plain.

"Manty maker. Prettiest girl in Spitalfields according to Darley—fact is, in all London—that is, since he fell in love three weeks ago. French father, pretty as a picture."

Her prettiness reigned undisputed, but at the sound of her name Darley removed his head from his hands and rushed over, catching his cane up with a sprightliness that said he was mending.

"Prettier than any petty picture! How could some clumsy oaf paint that figure, those lips? They can string pictures up in fancy frames and strut up and down in front of them all day, dam'me, at Somerset House saying *'pon my soul the very life* but if Martha walked in amongst 'em they'd know the difference!"

Mister Coats threw me a look.

"Madam, forgive us, it's heads-on she a'nt here, we've been given the heave-ho, and Dads is in a rant 'cos he laid out two guinea day before yesterday and ten the week before to have her likeness took, and it's clear she's made off with it. . . . By your bearing, Madam, you are not a mantua-maker yourself?"

"Is she? Stitch me sideways!" Darley, half-overhearing, stepped close, fully restored, hope shining so liberally through his thick powder that it was in danger of turning to pie-crust.

Only long practise at dissimulation concealed my indignation at being mistaken for a dressmaker, a thing scarce better than a *common* whore. Looking hard at Darley I was about to pronounce something tart when the street door closed with a loud bang. Everything in this nailed-together household conspired to everyone knowing everyone else's business. The two young men jumped up, in evident hope that their elusive Martha—doubtless laughing her head off on the Calais packet—might drop in for a spot of needlework, but I knew better.

"No," I said, smartly bringing Darley's attention back from my chamber door, on which his and Coats's attention was fixed, "you are right, sir, although my travelling clothes may have misled you."

Coats blushed so ferociously I had to bite my lip. "But by strange coincidence I am here to be measured by one—the young woman even now upon us, to whom these rooms belong."

At this dramatic moment, Victoire—blessed innocent!—walked in.

The dear girl, though well-practised in all manners of deceit did, like the best actors and actresses, need a morsel of time to get up her part.

Struggling with a straining basket, she was so new to this one that she had not even noticed our visitors.

"Sooth, Mademoiselle," I called out, to ward off her blurting something contradictory, "*are there no pins* in the whole of Spittle Fields? Do you dare call yourself *a dressmaker?* What a time you have been! I might have taken my own measure *for a gown,* stitched it and cut another, aye, since you have been gone!"

Victoire's back was to the room, settling her basket. A certain rigidity let me know she was debating whether her mistress had gone lunatic during her brief absence. Turning slowly, she took in our new friends at a swift glance. Who, oblivious to anything except her face and figure, lounged in easy postures, legs agape, dabbling in their waistcoat pockets as if trying to outdo each other in doltishness. She then curtseyed so low that I was afraid of her going into a dead faint, until her expression proved the profound trajectory a means to gain time.

"Begging madam's pardon, I took the liberty to examine some tambour'd muslins just come in a bale from Lancashire, at the mercer in Princes Street. Pure silver and gold thread, madam, no one would believe it was done by human hands."

"*Certainnement* not English ones," I quipped, under my breath.

"I took this liberty entirely on *madam*'s behalf," she went on blithely.

Again the wicked girl plummeted to the floor, so that I wondered if she was forgetting that we were not at the Opera.

"Yes, quite," I snapped, adopting Evil Witch to her Innocence Abroad; "One dares say that your ideas of the exquisite, *Trichette,*"—fixing her with a very hard look—"are not mine. I beg you remember that, before taking any more decisions on my part—however much *Her Majesty Queen Antoinette* praises you."

I stood up and the rakes leapt from their chairs like scalded whiting, faltering apologies for the intrusion, staring dewy eyed at the Prodigy from France. Any thoughts of Martha, I vouch, *bouleversées* out of the window.

The second they had gone, we fell upon the basket.

Letter I
Undated
To Lady Danceacre,
Hipp Street, Mayfair

Madam,

I write on the recommendation of Doctor Hubert van Essel in Amsterdam. He begs me present my compliments to your Ladyship. I am staying at rooms in Spittle Fields, but am anxious to improve my situation. My servant will call at Eight in the morning to request when I may call on your Ladyship.

Respectfully, Madam—

Letter II
Undated
To Sir Charles K—,
Russell Street

Sir,

I have the honour to write on the recommendation of Doctor Hubert van Essel in Amsterdam, who begs me present my compliments to your Lordship. I am staying in rooms in Spittle Fields, which are enough for my present needs but, since the occupants of the house are of the lowest sort, I am anxious to quit it. My maid will call at Nine in the morning and beg leave to await your kind instructions, whether I may call on your Lordship.

Respectfully, Sir—

Letter III
Undated, very heavily perfumed
To Urban Fine, Earl Much,
Salamander Row
near Lincoln's Inn

Sir,

May I present compliments and a letter of recommendation[1] to your Lordship from Doctor Hubert van Essel in Amsterdam. I add my own unworthy ones in order to advise your Lordship that the volume *Curiosities of the South Seas, and Fashions and Customs Peculiar to its Natives* is in safe keeping, until such time as your Lordship may desire it. I am at a temporary suite of rooms in Spittle Fields where I am not able to receive visitors. My servant will call at Ten in the morning and I beg leave that she may be suffered to await an indication of when I might call on your Lordship.

Your most humble servant—

[1] A forgery

Part One

May 4, 1784
From Sarah Beddoes
Housekeeper to the late Lady Danceacre
Hipp Street, Mayfair

Madam,

Your letter, requesting an audience with Lady Danceacre, lies before me. With regret I must inform you that her ladyship has not been alive this past month, having succumbed to a dropsical inclination that no Physick could allay. My mistress was, as you doubtless know, alone in the world except for her son, having lost her husband in the French Wars. Lord Danceacre, her sole heir, had been living abroad. He is very recently returned to London and Hipp Street is to be sold; the contents to be auctioned immediately, the day after tomorrow, once Lord Frederick has seen them. There may be things that you would wish to acquire, madam. Viewing of my Lady's effects begins tomorrow, at nine o'clock.

With great sadness in conveying this unhappy news,

Your humble servant—

Journal

May 4, 1784

On receiving the *woeful* tidings of an *unmarried heir,* I put off a planned exploration of the immediate neighbourhood to pursue this more profitable course. My bundled garments were shaken out and brushed. I advised Victoire to look equally to her own things, since I would not start my new life—*on which our existence depended,* I reminded her—with a ragamuffin trailing in tow like draggled plumage.

For supper there was a bottle of claret apiece and what food she had found—not unreasonable bread, although we were predisposed to find it heavy, a poussin, cold meats and potted shrimp. We ate heartily and retired at once; Victoire to the small room where, from the imprecations against our slatternly landlady and Flea-Bitten Scabbed Harpies, I understood that she slept badly on the floor, beneath her cloak. As the grumbling subsided I slept too, to be woken directly after midnight by an amorous kerfuffle in the street (Victoire's room faced towards the back). It was easy to hear what was going on from the enclosure of my bed; the boisterous couple might as well be frolicking alongside me, since neither bed nor windows had curtains, and the shutters had been removed—to which sorry lack I intended drawing Mrs Sorrell's attention in the morning.

All thought of sleep cancelled, I made myself comfortable with a glass of wine. Phrases that were impossible to understand, both from the coarseness of the accents and the filth they contained, floated up. Having just passed two years in exile in Holland studying English under a fine tutor, I strained to follow. There was one female voice and a series of three male, possibly four—there was a long period of rustling, provoking anxiety in case my new acquaintance had deserted her post—to which fear fresh footfalls put paid. Coins clanked, lacking the sound of silver. Then came the thud of a great parcel or sack dropt, and a repeated metallic noise that was surely spurs rasping stone, all accompanied by gutteral snatches, including *Chocolate Betty,* and a deal of muffled laughter.

English is a queer tongue. My own much-mourned language veneers dissolute phrases with delicate notions so that the trumpery stays hidden until, the ear having lost the words, the soul unravels their sense. By this means, insults remains misunderstood until the bestower is beyond arm's length, when mortification becomes a lonely dish.

English, on the other hand, assails like a blow. No subtlety—just plain facts, like currency thumped on a table hacked from the tree.

After a bout of further importuning followed by imprecations, the front door key turned in the lock. Despite sitting bolt upright ready for all-comers (in case we were about to be molested), there was no further sound. If someone climbed the stairs, it was on velvet feet. My next impression was of Victoire, waiting to dress my hair.

Journal

Morning of May 5, 1784
A Story in a Sedan Chair

Lacking the means to a carriage—despite having business in view—and since there was no hurry, I decided to go to Mayfair by chair, not knowing that London is bigger than Paris and Amsterdam together. Victoire had long set off on foot to fetch answers to my outstanding letters, before making our rooms more comfortable.

My own business was at the address of the lawyers Hubert had at last sent, at *Hol-born;* thence to *Mayfair,* and the house of Lady Danceacre. As I descended Mrs Sorrell's creaking stairs to mount my winged chariot, one of the chairmen lolling in the hall let out a whistle that I ignored, so he blew another, which met the same fate.

Betty was crammed fearfully under the stairs in the narrow passage to the yard, as if she had never seen a sedan in the hall before. I told her to sweep my rooms and bring linen and a pallet for Victoire, and look lively. From her motionless gawking there was no means to judge if the words struck home. The simpering way in which she twisted her hands behind her back and thrust out her roomy chest implied that she was in Venice, with two princes in a gondola come to whisk her to a masque. I gave her a tremendous clack to the back of the head with my enamelled fan. Victoire would need to talk to Mrs Sorrell.

The runners were still staring, clutching their poles. It would be a strange thing if a French noblewoman of eight and twenty, precociously skilled in all manner of arts, could not command the admiration of a pair of British carriage dogs. Happily, one was gripped at last by the whimsical notion of helping me in.

The morning had turned out brisk, we went forth at a fair speed. Sunlight sharpened a city I had never set eyes on, which now shewed better than along the river. Yet these streets were nothing against Paris, or those Dutch gables and canals I had so recently been forced to leave behind.

The men found a pace. As they jogged easily along, my thoughts turned to the rank and fortune I had lost two years before, leaving only a clutch of jewels to ward off destitution. For two years I had forbidden myself all thoughts of the past, but now, as we turned clumsily into Threadneedle Street, I cast back.

I had narrowly escaped certain death in Paris, creeping out at night on the road for Holland, with just Victoire to go with me into darkness and the unknown. Bandaged, bundled in cloaks in case we were stopped, in a closed carriage for which I paid ten times over, since my coachman had fled, we had scarcely rested till Compiègne. A *maid* as sole companion for a *Marquise* fleeing to exile. How far fallen! Yet this maid, bound to me since childhood, was the only person who would not betray me.

Even after the passage of so many months, the memories made me burn with rage, so that it was a wonder that my own indignant heat did not propel the chair along.

I had been wrongfully implicated in a scandalous affair that rocked Paris, in which several had died. For which—though it was no fault of mine—the mob considered hanging too modest a recompense. So, fearing the worst, I had the courtyard gates of my hôtel chained. After several days when the clamour showed no sign of lessening, putting my life in increasing danger, I saw that I might be arrested. Victoire let out the news that her mistress had been siezed by a smallpox virulent enough to satisfy the bayers for blood, Old Testament zealots. Drunk with prophecy, those yelping leeches nailed handbills to my gates, calumnies torn down by my servants in the night, only to have others spring like teeth. One portrayed me as the Whore of Babylon, which was an uninspired comparison.

It is well known that a smear on a master attaches to the servants. How long would my staff stay loyal? I should soon be at the mercy of a bloodthirsty mob. Fortunately, I have a disposition that revels in rational decisions and swift action: a military mind that, in such an isolated situation, is prompt in strategy. Thus, details of the dreadful contagion increased, seemingly spilled from my household but, in truth, all done by Victoire, who went in a variety of ingenious disguises to all parts of the city, seeding false accounts of my lurid condition in coffee-house and tap-room, mercer's and hôtel yard; which seeping stories she topped up daily with bulletins of fresh agony. All Paris knew I swung between disfigurement or death.

At that time, a paper was nailed to the gate containing a ditty whose threats were real and whose phrases revealed its author. I kept the vile thing by me, to remind me to stay vigilant—until the Harpy on the *Lightning Bolt* took it, along with the other papers in my purse.

Terror began to master me, as if the doors might be beaten down, the windows smashed, and fire thrown in. I was insane with fear. For five days I paced my prison behind tight shutters with just one candle, afraid of showing too much light. To those for whom dragging a superior woman through mud has more glitter than gems, my seeming illness must have threatened to rob them of vengeance. Such scavengers take nothing less than death or a crippling. My situation had become precarious. If it was death or disfigurement the filth wanted, I would give them the latter, from the monstrous plague they believed me to writhe under, more terrifying to beautiful women than outright death. Immediately, false news of my rapid decline made it imperative to send the servants off.

Victoire saw to the arrangements and gave me her account over supper, which we took in a small octagonal room with no external windows, where we felt reasonably secure and could dine by plentiful light. She had gone to my maids and manservants, her cheeks and forehead reddened and greased as if she was in a dreadful sweat, hair disordered, clothes disarranged and her manner wild, flailing at them red-eyed (rouge), as if she too was contracting the loathsome disease. She had described the hideous pustules bursting out over my face, raining down the left side and onto my bosom and arm, likening my delicate skin to the rind of a particularly pungent cheese; with the eyeball on that side suppurating, the pulpy flesh round it turning black; how she had tied me to the bed so that I did not tear my eyes out or scrape the chancres from my breast, and how there was such an ungodly stink coming from the leaking wounds that Death itself hovered over my blistered lips, licking its own leather limpet for a kiss. Laughing, Victoire wrenched another crisp wing from the chicken, balancing a piece of blistered skin on her nose.

As her speech progressed, the maids and footmen that were gathered in the kitchen crept backward, stumbling over each other to put distance between them and her—who, enjoying her role, advanced steadily, wringing her hands and, for good measure, drooling on to a large fowl and other delicious things set out that otherwise, she told me confidently, they would take once her back was turned.

Finally, fat Jacques advanced towards her with a broom. She put on a bold countenance and cried out my munificence in ringing tones. Drawing forth a bulging purse she declared: "For the love of God, your mistress begs you leave this damned house and spare yourselves!"

As tears sprang to her eyes (I fear she was embellishing events in her own favour), she went on, "Though your beloved, broken mistress can scarcely speak—so great is her nauseating disfigurement—her only thoughts are of you, dear friends, and the service you have done her. She sends you this gold, and wishes you God Speed." There had been a year's salary apiece in the bag, certainly enough to buy complicity. I doubt it all found its way to the kitchen.

Inspired by her own gibberish, Victoire cast the coins rolling on the floor towards them and staggered off, locking the door from the other side, staying without long enough to satisfy herself that they had all fled, before returning and bolting the heavy outer door from the street to the yard and that from the yard to the kitchen. Then she came to me with the magnificent spat-on fowl aloft.

These memories crowded so vivid upon me that I had lost any sense of where I was. We came suddenly into the shadow of a towering dome that must be St Paul's, as fine in its way as Nôtre Dame, certainly better than the Hanoverian churches, even though they are lofty. This part of the city housed many shops and businesses: banking, Doctors of Law, import brokers, tailors, tobacco merchants, coffeehouses. My chair was in constant danger from other sedans, as well as fast chariots, coaches, riders and wagons. Despite what I had been told, nothing had prepared me for such thriving enterprise, being prejudiced against the success of any nation other than my own—a characteristic by no means exclusively French.

I called halt at the lawyers in a nearby court and let the runners rest and guzzle ale for some half hour, before taking off again, greatly recharged, toward Mayfair.

Journal continued

May 5, 1784

Infusing one's spirits with nasty recollections gives an unhappy cast to any countenance. To liven mine I looked about at this prosperous neighbourhood, the houses of four or five storeys with spanking paintwork, finnicky metalwork, and footmen lounging in front. Carriages bearing arms passed on all sides with liveries hopped up on the back flexing satin buttocks and twitching their queues. Gentlemen and ladies stepped from magazines strolled on pavements raised up out of the dirt and droppings.

We passed through a vast, irregular square of grand houses, whose centre—a small park—was being measured. Strings were pegged on the still-bare earth. An overdressed gardener and his assistants preened in the middle.

Moments later a dainty sedan, grasshopper to my slug, passed rudely close. Framed against the linings lolled a small person so modishly dressed it hurt. Translucent muslin purfled at her bosom, diamonds and topaz spat on her breast, her hair such a soft shade and so brilliantly spangled it would have made any Parisian coiffeuse wilt. Even her runners wore powder-blue, matching their doll-like mistress and the gleaming chair. I nodded at her and patted a packet freshly pinned inside my skirts.

Without warning the rival sedan stopped; we heard the lady tap. Steaming with sweat, my lusty men jolted up its backside, scarce avoiding a direct crash, and threw me from the seat. With no thought to whether I was still living they began beating the nearest and most unfortunate blue runner about the legs and body with their poles, until he shrieked in pain.

We had collided outside a smart red house with stone facings, with a great portico like an inverted shell out of which, had Primavera attempted to arise, she would have plummeted on to the stoop. Iron balconies frolicked across the first floor, from whose tall windows Greek gauzes blew. This was the house of Lady Danceacre (as was, deceased); now that of Lord Frederick (sole heir).

So I was more than annoyed to see Miss Muslin mincing up the steps, ignoring the battle between her unwrinkled puppies and my scabby whelps that was gathering pace behind.

Letting myself out of my own chair—else I should have been

found Starved through Neglect, like some poor soul in the Château d'If—and ducking their fists, I followed.

Journal continued

May 5, 1784
A Guided Tour

The imposing door of Hipp Street, Mayfair, was propped ajar, braced for an onslaught, inviting all and sundry to step in. Its housekeeper, Sarah Beddoes—whom I recognised at once from her new black silk gown, apron and cap—stood deferentially at the back of the hall, with an inscrutable look.

The spangled vision swept in and tossed its gloves on a console with gilded legs and griffons. Round the claw of one of those monstrous animals—half bird, half door-handle—a parcel ticket attached with red silk twirled. Similar numbered tickets were tied to every thing—perhaps even the housekeeper had one tucked about her person. She must have wondered, alone at night knotting dockets to twenty years' memories, why she had not; or pinned one to her bosom, with the figure 1. For, unless someone bought her, what would her future be?

Catching sight of the sparkling visitor, Mrs Beddoes grimaced. No other word fits the contortion that tweaked her countenance like a November breeze, to be as suddenly replaced by one of blanket ingratiation. She came forwards, hands in apron pockets (where they were visible through the tucked black organza), head on one side. Her smile clearly stated, *I know you, you worthless little harpy; trouble since the day I first clapped eyes on you, the sooner you are out of here the better!*—but to the recipient, I imagine, it expressed servitude. Beddoes made a curtsey whose immaculate lines were congealed with contempt.

"Good day, Mrs Salmon, ma'am."

"Mrs Beddoes," declared the other lady, in a voice so high and carrying that it took me by surprise, having what I would later come to recognise as so much of the Estuary in it, mixed with the Fleet, that it was a wonder the Lady didn't have a tail flapping behind, and gills instead of a muff.

"Mrs Beddoes," she ricocheted again, extending a fin to the grimacing housekeeper, who instead battened her own mittened fists more firmly into their organza pockets, where the angry knuckles were curiously reminiscent of Honesty seeds, "what sad news, and how dreadful you must be sufferin'."

The object of her cod sympathy tried a smile as Mrs Salmon went on, blithe as butter, "How many lovely things, all waitin' to be *knocked down to the highest bidder!*"

She swept a look round: at the circular hall with its double stairs and a pendant lamp, the size of a barouche, on a massive chain from the grandest of *palazzos,* down which putti summersaulted; those gilded tables to rival Versailles, whose shining tops held Sèvres Elephant vases and pot pourri caskets like monkeys with perforated bellies; at busts of Diocletian and Caesar on pedestals carved *in the Doric style* as though hewn from potted meats; and a frieze across the ceiling three floors up, ramping down to where a well-endowed Apollo dangled his left leg over a cartouche whose occupant might well blush as she cast her eyes heavenward. On the first landing was a daub by the lady-painter, Cow-something, in which Lady Danceacre figured as a portly Diana, giving every appearance of having just taken a bite out of her headdress.

Mrs Salmon's *panorama* only lasted a fraction of a second, before roaming off past a handsome clock to a doorway that framed a picture on the opposite wall between the windows to the street, in which a pink slipper aimed a flying kick at a pair of oyster breeches. Beyond those windows' shining panes, under puffy chestnut blossoms, a well-drawn profile now passed.

To the millisecond at which the clock let out an acidic *ching,* Mrs Salmon caught sight of me observing her.

"Well *my Goodness*—," she had started when, abruptly depriving us of the knowledge of whom beside her had this quality, she broke off again, eyes flicking like quicksilver behind me, while I stood bolted to the Carrara by her performance.

"*Goodness* if it an't Himself, Lord Friderwick!"

At which, she genuflected.

Hearing his name squawked round his hall, the man whose noble features had only just traversed his own windows, stared at her.

"I don't think I—?"

"Poppy Salmon, *Actress*—" she began. Mrs Beddoes coughed. "—And Simultaneous Sensation! At your service, sir!"

Salmon's hoity-flighty manner and a second curtsey more ingratiating than the first, was so good as an opening act that I wondered what she could reserve for the next.

Mrs Beddoes whipped out a black butterfly of handkerchief and spluttered into it, while Lord Danceacre looked at Mrs Salmon incomprehendingly. "Quite, quite, simultaneous sensation. . . ." He trailed off and turned to me, raising a chestnut eyebrow. To establish, I believe, whether I was synchronised with the simultaneous sensation or might—as his expression hoped—be an independent, discordant one.

With a marked step to one side and cheerfully falling in with the theme *du jour,* I took his cue.

"Sir." I addressed him and, by default, the two ladies: "I learned the tragic news only yesterday of your dear mother Lady Danceacre's death." (A small, discreet bow put more distance between me and Mrs Salmon who, under a pose of listening, was seething with rage, while the froth on her bosom agitated continuously like two cups of hot milk.)

Monitoring that phenomenon out of the corner of my eye I went on: "I arrived only yesterday from the Continent. This kind lady"—indicating Mrs Beddoes with a nod—"suggested my visit today.

Yet—without impugning her noble motives—if I had known that I would perforce intrude on your grief . . . oh, *sir!!!*"

The theatrical mode was catching.

"Forgive me for coming at a time when you must be in such distress. How utterly unsympathetick!" At which I stretched out in a gesture of supplication, to show off the line of my dark green *redingote* (from which Victoire had bullied most of the creases by sleeping on it), then turned, poised for flight.

The great door stood open, casually propped by a head of Pompey, its ticket jaunty over one ear. I wondered if that general would have approved my tactics, for my *tableau vivante* was surely as moving as any portrayal of Diana and Actaeon—and a deal more so than the rather solid one in common view. Twisted in this untenable position, I was glad when Lord Danceacre stepped forward, sidestepping Frothy Salmon, to seize my other arm just before I toppled over.

"Egad, madam," he pleaded (twenty-eight or nine, I would say, and richly handsome), "this tender sensibility touches me mightily. Please allow . . ."

Ignoring a sound of boiling-over coming from somewhere nearby, he propelled me into the room on the other side of the hall, a well-appointed study with comfortable chairs and a fire—and pushed the door firmly to.

Journal continued

May 5, 1784
Refreshments

Lord Danceacre loosened his coat and made himself comfortable in the larger of two chairs by the fire, removing a small book on which I could make out the word *Otranto* that he tossed into the flames.

After so long abroad, his first impression of Hipp Street must have been like mine: a mausoleum of strangers. Here, in the private office of the housekeeper, were feminine things. A work-table with a frame for embroidery; a shelf of novels, and one above of graver works, amongst which were both Locke and Rousseau and several tomes by someone called after an ape. A desk held a neat pile of books that must be the household accounts; a porcelain writing set in green and yellow and a jug of primroses. All the belongings of someone intelligent beyond the expectations of their calling.

His Lordship rang for fortified wine and Mrs Beddoes brought tiny biscuits fanned on a napkin and a dish of hot-house plums quartered and pipped, sprinkled with Madeira and cinammon. I had not eaten since the night before and was glad that Lord Danceacre lunged upon the pastries with absent-minded greed. Under the astonished gaze of Mrs Beddoes, we ate ten between us and allowed our glasses to be refilled.

Meanwhile, Mrs Beddoes told Lord Danceacre of the stream of visitors filling the building, following the announcement of the auction in that morning's newspaper. A gentleman from *The Times* in the drawing room and the *Gentleman's Magazine* in the library, the *Monitor* by the barometer in the morning room, the *Salivator* drooling over the bannisters, the *Bon Ton* in her Ladyship's bedroom, the *Bon-Bon* in the dining room, *Tatler* in front of a conversation piece and the *Sunderland Gazette* in the coal cellar, all making pages of notes.

Footmen were stationed on every floor, she went on, in case anyone took a shine to something and preferred not to wait to bid for it. Most of those who came were Gentlemen and Ladies, she added, cocking her head, what knew of his mother's work with girls from the Foundling Hospital and the Magdalen.

A question had been hovering. "Mrs Salmon?" ventured Lord Danceacre, grazing on another biscuit. An intaglio glinted on his left hand.

Mrs Beddoes remained fascinated by her plain black slippers, so he tried again.

At last, in a tone under which suppressed triumph lingered, she answered that the creature had *flounced out the way she come in!*

But what I considered splendid news (and Danceacre seemed relieved by) was not what his Lordship meant: which was, in short, *who on earth was she?*

We both looked expectantly at the housekeeper.

Journal continued

May 5, 1784
A Fishy Tale

Mrs Beddoes moved the tray out of her master's questing reach before clasping her hands against her crisp silk, where they acquired a votive look.

"Five years ago, Salmon came here to be her Ladyship's personal maid, with a recommendation from a Lady Salts, in the village of Epsom."

Lord Danceacre suppressed an awkward snuffling.

"She was passable at her duties, although evidently untrained; whistling, or skylarking with the spice-man, if she got half a chance.

"Your dear mother—a *Saint,* sir—put up with it for companionship. Salmon's flightiness diverted her Grace, for there was no one else young around her."

Mrs Beddoes suddenly went red. She had accused Lord Danceacre of abandoning his mother and the number on her auction ticket had just shot up into the Hundreds.

Yet, why *had* he gone abroad, leaving his mother alone? But, overcome by her inadvertent charge against the man in whose hands her future lay, Mrs Beddoes was unable to continue.

"Go on," he said, touching her hand, ignoring the discourtesy.

Mrs Beddoes curtseyed.

"That girl had fingers so nimble they could make her Ladyship's hair and dress as fine as anything at St James's. So, her . . . her . . . *faults* . . . were overlooked."

I glanced up sharply at Mrs Beddoes' tone. What she was thinking was different to what she spoke, of which both she and I were aware.

"She was given dresses—too fine for her own good; and she fitted them to her shape. They gave her ideas. Shortly after she had been given an almost new wrapping-gown in Chinese silk, that fell loose on the breast, she stayed out all night. I am not saying sir, that it was the dress as encouraged her—those presents were an example of your mother's charity. It was what the girl made of it, quite without modesty.

"She was here a year and a half. Apart from a superior attitude that did not fit with the rest of the staff, who called her Miss Fishy, she gladdened her Ladyship's heart."

Lord Danceacre poured me a third glass of Metheglin, from which the perfume of rosemary came. Mrs Beddoes watched in a way that was either distressed or thirsty.

"Her Ladyship was very attached to Salmon, sir. One morning the girl didn't come to dress her. Gone! Her Ladyship told me she had dismissed her—which was not so, begging forgiveness—and bid me give her room to one of the other maids. There were presents in it from her Ladyship to the girl. An ebony table and a rosewood sewing box. They were never spoken of. I put them in the attic, and attended Lady Danceacre after. A few months later, news came from an under-housemaid who had it from a porter at Covent Garden, that Salmon had embarked upon a career as . . ."

Mrs Beddoes shuddered.

"She had set herself up as . . ."

Her meaning was unmistakeable.

"She made a great deal of money. Oh! She had rare talents! Some *gentleman* started her, and soon she was parading along the Row covered in diamonds, with a house he set her in at Marylebone Park. It was impossible to close our ears. The world knows of her goings on and her Evenings. Every week we hear her name, or see it salacious in the newspapers. Her Ladyship never spoke that Strumpet's name again.

"In the first flush of notoriety she called to leave her card—more than once. As if your mother would see such a jade! Impudence! My Lady never knew."

I glanced at Beddoes again, who this time returned my unspoken inquisition with defiance.

"Yes, I burnt them all, all! And threw the ashes in the street!"

Thowing *me* a stare that said *do what you durst, I dare you,* Mrs Beddoes left—taking the last of the refreshments with her.

Where was Marylebone Park? Was it smarter than Hipp Street? What were the Evenings the newspapers wrote about? I was turning these questions over, looking at the gloves in my lap, when Lord Danceacre interrupted my thoughts.

"You said that you came from abroad with the intention of seeing my mother?"

My wits were required, since a head-on collision of *his* familial interest with *my* inclination to secrecy could prove disadvantageous to my career prospects.

I smiled softly.

"Your mother's name was given me by a learned Doctor, on whom she had made a profound impression, many years ago. That noble gentleman counselled me to make myself known to her, that she might advise me in a city where I am *without friends.* Alas that I never met such a shining example of womanhood!"

I laid it on thick, for Freddy Danceacre was not one for subtleties. Bemused, apparently more interested in interrogating my lips than me, he was as wide open as the Sargasso Sea, which is why Poppy Salmon had flown across London to sink in her talons. Though her plan was foiled for now she wouldn't leave it there; but the bird was, for the moment, in my hand and nowhere near her . . .

"Poor, dear, child!" He grasped at my wrist. I let him be a while, before withdrawing with a sigh.

"You have come all this way to seek the protection of my mama and she has left you destitute!" He went on, inclining gently towards me, as if he was an obelisk of ice, and I the sun. Or perhaps the other way round. "Dearest girl!" I took sharp note of the exponential familiarity. At such a rate we should be married by tea-time. "Do you know anyone else in London?"

Danceacre's oily care for my wellbeing was merely to establish how vulnerable I was to his advances. His words made me shudder. There were people who thought me a disfigured fugitive, as good as a murderess; those who *knew of me*— and would have me tried for my life if my identity was uncovered.

"No, sir," I sighed, showing pretty white teeth, though I say so myself, "such joy is not mine.

"I had placed *all* my hope in your mother. Beyond her, I know no body."

I let my hand fall into my lap so woefully that Danceacre snatched it up again, creeping a little closer, his moleskin breeches denting my skirts. Now that he felt me to be unprotected I was fair game, as easy a prospect as a summer spinney stocked with pheasants to a seasoned poacher. Before I knew it he would be striding in knee deep. I let him stew in that absurd posture, calculating when he would lean over for a kiss. He eased a little, limbering.

Bolting upright I put down my glass with a ringing reproof, at which he bounded to the windows.

Frederick Danceacre:
—standing almost six-feet high—
with chestnut curls inclining to the poetic
and a slender figure; an excellent rider, sporting
high boots polished so hard I could have
seen my own expression in them
if I had bent to look

What a baby! Anybody's for the asking, like something in a plate-glass window, or an apricot to cram in one's mouth. But his brief indulgence as a lover might jeopardise longer-term uses. Furthermore, his brand-new coat with its dashing collar was unmistakeably the work of one of the finest tailors in Paris. And tailors are the worst gossips in the world. His cravat was tied in the French way, too. He might have heard of me.

"Damn me for a dog, madam, you must think me insufferable," he strode back, still in the high state that contemplating swelling May buds had not calmed.

"You came to see Hipp Street, which I have prevented by the most . . ."

With slow, soft sweeps, I was fanning my bosom.

"Most—most—moreover, madam, let me introduce myself."

He stood waiting for my reply.

Journal continued

May 5, 1784
A Quandary

Danceacre stood flapping his glove against his thigh and moving a plum pit around the boards with his shining boot-tip as if it might invite him to a gavotte, while I considered leaving on any pretext and quitting the country. My sudden flight from Amsterdam had left me unprepared to meet someone who might have heard my story.

He must recognise a French accent. My original idea, to pass as half-Dutch, would fool no one. Even after two years in Holland I scarce spoke that tongue, while my English, though excellent, still bore traces of my birth. How ill-equipped I was to move in society, without the risk of being unmasked!

I missed my real name. Would it ever be spoken again without loathing? Two years in the company of young men of the *naval* and *military* kind had taught me I was lost without it. Strip the silks and laces, refined gestures and haughty accents from a woman of title and she becomes—nothing. Or, rather, that thing whose sound echoes nullity—what I became and intended to become again: a Whore.

In Amsterdam I was *Madame Combien.*

It would not serve here.

He was still waiting.

"*Madame—de*—Mrs—Mrs—*Forks!*" I managed with a gasp, almost shouting the first name that crossed my mind, one that had been yelled over and over by a mob with banners earlier that morning as my runners fought their way through a large square.

"Bravo!" Danceacre exclaimed, clapping, "Spit it out! The same as the politician for whom the hustings are out! What a jolly coincidence! Tally-ho, what! Mrs Fox! May I call you that? I an't one for French, by and large. Do you give a fig for the Whig, Mrs Fox, ma'am?"

I had no idea what he meant. Nor cared. He accepted the absurd name and I breathed again.

"Evident you ain't a student of our politicking. Quite right, a bore. Hardly pay attention to who is in and who is out myself: change quicker than my man's shirt. If this fellow gets the job he'll have a devil of a time keeping it. It's no good belonging to the Pup when the Sire's still hearty. Have you come now from France, madam?"

"No."

My briskness startled him. "No, sir, I was living until recently at the port of Amsterdam, in Holland."

"But you *are Française,* madam, if my ears don't give me the lie? *Common tally view, hey?* Formidable, *hey, what?"*

He would not drop it.

"If only, sir, it was possible to take refuge in one nationality; but, in truth, having travelled since childhood—with, too, a Dutch mother"—a nice touch—"should I call myself French, Dutch—or even English? I am of Huguenot descent. *Something* of me I hope *is* English—that fine, tolerant spirit that sets your countrymen apart!"

I moved myself with this oration.

"Ah, yes," mused his Lordship, "how insensitive you must think me. I know all about the Hugnoses. There are many of them, Mrs Fox, some fat from silk and all manner of cunning, spinning things.

"I sincerely hope"—he made a bow from the waist, as if hinged—"that you discover yourself descended from *those* fortunate beings."

He dandled over to look at me earnestly. A pompous ass, despite finely turned legs on which the breeches sat as if painted.

"I had no right to wish to know your history. Lord knows madam, had you been a *Fugitive from Justice* it should be none of my concern. May I show you the house?"

We joined the small crowd wandering about, oblivious to the man by my side. No one recognised him. Some held a list, on which they jotted.

"That tall fellow with the rubbed coat," Danceacre whispered, "I'll wager he's one of those dam' Grubsters, come to reckon up how much the old Bird was worth."

I stared at him, in astonishment.

"I bet they've all got a gamble on how much the mater'll fetch.

"Reason I'm havin' an auction. Flog the old girl to the highest bidder—damnable enticing! Fetch a sight more than she ever would alive!"

"Let us go on," I said quietly, wondering whatever she could have done to him, to make him despise her.

He came to his senses and ushered me ahead.

It was a rare house, ripely furnished. What could be swagged was, to the apogee of swaggadocchio. Every inch of floor had a chiffonier, divan or vide-poche. The walls vied with the galleries in Bond Street and sculptures competed for gaps: a history of heads; four satyrs; full-length blackamoors bearing cornucupias or baskets of fruits, or juggling the two; a quarry-load of marble nymphs. In the centre of the library table loomed a mountainous carving with three naked Gods holding up a gilded girl by the buttocks. Lord Danceacre explained that this was Wisdom, that should be held aloft; in which case I agreed with the playwright that Wisdom was an ass.

We passed a pair of life-size naked bronze satyrs either side a doorway, guarding it aggressively, in a very novel fashion.

"They'll have to go," Danceacre observed, blinking repeatedly and steering me in the other direction, "Deuced modern."

The *Goût Anglais* of a devout old widow was not what I had expected.

It must have stung his mother that Poppy Salmon had launched her career from these rooms, wearing her Ladyship's clothes. Lady D would writhe in her sheet if she knew that that harpy had just come here, newfangled and spangled from Whoredom, to seduce her son and get her wealth into the bargain. She would thank me for pipping Poppy to the post.

We stopped at a half-length portrait of a seventeen-year-old in old-fashioned tan velvet, one hand poising his soulful chin, while a white and brown dog gave a competing performance. Books, scrolls of music, and a metal pointed object like a bent poker, littered the carpeted table.

Young Man in Girlish Outfit with Snivelling Dog could only have been ordered by a doting mother. This treacle spoke much of the painter's grasp that the boy was a Mollycoddle. It was by the face-painter Gainsborough, Danceacre told me with indifference, adding that *Maestro Buttony* had done him recently in a palazzo in a ferret-edged toga, which was a spanking likeness. But Gainsborough got my vote, for the look of the lurcher knew a fool when it saw one.

The picture must have been done just before Danceacre went on the Tour to shower his mother's money on harpies and charlatans at twice the going rate, teaching peasant girls a new meaning for the word *ruin.*

We visited the other floors conducting our own *petite tour.*

"So, Lord Danceacre, what of you these past years?" I asked.

"Ten years. Alps to Asia Minor, Casablanca to Copenhagen. If you've read that Shandy man, it's an afternoon jaunt next to me. Russia, Sweden, Austria, Italy, Spain . . . a year here or there, when something caught my eye."

He meant women. I ignored his smug look.

"France?"

"Had a good poke around. You can't say it has anything as decent as Rome. Places in Africa have finer architecture, don't know what the Froggies've been piddling at all these years. Versailles ain't bad, I'll give them that. Good drainage. That fellow, Nostril, the one who did our King's park: he knew a thing.

"Anyway, I was kicking about in Paris when old Beddoes wrote to come back. Only been there a week, barely time for a suit. Had to spur the tailor on, which was a bore—he skipped on the whipping, look."

Despite Danceacre's flippancy, I was relieved that his stay had been cut short.

As I took leave, he demanded to know where he could call. I lied without hesitation that I was staying at an Inn and would send a more permanent address later. He would not be satisfied.

"Let me at least offer you my carriage."

I bowed. "I have a chair."

"Honour me."

"My chair, sir, is waiting."

We bowed in unison, almost cracking our heads, trying so hard for ascendancy over each other that we had become exerted. Danceacre's face was flushed. Had there been sand in my pockets I would have flung it at him.

"Then," he insisted, "I must leave you here."

A minute later, a handsome footmen escorted me to the hall; Danceacre, I knew, watching from the landing above—to which end I showed an ankle and fanned myself, entirely for his benefit.

Journal

Afternoon of May 5, 1784

My chair was nowhere to be seen. Three coaches had usurped it. A canary yellow one with ebony strapwork had an Oriental in a black silk coat frogged with red a-perch the box, like a fisherman on a plate. I idled past, in case my idiot runners were hiding behind or in front—*inside,* for all I could tell.

The smirk of the livery on the step told me that my sedan had been paid off, to make me beg a carriage. I was determined not to be cowed. With thrupence in his pocket, he sent a boy running to a stable nearby, while I strolled to the end of the row.

The streets that had bustled earlier were now practically deserted, save for two crippled children cooking a cat, and a woman sitting darning her clocks in the gutter. There must be a Hackney carriage somewhere; I had seen several earlier, and many inns and stables.

Wishing to be out of sight of that smug nincompoop Danceacre, I set off in the direction I'd come. At the end of a deserted street, Dadson Darley rounded the corner at speed.

"Halloa! Whoa-up, Madam! What an unforseen pleasure, to meet you again so soon. What deuced good fortune brings you running straight into my arms?" He flourished his chapeau-bras, looking strangely familiar, in an overdone purple Great Coat, his hair teased disadvantageously horizontal.

"I am waiting for a carriage." My tone was stern. He must not conceive that I habitually walked the streets alone. Darley looked first one way then the next, his hair so peculiar that one could have been forgiven for thinking he had put his wig on sideways.

"Here?" The horizon was deserted.

"I have been at a viewing, at Lady Danceacre's."

Darley let out a whistle.

"Whoa once more and again, whoa!! Does that sort of thing interest you?"

Pacing easily alongside he missed my bewilderment. "Top girl, Mother D. Best bawdy house in Mayfair. Fifty guineas a go, a hundred for something peculiar. There was a red room, with a trapeze and a padded chair, and a couple of girls who commanded very high; and, with respect, some queer statues. All the world went. *Tout le monde.*" He giggled. "Princes and whatnot, right down to any one with the lolly. I was sorry to hear the old girl snuffed it, but they say she wore out her moving parts.

"General Beddoes, the housekeeper, was minded to keep it on, which was cheering, only the fool son has just come back and scuppered a worthy project, my opinion. Dim as a post, dandified as a doyly. They'd fed him the line that they were running some sort of charity for penitents and the deranged, to explain all the persons running about in a state of undress. If only he'd stayed away longer, the General might have persuaded him to join the firm. Well, that's the gossip, though it's being kept *sotto* so he don't cotton on by accident. From what you say, the sale's going ahead."

I was not so sure about Danceacre's being oblivious—rather that he was beginning to understand all too well.

But Darley took silence as an invitation to continue.

"You are remarkably ahead, madam, for one so soon arrived. I bow to you. One admits one wouldn't mind a look. There were a few things one had taken a shine to, might be rather amusing if. . . . *'ods nightgown,* ma'am, you're not related to the clan? It ain't the death what's brought you? Deuce if it is!"

"Forgive me," I disengaged myself. "Allow me to pause, I feel faint."

Mr Darley prodded his cane at some horse-spattered straw.

"*I say.*" He was all contrition. "God strike me, you didn't know anything about it! Look here, there's an agreeable coffee-house a stroll that way. Perfectly alright for the ladies, Blue Stockings and so on; above board, my honour. Everyone's milling about for the election. I should think you'd take to it—intelligent, what—it'll pick you up."

It was preferable to go anywhere than wander London hoping for a Hackney or, worse, be obliged to crawl back to Hipp Street.

We went along quietly, coming to the square where earlier, men had been marking the ground.

"What do you think of this?" Darley nodded towards it.

"Are they laying out some sort of giant game?"

He began waving his cane vigorously at one of the men, whom I now recognised as Mr Coats. "Let the fellow tell you himself," Darley said, "all his operation. *He* ain't just a pretty ninny, like me. In with the top brass, brains of steel. Hurrah, *here* he comes, waddling along, all the time in the world.

Pleased to see me, Joshua Coats took up Darley's thread.

"It's going to be full of trees." His factual tone was restful, but Darley interrupted.

"Great big ones." Balletic movements of his arms turned him into a nutcracker. "Idea's a bolter. We're going to club together and get up a statue of the Old Man for the middle, ain't that the case, Coats, hoist him on a pony. Subscription or what-not. They're measuring the ground to see how things will look. Coats has roped in a genius"—Darley gestured at a third man, far away—"to decide which is best. Then we'll go and talk to the money men. It *is* a sort of game, now you mention it."

He laughed, pulling his hair even further sideways. Beneath the profession of foppishness, he was articulate. Coats let him talk.

The third man was crouching in the huge, raked plot, turning one end of a long string round a peg, taking up the slack. The other end was right at the far side of the square, fixed to another peg pushed into the ground. Having secured his end to his slow satisfaction, he squinted along what looked like a quadrant and fiddled some more, teasing the peg from the damp earth and moving it an inch to one side. Then he set out astride the string, in a rocking fashion, as if beating out a melody. His too-big coat flapped behind. Head-down, feet apart and narrow legs clad in grey stockings, a crane searching out lugworms.

"Black!" Coats hallooed. Turning, the man peered towards us, then reclasped his hands behind his back and resumed the slow promenade.

"Black! God-dammit!" Mr Coats bellowed so loud it was amazing that the whole square didn't fling open its windows, or a beadle come running Nothing stirred. The houses looked quite new.

"Blind as a bat," Darley explained, joining in.

The Genius Mr Black, at last deducing that the caterwauling was for him, set out towards us.

"He ought to wear his spectacles but I daresay he's lost them. I've told him to tie them round his neck with a bit of galloon. Devil to replace, and he's quite useless without. So many of these clever fellows are," Coats observed, finishing just as Theseus, having picked his way between the guiding strings, arrived.

"This," said Mr Coats proudly, "is Nathan Black, our friend from America. Mr Independence, greatest painter in the world, exercising brilliance in the planting of trees!"

"One gets such a bloody introduction," Mr Black reflected laconically, without any attempt at a bow, twirling a couple of inches of twine to and fro between the ball of his thumb and his forefinger. Not nonplussed by such an opening, nor that we were strangers, staring as he spoke, as if the ground had opened up, leaving him, and me: Let me put things straight, ma'am.

He now bowed, carelessly. "Nathan Black, Barely Tolerated American Upstart, Impoverished and Unpatronised Painter, of whom all hope is not quite lost, since he is currently enjoying a sinecure of two days standing at half a guinea all-in as String Roller-Upper and Arboreal Plotter to His Moneybags, Joshua Coats, Bart. At your service in the peg-and-string department. Ma'am."

He topped this with a nicer formality, smiling on the way up. To which I made scant repartee; for my legs could not be relied on for the return journey. The day was becoming warm.

All three men looked expectant.

"Sir. I have always felt that our American cousins must be orators as well as soldiers."

Black took the compliment with eyes so dark it was as if I could see right inside his head, or they were hollowed from basalt.

If the truth were known, I had actually assumed that all Americans wore feather trousers and bonnets, with bare chests, and powder horns or arrows. On the whole then, Mr Black's appearance was disappointing. There was no point having a confrontation with a savage if they were as civilised as oneself, in possession of scientific instruments and cogent understanding.

"Excuse me a moment." Black turned to Mr Coats; yet—by what Magick—continuing to pay me unwavering attention, "Coats, it is surely the custom in this backward, useless country, for a gentleman to be introduced to a lady?"

"You have got me, Sir! I made the acquaintance of this charming person under irregular circumstances, breaking into her apartment and accusing her of hiding Darley's fancy—who has run off with the money for you to paint her, by the by! Forgot to ask her name."

Coats bowed to me.

"As in the dark as you, Sir."

They all beaded me once more, prime-full of expectation.

To be in possession of three fine young men and not profit is, to a woman of my worldliness, a bungle. I was faint with hunger and thirst. Someone had to master these toddlers.

"I know no one in this town, sir," I retorted, "no one, no-body, *personne!* Until I am sure of myself, it is preferable thus.

"I would be grateful for those refreshments," I added.

"Mystery!" Dadson Darley burst out. "Spirit and Originality! There's too little of it among the fair sex these days, they all seem to be patterns of each other, like those little dolls."

Black's head turned, like something badly oiled on a turret. "*Dolls?*"

"Yes yes yes, little dressmaker-dolls, flippety things in falderals and flim-flams, all the rage. Come over from Paris. . . ."

We had begun walking. "*Poupées.*" I supplied involuntarily.

Black exploded. "Dolls! Poupées! Great God, has this woman turned you and Coats *frocksters*? Are you *Mush*?"

"Steady!" Mr Darley looked shocked. "Only complimenting the lady on her mettle, no need to take on. Keep abreast, what? Fashion, what?"

His peevishness was not real. It was the English thing they call a dead-pot sense of humour.

Black cranked round again, with a brusque apology.

"Good!" Coats smiled. "Now we've got that cleared up we'll have something to eat. You in, Black?"

From his own side, while Darley dangled along behind, making great passes and lunges with his cane, a hand behind his back, thoroughly diverting passers-by with shouts of "Ho there, Frenchy!", Mr Black was at me even harder than before. After a deal of time on my face, his narrow eyes dawdled down and up again, as if once in the habit of measurements and lines he wasn't in a mood to quit.

"If Mrs Mysterious says so," he declared, finally.

Journal

May 7, 1784

"We will adapt our plans."

At my words, Victoire dragged her attention from a plate of Oxford John. The delicacy, a ragoût of lamb with parsley, in which hearty croûtons jostled, had been presented with a bob of dissimulated pride by our landlady Mrs Sorrell, who stood by to lift the cloth and lid, snuffing up the steam and claiming that she could also make a *Polard Besh-a-Mel* if we gave her the satisfaction, as she had a little knowledge of fancy cooking and was in possession of a book.

Here was a woman amenable to boiling a *ragoo* like the one she set before us, or even a *curry*—expressed with lingering wantonness—but if we desired anything more dainty than *those* dishes, we should have to go to one of the nearby taverns *and see how we fared then!*

I am not averse to a piece of well-done flesh; vegetables stewed or roasted; good bread with sweet butter; a pippin or other native fruit; cheese, fresh or rotten, and wine—which Britain cannot make, despite assertions to the contrary. Better that than have a cook run amok with flummery and spun sugar, or *Carp Ponds* leaking live goldfish from pastry coffins, to shipwreck a good table.

My maid and I adapt to circumstances, choosing between misery, that makes one sour and useless, or electing to change and flourish. Self-pity is an indulgence that excludes the weeper from preferment. Diamonds on the cheeks are fetching in the armoury of a young woman, but tears of rage in older women (for so they always prove) are a trial to the spectator. Loathing and revenge are not served by being prematurely advertised, and ugliness, all women should observe, is an end in itself.

Nevertheless, we were pleasantly surprised that between our landlady, shiftless Betty and the boy who ran errands when not farting under the stairs, such a supper had been produced. I restated my words, in case gluttony had spoiled their effect, and Victoire prised the tines from her mouth with passable grace.

"We have spent several days," I repeated, "in what unfortunately appears to be the only respectable house in the street."

There was a married couple at the top, months from their first baby. The sixteen-year-old wife took in mending. Her husband hurtled down at dawn and came back slower at eight. He had another woman. The young bride gossiped with Betty; they had fixed farthing bells at either end of a cord that went through a gap where the stair turned so one, by tugging it, could summon the other.

We had not seen the man who rented the rooms above. *The Scribbler* minded himself, Mrs Sorrell boasted, and had been away, coming and going being his custom; but was now back. We had heard a chair leg grate while we were at supper, and a slow footfall that might have belonged to an elderly or cautious man. If his name had been mentioned, in that whispering awe ordinary persons hold for literary types, I have forgotten. Were I Shakespeare, or St Simon in my own country, it would be irksome to be bundled in with all the pen-wielding flotsam with which both nations, sharing an enlightened attitude to literature, abound. The fellow was most like to be a forger, government agent, or spy—a criminal imposter who had once been seen holding a pen within striking distance of a piece of paper and traded on the admiration ever since.

Another room on his floor was used as storage.

"The only decent lodgings house in Spitalfields," I continued vengefully, taking a spoonful of root artichoke stewed with cream and too much mace. "We will have to be more cunning."

Journal continued after supper

May 7, 1784
The Story of the Pearls

Since I had just spent two years running an Amsterdam Cat House, the career I had sketched for us in London was that of straightforward whoring, in a sympathetic house. Given our skill in the craft, I anticipated rapid progress and betterment. Unfortunately, our precipitous flight had left no time to establish necessary contacts. That was my fault; in Amsterdam I had grown complacent, putting off the time to leave, half thinking to settle there. Besides, as the Flemish whore showed, Fate unknits man's efforts faster than he may secure them.

Beyond the idea of a life of immorality dedicated to financial gain, we would take things as they came. This part of town did as well as any to start, as nocturnal activity along the street proved.

In our Dutch notch-house we had employed up to six girls: one permanent, a sort of housekeeper; the others living close by, with their husbands, or other trollopes. They came when needed and gave up half what they took.

One leg's worth, you might say.

This was more even-handed than the practise elsewhere, and left them richer than they could gain honestly—which, to be frank, none attempted.

For our principle trade we attracted respectable men who did not wish to leave their family, nor had the courage to maintain the mistress they felt they deserved. Our placable whores were an acceptable alternative. The men were greeted and a girl arranged. They ate and drank with dignity, playing cards or politics. The decorum of an ordinary drawing room heightened their satisfaction. Nothing was irregular, no one became excitable. Other establishments catered for saltier tastes.

Every particle of our divers entertainments their own wives could have provided, had they taken the trouble to rise from their slack-arsed boudoirs and unglue their fat lips from rimming the chocolate bowl.

Aside from that stout clientele, we had a *specialité de la Maison.* The back stairs were used by sailors leaving port, who must show their embarkation papers to the doorman—a farrier or surgeon, I forget which—he still had a leather-apronish quality.

Our two sorts of culls never mingled.

The little house was a bandy affair squeezed on the corner of a cross-street with a pair of small rooms on each of its floors and a staircase front and back. Faced with neat black-and-white herringbone brickwork, it was enhanced by a family of piebald cats that grew from a basket of kittens and preened like chameleons on the sills.

We had a reputation of amiability, if such an unholy racket could. I was never recognised out of doors, although now and then I went, as veiled as a convent on the march. People believed me crippled. Victoire's was the face that was known, or so it was thought. Indoors, despite having plenty of her own hair, she wore a powdered wig in an ancient style and a great deal of colour, creating the arresting effect of a Watteau aspiring to be a Boucher, looking forty-six to her real nine-and-twenty. The corollary of this misinformation was a perfect disguise for going abroad—as herself—unpowdered and in servant's dress. On other occasions she sailed forth as a lady of rank or a slender footman; in which versatility I have already mentioned she was elastically adept. Under the title *Madame La Vôtre,* Victoire was our figurehead. The name's invention was a whim that became familiar, the house soon was nicknamed "La Vôtre", underscoring its homely, available nature.

If we had a single difficulty during those two years, it was of sometimes needing to turn men away, since we refused to scrabble after profit by dividing the rooms for custom, as other places did. There were never more than four young women working at any time.

Nor did we attract the displeasure of the law. With good reason. Our accounts and many other affairs were managed by a doctor (of philosophy, or he might have saved us much more money), called Hubert van Essel, who lived next door. Having led an exemplary life of scholarship, at forty-eight van Essel had become bored. When, as fate had it, we met.

Fluent in Latin, English, French and Spanish, he had published several treatises and was highly respected. He liked the *theory* of what we were doing, he said, but felt disinclined to test it; he enjoyed seeing so much life about the place and treated the Harlots retiringly. Eccentric—but this did not trouble us. A brilliant mathematical mind, kind heart, and tractable nephew in the town hall were all we desired.

Van Essel had studied at Leyden and travelled in his youth. He still knew one or two people in London (one was Lady Danceacre) and he taught me English.

I have noted that, as well as solid Dutch burghers (or anyone making a good impression), we catered to fired-up young sailors setting out on long journeys. On occasion we entertained soldiers leaving for campaigns. No men but these doomed souls ever saw my face. By the time they were allowed up to the top *to pay their respects,* they were too drunk to take in details. If they did, their memory of Madame La Vôtre's deformed sister was confused. Not one could have recognised me if we ever met again.

We let it be known that, living sequestered after being born lame, I had turned fanciful and believed myself a Queen, wearing and powdering white, in a sort of quaint court dress—only not so wide, since it was impractical in an attic. Victoire spent whole evenings engineering this garment; I would surprise her in the act of its embellishment, until she pricked so many holes it turned into a sieve. I made her start a copy.

In those white overskirts with meandering flounces, held out over hip-pads; a white satin petticoat embroidered with shells and twisted ribbons; a feathered fan; feathers in my hair and, as I have said, jewels and pearls everywhere, I was frankly alarming. English sailors liked it best. Some fell to their knees and called out Queen Bess; others other things.

They began to send presents: most often a pearl stolen or bartered in the East, in packets stained by grease and salt, sometimes blood, or swaddled in batik. One came wrapped in a leaf become skeletal on the way, another in chewed bark tied with uncured gut. The tokens arrived more frequently in our second year, so that by the end we had two hundred and seven pearls, a pair of fine pink pearls, two coral and one lapis necklace; a jade bracelet carved with dragons and a ring with a big black-foiled diamond that we were too cautious to assay. All from lonely men stuck on an ocean, certain they would one day redeem them in kind. Not one did.

Apart from its obvious meaning, my pseudonym, *Madame Combien,* stood for the game of guessing the number of pearls on my dress. I told my visitors that all were gifts, from Pasha or Pharaoh, Prince or Potentate—whatever conjured their imagination—until they swore to send better. Not hard, every one being paste. Each man was under the illusion that he was unique in this bold thought. Whatever the case, after a little time manoevring for a kiss or modest familiarity, enflamed to an absurd pitch, they were smartly escorted below, *where a servant would attend to their needs.*

I never attended to them myself.

The moment we had first arrived from Paris I had sold two bracelets that belonged to my dead husband's estate. They and a family necklace (his family, not mine) comprised my wealth. It took few questions to find a dealer who would reflect what might be called, by persons interested in regularity and legality, *indifference to provenance.* I swallowed his offer, a fifth of their worth, for the five-minute transaction gave enough to rent and appoint the house for a year, with a housemaid and other sundry needs.

Yet, despite a sort of dull comfort, I had no real wish to stay in

Holland for ever. Its very safety became a torment. Even growing financial security could not soften the fact of being an outcast pinned to society's hem, roiling with the pimps, tars and harlots. There were times when I could have thrown myself into a canal. Alas, picking death is not for the damned. Age would find me dragging the same burden.

But there were other days. On one occasion, watching an amorous couple kiss, I saw that my life could be redeemed: not by repenting my sin, *but by consigning it to oblivion.* Remembrance of old iniquities flooded over me, of abandon and unscrupulous indulgence. I could have danced, urging the lovers to deceive each other and know the bliss that betrayal brings.

What had I done that others did not compound? I had been one element in a chain reaction where gold, in a bastard alchemist's sorcery, had rotted into lead.

Watching that ordinary couple kiss once more, I knew that it was time to start afresh. Never in France, for there I was utterly ruined; but England appealed, once time had softened the scandal. Anyone who remembered would recall my being scarred and blinded, and look out for such a tragic woman. So, I grafted to the idea of England, but the date of leaving stayed unnamed. The second winter still found us in our magpie home, with roaring fires and roaring trade.

Journal continued

A Sailor's Story

The diamond dealer had given me van Essel's name as an honest man in a city of thieves and it was our fortune, having made that man such a handsome profit, that he spoke truth. Doctor van Essel let the house to us on reasonable terms for as long as we wished. He soon became more than our landlord. A man who, exposed to Harlots his for the asking, pats them and passes on, is beyond rare. I knew I would be sorry to leave—although never admit it.

Then, without warning, our tranquillity was destroyed. Two full years had passed when one cold day a sailor, different from the rest, came softly up the back stairs. Though dressed as an ordinary seaman he was older than the general run, with a countenance that set him apart.

Every young man who came to the attic sat and talked to me, mainly idly. Inevitably in cups, they had one purpose in mind towards which, whatever they spoke, they were driving. This man's otherness was clear the moment he stepped into my room, ducking where a low beam cut across. His movements belied his given rank: something in the way his hand touched the door-post in passing, the way he held his hat—as if it was the chapeau-bras of a gentleman, not the bonnet of an ordinary sailor. Everything was wrong.

I tried to collect myself, using my fan to hide my troubled face.

He was English, Mr Martin said. Might he use that tongue, *or would I rather French?*

"*Good honest English, Sir!*" I laughed, *or any thing he liked, Russian if he so pleased, and that I would understand well enough.* Speaking low to prevent my voice shaking, I rang for the best Madeira and glasses. In due course these were brought up by a man. That request was my signal to have someone stand by. It was the first time it had ever been used.

Sitting easily next to the fire, thin legs out towards me, for all the world as if describing the compass of his earthly estate—or mine—Martin stared unblinking, while I hid behind the trembling fan, back from the light of the fire, although greatly in need of it. He began to speak.

For years, he said, he had been a captain and travelled the world. Then he lost his ship, in disgraceful circumstances.

He told his story as if it had been rehearsed countless times. Although contained, there was great emotion in him. This, combined with his glance, made me very nervous. For no reason I was seized by the fancy that he might set me alight. All the while, his supple left hand held the glass with that elegance already noted. I saw how well his clothes had been fitted to him, a thing no commanding officer would allow. Mr Martin was neither what, or even who, he seemed.

I rang for someone to stoke the fire. This was my second reminder to my servants to post a man at the foot of the stairs and the door to the street. A pretty girl came, making a charming picture kneeling at Mr Martin's feet, face flushed, hair disordered, bodice astounding low for a housemaid. While the fair maid's attentions warmed me, Mr Martin was indifferent to all but his tale.

He told how he had put down a mutiny, on a passage from Brazil, that had come to a head at the Cap'Verde Islands. He hanged the ringleader and put the rest in irons. In this way they got home, but the legs of two men became inflamed, their feet so swollen that pus spurted, so the irons were cut free. Despite such clemency, they died in sight of port. Once on land, Martin's first mate spoke against him, that he had used undue cruelty, and so provoked the rebellion. The mate made himself a hero in his account. It turned out later that one of the dead men had been his brother. Mr Martin lost his commission.

He had finished his wine, so I poured again.

That was two years earlier. His family left him. His wife *had been the wife of other men*—he could not say what he really meant—and would not stick by him, dishonoured.

I began to think that his anger was at Whores in general and that he would rise and stab me. Yet, while his eyes stayed downcast and his hands steady, I did not ring. He began again. All he knew was sailing, so he took the first passage that offered, a short trip bound for Marseille. There he looked about for another, and a few days later was taken on by a small French merchantman. One of the crew had heard of him and betrayed him to the others. He feared for his life, keeping away from them as much as possible, staying on deck at night, certain that his throat would be slit if he slept.

The ship carried five passengers, two couples and a young man. Sometimes the couples came up for air, content in each other. The solitary passenger spoke to no one, even turning from the captain when the latter tried to engage him. Observing this, Mr Martin felt drawn to him, watching him stand gazing at the sea. Convinced that the young man intended to throw himself overboard, Martin determined to save him, or die in the attempt. It did not matter which, he said.

Watching Mr Martin stroke his hands as he might calm a bird he was about to dispatch, remembering that he had hanged a man, brought me to the point of crying out. But, sitting between me and the door, if he wished harm I should be dead before help came. That steadied my nerves. "Go on, Mr Martin," I urged, bent on putting an end to our meeting, whatever it proved to be, "finish your tale, tell me if you saved that unfortunate soul."

"There was no need, ma'am." Curt, as if addressing a master's wife. "We arrived at Malta, and he disembarked."

The strain went off him. He stretched, as if we were old friends.

"Thank God," I said, utterly perplexed. "And did the men treat you better after?"

"That I did not find out."

Mr Martin's manner made the rest of the room disappear into blackness.

"I was told to row him to shore, which I took for a hint, meant or not. I jumped ship and went along with him, after that."

There was a quality in my guest's eyes that I had only seen twice before. Once in my own, in a mirror just before I fled France, leaving my whole life trapped in the glass. One other time too, in the eyes of a man who had vowed before God to destroy me, whom, it was whispered, intended to join the Knights of Malta.

At noon next day, hoping to throw off pursuit, Victoire and I boarded the stage bound for Rotterdam, with just one bundle apiece and a few papers, to commence our circuitous route to England.

Journal

May 8, 1784

Over a late breakfast of cold pond pudding pitted with fruit peelings and pips I outlined my new plan to Victoire.

"Since we have already declared you a seamstress, it will serve as a front as well as any other. Furnish both these rooms in a seemly fashion," I told her, handing over a purse, "as the rooms of a successful mantua-maker—not a troll, or corset-cutter. Remember you are supposed to have the ear of our Queen, not the cunt of a rabbit.

"However small beer our own royalty is in this country, it still excites them, as you have already observed. Do not let this money undermine your common sense, and do not give me that reproachful look, either. Forget the past two years.

"Put a cutting table and some bolts of cloth in the back room. Get two made gowns from the 'Change and peg them up as if they were samples. While you are there buy laces and ribands and leave them trailing from a box. Take paper shapes from that gown (I pointed to the one I was not wearing, visible through the doorway, hanging on the wall) and pin them along a string. Make some up. You have seen how it is done as well as I, the rest is up to you.

"*This* room must have nothing of that business. The bed in red harreteen, with covers to match. Fix the other furnishings as close as you can to my smaller retiring room in the Place Royale; you remember. Nothing too bright. Worry some dust in if need be and rub the floor with sweet wax. When that is done, bribe someone at Mrs Salmon's establishment in Marylebone Park and find out every detail of what passes there. How many Whores she has rotting for her, how much, who, how often, how much to pay off the Watch. Everything."

Victoire looked at me.

"Yes, you are right: and who owns it—for certainly it is not her."

Before she could protest I handed her a piece cut from a newspaper, dated the day of the house viewing, with an indiscreet advertisement on its last page, for the Ultimate Simultaneous Sensation, including the Bed of Sultanas. There was an address in Marylebone Park.

"I have other business. I will find you when I need you, so do not even think of taking up employment with that puny fluffed-up harpy. I will let you know how to find me . . . *Mademoiselle Trichette.*"

Her expression made me laugh. "The name's irresistible, it fits. I should have thought of it long before. Your given name is far too inflexible for your numerous talents."

Lips pressed (but much mollified, I knew well), she handed over a folded paper, bearing a queer yellow-grey seal, the handwriting small, with an intriguing address: Salamander Row.

This was the last response from our enquiries since we arrived. I saved it to read till last. As I placed it, with its thin sharp corners, to one side I caught Victoire muttering something about *cutting cloth* that had aught to do with the trade of mantua-making on which she now found herself embarked.

Journal

May 8, 1784
A Fool and his Money

Victoire's diligence in procuring answers from the other two introductions I had written on arriving in London had finally paid off, in the shape of a conversation, and a letter.

She discovered that Lord K—, the gentleman I remembered from Hubert Essel's lost list of introductions, had married for a third time, to a chancer forty years his junior, whom he had met *incognito* at Ranelagh. He had been slumming it with some old cronies, looking for a dirty petticoat to tear another hole in, when love's young dream came swaying out of a threadbare bosket. A week later, immediately after the wedding, he took his bride up to his estate in Scotland. Not much after, they returned for the season, where the young wife thoroughly enjoyed herself, even though her new Lord's estate was one of the finest in Argyllshire and should have been more than plenty for such a cheap trick.

Alas, Victoire told me mischievously, across what had been touted by Mrs Sorrell as *terrine de lapin aux ceps* but was pig belly with burnt field mushrooms, his frolicksome bride had exulted in London a little too much, making a circle of friends from which her Lord was excluded, despite paying her gambling and dressmaker bills to the tune of several thousands of pounds without complaint, for he was besotted. A year afterwards, at the approach of their second season, when she was yet without child, his Lordship had an accident climbing a gate. He declared that he would follow Love to London as soon as he was mended, having sprained himself in such a way that he could only use a carriage with great discomfort. She was dismayed, forsook all idea of leaving and declared the stubborn intention of staying by his side. After a few days of pampering, the doddering old fool was overcome by an access of joy at her constancy. He had a paper made out, settling the London house on her with immediate effect, over and above what she could expect as his widow. There was no bar to such an act, since he had no children by previous marriages, although there was a younger brother with a living in Wigtown with four daughters in various stages of marital difficulty equivocal to the seasons, and their several children.

After a further spell of panderment, the young Ladyship came in with his breakfast one morning, for she insisted that no one else feed him. How pale she had become, how thin! It was as if the transformation had happened overnight. Her Lord was so alarmed that he summoned his doctor and demanded that she be bled.

Victoire was regaled with all this over a stimulating glass of posset by the lady's maid in the house next door to his Lordship's in Russell Street, who all the time kept her sharp-skinned eyes on the lower halves of passers-by out the window, in case her *own* Ladyship should come unexpected home, whose dainty silk ankles she knew as well as her own.

This maid then told Victoire how Lord K's wife had indeed got thin overnight, by the scandalous trick of having a bodice made bigger than her own size. So that, putting it on, she seemed all abruptly to be wasting away.

Which, the lady's maid observed, no *woman* would be deceived by.

"Nor no normal man neither," the bootjack cut in, having just slammed the kitchen door and come stamping down the stairs, "but his brains was so addled with it, he wouldn't know his fundament from his condiment."

"Addled with what?" I desired to know from Victoire.

The answer was not salutary.

On being thoroughly questioned by her alarmed lord, her Ladyship, alternately fighting tears and covering his scabby hand with kisses, said that it was not that she missed the ridottos (giving his hand an extra benison), or the fun, or the company of her dearest friend Mrs C (who was her own age, *and expecting to be brought to bed any minute, with much tribulation*) but that she was afraid for his comfort; and that being by him, day by day, watching his distress and *quite powerless to help,* was making her so unhappy that it was eating her alive.

At which the nincompoop immediately sent her to town in his best-sprung coach-and-four, lavished with every comfort: heated footstools, dainties, two footmen up on the rear to protect her against all comers, and a little black and tan puppy he had got off the keeper's wife as a companion, for he was a kind old fool. The amount of luggage she took did not surprise him; it was flattering that she travelled in such a grand manner.

A week later, when he was starting to mend and making his own preparations to join her, in the rackety vehicle kept for his attendants, he discovered what was missing. Plate, gold, and the fabled Boss of Cladich that had been in the family for fifteen generations. By the time he was able to get his Factor to London on horseback, three days ahead of the slow coach, she had stripped Russell Street and was long gone, some said to Panama, others Madrid.

Her footmen had gone too, one or both of them standing night duty, while the starving puppy was found locked in a bedroom, near to death.

Unmanned by one miserable bitch, the old lord was unhinged by the sight of another, and died within a fortnight.

The London house had since been sold for a knock-down price by an agent of the runaway bride, which sale went uncontested, since having a brain for larceny, she had the notary's papers by her. Those monies had followed her abroad. The Scottish estate and title passed to the brother's family, who were even now pretending to struggle over reconciling their good fortune with its acquisition, through the connivings of an adulterous trollope.

I turned Victoire's account to and fro. However fervid our imaginations, there was no profit to be had from it. I admired the young woman for her clear head and swift action, but like a fox with a chick she had gulped the lot. The puppy, at least, prospered, taken by the cleric to grow fat on raw liver.

We had not done at all well from the first two of Hubert's contacts. Put bluntly, they were both dead as door nails—although I had not yet decided what to do with Lady D's son, handsome Freddy Danceacre.

Journal

May 8, 1784
The Tale of the Collector

So it was on the reply to my least promising, third, letter (which strictly speaking I had had no right to send) that I bent all my attention.

It had gone to a collector called Urban Fine, whom Doctor Essel had met on his travels almost thirty years before. I remembered all about him from a vivid conversation with Hubert, on a wintry afternoon stroll along the Prinsengracht.

When they met, Fine had been little more than a boy, nineteen to van Essel's twenty. They had formed one of those connections only made when usual constraints are lifted, although by any account it was no normal friendship.

Unlike the majority of young squires who went abroad with funds and servants, poor Hubert had saved for years. He was travelling as a solitary scholar, taking a route down through Italy, after which he planned to visit Spain, returning through France. These were all places he had never seen and was unlikely to see again. Aware of this he spent time fruitfully, making notes and sketches in order to build a well from which to draw for the rest of his life. With little money, and none whatsoever when that was gone, he practised the economies of self-taught men, going from inn to inn with a sharp knife and his own silver drinking cup. He did not follow the swaggering fashion of carrying a sword, feeling that if he lost his senses enough to need one, he would be unable to use it, and die—not of sword thrusts, but humiliated by ineptitude.

On the slow journey south he observed moderation, studying in his room over a bottle of wine and loaf of bread, which was supper and, toasted on the knife-point, breakfast too; while the inn beneath became rowdy, simmering with travellers who spent and lost entire fortunes. Even though van Essel understood many languages, he pretended otherwise, affecting a dour demeanour, unwilling to be drawn into company he could not afford to keep.

On the first of May, on a day, he told me, so ravishing he would have cut his heart out as a memorial to it, he left Rome for Naples, arriving on the fourth. He spent a week there, in which he climbed Vesuvius. He then began making notes for his famous pamphlet on the temperament of man in relation to his environment, both natural and social, for which he is still rightly known, despite certain accusations of its having a heretical bent (when first published), fanned by some inflammatory doggerel in iambic sextameter, in which great mileage was made of *soul-searching* and *sole-scorching.* Nevertheless, in his exposition of what little power we have over our selves, how much we are empirical rather than rational, he was ahead of his time, and so not remotely understood. Translated into English and French it is now a valuable work for any student of human nature. Alas, I never got beyond the first page.

On the sixth day, Hubert was walking the port, at dawn. Through the glittering haze he noticed a sloop making ready. Its brisk preparations spoke of a dubious cargo, into which he made no enquiry, rejoicing at his good luck. Thus, he set sail for Palermo. It was an uncomfortable passage, troubled by a local wind called *scirocco,* which the sailors assured him was nothing compared with the year before, and shoved him below.

A man of wide knowledge who, nevertheless, had spent his life clapped indoors making sense out of chaos, Sicily turned him inside out. Where others hired mules he went on foot, cutting an olive stave from the straightest branch he could find and filling a knapsack with food. This, added to a broad hat and a dirt-coloured felted cape that doubled as a bed, made him self-reliant.

Van Essel walked from sunrise to sundown, sometimes skirting parties of English travellers stringing across the scrubby hillside on mules, their muleteers and mounts kicking up the gravelly dust, hallooing to each other, scattering wild goats and scree. He gave these groups a wide berth. One such, of four young men and a young woman in an inappropriate scarlet travelling suit, were already at the temple of Segesta when he arrived, just as the sun was setting.

The walk had left him dry-mouthed, panting, and Hubert wished to sit in peace to watch the drama behind the columns. Driven by high-up wind, small clouds raced each other. Behind the temple, red-lake and gold set everything aflame, billowing round the temple under the baleful influence of the scirocco as if it boiled in blood, or formed the backdrop for a monumental painting.

To suppress his irritation at the noisy interlopers, Hubert took out his sketch book. The task was hopeless. Between looking at the clouds and his paper, everything changed. He was almost relieved to have his contemplation of such a blood-bath disturbed by the group scrambling about, enjoying a noisy game of tag between the columns. From his motionless vantage point, wrapped in his cloak, merging with the dust, he could hear their words clearly. The young lady Jocasta had become prey to the English milords and was squealing to and fro, in and out, to prolong capture. At first, from his distance, Hubert found their childish oblivion to their surroundings contemptible. Then, despite his scorn, something like nostalgia took hold of him. For, while he reckoned himself only five or six years older than the huntsmen, their happiness in the silly sport mocked his lonely state.

Not far below him, servants were laying a picnic between the dry bushes, stretching blankets, balancing wine bottles in raffia slings and digging in flares.

Out of the dusk came the round sound of a bronze gong summoning the group towards the lights. They came gallivanting down. To his bewilderment, moments later Hubert found that he had got up, slapped at his cape, and was ambling towards them before the chimes had faded off the mountain.

Jocasta Verney and her brother John Verney were travelling with two Dorset landowners, Edmund Stuart and Roger Bullivant, having all made fast friends in Rome. Stuart and Bullivant were wealthy young men inclined to make the tour before another day passed, to collect ideas for their several houses. The Verneys came from near Worsley in Lancashire. While John had no notion except to get away from his father's mills, his sister aspired to paint watercolours, which she did badly, and to find a husband, which was going little better. No one observed Hubert's curious flapping descent except the fifth member of the group, who leapt up the instant he caught sight of the strange creature coming like Hecate out of the gathering dust and invited him to join them.

This slim young man in a rich rust suit embroidered all over in lilac, with spotless linen, flung out a thin hand on which there was a mole like a heart and introduced himself as Urban Fine. He begged the oddly dressed traveller to sit, himself stepping back on to a gilded plate, shouting at a servant, commanding another bottle, and sitting down once more.

Hubert, already attuned to his new companions, knew that the others were not impressed by his advent, and that Urban Fine did not care what they thought. There was an inhumanness about him that was shocking. Despite racing between the pillars with more speed and dexterity than his friends, leaving Stuart with a red face and John Verney's hair out of curl, Fine remained composed. His white stockings were immaculate and, Hubert noticed, whilst everyone else's shoes were spoiled by a thick coat of dust, Fine's soft-polished kid bore no trace.

Over brandy, Fine—who would soon become Earl Much—insisted that Hubert join their jaunt to the Villa Palagonia at Bagheria the following day. Consigning his own plans to hell, Hubert agreed. The moment of doing so brought ease and pleasure he had never known, under which he felt almost delirious.

There was something about Fine, he had explained to me, a compulsion, that no one resisted. It did not come from strength, for he was not especially strong. White skin that looked as though it had been stretched on damp, and a thin build, inclined him to appear consumptive, an effect that bursts of unexpected energy in the dry manner Hubert had already noticed reinforced. He never broke into a sweat. Under exertion his lips became even paler while his eyes, ringed with sandy lashes the same tint as his hair, grew so clear they were hard to look at. It was more a case that, accustomed to have everything he wished, he got it. Nor did he arouse envy. His companions took his money with as little apparent thought as he gave it. Wherever they went Fine paid, never quibbling a price that others would have beaten down. There was an unspoken rule that he must never be crossed, as if the result would be too awful to contemplate.

At last, Hubert saw this anger at an inn one evening, when John Verney, exalted from singing ballads, called out to settle the account. Fine stood up with what appeared to be the faintest movement towards his sword. One couldn't be sure; such an absurd reaction could have led to terrible consequences. Hubert often wondered if he imagined it, for it was never mentioned again. Yet everyone knew that that was where Fine's hand, with its dark blemish, was going.

While Hubert told me this, looking back thirty years, he had an odd expression.

"I still believe he would have killed him, without putting down the piece of bread in his other hand."

Hubert stared at me with freshly recollected horror: "Sat down and wiped his blade with it afterwards. He could not stand to be challenged; had to be the master of everything. The most arrogant as well as the most generous man I ever met—monstrous, but with the ability to be good, too—when it suited him. Frightening combination. Like gunpowder."

"But then"—I felt indelicate raising such a matter, since Hubert had strong views on how things should be done—"then I do not understand what possible attraction there could be between you?"

"He was *interested* in things. Couldn't bear to have anyone know more than him about a matter. Wouldn't wait for any thing, or any one—which, by the way, is how Jocasta Verney, the beautiful woman in red, fell foul of him—but that's something else."

I glanced curiously at him, at the word beautiful, which I had never before heard from his lips and which now, passing the back of his hand across his mouth, he seemed to taste.

"He took one look at me," Hubert continued, "and decided I was going to stay. That was that. That was how he was. He merely asked me to go on with them. I did. I am not sure I can explain . . ."

This conversation took place only ten days before my abrupt departure from Amsterdam. It was one of our too-rare excursions, walking slowly, like an ordinary couple still in love. In black with the addition of a veil, on Hubert's arm, I was the picture of a merchant's wife, the adumbration of vain frugality.

His young Viscount interested me. Why had that spoiled, demanding brat, having found such a valuable tutor, ever let him go?

"Did he tire of you?"

"You are cruel with your remarks, madam." Hubert honoured me with a satiric bow. "And prescient. It would be impossible for such a man to stick to any pattern for long. We lived and breathed the same air for six months, during which I profited from his generosity and he from my knowledge. The house you rent from me could be called a gift from him. My own house and library came the same way. Yes, he played catspaw with people, but when he dropped them—as inevitably he did—the landing was usually made soft."

I did not notice the *usually*—fatal inattention on my part. I was too interested in driving Hubert on, he too reticent to hold me back. Knowing his inflexible morality, his acceptance of being paid off seemed more than strange.

"You could reconcile his behaviour with your conscience, because of that?"

I wondered if he had heard. He was taller than me by a quarter ell. Glancing up in asking, I saw how he stared at the canal as if from a great distance. Finally he looked at me. "How else, madam?"

He had an expression I could not understand. It might have been exasperation at my slowness, yet was not. He scarcely saw me. If I had had to find one word to describe it, perhaps then despair; but that was not right: it was so much more. For some reason, Hubert was not telling the truth.

"He gave me the means to live as I chose. What greater gift for someone like me, with no hope except the same narrow existence I had known as a student? Can you imagine the torment of learning how to live like a lord but not having the means? Can you imagine what it is *to know*, and not be able *to do*? How could I fault him for making it possible? In forcing me to go, he saved me from becoming a lackey."

"I do not believe that ever possible," I reproached him. "Nor do you credit me with sufficient understanding."

We left the conversation, with all its concealed bitterness. It was as if we had just begun something, and as abruptly stopped. I had heard the torment in his voice, how he had gone over whatever troubled him so many times that he could describe it in this way, that would dupe so easily. God knew what was underneath the false covering. So we ambled on, eyes averted.

His remarks about how to live, stung. Contaminated by his malaise I fell to contemplating my own. My past hovered so vivid in the frosty air that it was all I could do not to recoil. I controlled myself. Hubert had never seen under my skin either. Nor, given how high and inflexible he held honour, would we be walking together if he had. We went a full ten minutes in the cold.

"Everyone has a price, madam, which your name illustrates."

The witticism ill-suited him. I changed the subject. "You still maintain a connection?" Levelly, as if the mistake had not been made.

He flushed and pulled himself together.

"Earl Much is one of the greatest collectors alive, with a library so extensive he bought a house for it. He owns a parcel of land and builds another when the first is full up. People around the world find him things.

"In the past I have found books. I have a particularly special one for him now, on the South Seas, that has taken years to acquire, years of patience, of diligence. The only one in existence. He would die to get his hands on it."

The South Seas! Dreary books were of no interest to me.

"The girl in red," I reminded him.

"Ah, yes."

Hubert could be incredibly frustrating.

"Then tell me what happened!"

At my sharp tone, he allowed himself a laugh. "Much could never hang on to people, as I have told you. He treated the living as if they were objects: picked them up and banged them down, ignored them, wrapped them up so they suffocated . . . she was a perfect example. He wanted her, so that you would see his hands tremble if she went anywhere near him. When she came into a room his eyes went black, despite being the colour of water. You could feel his desire, yet he could not voice it."

"And she?"

"Ah . . . money. The Verneys had wealth, naturally, but next to him they were paupers—in every sense; and of course she had none of her own. Her ambition was to make a match and escape. That was why she had come, and until Much joined the party she had been considering the two other amiable fellows quite seriously. Either would have suited. Then he arrived.

"Even so, she wasn't sure about it: he frightened her; she shrank from him as much as he fascinated her. That intensity would frighten most men, let alone women. It was as if he would destroy her as soon as let anyone touch her.

"Scenting a contest, Bullivant and Stuart threw their hats into the ring with renewed vigour. It was a game to them; they had that English way of taking everything as a joke, and could be very funny. Finding his hesitation amusing, they decided to give him a run for his money, shake him up. They were rich and—unlike Much—hot-blooded. Alabaster gave him warmth, he was so icy—particularly, as I said, when crossed."

We had started over a narrow bridge, and I reflected, following my thoughts beneath Hubert's words, that he and I might do worse than spend more time together. Even a life together. Looking towards the water I was surprised at how hard my hands clasped the rail.

"So?"

"He asked if she would have him, just like that, as light as that, in the middle of the Palazzo Palagonia. Under its ceiling, made entirely out of mirrors. They say there is a hall of mirrors at Versailles, but in the end I never went, I daresay there may be."

I kept quiet.

"We were all looking up, glimpsing ourselves here and there in thousands of reflections. It was giddying. Miss Verney liked bold colours and was scattered all over the ceiling wherever you looked, broken up into flecks of peacock blue. She was so bright—" Hubert stopped without warning and plucked at a yellow leaf that had fallen on his sleeve.

"No one was looking at anyone, we were all gazing at the reflections. Suddenly Urban Fine's voice came out from nowhere, without preamble: 'So, will you have me?'

"The room, madam, was soundless. Dead. Then her voice. 'Who is me?' she answered, teasing, sharp as a bit of glass, and still no one looking at anyone. She was joking, her voice sweet as a bell; charming. We all knew who 'me' was.

"His reaction was astounding. He grabbed her so violently by the arm that she cried out in pain. 'Damn you, madam,' he shouted, 'if you don't know me now.' And walked straight out, without another glance."

"But—" I was horrified. "Surely he could have just—"

"No."

Hubert laid his hand fleetingly on mine, in a sign that we should go on. "He didn't. She would have done so much better to have said yes."

Part Two

May 7, 1784
Earl Much, Salamander Row

Dear Madam,

What keen and unexpected delight, to hear from a friend of Doctor van Essel.

The unlooked-for news contained in your letter, of the book *Curiosities of the South Seas, and Fashions and Customs Peculiar to its Natives,* pleases me, having long put it from my thoughts. I believe it to be a work of great power; rumour has it that the drawings are unsurpassed in intimate anatomical detail, so entrancing that they drive men mad. For years I begged Doctor van Essel to find the only existing copy in the world. No price was too high: I would give my life to possess it. Yet I had come to believe that even if the only man able to discover it did so, he must fall under its spell and refuse to give it up. I should never have doubted him. His tenacity is boundless.

If one correctly understands the letter that your attendant—whom regrettably I was unable to interview—delivered yesterday to my house, you are recently arrived from the bosom of that noble Dutch scholar, and have therefore few intimates to offer protection until a proper establishment is made ready. Furthermore, you are unwilling to receive visitors until then. Might I be of service in the meantime, by putting a house at your disposal—which trifling offer I beg you consider. Should this simple act bring the slightest ease to your circumstances I should rest happier, which condition cannot be established until you honour me with your opinion.

Your servant,
Urban Fine

Journal continued

May 8, 1784

Fine's letter was written on the sort of flimsy stuff that comes from the East, brown handwriting dancing across it with a mixture of delicacy and boldness that blent the light touch of a woman scattering embroidery across a muslin with the strokes of a Janissary along a row of heads.

Nostalgia for such a hand swept over me—and hatred too, for it is a fact that the cruellest men may write the most dainty. I had to steady myself before folding his letter with its unknown scent and placing it deep into my skirts.

Callously indifferent to any effect that the contents of the missal may have had on her mistress, Victoire had already closed the door and was on the way to carry out her commissions. I called her back, thrusting a few coins into her hand. "Forget the decorations for now. Run down and see who knows where that girl, the one who lived here before, has gone—Mary, or something similar. I very much doubt she had the common sense to crawl more than a few yards. It would not even surprise me to discover her in the room above our heads.

"Wherever she is, whatever she is doing, get her back. I need some clothes. She may even prove useful in other ways, it depends how she looks. If I am not mistaken, you will find she is an easy-going nothing with a passable figure, sodden with gin and buried beneath a paying customer."

"What am I to say?"

"We know she is a fool, since she could have had the bauble Darley on tap if she had played him better, rather than getting his money just once—which I don't doubt has already been palmed off her. Of course she will pretend otherwise. She is no use to us if she does not; the world is not run by whiners. Wait until she starts to give herself haughty airs: that will be your cue to know that she is destitute. Then give her this."

I produced a further coin.

"Make certain she feels how fortunate she is to get it, and ensure she brings scissors and needles. A real dressmaker on the premises should make your life easier. I know how much you dislike putting on an act."

I ignored Victoire's scathing expression.

"She can measure me the moment she comes. I need a close-fitting redingote, buy the brightest red cloth you can; then a silk a little in the Antique mode, white, sashed with . . . lemon"—Fine's seal caught my eye—"and a cloak. The colour of mole-fur, to set off my eyes. Ready-made will do. Slippers you may get from the 'Change. A pull-on muslin for the evening—that silver-figured stuff you saw, or something equal.

"Push her, since I am a hard taskmaster, which she must understand. There must be no intoxicating liquor concealed about her or her work things. Lock her in the back room when you go out. She may sleep on the floor there, if she earns it."

May 12, 1784
Joshua Coats, Conduit Street
to Mrs Fox, Warp Lane

Madam,

You have already returned two letters.

If you will not see me when I call at the house, and refuse to accept my person or my notes, how is one to make peace? How explain? Would you deny me the chance to prostrate myself in an agony of guilt and remorse for what my friends and I inadvertently made you suffer last week?

We did not take you to the coffee-house Diavolo's with the intention of offering insult, but in good faith that it would refresh you. Your abrupt departure was mortifying. I write again in an—I dare say hopeless—attempt at reparation.

You will do us great kindness to concede the impossibility of our knowing that the Tories had chosen an erstwhile blameless coffee-house for shameful uproars and exhibitions of that sort. Elections are unpredictable and the men were in a buoyant mood, no doubt spurred by the daring appearance of Her Grace the Duchess of Devonshire walking in their midst, scattering kisses like rose petals, to curry votes for your name-sake, the polititician, Fox.

Your reaction to those salacious fly-sheets pinned up about Her Grace in Diavolo's was generosity itself, all the more so since it was expressed on the behalf of a woman not known to you, who had been drawn in a frankly disgusting manner. But the debauched insults circulating about her are unfounded. A woman of such rank could not do those things. Only men at the palest ebb would portray a noble woman in undress and show it in a public place. And the scandalous uses to which they were putting her likeness, in front of you! Flay me to the Bone, madam. How can you forgive us? But it was mere horse play. English men would no more defile their own daughters. Believe me, ma'am, your pallor at their repulsive demands *to kiss them like the lady in the picture* won my adoration.

Hold me entirely responsible. Black's insistence on it being his fault, for which he says he will make amends or die, must be discounted. Indeed I actively beg you so to do. He is young, hot-tempered, and foreign to boot; a blaggard—albeit a genius—quite without malice or means, not even in possession of a sword. Moreover, his career as a painter has lent him a morality one does not recognise. I must advise you against him, other than in company. Days spent drawing from the life have inured him to such abandonments as those you witnessed. He is no fit companion for a lady seeking the approbation of Society!

I, on the other hand, am so engulfed by shame at your exposure to that unpleasant scene whilst under my protection that, with your permission, my carriage will wait on you on Thursday after next. A small party goes to the theatre and thence to a supper at Lady Brittleton's. Black will be of the number, as is—if I may take the liberty—your second most ardent admirer, Mr Darley. Favour me, least worthy, with the delight of your company in return for the ordeal to which you were unwittingly submitted.

In the slender hope, madam, that when I next see my worthless ha'penny carriage, you will be in it.

Until that time, I remain,

Yours, etc, etc—

May 12, 1784
Mrs Fox
to Lord Frederick Danceacre
Hipp Street, Mayfair

Lord Danceacre,

I would see you at once on urgent business—send note when, by return.

Yours—

May 12, 1784
Amsterdam Post
Mrs Fox*
to Hubert van Essel, Amsterdam

Dearest friend,

Forgive my delay in sending you a fuller account of our arrival.

As far as Rotterdam the journey was no more uncomfortable than expected; the crossing was another matter. The thieving whore that took my pocket book used the shuddering vessel as her ally.

We felt the lack of a friend to meet us, and witnessed lewdness on the quays that I never expect to see equalled, as if hell sprawled its guts on the cobbles. Yet, had I not already lost my purse, we should surely have been molested for it later, parts of this city being so rough that even a man of your tallness would set foot with fear.

Finding accomodation was harder than anticipated, even without the blow of having been so foully robbed, so that for days I was greatly perplexed.[1] Had you not come to my aid, our circumstances would have been straitened beyond endurance. Leaving the best half of my goods in your safe-keeping, as you advised, has been my salvation. Yet, becoming the example that proves your unerring wisdom so swiftly would humiliate a lesser woman. Further, your arrangement with the lawyers is admirable, I may draw on them for funds as required.

We are now settled, in a house in a mixed part of the city, in lodgings on the piano nobile: two rooms, south and north. There are plenty of industrious souls around these parts, mainly in silk-cloth. There is a tenter ground nearby, but it is not currently in use.

As well as that honest industry, the area is one of flourishing vices. I have heard night-watchmen (which they call the Watch) bribed off outside my windows; also laughing talk of "beating the

[1] This is an out and out lie. Mrs Fox held back more money than she lets on.

Watch"—although the speakers fell silent as we passed, certainly bent on mischief. We have not been offered violence, and are ever on our guard.

Of the names you provided, I had committed two to memory. In addition, from one of our walks I recalled that of a nobleman, Earl Much, whom I felt certain you would wish me to know.

Lady Danceacre (whose charm, if her painting is anything to go by, you elaborated) is recently dead, but her son Frederick lives. Having sent him abroad, she devoted her widowhood to good works, helping young men and women find temporary oblivion from the cares of the world. At Hipp Street, girls on the threshhold of life learned from her *particular* feminine understanding, while young men found a conduit to the expression of their manhood that their mothers could not supply. In return for which incalculable pleasures they gave sums to her institution, whither, having enjoyed plentiful good company, they returned often. *Did you know nothing of this goodness, spread so wide, so impartial?*

You have insisted many times that you do not consider me tainted by the business I had recourse to in Holland, arguing that it always seemed as if I was out of my true station—indeed, treating me as a lady of the blood, and pleased to say I should have been, had not chance thrown me to my knees. Yet, surely you would not speak of me and that stanchion of society, Lady Danceacre, in the same breath?

With further regret I must tell you that Lord K is also dead, howsomever at a good age and following a felicitous—if short—knowledge of a very young wife, in pursuit of whom he died. His Scottish estate did not go to the widow, but to his brother's family. I believe that you will take comfort in this proof of kinship. It is all too common that a newcomer wrests the fortune from those who reasonably expect it, leaving a trail of rancour and destitution. Not that he would have been in danger of such behaviour from me, had he lived!

However, given such misfortune, I know you will be pleased that I have made contact with Earl Much. By his reply—expressing the wish to be acquainted—he, evidently, is lively enough! Be so good as to send the book about the South Seas, so that I may present it in person. I mentioned it in passing, and he appears taken with possessing it. There is no other seemly way to go forward, and I admit to curiosity concerning him that I would prefer to satisfy in a way you approve.

His immediate response to my introduction pleased and astonished in equal measure: unexpected courtliness in a world filling with insolent attacks against modesty and virtue. He has put a house at my disposal until my own establishment is ready. Who knows when that might be, now that half my wealth is gone? His generosity towards an unknown stranger can only be ascribed to the esteem in which he holds you. Your difference from other men, that has long secured an unchallenged place with me, must be noticed at once by anyone sensible. Much's cordiality proves his estimation and in return renders him worthy of your praise.

In short, dear friend, every moment is wasted until I have news from you. I beg you not delay, lest my tardiness in replying to Earl Much be interpreted as indifference.

Your—

**By the by, I am known as Mrs Fox here.*

May 15, 1784
Frederick Danceacre
Mashing, Suffolk
to Mrs Fox
c/o Mademoiselle Trichette, Mantua-maker,
Warp Lane

What ho!

Mrs Fox, ma'am, a letter from your earth at last! Although deuced short, if you don't mind me saying—on the windy side of a whistle, almost blinked and missed it.

Longing to call on you in your Bolt Hole, as you request. But alas, dear lady, torn up about not being able to see you straight off, profound regrets, but can't now be done for a week or more. Having heard nothing from you (for which I curse myself for a simpleton, for not banging on every inn door the length and breadth of the city until they handed over the most fascinating creature in London), the only way to avoid death and despond on account of your absence was to hole *my*self up, in Suffolk; so the fact is, I have missed you by a nail.

Post-boy came galloping along so hard with your delightful letter that I thought his weevily wig a-fire, but it was only the dust harrowing behind. He brings me your affydaffy, waving it about, seems old Mrs Beddoes thought I might want to have it, which shows her good judgment. Knows things to a nicety, gets people right off—jumps at it and gets it—without so much as glancing at them. Not that she would have read it, you understand, but I dare say her feminine wiles winkled out the gist.

Can't think why the rider didn't set you up in front—would have been a sight wholesomer than his ancient sweaty face when he finally comes tooting along-side trailing bits of splotched velvet, too exhausted to manage above one sad wet splutter like the last fanny of a fish; so I snatched the paper out of his hand, pressed a crown to the damp spot and let him flap back to London out of pure compassion.

And that's the truth. All alone up to the boot tops in mud, I swear.

After the auction, Hipp Street looked plucked as a pullet, more echoey than the Matterhorn. Was bored in five minutes. Left General B in charge to clear up, legged it here, to Ruralitania.

Extraordinary crowd at the sale of the maternal things. I had hoped for a glimpse of your lovely profile. Wish you'd come, you would have agreed you'd never seen nothing to beat it. That odd personage Mrs Salmon was there for all the world to see, bang at the front in a group of six that wouldn't stop making a hubbub. Three men and two women, fancy two-seaters lined up outside. The women were very fly; I recognised one from Bond Street yesterday. *Popular* girls, I'll venture. Mrs Salmon was bidding through a gentleman. Raised a riot and a wad of cash, then rode off in a cloud of dust, waving most brazen all the way. Beddoes has never looked so pursy, although I don't know why, since, among other items, I believe she sold Salmon the very two things my mater had already given her, years before.

I was stood at the back, keeping an eye and saying halloa to those few of my mother's older friends. Some fellows hung back with me; amongst them Coats, know him from Boodles; surveyor, pleasant fellow, who confided his hope of seeing someone there—lady—but she weren't among the fine selection on offer. Then there was a spectral, pallid gentleman in lilac that I vaguely recollect from long ago. Must have been a friend of my mama's. Didn't say a word and when I went to how-de-do, he was gone. Oddest thing, the footmen couldn't find him, even though he had a scented suit and a cane so cutaway you might have took it for an épée.

Swear ma'am, knocked me sideways the old girl was that popular. Any one would have thought, from the rowsterers and flibbertigibs, that she'd been a pretty thing of five and twenty—like your self, except you're a deal younger, scarce out of strings—not an old used-up one near fifty-and-two. But it's the way of the world. No shame making a pile from it.

Which subject has drawn me to Suffolk. I don't think I mentioned this place at our too-brief meeting (which I assure you is engraved on my innards).

Mashing's a solid old wreck, offers a bit of shelter from the wind whipping in, considering that it has hunched on this bit of land for aeons; but it needs licking into shape. My mother hadn't set foot here for years—not since I hopped on the packet-boat. Her works kept her in town.

In the meanwhile, the manager, Tutton, had been polishing the silver until he could see his own face in it a sight better than hers. Thought I ought to come and get the cloth out of his hand, before he decides that his crossed matlocks and mangolds rampant look better there than my Leaping Ram.

On my honour, Mashing's a nice place. A lot more trees than London, different colour dirt, and the stink's off. Why not come and take a look? You seemed to have the dress for the country in that green get-up, if you don't mind my noticing; and I will admit it's deuced quiet, after all the excitements of abroad. Beddoes'll have you put into a cosy vehicle with a rug and pick-nick in no time. There's a fast road. I need a woman's touch to shake things up.

Here's how rapidly I've decayed: all yesterday was spent dobbining round the perimeter with Tutty, bashing at a few posts. He said it was a local custom that had to be done, to get everything shipshape. Then called on the parson, who told me who was dead that I might have remembered, and who had left the neighbourhood that I might have wanted to visit. Unremarkable sort, made no impression.

For want of sharper-flavoured company (which you must take as the compliment it is meant) I gave a dinner to those same neighbours. Came in off the fields pretty early next day, at four, to find them kicking about in the parlour, where they had been for a good hour! There's no keeping up with the oddities of country customs. All of them looked as if they had been gnawing the furniture.

Father, Justice of the Peace, bothered about his newfangled hogs called Tamworth, whilst he should be more worried about the one he's married to, Little-Worth. Said portly creature as peevish on the subject of creams and jellies as her mate on modern methods. Two young girls, and a third almost out.

This last, Miss Pert-Intent, gave me a good going over, questions about Italy got from her books, inbetween sighing at her parents to remember they were in the company of someone who had *Been To Pompeii.*

"And back!" I sang, hoping for a blush to breach the tedium. Of course, *Violet* knew a dam' sight more about it than I did. Couldn't keep up at all with her Rhomboids and Rebuses. Tried the experiment of getting fond with her after dinner, but the mother was a kestrel perched on the back of the settle, no amount of brandy would topple her, though she was sinking it out of a wine glass without even pretending to flinch—that steady influx without breathing that only belongs to a souse-head.

Shame that. Rather took to her; soft under the sharp stuff. Not the mother, I mean.

I have to tell you, Mrs Fox, that these country girls aren't called so for nothing. They know the tricks of the wild. Sire's whip didn't stop twitching all night, but whether he wanted to give me a good flick or regulate his own brood was impossible to tell. I favour the latter. You wouldn't wake up to the eyes on that ox his wife without wanting to buckle a hood over them. Piss yellow begging your pardon if they had any colour at all.

His kittens finally started yawning and mewling at ten, and he got them into their cart for the toddle to their own basket. I helped them up. They all sprang like steel except Violet, who had determined to play cat's cradle with my hands. It was a wonder my fingers weren't pecked off, since Violet hasn't learned to keep her manoevres to herself and wouldn't stop wriggling. The old gizzard her mama was on to her anticks in no time.

I swear on my life though that that is all there was to it. None of the fault was on my side. You might say I was as much sat upon as put upon. Nevertheless, you could hear her Worshipful father, the Justice, yodelling like a stuck bullock half a mile down the drive, frightening the sheep out of their curl-papers.

But you have already taken my measure: as harmless as a stallion at a saucer of milk, unless there's someone worth lapping—and these young girls are so fresh they're still dripping whey from their whiskers.

I shall not now come back to town until the London house is ready to sell, which may take longer than expected, now that the lawyers have decided to start rummaging. So I beg you, Mrs Fox, spare me from going mad! Tell me how to bring this hut up to scratch. I risk becoming the talk of the neighbourhood as a solitary bachelor, ripe for a visit from every unmarried woman under five and forty.

Your note said that you wish to talk to me urgently: I have been speculating what can be so deuced urgent in such a short acquaintance—although I am damned eager to find out! No time is needed to validate your charms. A glimpse of that profile enslaved me. Surely, one place must be as good as another for a chatter? You might take to Mashing. It is commodious, a different room every week, if it please you. A chamber has been got up against your arrival and the views have a certain greenishness to recommend them. I shall look out for your carriage. Charge it at the stable. Have Sibbald the squinting footman with you, he is the only one who shoots straight, and bring your woman, if you won't trust my lazy trollopies.

Yours up to the hilt—
Danceacre

PS: Turn left at the chained gibbet at Danceacre Cross. Right takes you over the cliff. Tally ho! FD

May 17, 1784
Hubert van Essel
to Mrs Fox

Dear *Mrs Fox*

How shall I become accustomed to your habit of changing your identity as easily as your dress, as women do the world over? You should not be blamed for doing what is customary: while I had put you outside the general run, it is apparent that in this one respect, you have everything in common with the lowest of females.

Such has been my debate on my walks to my nephew Albrecht Oeben's house, and the small circle of his wife and four children, where—since you left me nothing but my own company—I am increasingly drawn. A stroll of only twenty minutes; the exercise is congenial.

They live quietly. Civic duties occupy Albrecht, while his wife keeps house with the help of the girls and three maids. The youngest boy is twelve and apprenticed to a glove-maker, having tried leather breeches but found the work cumbersome. His hands are delicate, the fingers as nimble as his mind. I am determined to see him employed better before too long. We have commenced a course of study together in the evenings, at which his eldest sister joins, when she can be spared from affairs of the household. This is rewarding work and makes me forget—

May 17, *continued*

Forgive a momentary lapse. Your absence weighs more heavily each day, which is the reverse of how I sternly told myself it must be.

I have had your house shut up. A watchman guards it in the evenings, so have no fears for the safety of your remaining effects. It is as you left it and will remain so until your return. Your cats made a sulking entrance at my nephew's, protesting the indignity of being transported in a closed box. Next day, having adopted a child apiece, they were in possession of the field—with new names, better suited to childish tongues.

Two of your former employees made a play to continue the business much as you and Madame La Vôtre had. They argued that it would be folly to allow such a well-organised system to fail through neglect; that the town benefited from its wholesome provisions; that its decay would force the women to seek less salubrious employ elsewhere and open the door to others of less principle. There was more than a little sense in their reasoning. At no point did I attempt to stop them, finding myself considering their words in the light of a moral conundrum, rather than a financial proposal—for I have no need for money.

Yet, either their next suggestion (of adopting the very identities of you and your *sister* Madame La Vôtre), or concern over the reputation of my nephew's family, that would preclude such association . . . howsobeit, I fastened the shutters with great care that night and took leave of the rooms one by one, with no plan to open them again.

All your women have received compensation in gold for the abrupt ending of an employment which they reasonably expected to continue, metal computed as Jenever even as they counted, illustrating the fickle nature of their species. I talk of them thus, safe in the knowledge that you took no part in such travail yourself. Whatever my nephew says (with increasing impudence, now you are gone), I will not see disgrace in your involvement in that business.

You asked if it is possible for me to consider you in the same breath at Lady Danceacre. What you could mean by this—or, if it was a momentary (and I cannot help but remark, ill-judged) whim—has absorbed me. It is not wise to set the living against the dead. As your tone was playful, my answer must be the same: you are two women as far out of the ordinary, as captivating and as untouched by the taint of corruption, as each other. I cherish the memory of one and the friendship of the other.

Of your declared interest in Earl Much, I read soberly. Jesting never touches matters that concern him, for whom humour is as alien as the Antipodes. Although your curiosity is understandable, I would never willingly see his attention attach to you, and feel trepidation at your proposed meeting with this compelling man. His wealth and power, compounded by his nobility and his assurance in it, exert a fascination no woman has ever resisted.

How keenly I regret not having enumerated your qualities when we were together, never daring trespass on your patience for sufficient time to do them credit! However, when so much distance lies between us that we may never see each other again, and you propose to see such a man as Earl Much in the tone in which you would suggest a game of canasta, I will at last express the esteem in which I hold you, in the hope that if it may not change your hand, I might at least delay your play.

There is a light in you that pricks dark places and drags forth secrets. Such clarity may blind or kill, just as it can illuminate. One so dazzling endangers herself as often as she endangers others. For that reason you should not go unprotected. Wherever you are and whatever you do, I have offered my assistance, which service I will continue until you order me stop, or until one of us dies.

But beware. Rare though you are and precious to me, Urban Fine is your equal. You cannot deceive him, as I hazard you may wish to do. He fears nothing; he has given his life to taking men's souls. Though unmarried, he is far from unknown to women, or they to him. You are bent on an encounter without guidance or companionship: I beg you, reconsider. He is a libertine of the most dangerous sort. No one withstands him. Despite his years, that must be near fifty, his powers are undiminished.

It is possible that your unusual knowledge of human nature may offer some protection. I have pondered whether your circuitous route through life could have been directed by an all-seeing power, for just this eventuality; but the startling impertinence of the idea made me put it away. Heed my advice and put off this foolish notion.

The story of Jocasta Verney that interested you so much is still unfinished. Come home, let me recount the remainder over a bridal feast the like of which this city has never seen. Your safety would make my life complete.

You asked me to let you know at once if anyone asks for you. I have instructed the watchman to report everything, however unimportant, but so far, nothing of note has taken place.

If, after this letter, you still insist on having it, I will send the *Curiosities.* I wish that you were not the agent to deliver it; that I had the courage to withstand you, or that you had the courage to withstand yourself. You say that you would satisfy your curiosity about Earl Much in any way I approve.

There is no such way. I cannot! Madam, there can *never* be approval for the appalling course on which you are stubbornly bent.

To meet him is a passport to Hell.

May God go with you.

Journal

May 17, 1784

I was in an agitated mood on the cusp of action and inaction, waiting for Hubert to send *Curiosities of the South Seas* which, for one reason or another, was delayed. The weather had turned stormy, what havoc would that wreak on those freezing waters? Every hour of no post increases my unease.

Although the *actual* reason for coming to England had been the threat of Mr Martin, I found, once arrived, that one change inspired recklessness for others. All women are born knowing the method I had settled on to conclude a journey already half-travelled: that twilit crossing, between *demi-monde* and *mondaine,* where mysteries turn marvels and duchesses rise from doxies. Having been at an ebb from which, short of death, I could sink no further, I now anticipate a reversal. If others are crucified in my rehabilitation, so be it. I will take up Mr Coats' offer of the theatre.

Journal continued

Last week, the missing Whore-cum-seamstress Martha was found by an astonishing coincidence. Just as Victoire unfastened the street door at Warp Lane to set off on what we both suspected was a fruitless search, our landlady's own door opened further along the passage, whereupon a young woman was half pushed and half backed, into the hall, only yards from where Victoire stood transfixed.

"It's no good snivelling," came Mrs Sorrell's bullying voice, her person following close after. Neglectful of propriety in the triumph of a parting shot, one of her raw hands clenched a rolled pair of blackened leather stays like an advocate's brief, while the other grappled a grey morning gown round her unrepentant bosom. In this magisterial pose she was oblivious to Victoire, stock-still, thumb on the latch.

"*They're* a higher class all round than you will ever be," our landlady went on, strands of greasy undressed hair on her shoulders, jerking a thumb in the direction of our floor, "so you can whistle for your room, you splay-legged little *Con.* They pay double, and in advance. So what if they are French muck. *You're* French muck, don't pretend you ain't. What do you want me to do, turn them out and have a shiftless fourpenny drab back? They've taken over your *Noodlemen* as well, your *Macaroons,* so that's you on the dung heap again and no mistake." Remarkably gently, the door closed.

For a moment, the young woman stood still, competing forces of rage and resignation cancelling each other out so effectively that, in her small, pinched face, no expression was left. She went to push past Victoire, who swiftly pinned her to the wall and gave her a belt to bring her to her senses.

By that lucky catch, I was measured for my clothes within two hours of desiring them—which a fifty-guinea wager says is swifter service than the finest mantua-maker in St James's Place, not counting getting there and cajoling an appointment.

At the outset, the gratitude of our young charge, Mademoiselle Hublon, who turned out to be merely fourteen, knew no bounds. While she told her story, my attempts to discover *the prettiest girl in all London* were defeated by the string-haired shoulderless object hunched before me, with a ripped and fouled dress, a badly bruised arm and a freshly blued eye adding colour to its surrounding pallid charms.

She said that she had been turned over by three older whores in a flop-house in nearby Frying Pan Alley that she had—mistakenly—selected for a new start. One plied her with a large cup of gin, another let her share her straw mattress in order to cuddle her closer than was proper, while the third dipped her pockets and stole from her petty-coat as she slept.

Over a glass of sack, Martha then recounted how she had been woken by the sound of that third woman dropping one of the guineas she was cutting out of the petty-coat. A fight broke out. Martha was smacked a bit and stripped, so she couldn't give chase. Shortly afterwards the landlady's Bully (tipped off without a doubt by the departing thieves) discovered her, in the room whose rent had not been paid. He took swift pleasure for it, embellished her eye as a makeweight and threw her onto the street, twisting her ankle, in which sorry condition we acquired her. She pointed out that the three Harlots, who had been no more that twenty themselves, had tossed her cheap print dress back into the room at the last minute.

"They needn't of, there's some wear left, look, and the colour's a nice one. They might of got a bob on Petticoat Lane."

The sobbing stopped remarkably quickly, given the state she was in. A life spent in immorality has certain compensations—one being the recuperative genius of cactus. While she was compressing a second slab of bread dipped in a third glass of watered wine to swallow it quicker, she stopped and stared at the ceiling, saying that her sewing things were upstairs with the Scribbler. I gave Victoire a kick and went and sat on a window seat with a novel, pretending to find the proceedings beneath my notice. The book was that same *Otranto* I had seen in Mrs Beddoes' study, but with only two pages cut. It wasn't worth blunting scissors on. These days you could get a tale anywhere, but a knife-sharpener was another matter.

"We will go up together when you have done, and recover them," Victoire soothed, misleadingly. "What manner of man . . ." She had pulled a chair to, and was stroking Martha's draggled hair with the cup of one hand, while the girl finished her bread and cast about for another piece, which she was given, and some butter for it, and a piece of pie with slivers of duck that appeared from under a napkin, next to half a pear, that I had been privately looking forward to.

Having tucked these away, Martha became more expansive. "Keeps in his room a lot, goes out sometimes for days at a stretch. Weeks. Sleeps other days. Has a big locked cupboard I never saw into, big enough to get inside. I never knew anyone call on him.

"He was all right with me. Once showed me his books, they looked like they cost a lot. He liked to watch me pretend to read them, got his dander up, especially if I held them the wrong way on purpose to tease him."

"How do you know they were the wrong way, if you can't read?"

Martha gave her a withering look. "I aren't *blind.*"

Victoire didn't waste further pretences. "So if he was good to you, why did you take up with the other two? More money?"

Martha jerked her head out sideways from under Victoire's palm and smoothed her hair furiously. "I didn't take up with them *two*—just the one, Mr Dadson, and he came after me! What would you have done? He loved me, he said so every time." She was taking Victoire's measure as the food and wine brought her courage back. I had to keep my face towards the window so as not to laugh, since it was obvious that Martha's tone was putting Victoire into a terrible temper, in which she was as like to slap as stroke.

"Don't tell me you don't have gentlemen friends," the girl darted out.

That's it, I thought, now she will get another whack to make a matching pair with the Bully's handiwork. Nothing happened.

There was scarcely a pause before Victoire spoke again. In my imagination I heard her swallow.

"You were saying, about this man upstairs?" Victoire voice had stayed even. No one but a connoisseur would know how angry she was.

"He's mean. Mean as Moses. Liked it all right, don't they all, but thought he was so fancy he should get it for nothing. Give me a sixpence sometimes, as grand as if he was the Prince of Wales. I was doing him a shirt. He made me sit, and stitch, in front of him. *You* know. Same as with the book."

We both knew. I kept my forehead pressed to the window.

"It was taking a devil of a time," she concluded unnecessarily.

"What did you do?"

"What do you mean, do? I couldn't do anything, could I? What could I do? No one would care what he did to me. He could of done me in like that if he'd of wanted, he's got a sword up there that he used to play with sometimes, and a dagger that was always near him, no matter what." She winced. "I was glad when Mr Dadson turned up, he could see I was worth having. He was a gentleman."

"And Mr Scribbler isn't?"

"Mr Scribbler? Love you, that isn't his name! That's Mrs S's jest. Laforge's his name, I seen it on some receipts and on a counter for Vox'll."

I felt Victoire's face turn in interrogation in my direction, but kept my head bent. So the girl *could* read a little, after all. Which meant that she could be taught. Martha licked her plate and put it down so the pewter rang.

"Done. What do you two *ladies* want to do with me?"

Martha agreed without complaint to the work we gave her, perfect proof that if such women are offered wholesome employment they will not turn to vice, preferring dainty pass-times, such as sewing or laundry-work, to the unhealthy profit to be had from men. Which, like mackerels in thunder, is sudden but not steady; whose ungodliness lies not in the Act itself, but in cheating God of his omnipotence by causing death quicker than He would have it, on account of the Rot and Pox, and the White Flux.

~

There was nothing of value in our rooms where Martha could find it, and I wanted her to feel at home, so that she would work harder. We left her in the back with a pitcher of cold water and the last crust, while we went to pay a call upstairs to recover her sewing things.

I told Victoire that I would go too *in case there was any difficulty,* at which she gave me an elevated look. Something was altering between us. Yet, the natural boundary between us will hold; I do not fear her insurrection. Victoire's parents signed her into my care in her infancy, giving me the absolute power of life or death. Besides, between master and servant, the latter is aware of his inferior nature and tendency to violence. He observes the perfect decorum of the superior class and takes pleasure in being assured kind treatment and protection from the savagery of erstwhile peers. In contrast, among my own station, only rarely do we resort to the violence of sword or pistol, balletic parlays that can be stopped by a graceful capitulation of either duellist. And in the case of pistols, the distance between combatants is so far apart that the risk of a scratch is less than being shot dead taking the air out of a bedroom window.

Which is why my original exile, from Paris, had been so unjust. How could a frail woman be held accountable for two enraged men fighting to the death, as I was? Should I have interposed my bosom—had I even been near the fateful encounter? No law can control a man committed to blade over tongue, and rightly so. The sword has absolute mastery over its poetry. Let no one interfere with the interior workings of a duel. Two skirmishing swords flashing in awful beauty, harmonising, counterpointing. Let anyone, as I say, thrust soft flesh between and imagine the consequences. Yet my life was brought to nought by failing to do just that! Foul injustice—from which I absolve myself.

I had refined this argument in numberless idle moments over the preceding two years. It convinced me that it would not matter if I danced up the stairs a pace behind Victoire to retrieve Martha's things from the Scribbler.

I stood well back while she knocked. The dun-painted lintel was lower and broader than ours, projecting like a slate, more like an outer door than an inner one. Victoire tapped again.

Primed that Mr Scribbler sometimes stayed within doors for days, and not wishing to alert the mother-to-be on the floor above, we tried for a knock sufficient to ascertain the departed, but not trouble the living. After a restrained fusillado we regrouped, while Victoire nursed her fists. The door was locked. I directed her to the lintel. On tiptoe her fingers just reached, but not far enough to search all the way. A stout trug of kindling stood at the foot of the next pair of stairs that the slattern Betty had been too lazy to take further. Victoire hopped up. A moment later she handed me a key half the size of her hand which we stared at, mesmerised. But whatever convolutions she put it through, the key would not work, so I sent her back up to discover a second, similar in shape. Slipping the first into my pocket, we pushed the door open.

No one was at home. The Scribbler's apartment (for I preferred this title to that of Mr Laforge) was laid out on the same pattern as ours, the door to the back standing open. Brown curtains moved at the unshuttered windows; with the sashes down it was airy and cold. The grate had not been swept; from dust everywhere, it was clear that the Scribbler did not allow anyone in. Mrs Sorrell was poking about in our rooms the moment our backs turned: why tolerate his privacy?

The apartment did not yield whatever horrors we expected; neither a dark torture chamber full of evil implements, nor a room so rich it could only belong to an Emperor—just disorder and neglect. Yet, I was left with a sense of unfulfilment that a philosopher would liken to the ashes in the grate: proof of a fire.

We went straight into the smaller room. There was a bookcase with an atlas and volumes of military history on the top shelf. The bottom one held three glasses, two plates, and a slender-bladed Japanese knife, imperfectly wiped, a dirty cloth under it. In front of a dead grate was a chair in once-orange brocade. The matching stool held a work basket that Victoire caught up. Now we had our passe-partout, we turned to leave. Stepping back through the connecting doorway I let out a cry so sharp that Victoire screamed in sympathy and dropped the basket with a bang. I told her not to be so stupid and pick it up at once.

Diagonally opposite loomed the cupboard Martha had spoken of, that we had walked straight past on the way in, its enormous presence as startling as if a man stood there. Eight feet wide and six high, of black oak carved in the Dutch manner, it was more than a hundred years old, polished very high, with bas-relief figures cut in a way I had never seen, projecting so far that it would be no surprise if they flexed their elongated toes and stepped off their plinths. An Adam and Eve such as one might find aside a fire flanked the gleaming structure, a trifle less than life-size, rendered by a great master. The rest of the surface was taken up with all manner of birds sitting and calling in the brances of a tree spread over the front. Several had turned their heads outwards, beaks wide, to call song into the room, whilst a pair of turtle doves stretched their wing-tips so longingly that they might fly from the timber at any moment. The leaves were carved so well, they fluttered.

Unusually, the cupboard appeared to have three doors, the cracks scarce disturbing the creatures running across them, and whose locks, almost invisible among the carving, were too small for the key banging against my leg. These doors must be cleverly sprung, for there were no handles to be seen.

The effect was disturbing. If I had had a fanciful nature I would have said that Adam and Eve were watching us. My heart beat high and Victoire was deathly pale.

"Come." I squeezed her arm, the spell broke.

We took the rest in at a glance. The bed had been left thrown open, linen and camlet dragging on the floor. It had no hangings. There was a table with two rush-bottomed chairs. Between the windows was a locked chest like a seaman's with a spotted Venetian mirror above. In the corner, a washstand held an empty bowl and pitcher covered by fraying green damask. A black-sheathed rapier with a wrought grip done in Aleppo work rested beside it, with a limp black ribbon hanging from the guard. I did not like the look of it, and what Martha had said about Laforge's liking for it made me uneasy, a reminder that we should leave.

Before we did I glanced again at the table, piled with books it would be imprudent to disturb. Some titles were visible. French novels, more history, and a small, old volume—Ovid's *Metamorphoses.* A Boulle inkstand crouched in the centre of this disarray, between blackened candlesticks. Any papers had been put away—yet there had been some. The books and stand formed a sort of horseshoe where someone had sat writing, dripping spots of ink. I put my finger to the largest and pushed: not dry. A little glued itself to my nail. Suddenly I was terrified by an unfathomable sensation, as if someone stood behind my back. "Go," I hissed in Victoire's ear, "go, now!"

We ran, tossing both keys back to the lintel, praying that they would land at the first fall, and that this man was not tall enough to see tell-tale marks in the dust.

We had scarcely entered our room when the street door slammed very loud and footfalls started up the stairs. With our backs pressed against our own door, that we had not even bolted, we trembled. Nothing for a quarter of a minute, then someone cleared their throat and the steps continued. We waited to hear movement above our heads. A look of concentration came over Victoire and she shook her finger. "It's not him!" she whispered. "Listen, they are going on up. It must be the man at the top."

We were so transfixed, listening, that our own room was a mist, which now cleared. Framed in the doorway into the small room, Martha straightened, clasping her pinkish-red dress against her where she had been using it to dry herself. She smiled. Her hair clung to her head in places and stuck up gleaming in others. We stared at her, at where deep gold light flared round her from the window behind.

"You got it then," she said, matter-of-factly, resuming her drying, nodding in the direction of the sewing box, unconcerned by our eyes on her body.

"Give it here, so we can get on."

May 25, 1784
Mrs Fox, Warp Lane
to Hubert van Essel, Amsterdam

Bridal feast! Your jests are vastly amusing. Do not let it grow stale on my account.

I am still waiting for the *Curiosities* to arrive. Do you tease me, or has some misadventure befallen it? It is my cherished expectation that even as you read these words, the book will be safe in my hands—and I may understand what you once called "a work so dangerously rare it should never leave the vault."

Feel my anxiety: a week has passed since you agreed to send it. How to understand such delay?

I have had a second note from Urban Fine, repeating his entreaty to take up one of his houses—yet in a different tone. Though the letter lacks nothing owing to a gentleman, there is an underlying impression that my silence has been taken for discourtesy. Beration, where before only approbation fell to my lot.

Given your extreme truthfulness and attention to matters that affect me, often at the exclusion of responsibilities proper to the felicitous running of your own affairs, I am full of disquiet that something else has happened, more serious than mere *absentmindedness* or *neglect.* On which account, I beg you, put my heart at rest.

Meanwhile, let me describe life here.

We are forced to stay a great deal within doors, improving our English with novels, reading to each other turn and turn about, or studying the news-papers. I have been once to one of the Theatres Royal and learned more in one evening than during all our study. But otherwise, while my clothes are attended to I am not fit to make any appearance of note. Amsterdam, sir, is not London!—my travelling costume has been laid away; leaving only a close-fitting suit that can not be worn in the evening, or company, having been remarked.

Receipt to Make a Woman

or

A Paeon to the Mantua-makers

A man is only as good as his tailor—but a lady does not *exist* without her mantua-maker. Where *he* may be indifferent (like the politician, Fox, going to his club in a foulled night-gown), *she* dares not have a pin misplaced. She is as if blown from glass, made visible by the breath of man and, as the breath fades, vanishing. Imagine a handful of humours: shaped into the loveliest of creatures, evanescent as dreams. Then build a suit of clothing hacked from whalebone and horsehair, of buckram stiffened with stinking fishes; a skin of silk and lace stretched over all and stitched by women too poor to step out doors except at night, shifting along walls like crabbed shadows. Should these genii be noticed, it is by some drunken soldier investigating the quality of their work by flinging up their skirts and looking at the nether side. Yet, when those nonesuchs have made a mansion for us from cloth and splinted bone as cunning-done as their own skins and skeletons—then we go forth, transformed by a beauty the world believes ours. Those women should be paid their weight in gold, for they form and shape us more than dance masters or mothers. Eve was a seamstress, that wanted Adam's rib to splint into staybones and fashion herself from.

Fops and dandies maintain extravagances mocked as "Frenchified"—my countrymen are reviled while being imitated. I dare not defend them, but must tolerate instead this German *Riff-Raff.* The father is whispered mad; the Prince has a hundred pair of shoebuckles, more affairs than his father's foreign minister, and is setting up courts in Brighton and Pall Mall with an actress who will never get the one part she really wants.

Young men dress in manure and lichen, while women pull muslins on over their head, like infants. At Drury Lane last night, several ladies were not wearing stays, their bodies distinctly visible under their garments. These grand ladies know to a nicety how much bosom and belly they expose, just as they know to a mouthful how much mutton is on the shanks for their dinner. If it were not for coronets plastering their coaches we should call them *Strumpets.*

Telling ladies of the *ton* from those *of the town* exercised all my skill at the theatre. The carriage was twenty minutes late, rattling along so hard that I thought it was a storm, not Joshua Coats, who had got a new pair of yellow horses and commandeered the whip, putting his enraged coachman so low into his collars that you might confuse him with a volcano. My relief at Mr Coats being outside the conveyance rather than in (for I had anticipated amorous overtures), soon turned to dismay as I clung to the straps for dear life.

We were eight for *The Belle's Stratagem,* in one of the best boxes on the front of the stage; the finest seats, short of the Prince's lap—which was already occupied. Our benefactor was Mr Darley, to whose purse the finest of everything is as nothing and the finest of nothing everything. He has the judgment of an atom, a particle of sense, and an immense sensibility—such a striking amalgam of wealth and witlessness that someone should sell it as Essence of Englishness.

The red box set the women off, like teeth. Coats flung himself next to me. On my other side Nathan Black had a brand-new neckcloth, that made the rest of garments more derelict. Behind, Darley was dressed as a humming bird, wafting an eye-glass on a peridot handle. Lord and Lady Brittleton commended the decorations at their new house to no one in particular, while the dreary musical sisters, Bathia and Sarah Loyde, stood in for Hope and Charity (having given up on Love or Money) and were gazing at everything. To which only Mr Black was insensible, so busy pleating a miniature paper fan that it would have taken bows and arrows to divert him.

The English theatre is no different from the French. Everyone in the audience stares at everyone except the neglected actors, who fluff their lines and swig from bottles thrust down their breeches. More than once into the breeches, from the way some of them were stumbling over their parts.

I was at first oblivious to a great bustle on the other side of the apron, in a box that had been empty. But at an increasing commotion, I dragged myself from wondering if clever Letitia would overcome Doricourt's prejudice against superior women (and prove that this was indeed a play) to encounter, directly opposite, Mrs Poppy Salmon *gazing straight at me.*

Head to toe in shining yellow satin, her diamonds outdid those scientific marvels lighting the stage, so that, had she been wafted about in a harness, no other illumination would have been necessary.

I looked down, with what I hoped would be taken for modesty (rather than intense irritation), but her burning eyes were still on me, so that the actors inbetween were at risk of their vitals catching fire. At last, her attention attracted Coats's notice.

"Ma Foi!!"—in such poor *sotto voce* that the whole theatre swivelled round. "I say, Dads, who is the lady with such a determined look for Mrs Fox?"

As the whole box broke off to look, I redoubled my attempt at appearing nonplussed and was on the point of pronouncing her a stranger—when she agitated her fan at me as if to shake Niagara off it, adding a wave like fireworks, and several nods that made her necklace come and go like a solstice.

"It is—it is—" I began, wishing there had been a hot-air balloon to carry me away, when Black leaned over so that only Coats and I should catch it: "It is Mrs Salmon, the Simultaneous Sensation of Marylebone Park."

After which he drew back and appeared to take a nap. Though not before I felt him against me, and the folded paper he put into my palm.

"Zeus it is, by Thunder!" Darley dropped his eye-glass in his haste to squint at the marvel. Mr Coats, who missed Black's sleight of hand helping Darley recover it, fell to chewing his lips, staring at me and Mrs Salmon by turns.

How to repair this latest breach in our understanding? Being observed in open correspondence with a reknowned courtesan, after the smoke and fumes I had surrounded myself with, would surely lead eager gentlemen and ladies to only one conclusion about my character. The play passed as if through fog. I lost interest in Letitia, letting my eyes wander towards the opposite side.

Having settled on its perches and distributed bon-bon boxes and decanters to its satisfaction, Mrs Salmon's party was as agitated as a flock of poorly caged coloured birds. The five women, all of a flighty inclination, trilled without restraint, pinpoints of light flashing across their flimsy garments. From Coats's rigid posture and clenched hands, it was evident that he did not cease watching either. I was sorely troubled by how to avoid Poppy Salmon when we went out, as soon we must.

Meanwhile, the talk on stage had turned to a ball, and my thoughts to what I would give to be concealed under a domino, when Mrs Salmon received a visit from four cavaliers. A *sforzando* of agitated fanning was followed by the disappearance of two parakeets and two gallants to the back for ten minutes where, from an occasional scuffle of plumage, they were enjoying refreshments. Seeing how this took Mrs Salmon's eye off the ball, I felt a faint hope of slipping away in the crowd at the evening's end.

But Mr Black, bored of watching me slantways through his eyelashes while pretending to sleep, broke my reverie.

"Can you guess the profession of the fellow next to *your friend* from Marylebone Park?" He spoke so that no one else would hear. I dared not snap back that she was no friend of mine. Mr Black was as comfortable as if he was lounging in his drawing room after a hard morning on the Gallops. His indifference to Mrs Salmon's knowing me was perturbing. The paper inside the prison of my gloves was like a brick. What did it say?

"Cleric." He went on regardless. "Good living in the country. Spends his time prodding penitence into Marylebone while his proper flock goes hang."

He leaned back while I imagined his eyes with the devil in them, and tried not to appear to care. "Why do you insist on telling me this?"

I did not risk looking up, his nearness laying siege to my frosty intentions.

"Why do you refuse to meet my eyes, Mrs Mystery?" He shot

back, so full of mockery he might spill over. "Or, *Mrs Fox,* why not a glance?"

"Sir, you are cruel. My name *is* Fox. Why do you torment me?" I looked at my interlaced fingers, in case the paper showed. So did he. I clasped them harder.

His voice went lower, his breath so warm I could not breathe for fear of catching him. It was impossible to tell his intentions. My own response was mixed, somewhere between love and murder.

"You find these women as interesting as I do."

The shocking words, spoken bland as sorbet, were true. Any honest woman would have fainted at once at his appalling suggestion. I did not bother trying.

"You see them with the eyes of an artist." I tried to dismiss him with flattery. "You grant me a sensibility I do not merit."

We both returned to the stage, his presence still upon me. Behind us the Loyde sisters smouldered and Darley repeated every clever phrase.

The time came to leave, but there was no chance of slipping away in the bustle, for a lady must always be accompanied, in case she collapse in a babbling fit, and Mr Black, glittering at me, had taken firm hold of my arm.

Just as we arrived in the lobby, tremendous shouting broke out. Two of Mrs Salmon's friends were wrestling with a pair of beadles, in such a frenzy that their hair was disordered. On the side of the head of one, a piece of padding like a large hair-wrapped puffball jerked. The other was biting her would-be captor on the ear, so that he threw back his head and howled at the chandeliers. It was these same Whores, straight off the street, who had vanished into the back of the box with their paramours and were now being arrested, for plying their stratagems indoors.

The confrontation was causing sufficient uproar when, from nowhere, Mrs Salmon landed like a meteor on the backs of the officers, clipping them in quick succession on the head with a loud clack of her fan, which aggravated them so much that they dropped their almost-vanquished charges to face the fresh assault. At which the Harlots turned tail and headed for the other side of the lobby, and Mrs Salmon let go and took refuge behind the men from her box, who rose up like spikes to protect her. From there she slipped back so smoothly on the lilac arm of a man I could not identify that the officers had no idea what had hit them. Enraged, they stood stock-still, blood coursing freely from the ear of one on to his linen, resembling nothing so much as a tagged pig, while their opponents brandished canes in a way that promised a scuffle. Twenty yards off, the Harpies delicately rearranged their bosoms and vented obscenities, parading themselves to the relish of every man, while the Law looked on sheepishly.

"Why do they not arrest them?" I asked Mr Black.

"They cannot," he explained, pointing an illustration on the marble with his own cane as he spoke. "The women have crossed into another jurisdiction, for the theatre stands on a dividing line, from here (*tap*) to here (*tap-tap*), although there is nothing to be seen that marks it (*tappity-tap-tap-tap*). These officers have no more right to arrest them now than they have you or I. We could stand each side and offer to murder each other in cold blood—if you like?" He grinned, showing sharp teeth and giving me a fraction of time to decide, "and they would be strongly disinclined to help you. It is another country over there. Come."

"But—."

"The Law," he repeated patiently. "This is the finest trick against the statute book. Each side knows it. The most perfect example of the triumph of absurdity over common sense.

"Look now," he continued, taking my hand, apparently thoughtlessly, "since you are determined to be a student of these matters, watch and you will see another transaction take place."

At that instant, a thick fold of money got free of a diamond clip and passed from one gentleman in evening dress to the hand of the more superior-looking of the Watch, so fast that no body but someone such as I, skilled in that kind of treaty, would have caught it. A game had been played out, and I knew what sort of game, and how everyone involved was now ready and cheerful to disperse.

And Nathan Black, who had slipped me a paper in just such a practised way earlier, knowing that I would take it, rather than bridle and throw it in his face, had understood that I would understand it.

"Come," he repeated.

I went in silence, forgetting my gladness at not being accosted by Mrs Salmon in this fresh cause for alarm.

May 26, 1784
Nathan Black, The Strand

To Mrs Fox, Warp Lane

Your refusal to sit for me[1] does not satisfy me, Mrs Fox. I cannot believe it was written in sound mind, but by a spirit harried by the injustice of its action. Reconsider! Beauty of the order you possess, combined with such fire and spirit, does not belong to its physical owner, but to God, and thence the world.

You have a sacred obligation to sit for me, for the panels for the Church. So pressing a duty could only be dismissed by proving my skill inferior to the task. By withholding the delights of your countenance and figure from generations of worshippers, you commit a crime. Further, since the work is religious, you would entail posterity with a needful guide to the Scriptures.

Consider what I hold out! To be a ray of light in this murky world; to offer beneficence to beggars; illumination to poor sots un-

[1] Black's request and Mrs Fox's reply are missing.

able to read and balm to cohorts of lost souls. If you repudiate this, all who learn of it will shrink in horror and call you monstrous.

I cannot finish the work without you and will renege, desert my solemn undertaking and break my contract with the Church Commission, filling the blank place left by your cruelty with a gaping void. Down the centuries, all who pray there will point an accusing finger and say: she deserted us, she, unnatural among Women, left art with an unplugged gap.

Only a criminal could refuse this appeal made on bended knee direct to your shining Soul, that makes you move in a cloud of Celestial Light—in which pose I would most like to paint you.

Agree to come at once.

Yours—

Journal

May 27, 1784

Nathan Black's importuning, first at the theatre and then by letter, pleased me, yet it was impossible not to laugh. His dark looks, and what seemed supernatural understanding, turned out to be nothing but the amorous intentions of a romantic young foreigner, too long shut up in his studio indulging the hot-house fantasies of an underfed artist.

Thrilled by this false alarm and touched by his ill-written outpourings, I still did not feel inclined to capitulate. His eager claim that I was *the only woman in the world* struck me as hasty, even by my standards. Willing though I was to accomodate him if it proved so, I decided to set the simple test of exposing him to the charms of Miss Hublon, to see if he remained steady—and to test too if that young woman was as deadly to men as I suspected.

Mr Black certainly pleased me well enough to employ him in the thing he yearned for, but the extremity of his intensity recommended restraint. Profound young men, with their harsh whispers and looks (who often have dark hair and eyes to match)—satisfy above the general run. Indeed, I cannot help observing that the otherwise charming habit of a perruke has done all civilised ladies a disservice, disguising the hair-colour—and hence temperament—of prospective gallants. In many cases, having gone energetically forward it is too late to go back, and we risk being saddled with a lover who turns out grey, rather than Black.

What a mercy, then, that God made eyebrows.

However, to return to young ravens: they are tiresome to disengage, not willingly comprehending that once on board, they will be required to disembark at the captain's discretion. Though the attraction of such headstrong youths is too stimulating to repudiate long, it requires concentration that, at that moment, I am too preoccupied to give.

Matters more pressing than pleasant sport occupy my thoughts.

To wit, I am not at all satisfied with my establishment.

Once that is remedied, there will be ample time for Mr Black—unless, unique in the male universe, delay cures his appetite.

Meanwhile I have investigated his artistic claims, since they are by no means petty. The commission to paint church panels exists and what he proposes, however clumsily couched, represents honour, and pleasure into the bargain. Had I a shred of Christianity about me, rather than the tatters of Confirmation vows that will not bear a wafer, I might have given in on a whim that would please us both.

As it is, knowing the uses to which great painters put the same model—the evening before, Persephone, the morning after, Medusa—I am more than certain he will soon find a willing body to fill his wall.

Leaving a note at Warp Lane for *Trichette,* whom I hope is busy learning the secrets of Marylebone Park on my behalf, I am heading for the country seat of Frederick Danceacre.

June 4, 1784
Albrecht Oeben, Amsterdam
To Mrs Fox, Warp Lane

Honoured Madam,

Forgive this intrusion. You do not know me.

One related to me is, I believe, beloved by you. Since you quit Amsterdam, my uncle, Hubert van Essel, has spoken of only one woman. A letter from you now may do him a service that, if it fail, will be superceded only by those of a priest.

He has fallen into a dreadful distemper, madam, a grave *Melancholia* we do not know how to treat. He stays shut up in his rooms at my house refusing food and drink, taking only the water and bread we leave outside his door. He studies deep into the night, refusing the attention of a surgeon, declaring there is nothing the matter—which the pallor of his countenance belies.

This declining came about suddenly.

My uncle had fallen into the habit of walking to our house most days, rejoicing in my children's welfare, whilst they in turn delighted in his solicitude. We were pleased by his familial attention, since he has always been a private man, his personal life a mystery. We felt ourselves blessed and flourishing.

Your former house (that was leased to you by my uncle on the most generous terms) holds many dear memories for him. He was in the habit of stopping there to gossip with the duty man on his way to my house each day.

A fortnight ago, having deprived us of his company for two days, he arrived in a state of great agitation, holding his hand to his side, as if from exertion. However, in answer to my enquiry he said nothing was amiss, and busied himself in a game with my daughter and her cat. That evening he went out again. He was gone above an hour and a half and on his return carried a bag which he refused the servants' taking up. Calling for candles, he retired. The next morning he did not come down, nor answer his door, saying that he was not to be disturbed; that he was in perfect health and we should not worry, merely humour a scholar who now had an inclination to work.

Imagine our happiness! My uncle is respected the length and breadth of this land, but has published nothing for years. That he should choose to recommence under my roof made me proud. But as the days of self-imposed sequestration turned into a week, and the dishes outside his room stayed untasted, I begged him—for, since he was in my house, I had an obligation to his well-being—to let me talk to him.

I will not pain you with the state I found him in. He was evidently in the throes of great distress, whose cause he would not reveal, saying only that it was something no surgeon's knife could excise, and that he must be left to manage it as he saw fit. In talking, he mentioned your name. Thus, madam, have I taken the extraordinary liberty of this letter, in the hope that you may write to my uncle, or shed some light on what may ail or aid him.

Your servant,
Albrect Oeben,
Nephew to Doctor van Essel

June 11, 1784
Mrs Fox
to Hubert van Essel
By urgent messenger

What in the name of God is the meaning of the letter just come from your pathetic nephew? I have been in agony every moment, praying that he is deceived in the severity of your situation; that, though he is a half-wit, he is correct that it is not some dreaded plague that has laid hold of you, but a melancholy to which you are irresponsibly giving way.

Why? Reconsider this ill-advised course and heal yourself. Only let me know what has caused your sudden affliction, and what I may do to help you! Dear God, sir, do not allow yourself to die! You have saved me more than once. Should I lose you I would come undone myself.

Command me and I will act.

In haste—

June 12, 1784
Mrs Fox, Mashing,
Country seat of Lord Frederick Danceacre,
County of Suffolk
To Nathan Black, Painter, The Strand

Thank you for your fine offer of sitting for you, sir! But, since we scarcely know each other, how can I have merited it? Or is it of some other woman you speak, and the letters have become confused? Blandishments rain so smooth from your pen that they tell of a felicity born of repetition. How long is the list of lovelies you have lured to *pose* for you?

Sooth, the country is very fine heareabouts. This Mashing air does me great good. I am in less hurry to quit it with each breath, as if its aery touch were the verdant embrace of an impassioned lover. My humour expands, I meet all comers with anticipation: the dullest fellow entertains vastly. These country souls endear themselves to me, until I could pin on bib and apron to churn cream with brawny-armed maidens, spending the evenings in strenuous country dances to flute and fiddle, whirled like a match stick, powerless in the huge hands of lusty yeomen. All my London cares and obligations slip away!

Your letter does me honour. Yet, how can I allow myself to believe that I am the one woman you would exalt by your artistry? The mere thought of being so singled out, so captured *for posterity*—makes me blush. I had heard that artists live like hermits, in a chaste world peopled only with imaginings—and so am doubly privileged by your offer to enter me in that Sanctum.

It is too important a question to answer now, let us discuss it on my return. Meanwhile, I should be grateful if you would deliver the enclosed note at once to the misses Trichette and Hublon, my dressmakers, at Warp Lane, Spitalfields, the granting of which favour will, I know, inform my response to your request.

Your friend—

Enclosed under cover with the foregoing
From Mrs Fox
To les demoiselles Trichette & Hublon

[A blank sheet of writing paper]

June 16, 1784
Hubert van Essel
To Mrs Fox

So then, Madam, you are in haste.

I AM IN HELL.

My spirit writhes under the gravest penalty.

Damned! There is no salvation, do not come near me. I shall stay in this room until I die, when God will revenge the wrong I have done, casting me from merciful darkness into fire.

Let me explain.

A man came in search of you, just as you feared. Though I confess I did not believe your concerns when you expressed them, even so, a watch has been kept night and day as promised.

He came, a week after you had gone. I did not tell you then, wishing to spare you the dreadful worry it would put you to; nor knowing what the matter was, but fearing that it must be grave.

The watchman, having listened to the stranger's enquiry, said (as I had taught him) that you had removed *to the house of the worthy Doctor, that was soon to become your husband.* If he would be pleased to call later in the afternoon, I should offer him every assistance.

My man told it word for word—I pay him well—coming to me without delay the moment the stranger was gone from sight. He described every detail, particularly how the man started at the part about my soon becoming your husband, the blood rushing from his face so that he looked inhuman, with staring eyes; but speedily collected himself, thanking my servant civilly, and saying that he would indeed call that same afternoon.

I was prepared—if such a condition can exist in such a circumstance. When he came at the appointed hour, as I knew he should, I told him that you were at the Hague, ordering linen stuffs against our nuptials, but would only be gone a day. I let him know that I was the proudest man in the world, and that the stuffs were for a trousseau, as nothing but the best was good enough and even then it should be wanting. In devilment, I pretended the folly of an old man bewitched by a charming young woman, and said that it was as if you had magicked me, and that I had not known what life was before I met you; that whatever you commanded I should do; so in slavery to you that *if you bid me destroy someone I should,* as proof of my love.

The effect those words had! He almost tottered against the wall of the house and flames seemed to rush into his face. He wiped his brow repeatedly, as if he was burning.

To all of this I pretended easy indifference. Continuing my pose of a purblind old man, I declared my ecstasy at having the chance to boast to someone who knew you, knowing so little of your past myself, on which subject, I said, scrutinising him, *you had been strangely silent.* I then offered him the hospitality of my house, giving the impression that I believed he was an old friend of yours—in which deception he did not disabuse me, vigorously agreeing that *he wished to surprise you.*

Scenting extreme danger, I did not enquire into his particulars, recognising him for the man you feared would come. Well dressed and well spoken, there was the gleam in his eyes, of purpose or torment, just as you had described. Without doubt a gentleman, though his skin was brown from the sun. It was easy to tell that he spoke languages; inmixed with a learned vocabulary his accent bore scars of travel.

I repeated that my house was his if it pleased him and he should not be troubled while under my roof—but hoped that he would do the singular favour of supping with me, and taste wines the like of which no living man has ever known.

We dined well. I served vintages that have lain untouched, some of them so rare that I doubt there is one bottle more in the world. He took his as if it were a cordial and I matched him, determined to find out what it were he held against you, in order to protect you from it. So I brought another bottle, even better than the first, and then another. As the evening wore on, liquor loosened his tongue. Over a period of hours he mentioned things that filled me with such horror that I should as soon have spewed bile as breathed. Finally, he became so bound up with drink that he thought only of the matter that obsessed him. Perhaps imagining me a Father Confessor and he under the obligation of the Sacrament, he spoke more wildly with every second.

He recounted a story with which I was already familiar, having heard it in the coffee houses round the harbour a short while before you came to Amsterdam. A terrible account of how, in Paris, the callous whims of two debauched libertines, former lovers, led to the ruin of a convent girl and the death of a virtuous wife; how the evil man, a Viscount, received a fatal wound duelling with the lover of the girl, when the latter discovered he had been a pawn in the games of the vicious pair; and how the evil woman, a Marquise, fled abroad, after smallpox ravaged her so badly that many called it a fate worse than death. She, they said, would be torn limb from limb if she ever set foot in France again, however many years passed, such is society's loathing of unnatural women.

The tale was so appalling that I had always considered it fictitious, a sort of putrid stimulation for the depraved, and never thought of it again. However, it was clear to me that my visitor spoke not from hearsay but knowledge, and had been in search of revenge against the Marquise ever since.

With horror mounting at every word, I soon knew at whom his vengeance was directed: understanding can, at times of tremendous strain, overleap the logical application of the brain, so that even a fool may outrun a scholar—although happily not, in this case.

But I was sorely puzzled in one particular: I mean, concerning the disfigurement of the woman he sought; for here the story did not fit. Then, as if struck by a deadly thunderbolt, I realised something else, of which the young man was oblivious. While I had jumped, in one moment, to a complete recognition of your horrible part in this story, he on the contrary did not know how close he had come—only believing you *connected* to the Marquise, and that you would lead him to his prey. Comparing *your* situation with *her* former circumstances, it is likely that he took you for her servant. You told me that when he called on you, Madame La Vôtre had been out—is it not probable that Mr Martin was under the impression that *she* was the one he aimed to destroy—and the woman I intended to marry?

For the first time that long night my alarm subsided, so that it was possible to think more clearly. I was ahead of him, even though he had spent two years debating the matter and I only an equal number of hours.

Still recoiling—knowing, my heart like a stone, that it was all true—*and knowing too who, and what, you are, unspeakably worse than those women who worked for you*; instead of reacting as one might expect, I found myself unable to feel any compassion for him. There was nothing whatsoever in my breast, except cold loathing and a wish to be rid of him.

What he described had acted on him like a brand. He had become deformed by contemplation of injustice, damaged inside. However badly he had suffered—and that this was so was not in dispute—rage had suffused him with such hatred that he was no longer human, but a form of living death. His very blood was gangrenous, his flesh molten with anger, his entire being rotten; a pitiable mechanism whose sole ambition was your destruction. To this end he had vowed to search the length and breadth of the earth for you, quartering and cross-quartering, circumnavigating and counter-navigating, until he achieved his aim.

Yet his aim was wrong and I, sober as Death, was determined that he should never right it.

All the time he spoke, it was with eyes made inhuman by hatred. He felt that he was saving me by telling me the true nature of the Harpy I planned to embrace: not a woman, he said, but a monster that must be destroyed. No emotion moved him as he voiced these words, so burned up with the exultant justness of his cause that he had lost all sense of whom he talked to, displaying the fanaticism of a mercenary who only rests when his job is done. He froze my blood.

I had discharged the servants, telling all but my man to take the next day as a holiday, giving them a gold florin apiece, to treat their families. Alone for the first time in years I served the visitor with my own hands, finding it almost impossible to hold a glass without snapping it, or spilling its contents. Carving the meat, the sliding knife gleamed among the dark flesh. He did not notice my agitation, but ate and drank, and drank again—then told his tale.

At two or three in the morning, when fresh candles were stumps, I suggested a nightcap. I was old, I said, and too shocked to sleep without it; and I wished to offer thanks for his timely warning. He drank a bumper to my health and shortly fell asleep at the table. Leaving him there, I retired to bed.

The next morning a man, believed a sailor, was found drowned quite near my house. There were no papers or rings to identify him, although since he had a full purse, he had not been robbed. Nor was there any sign of violence. By coincidence, it was my own servant who happened to spot the body and raise the alarm, having first tried to rescue and revive the unfortunate soul, almost destroying himself in the attempt. I insisted that the corpse was brought in, to rest with decency before being removed for burial. We laid it on the dining table. There will be no inquest. Despite having been in the water for several hours, a pervading smell of drink made enquiry into cause unnecessary.

My nephew, concerned at what effect this sorry affair might have on my spirits, begged me to have some personal effects brought to his house.

Thus, madam, events have occupied and overtaken me. I no longer know what to think.

Far from diminishing, my perplexity and horror grow by the hour.

It is not so much that I have killed a man, although that is grievous: *but that I have killed the most perfect example of my life's work and argument.* Here was a creature absolutely transformed by experience; the living proof I had searched for so long and fruitlessly in order to dismay those critics who have laughed at my theories and dogged my career. *And I have murdered him!*

By choosing regard for you over interest in this phenomenon, over what could have been the crowning glory of my life's work, I have sided with flesh over reason, indulgence over consideration. I have become that thing I destroyed—and, now that I have discovered the ease of killing, where will it end?

You said, when still ignorant of the contents of this letter, command and I shall act. Yes, I shall command you . . . but not quite yet.

I will enclose the *Curiosities* with my next letter. They are so frail that you must swear on your life not to disturb the wrappings that will be bound carefully about them. Let Earl Much undo these bindings with his own hand. I have told him that there is nothing on earth like it. Do not come between him and his destiny.

Your friend, in deed,
etc—

June 20, 1784
Mrs Fox, Mashing, Suffolk
to Hubert van Essel

Dearest Sir,

I have not yet had answer to my letter regarding your health, but trust that all will be revealed as the vapourings of that pompous, lily-livered nephew of yours—for what can possibly ail such a man as you? Meanwhile I have come to the countryside, where your letter will be forwarded.

I hope you will be pleased that I have thrown off all taints of the city for a while—compared with the bustle and dirt of London, your own town increasingly appears as a paradise of life-giving properties. Yet, Suffolk country life, while rustic, is not without amusement.

Lord Danceacre is a spoiled young man who, now he is back from a Tour so long it was in effect a career, does not know what to do with himself. He still intends selling his mother's London house, which he has rashly emptied of almost all its furnishings at auction, but his lawyers have just discovered irregularities in the deeds. I had toyed with buying it myself, and came to the country to suggest that idea, since he would not come to me. However, it now seems more prudent to discover what the problem is, in case there may be any advantage to me that disclosing my intent would remove. I have therefore instructed *my* lawyers to make enquiries[I].

Whatever the outcome, at present no body understands quite what is the matter, least of all Lord Danceacre. Uncertainty has put a stop to the sale as if someone had tied an anchor to it and thrown it into deep ocean. Things would go quicker if he would only go to London, or have his Silks here; but he claims that this is not Chancery, and he does not want fusty old scratch-bottoms scaring the geese from laying, strewing clouds of flour over his floors, nor an infestation of Ear-Wigs. Beyond that he will not discuss it. Therefore any prospect of a sale seems a deal farther off than formerly—in direct proportion to his enjoyment here.

Seized by the notion of becoming a model farmer, he has acquired sixteen red cows and converted an outbuilding into a dairy, with pretty coloured tiles inside and a thatch outside. Though not practical it is quaint, copied from one the French Queen has, that he heard described at Paris. Equipment for butter and moulds for cheeses, several in the shape of pine apples, came yesterday, on two carts. They took the best part of the day to unload and install, his Lordship greatly absorbed by the mechanisms for turning and paddling. His manager, Tutton, had set out before dawn, since it was the half-yearly statute fair at the local town. He came back as the sun was setting over the stand between kitchen garden and park, with two fetching dairy maids propping him, a boy and kitchen maid bouncing in the back, and five geese. All but the geese taken on for a year.

We were still finishing dinner with the parson's brood, their mother being gone into Nottinghamshire to visit her own mother, a

[I] This letter to Relling and Squire, Lawyers, not included.

rich widow that married a lace manufacturer, the father on business in London. Nottingham Lace is considered the finest in England. It seems that the parson sneers at a fortune built on lace, yet has no money of his own. While he doubtless rails from the pulpit about *pillow work*, it is pillow work that buys his piglets.

Freed from their parents, the parson's daughters quizzed me in relation to his Lordship—if I was his sister—to which I quipped that *I* had never had the good fortune to have a sister, as they all had, but should look forward to them telling me about it when we left the table; in such a way that they all fell silent. The discussion till then had been whether it was possible to get four hundred pounds of cheese and twenty of butter out of his Lordship's herd every week during summer milk, as he insisted to Tutton, who dined with us as makeweight; followed by a short course of pigs and a dry dish of politics.

Afterwards, as the light had not gone and it was a nice evening, I removed the girls for a walk round the pond. The youngest ones soon lagged behind; they had drunk too much watered wine when Danceacre was not looking, and were very merry. Violet, the eldest—the sharpest and by a long way the prettiest—kept pace in order to renew her childish questions, so clumsily that her ambitions towards Lord Danceacre were very plain. When she asked me again how, if I was not his sister, perhaps I was his aunt?, she got such a box on the ear that she lost her footing and would have tumbled among the baby pikes, had I not snatched her up. She cried out in fright, tearing a jagged rip in her sleeve where it joined the shoulder.

While I was helping her up, ripping her muslin a great deal more, so that I fear it was irreparable (for she had collapsed in a sorry heap on a patch of untrimmed lavender), and before her sisters managed to weave to her assistance, I hissed in her undamaged ear that if she wanted to steal my betrothed from under my nose, she would have to learn to dress better than a milkmaid who made her own garments in the dark with a bodkin, and stop waddling, at which she burst into tears. In this state I delivered her to her siblings, with a final friendly shake, for putting me into such a scare over her almost drowning herself.

Before you ask—Lord Danceacre is not my betrothed. Nor like to become so—though increasingly pleasant to look at; and Mashing, once improved with a new wing and farming methods, combined with Hipp Street and fifty per cent in a canal, is a not unconvincing proposition, and one he urges me to consider.

He is very pleased with my suggestion that Mr Coats is the man to draw up the plans for this new building. Let me tell you how, though scarce two months in the country, I have architects at my fingertips. Danceacre had mentioned a slight friendship with a gentleman by that name and so, under the guise of asking questions about this Mr Coats, I added a few suggestions of my own, so that Danceacre soon came to the opinion that here was the very fellow, and how glad he was to have thought of it. He decided to add a chapel as well and drafted a letter on the spot.

You know as well as I—better, since you are a man—how, once stoked, a gentleman of imagination can run away with himself as if he was fired by steam rather than more moderate coursing of blood; and that once set in passion there is no knowing what he might do, or where stop. So it was that his contemplation of enlargements in one direction led to other matters; in short, that I was the most beautiful woman and the most intelligent on earth, and he took my being at Mashing as some form of agreement. I was glad that the table stood between us, for the forwardness was an outrage. Had he been within reach I might have struck him a painful blow.

Next he invited me to the parlour. The maid brought port wine, and I saw how my situation was rapidly becoming intolerable, for we were in his private house, at night time, and if he was inclined to do what he wished it would be a task to stop him. Announcing that I must retire at once, having certain matters of business to attend to, and letters that would not keep longer. I stood, at which he got up too, rushing towards me impetuously.

"Sir," I said, holding him with some difficulty at arm's length, "I have made a grave mistake coming here, even though it is a delightful spot. I beg you remember that I came at your insistence and so under your protection."

By then he had got hold of my arm above the elbow, sending a shiver through me that was entirely agreeable.

But I shook myself free, before he noticed that I was scarcely struggling, and adopted a harsher tone, while he gazed at me brown-eyed.

"Your mother," I began from a fresh distance, relieved to see that I had his attention now, since his eyes had stopped wandering about like a cow in a field, "your mother would have offered me the protection of her house. If she were still living you would not treat me in this familiar way, abusing my trust. I did not come here, as you earlier dared suggest, with any intention of behaviour of which that saint would not most heartily approve."

This last part was criminally disingenuous, since I could have swung naked from the meat hooks in the pantry and his mother would surely have approved. He did not know how close he was to a complete advantage and the immediate satisfaction of his every desire: my sudden nunnish conversation unmanned him. Taking a pace aback, rubbing at the sides of his coat, he bid me goodnight.

At that moment, had he but beseeched me once more, I would have turned on a halfpenny, but instead stuck fast to my advantage and retired to bed, from which haven of blameless tranquillity I write this.

I long to get an answer to my previous letter.

Your devoted friend—

Part Three

June 22, 1784
Mrs Fox, Mashing, Suffolk
to Hubert van Essel

Sir,

Your letter has just fallen from my hand.

Such violent trembling overcame me that it was certain I should faint. Against my will I have read it again and again. With it, mingled with shock at your cruel words, all the horrors I fled France to forget.

It is clear that those long-past events, that I had prayed would always rest forgotten, must now be spoken of to ease your mind. I will lay my troubled breast before you, so humbled by your clemency and disregard for safety that were you here I should fling myself at your feet begging protection and forgiveness.

Yes, the sorry affairs you refer to happened. But, contrary to your account, they *did* leave me disfigured, eternally crippled by scars to which your friendship in Amsterdam—which indulgence I never dared expect—was balm.

Having been forced to flee my birthplace, to give up property and friends, I believed that the remainder of my life would be spent as an outcast, scouring the world for a dark corner, recoiling from the light; shrinking from ordinary pleasures like a diseased speck, not allowed to live, nor yet to die.

Not once during our acquaintance, begun shortly afterwards, did you ask my history. For that, I daily offered the Almighty thanks—a fact that may surprise you, knowing how I made my living. Yet perhaps not, for along with your belief that I carried myself nobly, you expressed the conviction that I could not be party to those shameful activities to a degree that would bar our intimacy.

You were the one man on earth who did not think me depraved beyond the name of female. Your trust gave me strength to live. From that slender thread, my life began once more.

Sir, here follows my true tale, of which you shall be sole judge. Therefore, all alone, with only your trust as spur, this is the truthful account of my life.

My unshakeable faith developed in the convent where I passed a dreadful childhood, a modest-looking place near Aix.[I] I was immured there by parents who had no interest in a sixth—female—offspring, nothing more than another *dôt* to drain their untrammelled pleasures, best left in a quiet place and forgotten. There, in preparation for a loveless marriage (the dowry reduced against my pliant youth and good name), I found myself at the mercy of those for whom a sensitive girl is as tempting to the abuse of sacred trust as any bait imaginable. Violence that would make you recoil. Not only at the hands of those so-called saintly women, but also the older girls, whose depravations the nuns liked to watch. Yet, bathed in God's all-seeing love, my faith held steady under subjection to actions that, even now, cannot be pronounced. If only I were with you, my hand in yours, meeting your eyes' unflinching probity, drawing on their shining goodness!

Alas not so. Let me go on.

The horrifying story you say you heard is founded in truth—as the most dreadful tales always are.

In Paris, two noblemen fought to the death over a girl each had secretly enjoyed, who was promised to a third in marriage. The challenger, having dealt his enemy (a vastly superior swordsman) a fatal thrust, was obliged to flee France, duelling being a capital crime. The slain libertine had also tricked a virtuous woman into adultery, before deserting her. Losing the will to live, her racked spirit flickered

[I] Most of this account is fabricated.

out with the softness of new-born breath. Yes, such scandals took place.

To my horror, I was implicated in all these disasters. It was laid at my door that I had conspired with the duellist who died, my former lover, to set the characters of this black play against each other. Calumny! But, since *he* could not answer, the charge stuck. I was held solely accountable.

My real part in this sorry business was so different from the slanders that were spread. Where to begin my defence?

Speaking unvarnished truth is a rigour from which we shy, preferring the smoother fit of dissimulation. Yet, since you, fairest of men, are the judge, let me proceed without fear.

My former lover, whom I shall call V, was the most depraved wretch ever spawned. In childhood he drowned his elder half-brother, Hugh, in what was called a fishing accident, in a shallow stretch of river on the other's estate. By this means V not only acquired a title that nature had not decreed, but eventually acquired the whole estate from that side of the family. His brutish action left the dead boy's mother, already repudiated by V's father, robbed of her only child, and comfort in her old age. V offered no solace—the reverse: he tortured her into a fatal decline. There were rumours, so scandalous that they may not be countenanced: fortunately her death closed that enquiry. All her considerable bride-portion, land and property, went to V's father, which V shortly inherited. It was his stated opinion that there was nothing he could not have, once he desired it.

His accomplice in his half-brother's murder (since at the time he was just eleven) was the under-gamekeeper, to whom he gave a sum of money and a promise to take the man's son, a boy his own age, into service once he reached his full estate. This he duly did. The servant, as corrupt as his new master and morbidly inclined to learn by example, was instrumental in his master's later misdoings.

Years later, rehearsing the arts for which he would become notorious, V seduced me on the eve of my wedding. He sent his servant to my women, dressed in my *intended* husband's livery. With a falsely crested purse, the impostor bribed those good women to leave me, telling them of a delightful plot, involving no less a person than my appointed lord. The false messenger's youthful face and urgent appeals in the name of love swayed them. The sound of gold convinced them.

Thus it was that the evil V found me sleeping, ungirded, without defence.

Twelve hours later I was married to a cuckold.

How to describe those events, never murmured to a soul? Though there was no proof of the insult done to him, my husband, with the suspicious instinct of all cruel men, punished me from that day on with unspeakable coldness and far-flung infidelities.

Know that the popular accusation, that I was willingly the lover of V or, worse, helped plan his defilement of both a childish virgin and an honest wife—is a slur. It is all too true that as long as my husband lived, V used threats of disclosure to make me render him abominable services whenever he was inclined. Do not make me write more, lest I take my life rather than endure fresh remembrance.

My husband died unexpectedly, releasing me—or so I thought—from my tormentor. Fool! That devil appeared at my master's funeral and, pressing against me under pretence of condolence, whispered, "Madam, if I am not satisfied this evening by a sufficiently *touching* demonstration that your attentions will not only resume but improve, be prepared to read such ingenious accounts of your repertoire throughout the city, that you become a new wonder of the world." Then those cruel lips brushed the cheek I turned from him, and he was gone.

I hear you say, what of the reports of an evil correspondence between us? Dispel such anxieties. Scandalous forgeries that would hang a woman, but for which a man of V's rank would scarce be chided! Consider this well, for it was the certainty of going unpunished that made him so despicable. Young gentlewomen are convent-trained to write the hand of a child, alike as peas. Scurrilous letters, seemingly from me to him, bearing my veritable seal—were all written by him! But do not rack me further. I have told you of his crimes: murder, imposture, rape. Can you believe *for one moment* that the woman who adores you, loves you, worships you, could have written those letters? Their vicious turns of phrase, their blood-curdling carelessness over the fate of unproved girls, or blotless women?

There is one further thing you will desire to understand.

Following my husband's death, years of spotless widowhood passed. Then, I became interested in the preparation for marriage of a charming girl (now, I trust, safe in her vocation as a missionary nun). At that time, a serious young Chevalier, of such an intellectual disposition that he could surely pose no threat to propriety, became her music teacher, with my agreement. He was soon enamoured of her. Serpentine, he drew the girl into subtle deceptions, until she gave in—all too easily, as it turned out.

Having satisfied one corrupt ambition, he turned his unsated attention in my direction, blackmailing me with the threat of saying that *I had procured his mistress for him.*

Exhausted, abused, haunted—tossed from one reprobate to another, like some plaything—after endless battery, I became his lover. What else to do? How protect myself? I was defenceless! I told myself that if I sinned, it was the sin of pride, that a mere woman could attempt to resist masculine superiority. There was no choice but to submit.

But I was not enough.

The Chevalier, discovering that V had deflowered the girl before him (a girl, one is forced to remark, hardly fit for a life of piety), provoked a duel. Both combatants were close-matched in evil. The younger man, contrary to the saintly image he touted, was a vicious libertine. Given time, he must have become worse: his treatment of me illustrated such a propensity.

The only surprise was that he managed to kill an adversary so superior in swordplay, for V was unmatched in France.

Of the murder of Mr Martin—who was certainly the Chevalier's agent—I have no regret, for Martin's own disappointments and the desertion of his wife had turned him mad. My reservation is that it was not the Chevalier himself. The fear that he might pursue me until one of us is dead is ever present. He believed that I urged the debauching of the girl. Which untruth—as I have proved—is V's deadly legacy to me.

For *that* monster's death I give thanks that I shall repeat before God. He abused my person and used forgery to impersonate my character and name, defaming me more thoroughly than any creature in the history of mankind.

Yet it is I who am cursed! I who must spend my life in hiding! As God is my witness, long after Hell plucked V from the sting of punishment, he reaches from beyond the grave. Only my own end will give me rest. The Devil knows if he will pursue me then.

My life belongs to you. I am indebted to you. Whatever you demand I shall undertake. Yet again, tears coursing down my cheeks I say: command, and I shall act.

Your weeping, devoted, friend—

June 23, 1784
Mrs Fox, Mashing
To Mademoiselle Trichette, Warp Lane

Victoire,

I am surprised (to say the least) to have had no account of your progress with the little French tart, or at Marylebone Park. While pleasure in Miss Hublon's company may outweigh that of my purse, I do not pay you to lard your sides, but to send me daily bulletins.

Put plainer, since your attention is evidently elsewhere: are my clothes ready? How fares the girl? Have you managed to teach her anything? Where is your account of *our friend* Mrs Salmon? Have there been letters or callers?

Take care how you answer, for if I find you remiss, you will discover with what smart slap an open palm shuts.

I am doubly angry at your silence, since I would rather have you here. The maid that has been given me looks and moves like a heifer. Hauled in from reaping mangle-worzels, she pulls me apart every evening and yanks me together again of the morning. I have been so stuck with pins that at times it has been a temptation to start tatting on my own breast. She has only half a tongue, after licking a frozen railing as an infant—for reasons that are, in the event, incomprehensible.

I should get along fair enough even so, but am alarmed by the behaviour of my host, who, while not absolutely offering molestation, chases me in decreasing circles round garden, ha-ha and park, even when we are riding, as if I were indeed a Fox and he the Hound. His childish delight is wearing, while his ploys to seduction giddy me with their inanity. Yesterday I almost tripped over a still-warm pair of duck laid tenderly outside my chamber door. It amazes me that a man with every conceivable advantage, wealthy and well-favoured, displays no inclination to learning or politics and is painfully clumsy at elegant conversation: is, in short, no more sophisticated than a boy of six.

By the by, in extenuation of the temper I am in (steadily mounting, as writing revives your numerous failings), go and present my compliments to that dear lady Mrs Beddoes, and take our protégé with you. A note for Mrs B is enclosed. Accompany it with an excellent fortified wine or plum-brandy, as soon as you have dispatched a reply to me. Hire a conveyance. Hurl my money about as if it comes in so fast we fear being buried by it.

Take careful note how Martha comports herself, and how Beddoes responds to her—but do not let her out of your grasp, nor allow Beddoes more than a glimpse. Harlots such as Martha are born more than usually slippery. I will expect a full account.

While I shower exciting entertainments and diversions on you, and to prove that I am neither grieved nor scarce exasperated to have received no enquiry whatsoever into my comfort or needs, *you will doubtless be anxious to know how your mistress fares.*

Let me at once disburden you of a moiety of the ignorance under which you writhe: I become dreary here in the country, and impatient to be gone. My initial enthusiasm is waning. There is little company except the parson's daughters, who are allowed to run riot, since their mother wishes a marriage, and their father is absent on episcopal business. The eldest, Violet, is the same age as Martha and bursts to be out, towards which lowly ambition I toy with assisting—only it is such easy game. So bent is she on achieving under her own gushing steam what I could contrive, that my reward would be a brief candle. Yet, the more I think on it, she will be so poorly spent in marriage to a country squire that I have decided, in a rash of disinterested admiration, to rescue her. I will create a more interesting opening, enticing and rewarding in equal part, and let you know when I require assistance.

There is also the manager, Tutton: not uneducated, very keen to help Violet in her ambition; and two land-owning families with whom Lord Danceacre has taken a dish of tea.

To enliven this dismal throng, Mr Coats, one of the gentlemen who called on us at Warp Lane the day we arrived, is expected hourly with his rules and set-squares, and news of town.

Lord Danceacre has rusticated alarmingly and taken to wearing a suit of nappy green-stuff, lending him the appearance, lounging with a book, of a moss-covered log. His favoured reading-matter is cheese-making, resulting in spells in the dairy house (although it is not cream he is sampling, since the *cows* are not yet in milk). However, his lactic absences provide opportunity to write to you as well as other—stimulating—correspondents.

I have read the same magazine so many times that I may decide to try my hand at journalism. If a sharp tongue, tolerable wit, diligent eye, effusive pen and complete disregard for truth or accuracy are the principle requirements, then, could I but add an Esquire, I should flourish. Put the latest copies in the packet, they will leaven your ill-considered, hackneyed prose—which literary anniversary, even so, I await impatiently.

Send all by the next courier, or you may be astonished to find me in place of my next letter. We grow stale as toast here. You have enough to do without answering tangible displeasure also.

YET in Arcadia ego, etc—

June 28, 1784
Hubert van Essel, Amsterdam
to Mrs Fox, Mashing

I have mused long over what you say.

What difference a few innocent words are supposed to make.

Does one believe things because they are *professed before God*? One word over another, because it is chosen? What of slips of the pen—death instead of breath; *loathe* instead of love. Might verse reveal men's real thoughts closer than the lies in which they clothe apparent truths?

In my own youth I believed everything, which is a fault the reverse of noble. Good is not implicit in gullibility. Now I veer from one extreme to another, both wide of the mark—supposing a mark exists. Once I was sure that there was no secret that logic could not unravel or place the mind penetrate. I was young. Logic does not obtain in human relations, only for metals and alkalis, planets, rhythms of music. Da Vinci showed us that undulant shapes form what we see and hear. Then, too, I have followed Newton with prisms, and scattered sunlight into colours that may be combined again—yes, I have done it; and shewn that by using glass instead of violence I can throw you across a room, perfectly, without magic. Transmogrify matter, one thing to another and back again, unbroken. It is so.

Then, I have looked through the microscope you saw in my rooms, and observed a world of minuscule animals which the imperfection of our vision conceals. From here it is a small step to conceive of other patterns and activities, invisible yet commanding elements of our sphere of wingless flies, thinking ourselves kings.

So, might it be that in affairs of the heart we are also ruled by unseen mechanisms? Is this what you would convince me of? If emotions follow destined paths, if there are no freely willed actions, how could there be blame in misadventure? It is a short remove to abnegation of responsibility. . . . If, in these horrible events you relate so matter-of-factly, you were acted upon like a mote of dust picked up by a breeze—in other words, the toy of Fate (which is the crux of your argument), how can blame apportion to you? Is this not your plea?

For my plain speech henceforward, *spare me your blushes.*

You know that you are the woman that I should have chosen above all others. Indeed, that by the tacit bond of an abhorrent crime, *I agreed to marry.* That is as like to happen now as for the sun to spin round the earth.

My dear, you no more believe yourself without the strength of a tine of grass than an elephant. You took each step with fuller knowledge than those whose duty it is to explain our consciences to us!

My mind has heard your voice speaking the words I hold before me: false-dropping mellifluence every one. Good God, did you think I would sip your poisoned pap like a feeble old man, grateful for crumbs? Are you so fortified in estimation of your wit that you picture me plodding behind, blinded by love? I have read your letter so many times I know by heart how you twist truth into something closely resembling it but insubstantial as shadow. Your dexterity is marvellous! The woman I love is false, through and through!

How did I discover your counterfeit? By an error that has caught many: casuistry. What, in a surprising slip, you called, *your defence.*

Dear lady! Your position was unassailable, with me. There is no need of defence when there has been no crime. Nor judge, nor jury, neither. I believed you unflinching honest. Why—unless it was not so—defend yourself to your chiefest defender, who cherished you above judgment, above truth and, as my misguided action shows, even above Law!

Defence. You tore down the faith I had built for you with just one word.

At last, the full extent of what you are capable of is clear. There is nothing which you will not attempt.

Have no fear of betrayal, I have grown to love you too well. Whether you progress in deceit or honesty, my connection is too familiar, my life too closely bound to yours to relinquish you easily. Moreover, guilt puts me in your toils: why should I turn against you, when I have gifted you power to betray me to the hangman?

Appreciate, then, my dilemma: something I did not anticipate, more invigorating than anything I have known for years.

Do I destroy you, so risking my own destruction? Even in the midst of horror, you inspire doubt and quandary—in short, you captivate.

But one word of warning. That cloying falsehood of claiming me your saviour—never again draw so hard on my indulgence. Repeatedly, you bid me command—flattery! a further attempt to bind, believing that all I should ever dare ask is a promise of love, and scarce have the courage for that.

So arrogant a hand deserves to be played.

I COMMAND.

Here is your task: destroy Earl Much.

A simple game that should amuse you, just as your letter has beguiled me; the subject one for whom you have already expressed an inclination. I do not disclose my reasons for this un-negotiable request. When you give me satisfaction will be soon enough. You know that I once cared for him; an anomaly that should intrigue you. . . . My expectations are high.

Last, know this. Your account of the duel between V and the Chevalier tallied in every particular with that which circulated freely at the time in all the capitals of Europe—except in one detail. The deadly thrusts came from your hand, not theirs.

So, on a whim of like for like, I present you with a notable swordsman, twenty deaths as careless on his back as trapper's pelts. Fatal with steel as with skirts. Does that please you?

You have been too long in the nunnery. Engage him. Beguile him, do what you wish, merely leave him dead, or dishonoured. They are the same. Manage at least one, it is child's play, the work of an afternoon!

Do so and regain my protection and love for ever. Fail, and a scholar's hands will shape your last caress.

Dearest—

June 24, 1784
Victoire, Warp Lane
to Mrs Fox, Mashing, Suffolk

Mistress,

Had I a groat for every service rendered you, beyond those my hire demands, I should now be set up in a comfortable staging inn, polishing foreign coin, and speeding the post. Not Harlot one day, haberdasher the next, until I scarce know my nature—except I ought rather be on the stage, where there is not only better money, but Royal pickings for anyone able to warble a pretty song, wear skirts sopped to make them stick, and grasp why God made bosoms.

Since Martha has been here she has had several low callers, that I have shooed off without distinction. Her honesty is a fig-meat of her imagination. Six were on naming terms with her, including a grocer, who offered me a lump of sugar *as my own sweetness was run out.* He has a provisions shop with blue shutters by Christ Church. I shall go elsewhere.

When I turn them away, they tramp off bold as anything, down to that cunny Betty, whose exertions start up at once. No objection from Mrs Sorrell—she has her own squires to tend—and her stays more off than on.

This has *never* been the honest house we took it for! Mrs Sorrell, Betty, Martha . . . even the woman upstairs, for aught I know, although now she is so blowed like a bladder they would roll off. Business was quicker here before we arrived than you supposed, they were spinning the culls like tops between them, each taking up the slack when demand outstripped supply.

Nevertheless, following your orders to improve her, I have kept Martha bent to her needle dusk until dawn, and then we set to lessons, so she goes to bed exhausted. She has a fine hand. Your clothes are as good as any in Paris: stitch her mouth up and there would be something for everyone.

Yesterday afternoon, a young man called Mr Black, in dark cloth, came—but no parson, having a roving eye and curls.

He pushes past the boy and bounds in, twirling a letter made out in your hand to me and the sauce-box—altho' since Martha can't read, she was obliverous to being so highly favoured. The door wide behind, he darts bold looks all round, flicking the letter to and fro out of my reach. Soon there was muffled shuffling from the stairwell, which was Betty, the boy and the landlady, greasing up to eaves-drop.

Martha (whom I had allowed a rest) was sitting on the window-seat, shirring a bit of yellow riband for your Livorno, gawping all the while out of the window.

The moment this young buck hove in view, she plucks her cheeks, smooths her hair and hauls herself manfully out of the top of her dress—and he had only blinked once! Scarce dared blink again, lest she make another attempt at levitation. He was well-favoured, but too thin and in need of scrubbing.

I kept one eye on her while I broke your letter, but while I was busy she must have give him a look. He slipped round me to her and whispered something, at which she coloured.

At that moment, just as I caught the fluttering behind me, I saw as how there was nothing at all written in your paper, but didn't let on, realising you must have a reason for it, although I could not begin to guess what.

So I bid Master Black farewell, shoving his bony chest, saying we had no answer to the letter and he should be as pleased to take himself off as should I to see his heels. For the benefit of the gallery, I shouted this part out louder than necessary, occasioning a tremendous tumbling outside the chamber and a shriek, like someone's foot being trodden.

In the street, this Black turned for a last glimpse up at our windows. The two of them had been so Magnetic to each other, like iron filings, that I was expecting to see Martha bumping down the stairs on her skinny backside after him.

Then I shook the living daylights out of her. What did he whisper, you worthless little trollopy, says I, till her teeth dance; and what was your reply?

She is rattling in front of me with hair tumbling round her face, so I give her a good slap to steady herself, and sit close in front on a hard chair. "We can stay here all night if you like," says I equable, pouring a full glass of wine from a bottle near to hand, and none for her. "It's no difference to me, only you shall go without, and I sha'n't; or you can tell me what passed between you, and I will let you up—and I may do more for you besides."

At this hint, a calculating look replaced the sullen one.

"I didn't say nothing he didn't want to hear," she simpers, a sample book for a Trollope if ever I heard one, still fiddling with the ribbon that was meant to set off the gown, now grey from her filthy thumbs. I leaned forward so sudden to take it that she thought I would strike her again. Such a child.

"It's all right," I soothes, going ahead of her, since I was wearying of the game, "of course he wants to see you. Any man would. Did it get as far as money?"

Said very sweet.

She didn't so much as flinch. Criminal through and through, whatever nice ways are shown her. I begin to wonder if we are trying to put good French wine into a pint pot. A smug expression appeared, giving her dimples.

"He doesn't want that," she says, with a look I could have taken off her face with the bottle, "he says I am a goddess and he wants to paint me, for the benefit of mankind."

Madam, this was flummoxing, as I had not imagined such a thing being asked of someone so worthless. Yet it was a great relief that she had not shewn herself in her true colours, and that he was so blinded with amorous intention that he had gilded her. Then again, it might be his ruse to soften her up before having her, so I asked afresh, in a way that made her cry.

"No!" she blurts, one hand clapped to the new red patch rising on her face, but glinting through the fingers, so I began to believe her, "no he didn't offer nothing like that, no more did I. It's true, he wants to paint me for an angel! He swears that accounts of my beauty have reached the ends of the earth."

"Very likely," says I, doubting that her fame could have got beyond the end of the bed. Yet, what if this painter-nonsense is so—or even part of your intention, madam?

"An angel." I pursued, "How is this to be done, cherub, since you are under lock and key? Shall you fly?" She started snivelling, so I poured her a small glass of wine.

"Come, child," I softens again, prising away the spoiled riband, at which she gets the glass in both hands (which I thought I had trained her out of), marvelling all the same at how weeping makes her glow. "There is no need for secrets. I wanted to be sure he offered no insult, and whether you can be truthful. Your answer pleases me."

It wasn't hard after that to make her hand over the bit of paper he had slipped her, pleated like a tiny fan, so small I had not noticed its passing. There was an address, black-spidery as him, in the Strand.

If she went there at all, I told her, adding that it should be considered by and by (after discovering your wishes in that direction), it would be in God's honest daylight; and that if she did as she was taught and behaved like a lady, she might be treated like one.

There is less to report of the Scribbler. I have heard him once, stirring above in the early hours, scraping his chair, but so soft. I have never heard him come in, nor set eyes on him. He must move very quiet, otherwise I should catch him. It is curious that we have never seen him, however hard I keep watch; you would think there was a back stair. Of course I am not always here.

I lock Martha in when I go out, although she has no wish to escape, since her thoughts run entirely on Mr Black. It has galvanised her into learning manners and courtesies, not wanting to look like the common strumpet she is in her ambition to be immortalised on the wall of a church, doubtless as Mary Magdalen.

Here is the account of her progress. In one day she has advanced more than all the last week . . .[I]

[I] A dreary account of Martha's progress follows and has been removed.

continued later

You commanded me to call on Mrs Beddoes. We have just returned.

I followed your orders, purchasing wine off of a Mr Berry in the Hay Market. I told him that I should carry it myself, to ensure that the lady in question got what was paid for and not some vinegar, at which he puffed up, drawing my gaze to the carved and painted crest over the counter, and demanding to know if I supposed *that* family got vinegar? *Judging from their sour faces,* I replied, setting his clerk choking. Then we took off for Mayfair.

Mrs Beddoes was in a flutter, more than I have ever seen. The sale of Hipp Street is suddenly going ahead, and won't have to wait until her master comes back. He left her powers to conduct it, which she is certainly able to do, being of great cleverness. She was eager to boast about her importance. Some irregularity has been overcome, there has been a bid, and all seems well advanced. I asked the buyer's name, in case you might wish to know, and she replied she could not give it, since all was being done through the lawyers, whose name was Squirrel and something.

While this was going on I had left Martha outside in the vis-à-vis, with instructions not to talk to anyone. She is become so intent on being ladylike that all I could see outside the window was a poker back and haughty profile, for the world like she had cut herself out with a pair of scissors, provoking every man as went past beyond endurance. Mrs Beddoes came alongside me at the parlour windows, and asked her name. I did as you bid, saying that she is a young lady from Abroad, distantly related to you, and just come into a vast fortune.

I then give Mrs B a smart good-day and hurried out, noting with satisfaction how a pair of Loungers stood rooted in admiration of Martha as if they were auditioning for gate posts.

All this is done, madam, according to your wishes. The magazines are enclosed.

Your *tireless* underpaid servant—

June 27, 1784
Mrs Fox, Mashing
to Victoire, Warp Lane
by Messenger

Expect me before dark. Do not let the girl out of your sight for a moment, she is not to go *anywhere.* Certainly not to that lovesick puppy, Black. I have learned what I wished to know about him! Never admit the scoundrel again.

How could I have *ever*—

Bah!

Your mistress

June 27, 1784
Mrs Fox, in transit
to Lord Danceacre, Mashing
By courier

Sir,

Forgive me for leaving you without warning. I am in my carriage, at the outskirts of London.

At dawn this morning, urgent news came that allowed no delay. I set off with the courier who had ridden the night through to bring it. You have shown great generosity, granting me brief respite from London cares. The country air has been refreshing. I regret there was no time to bid you nor Mr Coats goodbye, and trust that the plans for the wing and chapel go well. This sudden business may detain me for some time.

In haste,
Your friend—

June 29, 1784
Mrs Beddoes, Hipp Street, Mayfair
to Lord Danceacre, Mashing

Sir,

Yesterday I went to Relling and Squire, your mother's lawyers at Holborn, to complete the sale of Hipp Street. A feather-cap flew down as I went up. After some minutes, one of the clerks shewed me in. The lawyers sit either side of a window in a room covered with oak. Both have freckles, and red tufts sticking out from under their bags.

They told me that a small, quaint-looking stranger had come unannounced the day before yesterday and made a much higher offer, which he had bonded in gold. The lawyers put this challenging offer to the first party, which apparently raised its bid, and that went back to B (who was *exotic,* according to Mr Relling). The exotic party raised its offer without hesitation, which went once more to A. "Like lightning," Mr Relling observed, offering me a dish of tea.

I was in need of refreshment, sir, as you can imagine. I noticed that the cupboard he took the urn from had a large sprigged dress in it, hanging next to a ham, which struck me as curious.

Mr Squire beckoned me to the fire, where he read the paper over a glass of Portuguese. After some minutes, while his partner shelled nuts, there was the sound of a heated discussion beyond the door. Then Mrs Fox appeared, cloaked to the chin, with a clerk right behind.

We looked at each other.

Mr Relling threw his shells at the floor, while Mr Squire quartered his newspaper and started down the boxed announcements, without so much as glancing in her direction.

"Unlooked for pleasure, ma'am, "Relling said softly, "although, as you can plainly see, we are engaged." A nutshell fell from his breeches. "Alas." He raised an eyebrow at the two hovering young men.

Mrs Fox stood like a statue. "I am sure this lady will allow me a trifle of her time," she said, nodding at me. I granted her request, believing you would wish it. At this, she and the lawyers went out for five minutes, then they returned alone.

"Generous to allow the interruption," observed Mr Relling, scuffing at his shells. "You never know."

Your Lordship's business in finalising the details of the sale absorbed all my attention after that, sir, as you can well imagine. Clerks came in with a large pasteboard box full of papers, and Hipp Street is now sold, for twice the original sum.

The relevant documents are enclosed for your inspection.

I do not know what brought Mrs Fox to Relling and Squire.

With the greatest respect—

July 6, 1784
Mrs Fox, Warp Lane
to Urban Fine, Earl Much,
Salamander Row

Your Lordship, daily absorbed by affairs of great moment, must have forgotten a trifle of no consequence, an unimportant work in a binding that feels so frail through the outer wrapping of parchment that I have been put under strict instructions not to untie it.

It is *Curiosities of the South Seas, and Fashions and Customs Peculiar to its Natives,* found for you by Dr van Essel, Amsterdam, for which you have been kept waiting an unconscionable time, due to delays of weather and the Customs. If it please you, the volume has at last reached me, which I would be happy to present at your convenience, if you will send word by the servant who carries this letter.

Respectfully—

July 7, 1784
Mrs Fox to Victoire

Dear Victoire (or *Mr Voster!!!*)

Everything is to be done to reopen Hipp Street as I instructed you in detail a week ago, and repeat here[I], since I cannot understand where that letter has gone, or how the post can be so unreliable.

The trust I place in you is unequalled, of which you have long been aware, having been nursed at the same breast—which created a bond from our earliest days. Were learned men to be believed, our differing estates at birth would be annihilated by that shared intimacy. Which is of course nonsense. Nevertheless, were I in the fortunate position of having blood relatives in London, instead of relying on subordinates and strangers, they would doubtless interpret my wishes even worse than you.

[I] Mrs Fox, having bought Hipp Street secretly, through Victoire dressed as an exotic-looking young man (Mr Voster) now uses Victoire as a front. Her first letter of instruction was evidently lost in the post.

Mrs Beddoes is to take charge of running the business side at Hipp Street, Mrs Salmon will be the figurehead and right hand, and they will employ whom they like beneath them. I do not care to know more, as long as you express satisfaction in their choices. With the extra authority you will have dressed as *Mr Voster,* my secretary, ensure that peace reigns. Which I believe you will find easier than you suggest—particularly once you make clear that you are their sole route to money, with which they may be showered or straightened, depending on the reports you send *to their new master,* the "mysterious foreigner" who has purchased Hipp Street.

I leave the embellishment of that part to your fruitful imagination, within the guidelines of practicality, and as long as you make sure that however wild your flights of fantasy are in respect to this *gentleman*'s identity, your story stays consistent. In disguise as the effete servant of my exotic self, any peculiarities in your manner will be discounted as proper to a foreign lackey. Nevertheless do not lose sight of Mrs Beddoes's intelligence, for although it is an undoubted truth that one reprieved from execution—as she has been, to all intents—is prepared to believe anything, that humbled condition quickly wears off.

I am certain that these two former enemies, once reintroduced in fresh circumstances, absorbed by the task of establishing Hipp Street as the miracle of Whoredom it is destined to be, will soon become comfortable in each other's company and confidence. The speed with which animosity turns to love is a well-reported fact. Mrs Beddoes's recent expression of dislike for Poppy Salmon was no more than the jealousy of a usurped servant for a younger and more talented rival in the affections of her mistress, rather than actual hatred. Between feelings of rejection and those of a lover thrust from the palpitating embrace of a mistress by a fresher, livelier amour, there is no difference. Grievance; wounded pride; blood whipped to fatal deeds but as fast abated by new employ or encounters—whichever the case—all qualities matched one for one. There was so much admiration, did

Beddoes but know it, mingled with her every abusive word about Salmon, confirmed by her lingering on the very object she professed to scorn, that her true feelings were transparent.

I would go further, that Beddoes nurtures a sort of maternal diligence for the younger woman. It is a marvel that Danceacre did not see it. What provoked Beddoes's wrath was a sense of inevitable betrayal, that the girl was breaking away from her to fly into an independent sphere—the same feelings of a mother at an assembly when, in her most becoming dress, eyes sparkling, responding to the thrill of the evening air and scent of camellias playing duets with violas, her child whirls away while she watches, invisible as the chair she is compelled to sit in.

You will have no difficulty bringing Mrs Beddoes to a nicer understanding of her feelings, and the relinquishing of any residual murderous ones. At least, I trust so, for a misjudgment on that score would prove costly.

So long as Beddoes thinks that she has the superior role, she will be content, and make friends with Mrs Salmon. Give her back her amusing title of General. Restoring her rank will let her know what is expected. As a final lure, she may reclaim her old study and furnish it as she pleases, to which end a bill for two guineas is enclosed.

To help ease the breach between Mrs Beddoes and Lord Danceacre, and to guarantee the greatest profit, the *world* must be in no doubt that it is Mrs Salmon who has the upper hand and that she overcame stout resistance to woo Mrs Beddoes into her service. Mrs Salmon's is the name connected with this particular style of entertainment. Ensure that this is the impression abroad, a task that will be aided by Lord Danceacre's blind indifference to the value of the commodity he had at his disposal in Mrs Beddoes, yet let go; a woman pining to be employed by him.

His continuing folly amazes me. His error, in not at once securing her to run Mashing in place of his thieving estate manager, Tutton, left her at the mercy of the first bidder. Not even the highest, I suspect. She would have done it for a crust, if he had only asked: really, he should have auctioned her. Thus whimsical is a servant's life, no better than a slave in the Egyptian market place, where the best teeth win. Take note.

Danceacre's not dismissing Tutton is astonishing. The man had been stealing land behind his back for years, for which a brisk fan-dangle on the gibbet at Danceacre Cross would have been too rapid a recompense. I learnt the extent of the malpractice from a neighbouring farmer who mistook me, walking in my outmoded riding dress, for my own maid, and so enjoyed a good gossip. Over the years, Tutton had fenced off a large piece of land and a length of stream, on which he built a modest house and barn—at his lordship's expense. Easily done, since Tutton audits the accounts. Lady D had never wanted to know anything about Mashing during her manager's twice-yearly visits to Mayfair, beyond whether the fish were jumping, which shameful indifference her son has inherited: Lord D only understands figures on bits of card illustrated with kings and queens.

Lord Frederick's absence abroad, and Lady Danceacre's having stayed in town, meant that even the local people lost a true sense of where Mashing ended and imposture began. As a final act, some weeks ago, clever Tutton made his Lordship take part in an *ancient rite,* apparently to confirm the old boundaries but, in fact, to legitimise his new ones, legally dividing off the property he had stolen, by which ruse he now has fair title, and a paper signed by his master to prove it.

Even though Lord D's stupidity worked in our favour as far as Hipp Street is concerned, since he could not bear the discomfort of coming to town to meet the new purchaser and let it all be done by the most crooked pair of lawyers in Christendom, the case of Tutton irritates me. For while being duped by one's superior is bearable, an inferior attempting a similar trick must not be allowed.

Since Danceacre is incapable of protecting himself, I will take an interest on his behalf. If that smirking Tutton is striding about getting bastards with the dairy girls, there must be some corollary advantage to be had. When one shakes a tree, more than one fruit should tumble down. It should be possible to advance Violet's career at the same time.

During my stay at Mashing I let Violet into the details of Tutton's theft—tho' neglecting that bit about him now having due title to the land. Miss Cosmopolitan considers herself shrewd enough to use this partial information, believing, after what has been planted in her greedy mind, that she will insinuate herself permanently into Lord Danceacre's affections, and lord it over her sisters.

Alas, this will not prove the case. Only extreme youth (her main attraction) misses the fact that forcing a man to see that he has been conned by his hireling and made the laughing stock of the county is not the way to win him. She may find Tutton, cornered, a robust adversary. Particularly as he had got the fancy of offering her the run of his barnyard and could, if roused to anger, try to hurry things along.

Then, too, it was only fair to inform Tutton of her tendency to defamatory falsehoods, telling him something she appears to have said about him, which made him turn very dark. Next, there is the question of two scribbled notes, that would certainly appear to be in her childish hand, in the instrument case and pocket of Mr Coats, the surveyor. The contents of these will, when they are discovered and shown to Lord D—in addition to the girl's growing history of malicious slanders—make her feel very sorry for herself, and resentful of her elders.

I anticipate that Lord Danceacre's anger at her using his hospitality to attack his manager and seduce his architect will be short-lived; the man possesses a disposition both amiable and accommodating to the highest degree. Even so, it will make her smart, and she will despise him with the vigour of youth. If I judge correctly, should she learn, by any means, how easy it is to get to London with just a few coins in one's pocket, she may feel that she will receive kinder treatment there, and her gifts be better regarded.

I am taking this benign interest in Violet because I agree entirely with her estimation of her gifts. A girl so naturally full of energy and high spirits will adapt quickly to the ways of Hipp Street, where her exuberance will have full expression, and she will be a source of untainted pleasure—for a few nights—to so many.

Your mistress, and new master—

July 13, 1784
Mrs Fox, Salamander Row
to Hubert van Essel
c/o Albrecht Oeben

Yesterday I handed Earl Much the packet containing the *Curiosities*—although you had swaddled the book in so many wrappings that it might as well have been a piece of balsa wood. Do you really think I care a farthing about looking at it? You treat me like an infant.

Earl Much is a great deal smaller than I expected.

Following your warnings to be resolutely on guard against an unmatched skirtsman, I had imagined a bigger casing to be the habitat of such a dangerous creature—at least six foot tall, with the strength of two men; a flesh-eating Colossus, sparks flying from his eyes, spitting limbs and lace along halls clogged with corpses and whale-bone. Not the elegant creature with transparent skin and girlish hand that greeted me. I struggle to comprehend why you placed so many obstacles in the path of our meeting—before, that is, your dramatic change of opinion and renewed interest, nay, insistence on it.

I had girded myself well against his advances, requiring to be stitched into my gown more firmly than usual, so that those delicate parts, at least, should have nothing to fear unless from an indentured seamstress. From the moment the light carriage that he was thoughtful enough to send deposited me outside Salamander Row, anxiety reigned. My breathing turned shallow, my hands clammy, while my heart began an alarming shudder. It was barely possible to totter up to the imposing portico between footmen on whose youthful strength and hyacinth arms I was forced to rest for a considerable time. A dozen steps took as long as the Himalayas. Had they snatched me up and carried me, protest would have been impossible.

I was certain death was near, and that I should scarce be shewn to the drawing room before the fatal onslaught began. Cast to the ground, my reputation destroyed, my life-blood sucked out and one more empty carcass tossed on a heap, a husk for the night-men in the morning.

In truth, I was so prepared for this encounter that, when unseen retainers pulled the double doors open from within—as if the tomb itself fell agape!—I near screamed from disappointment, finding nothing but shining stone, twinkling lamps, and a towering display of orchids and other exotic blooms, acid-green striated with cornelian and vibrant pink spattered with white. These rarities glistened from an ethereal penumbra, cast by a ribbed dome swooping up to where a light-well cunningly let into its top dropped coloured lights below, man-made rainbows of shivering spits and splashes.

Standing thus entranced, observing the colours play on the floor around my skirts and blossom on my hands, the servants melted away through mirrored doors. I was alone. Tall glasses to every side played further tricks with the light; I caught sight of myself, a column of red in a close-cut redingote, eerily suspended in the glittering perfumed gloom like the pistil of a gigantic lily. Throbbing, in that intense silence, to the come and go of my blood.

Only a moment passed—although one so remarkable it is engraved on my memory—when, in another mirror, from out of what I had thought merely broken light and shadow a man stepped, taking me so unawares that I almost dropped the *Curiosities.* How long he had stood watching from a dappled pool, half-concealed by waxy blossoms, was impossible to know. He came briskly forwards. Even in the subdued light, the intensity of his eyes was notable. Specks of colour drifed across his suit as I was caught up in returning his greeting.

There is little more to tell that could be of possible interest, except that his civility is unparalleled.

"Tut, is that all!" I hear you say. Very well.

He paid me the compliment of a tour around the house, apologising at every step for defects that did not exist, rooms he considered too small, effects too simple or colours that must disappoint—if they did not cause actual pain. He demonstrated consideration for my comfort and pleasure as if nothing existed but I, round which the world revolved. That one so superior should be so humble, so faultlessly courteous, provoked sensations impossible to describe.

As he drew me on, his delicate hand marked as if by the petal of a wild violet, which threw the skin into purer white, I became spellbound by the unrolling kaleidoscope of novelty and diversion.

"My life's work," he sighed, as we went through a narrow passage of Egyptian paintings, stiff figures glistening with pure gold, the whole flecked with gems crushed to pigment. "Tragic," he continued, gesturing towards the figures of a Pharaoh greeting his Pharaee, or possibly a master decapitating his servant, "that one should achieve so little, be so reduced by one's puny effort. Wherever one tries to touch the sublime, the result is derisory."

I halted in wonder at his appeal but could trace no irony. His face bore the expression to which I was already accustomed—nothing but my own reflection and attention to my wishes, as if he was a mirror held up to my every desire. Yet, he sounded as indifferent to his treasures as if he would as easily take a torch and destroy everything, as to set eyes on it again.

The house was like a symphony, every section modulating to the next. Had young Mozart scampered through these octagonal and sextagonal chambers, he must have burst into a lively air on the spot. Each room has its particular flavour. In one, dancing girls and boys from Greece and Rome flirt with the breeze of centuries; in the next, rigid Assyrians. Further on, naive carvings of pattern and symbol refresh the eye. There are miniatures one may only observe through an optic, traced with a single hair in nacre or lapis; manuscripts miniaturised on rice papers on which whole lives have been spent. Panels depicting lovers and battles from every great master flashed before my gaze, dismissed with a wave of his elegant wrist as if they must bore me: Coptic embroideries; Renaissance jewels; Peruvian daggers; flasks from Samarkand hollowed from rubies. . . .

At last, stumbling from exhaustion, I begged for mercy. With the lightest touch, the Earl directed me up a second flight of stairs, towards the salon. Here, away from the cacophonous treasures below, all was Parisian taste. He wanted to know if the double room with its slender balcony overlooking the tree-filled square pleased me, since its decoration was only just complete. He was anxious lest the colours were garish, the silks coarse, or the precious inlays obtrusive.

"A hint," he beseeched me, "a breath of dissent, would convince me to begin again for, while it might do for me, wholly indifferent to my surroundings, I should be ashamed to make you endure it."

The room was yellow, like being inside a canary. It pleased me.

Much allowed himself a bow, his lilac suit queer against the vivid upholstery.

"Then," he took a sip of champagne, never removing his eyes from mine, "you cannot know the balm of your words, for I have been sleepless with anxiety, ever since your first letter."

At a loss, I asked him to explain.

It seems—although I felt uncertain of this part, so he repeated it, muttering that he should be taken to the steps of his club and whipped for my confusion—that this house is for me. His own is next door!

We are very late for the Opera. I will write again.

With every hope that your health improves,
Your—

July 13, 1784
To Miss Violet Denyss
The Rectory
Village of W—
Suffolk
From an Admirer

[The enclosed piece of newspaper had been neatly cut out]

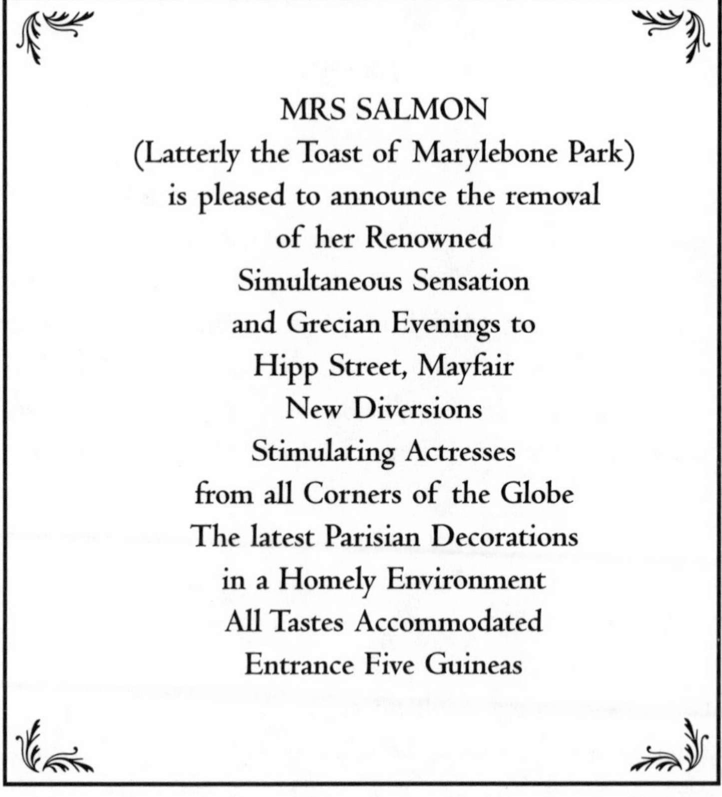
MRS SALMON
(Latterly the Toast of Marylebone Park)
is pleased to announce the removal
of her Renowned
Simultaneous Sensation
and Grecian Evenings to
Hipp Street, Mayfair
New Diversions
Stimulating Actresses
from all Corners of the Globe
The latest Parisian Decorations
in a Homely Environment
All Tastes Accommodated
Entrance Five Guineas

[On the reverse]:

Special Herbal Pills and all manner of Useful Advice for mothers-to-be, including Consultations with a Female Doctor in Comfort and Privacy; Layettes of the Finest Quality (second hand); Advantageous Rates for Lying In at Clean and Hospitable Nurseries in Leafy Countryside; Recommendations for Wet Nurses in Full Health and under Forty years of Age (positions available for suitable applicants with Firm Well Shaped Breasts and Full References); Dentistry and Tooth Extraction (incisors only) by Woman Surgeon; Pink Hysteria Pills to correct Enlarged Stomachs; Apprenticeships for Young Orphans. Apply Mrs Masters, Seven, Three Kings Yard.

July 18, 1784
Hubert Essel
to Mrs Fox,
Salamander Row

Obstacles? What Obstacles have I ever placed in your path, and what notice would you take if I had attempted it? You are wilful, as your previous history amply illustrates. Were you without the redeeming qualities of spirit and resourcefulness, what interest could one possible take in you, madam? Where would be the allure of someone so contrary, outspoken and manipulative? I accept that it is these that shape your fascination. But your quick enthusiasm for your new friend demonstrates that you are not the only one to practise them. Moreover, whilst I took more than a year developing an appetite for your peculiarities, it seems you have fallen *in minutes* for those of your rival—which is in very low taste, best suited to the quayside brothels you once professed to be sickened by.

I do not know whether you are in jest but, if so, your last letter was ill-judged. This man is deadly, yet you talk of him as if he was a child at skittles, with his *amiable smiles* and *elegant hands*, his doing everything to please you . . . really, I am so infuriated by your nonchalance, threatening as it does your life, that I can hardly see the paper to write. What were your exact words, that he is a mirror held up to reflect your every desire?[1]

You have seen young cats, when they first encounter a mirror, how they rush behind to find their playmate, only to bang their heads severely against it, or face the worse perplexity, that there is nothing to be found except dust and dead cockchafers. You think he is holding up this glass to please you. Have you gone mad? He is holding it to magnify your vanity, so that you make no attempt to see what he is really thinking, so that you cannot see behind. Dear God, if you could, I swear you would run screaming from a Gorgon.

I cannot believe that you have swallowed such a simple ruse. He is turning your conceit into a weapon. He will lure you into his confidence, make you feel safe in his company and then when he has worn down your reserves—which you seem to have tossed aside already!—do what he likes with you. Never lose sight of the reason why you have made contact with him, lest you are the one destroyed. Tease me to your heart's content if it please you but do not, by making light of the matter, fall into the trap of believing it so.

Think more clearly. Why would he embrace a complete stranger, putting a house full of irreplaceable things at their disposal? Apart from a slender link with me, about which you know nothing, what is there to connect you? You do not know the terms on which he and I parted, or what may have taken place between us in the intervening years, during which an entire life—yours—has passed! You are the age to be his daughter . . . does none of this concern you?

He has no way of telling who you are, or what you might do. Did he know—and such a thing could so easily happen—I am certain he would find you a great deal more interesting.

Imagine hanging at Newgate: what a change of scene, a novel view. Even *burning* can be put on for a murderess; are you aware of

[1] Not her exact words.

that? You enjoy new horizons: does the thought of fresh prospects and companions please you, albeit short lived? Sufficiently to focus your attention on the game in hand? Or do you believe that this sweet lord, only concerned with your comfort and pleasure, would be *charmed* by your illustrious history? Even he might be taken aback by the accreted villainy of one still so young.

But no. You think him disinterested, blown by the breezes, carefree and careless.

Only my admiration for you prompts me to explain his true nature, before it is too late to save you.

The world is full of charlatans. He chief among them, you may be intrigued to learn. It might provide hints for his future. If you have leisure, examine some of the paintings and sculptures you describe so tenderly, when he is not hovering like a lavender cloud at your shoulder. Some of the very things that impress you are pitiful imitations.

Take, for example, a rare bust of Apollo.

I once told you how money is no object to Urban Fine, and how he stops at nothing to realise his ambition. He scarcely knows how to tell bills apart, handling them so infrequently. The inevitable adjunct to such largesse is avarice; there is no exception. The most wealthy are the meanest, stake your life on it.

Here is proof. Much saw the genuine bust of Apollo in a palazzo in the Grosseto, where it took pride of place in the collection of an Italian, Signor Piestre, and was something of a point of pilgrimage. Much suggested to Signor Piestre that he would be pleased to buy the bust, at whatever price that gentleman named. I was there.

We were all strolling along a very windy parterre, the sun was on the point of setting. I longed to go back inside. In his usual manner, Much expressed his wish and waited—forgive the levity—for capitulation.

Instead, the other man seized his arm, laughing out loud. He had heard how the English Milord took revenge on those who refused to grant his desires, he said. Humour rippled in his voice, he knew no fear. Piestre added that men such as Urban Fine cast things aside once they have them, their pleasure desire, not possession; yet, until they get ownership, they never rest.

I had fallen behind, fastening my cloak. Much was cringing in the tall man's grip, writhing under what were unpleasant truths. Signor P (a financier) continued that he would not sell at any price, no, not for the Milord's entire estate, since money was nothing to him, either. He laughed again, before proposing to give the bust for three days, so that Much might wake to it and go to sleep with it. After which, the banker said gleefully, he was heartily convinced that his new friend would be as bored as of a woman, having enjoyed all the pleasure, at no cost.

"Three days on a woman?" Laughing feebly, Much released himself. They shook hands, adding the proviso that on Signor Piestre's death, Much would get the Apollo. A paper was drawn up to that effect. When I saw the ink sanded on the parchment, which was afterwards put into my hand for safe-keeping, my mouth went dry.

Next morning the bust was delivered to our villa, not far away. The Earl summoned me and told me to have a copy made. That took me by surprise, since I had assumed we would keep it and face the consequences, presumably a duel that my master would win. That was his preferred method of solving problems.

He had been up since dawn. After firing those orders at me he set off hunting, with servants and provisions for three days, tapping the Apollo with his knife in passing.

Making the copy was difficult, since there was so little time and the original was well known. A marble at such speed, in secret . . . of course, the job was done, although the stone had to be stained. The result was superb.

As the third day drew to a close, I kept a look-out for the hunting party. Urban Fine and I had agreed to breakfast together the following morning, before returning the bust. Near midnight, torches came stumbling through the trees at the edge of the park, moving as if the men were exhausted. This can happen with a long boar hunt. As they approached, it was obvious that something was wrong. The group was smaller than it had been on setting out. Rushing forwards I was relieved to distinguish Much's slender figure, and ran up to him.

Signor Piestre had joined them that morning, the Earl lied, carelessly, waving a languid hand in a sort of valediction; but met with an accident in the afternoon. Some men had carried him to his own estate, his life in the balance.

There was no point asking how the accident happened.

We retired.

After a miserable night I met him on the steps with the wrapped copy of the Apollo and we set out.

At the palazzo of Signor Piestre, black streamers flew from every window, and scores of doves that had been hastily dyed black, but turned purple, fluttered in agonies on the lawns.

Once inside, we learnt that the recent bride had just returned from Milan, to the sight of a priest robing for the last rites. In a voice of hollow sadness, Much requested an audience with the widow.

We were kept waiting. The great chamber was unlit and unheated, every mirror draped black. The head sat in a lake of its white wrapping linen, like that of the Baptist.

At last a door closed somewhere. Head to toe in weeds, the solitary figure of a woman came the slow length of the long chamber, reflecting like a smear in the terrazzo. In her fist she held a paper; the duplicate, I suspected, of the one I had. It was the only relief in her mourning.

She came to a halt at some distance. Much began a speech about tremendous sadness, bravery, and the bust; and how he could not, of course, accept it from her, *even though it now belonged to him,* as the paper in her hand—*he believed that that was the paper?*—proved.

You cannot imagine how dreadful it was as those vipers slipped from his mouth. I knew he had engineered her husband's accident. My only consolation was that Much believed the head between them to be the copy, not the true Apollo (for I had had the wrapping of it and clung to the grim intention that somehow it would return to its rightful owner).

As he continued sneering, defying the young widow, ignoring how her heart must be breaking, my own heart went out to that shrouded figure—which unlooked-for compassion overwhelmed me. Taking a pace back I sat, at which Much glanced coldly at me, before resuming his attack.

He pushed the loosened covers clear of the Apollo with the heels of his hands, prised the head up, and took three paces, that thing glaring from his arms all the while.

"Have it, madam," the hypocrite insisted, caressingly, as if offering a love token, "one word and I relinquish my claim. Your husband valued it above life itself. Just one word."

At his disgusting tone, the widow threw the paper on the floor and stamped on it.

"*Murderer,*" she spat, through her mourning.

We looked at her in amazement.

"I hope you choke on it."

She tore off her veil. Signora Piestre was Jocasta Verney.

With a horrible crack, the priceless bust shattered at Much's feet.

Carousing in the blandishments that man offers, you may have already cast our pact aside, believing of an old man in another country that, though you owe him your life, your promise can safely be discarded.

Consider such a route carefully before embarking on it. It would not trouble me to come and hold you to account; or reach you through others, if I do not care to see your face in its dying throes.

Be in no doubt of my power to do so. You know that I can—but will not. Coercion is not justifiable. No servant, child or woman—none of God's creatures—should be forced into actions not of their choosing. Making others do things unwillingly may well be the spring that drives the world—and, it seems, fascinates you—but the price is too high.

Refusing that way of life excluded me from most professions, except artist, scholar, or priest. From marriage too, which is the only part I regret. Women need excitement. What little I had to offer . . . I could not compete.

It is not merely for myself I seek revenge, but for a woman Earl Much wronged, now dead. She was the one woman I loved, apart from you, and he destroyed her. You will know who she is, by now.

My life has passed wondering what I could have done to save her from the life he forced her to. At times I despaired, but used study as a distraction, hoping that if I made important discoveries, or influenced other men to do good, it might counterbalance him, or redeem my failure.

So I watched from a distance as he went about her annihilation, telling myself that I was powerless. . . . God help me, my heart is too heavy . . . nor will I dishonour her a second time by exposing her story to you, full of mocking indifference.

Let me know if you will keep our agreement. I shall not lift a finger to enforce it, preferring to discover your true nature, rather than what it might be, under duress. Whether you hear from me again depends on your answer.

May God influence you, since I cannot—

July 23, 1784
Mrs Fox, Salamander Row
to Hubert van Essel

You are in such a rage that your much-vaunted reason and logic have fallen into a canal. How interesting!

Whilst you are the professor, I a mere student of human nature, one cannot help but suggest that the pupil outdoes her master in skill and understanding.

Your reason is rudderless. You cannot decide whether to threaten me with death or grant me pardon, in a saintly turn that is both sickening and inappropriate since, unless my memory fails, *murderers find the gates of heavenlocked.*

Hanging! What betrothal gifts you offer! And at Debtors' Door, with the mob cheering, too! An audience! You know, Doctor, you are irresistible breathing brimstone—so well informed, painting such a moving death for your *recently beloved*! Why not come with me, it is easily arranged for us to *swing together*! They say that criminals dance in rows, men and women in a line, the only time in their lives that they do something in unison. What a fine thought, to provide amusement for those Londoners who find the theatre bloodless. I have been to a play recently, and am forced to say that poisoned looks and ridottos offer so much less than poisoned books and stilettos.

Do not turn confessor either, rushing to absolve every sin I ever committed: we will be at it so long I shall have time to get up new ones before you are half-way through. What is more, the priestly garments do not suit you. Old-fashioned you may be, but at least you wear breeches. There is no space in my memoirs for another skirt.

Can you really have so little faith in me? It shakes my opinion of you. I thought you—for so brief a time, it is true, and then I was under the spell of your direct influence—the best and most intelligent of men. Now, deceived, I too am floundering, all at sea. Look at us, both awash with indecision. A sorry pair—some might say suited. But, there is no chance of that in our current misunderstanding.

I see I must be patient: take a closer look at the seal on the letter from me that you recently reviled. You will have it within reach, I know how carefully you open letters—especially, I flatter myself, when they come from me. Tear your other correspondents to shreds, but am I not pressed between petalled sheets?

Did the wax have an irregular indentation at the bottom, almost like a bird's foot? Of course not . . . I doubt he even saw it, in his impatience to get inside my thoughts. How my slavish admiration must have pleased him, running panting to tell you what a great man he is and how I am already in thrall, my blood quivering in trepidation.

Do we understand each other yet? *Earl Much read my letter before you!* Is it possible to be so blind, so slow?

Victoire is furious with you, she has rings around her eyes from staying up day and night two full days to intercept every messenger who came near the house, to get to your reply before Much's henchmen, since a toddler could guess at its unguarded sentiment. Needless to say, he may be quick, but she is quicker. A genius at these matters—at so many—she soon made a friend in the kitchen, a perfect vantage point. Victoire possesses the attention to detail of a forger . . . which gives me fresh ideas.

Send a note parting from me forever, bidding me farewell and good health. Praise my happy situation, whatever you see fit. He will of course read it. Then, if you wish to write for my eyes only, send to my former address, at Warp Lane.

By the by, do not dismiss me yet, since I have not done with you and your delightful slip about *my* rival . . . don't you mean *your* rival, of whom you are thoroughly jealous? For he is near by, and possession so large a part of the law that there is always a risk of its becoming complete. Note too, before you scorn him again for the senility of being "almost fifty," how decrepit that makes you!

Now he is no longer a stranger to me it will not be easy to humiliate him, unless I fully understand why I should. I am no more blind than you, and will not be led. You are unfair to say so much and yet so little. A cracked statuette is hardly enough reason to destroy someone who has been so kind to me!

Striking down an adversary one has begun to know is difficult. From then on, only complete understanding makes it possible in the fatal moment to close one's eyes yet still hit the mark. Thus it is with the archer and marksman, thus also with me. I must have a reason to harm him.

However willingly I agreed at the outset, the situation has changed. So, he is murderous and unprincipled, you have made that clear as day. But then so are so many! Look at yourself! It is a broad church among my acquaintance. There are plenty of men and women as bad, and I cannot become a ubiquitous avenging angel on your distant whim. However we scorn it, that is what the Law is for.

Nor is it fair to enclose such a hasty account of his misdemeanours in relation to Jocasta Verney. Why stop, when you should have gone on? Why start at all? I deserve better treatment. Fortunately, I am not so hurt by your insulting reason for stopping (doubly irritating for its disingenuousness), as to be unable to speak. Finish, or the bet really is off.

That no man should reveal too much about a former love is well understood. It is prudent, too, from the intended's point of view: for women are so competitive that praise even for one in a lead dress ruffles our feathers. Then, men have a dreary habit of getting fonder of a mistress once she is gone. Whether to death or fresh pastures is immaterial; from the moment she slips a man's grip she achieves the halo'd status of wife, her rating goes up, and all without any of the rigours of the position.

Since, against my judgment, I retain a tatter of affection for you, the only way to persuade me to the favour you demand is to explain how he has injured you, so that I may develop a personal grievance. If perforce that involves the tale of my former rival, *glorious in death etc, etc,* so be it. Only keep your flattery and worship within bounds—so that I do not, in a fit of misogyny, side with him instead of her—*and you.*

Yours—

July 27, 1784
Hubert van Essel
to Mrs Fox,
Salamander Row

Very well.

I loved her. She stood out in any assembly. I thought I should never see such a woman again, which held true until a freezing January two and a half years ago, when I first set eyes on you. Remember that she is dead and you are living. I make no comparison, she offers no contest.

Jocasta Verney, with her brother John, whom I liked, and their two servants, quit Earl Much's travelling party the day after his explosion at Bagheria. I still recall my elation: not because she was leaving, but because, repulsed as *I* was by his treatment of her, it seemed impossible that she could care for him. I began dreaming about finding ways to possess her.

After they had gone, I did not sell my soul to Urban Fine merely for a house and library, but to get the means to court her. There is no shame in it. However, for the moment there was nothing to be done. I was penniless, and she was hardly aware of my existence.

The Verneys set off for Florence, where they planned to stay for some time.

We—what was left of the original group—went on, to acquire as much Italian treasure as time allowed. I became fascinated by the difference money confers. We could go anywhere and do anything. Every court welcomed us, every one sought Much's opinion, whether he had one or not; no collection was barred. Occasionally he bought with discernment; but more often on a casual impulse; for fun; to spite someone else; even from boredom—since it was what he did best, at the time. He also gathered experts who might be useful later, shaking their hand while I wrote them down, like any other purchase. I basked at being frequently consulted, kept his diary and noted our purchases in a ledger, vain of my precision. I found out provenances, arranged shipping, and resold inadvertent duplicates. I knew what was on offer wherever we went, not through genius in tracking masterpieces, but because I let it be known in advance that the *English Milord* was coming, and that I was the one to approach.

It is a fact that the less variables there are to any formula, the more dependable, thus in our case:

$$X = Y \text{ when } Y = X\ (\pm)\ Z$$

Put another way, the combination of him, me, and a bottomless purse, was infallible. Ticketing and docketing occupied me far into the night, during which time he disappeared. His reputation as a lover had also preceded us. Women could not resist having their hand filled with raw gems, an Etruscan necklace, emerald earrings. Although he was a thin, dry, conceited man who rarely laughed unless he smelled blood, it made no difference to the overwhelming spell his fortune wove. He was famous for offering to cut himself out of romantic difficulties. There were very few takers.

We spent occasional evenings together at cards, at concerts or a dance, for which he gave me suits of clothes.

Five months later, our group split up. He and I went north.

After we had seen Miss Verney in mourning (or Signora Piestre, by which name I never once called her, even in my mind), we rode back to our rented villa in silence. The rooms were baking. He ordered the place shut up. Having nothing to say, I announced my intention of returning to Amsterdam and my neglected studies, at which he went out and came back with a letter of credit to draw against him, then went off again; I heard impatient calls for a mount. With that money he dismissed me.

He returned two hours later; there was a line of blood on his neck.

We never referred to what had happened to Signor Piestre. It was clear that he would smooth it over, his servants would swear to the accident being just that. I did not care what he would do when he discovered that he had smashed the genuine Apollo—or if he would even be able to tell the difference. My disgust and hatred were boiling over.

You ask why I took his money? I had earned it. My only thought was how fine she looked, cursing him. His money might make it possible for me to see her again, once the period of mourning had passed. I quelled the desire to go to her palazzo and throw myself at her feet, there and then. I should not have done.

In Holland I resumed my studies, yet, however long I sat barricaded by books, no thoughts came, except endless versions of how it would be when we were together. There was no doubt in my mind that it would be so. After six months, I wrote. Weeks later, the letter came back, with *England* on it; nothing further, no forwarding address.

That same day I arranged a course of work for my students—the research that day-dreaming had left me unable to do—and set out for London, hoping to find her, or news of her. After a week wandering the streets I remembered the name of her part of the country and, like a deranged man, convinced myself that that was where she must be. The stage took days: I took the first available. There was only space on top, but the discomfort was nothing. Nor did the size of Lancashire concern me, for I knew her name, and was convinced that I remembered that of a nearby town into the bargain.

Her parents treated me with suspicion. I daresay I looked mad. They had not heard from her since her marriage to "the foreigner." Even the news of that man's death appeared to have left them unmoved. They did tell me that her brother John had just set off on mill business, so I decided to wait—whether for a day or a year. I would not be turned off again. She was my destiny.

The nearest village had two inns. In the better one I took rooms with a narrow wooden balcony that ran round the entire first floor, looking over the yard. The chambers were decent. Many travellers passed through, mainly in the cloth trade, the same as her brother. Finding the comings and goings below diverting, writing notes for my treatise passed the time. I walked for an hour or two every afternoon.

Weeks had gone by when one of the potboys rattled at my door. Mr John Verney was waiting downstairs, he said, if it pleased me to go down. The boy went ahead in his dirty fustian, towards the back parlour.

John Verney and I renewed our acquaintance easily enough, as if we had scarce parted, and were shortly served a dish something like the *hutspot* I had eaten in Leyden as a student. We drank a great deal of wine.

"Don't mind them." John Verney spoke at last, beginning with his parents. "They were always close-lipped, and Jocasta never wrote once she was married. They were disappointed at her unnatural neglect; they washed their hands. It isn't that they don't miss her, but that she wanted a different life, away from them, away from this place. She was determined to go and marry abroad. She did. He was Catholic. She went against them at every turn. What more is there to say? They are ordinary people—though very rich. They did not understand her *London ways.*" He laughed drily. "Certainly not her Italian ones. They felt that she had made her bed, if you know the expression."

I did not, but understood his tone. "Do you?"

In Italy I had observed his fondness for his younger sister, his protectiveness when other men became too playful. He was good company. Now twenty four, Verney was inventing a superior twisted thread. "It will revolutionize cotton," he said, "the mercers'll rise to it, mark my words."

We drank a great deal more, in silence, watching the turning of a couple of coaches in the torch-lit dark that was itself threaded with light rain. The unloading and reloading, the harnessing of fresh horses, the jockeying of new travellers for the best seats, the trimming of the lamps. Verney looked at me quite hard.

"I was always of the opinion that you had a liking for her," he said at last, with a particular emphasis.

I had thought he was going to stay quiet for the remainder of the evening.

"I expect that's why you are here," he went on, "but it is too late."

The words fell on top of me as if from a height.

She was dead, that was the only explanation.

Not able to meet his eyes, I rested my head on the table. Given the amount I had drunk, it seemed the best course. The next thing I knew I was weeping.

A hand came down on my back, harder than necessary.

"Dead? Good God, sir, pull yourself together. The drink is making you maunder, you must get a grip. I know just the thing."

He called vigorously for even more wine.

"Dead? Not dead at all! She's had—" Verney turned the empty bottle to and fro against the light of the candle. "She's had her fill of foreign parts and set up in London. I've just come back."

I left in the first coach to leave the yard in the morning, when it was dark. Verney told me to call on his sister the minute I arrived, but there was no need for telling. I determined to waste no more time, having wasted so much before.

But although I found her, nothing had any effect. I ran off her like water. She laughed at the notion of marrying again; or if she did, she did not want another foreigner. I was too serious, or too tall; I wasn't wealthy enough; my hair was too long. Every day I renewed my suit and each time there was a different reason against it. My pursuit continued, at her morning levée and sometimes in the afternoons when we walked together, or at an assembly, or a card party (which was a labour for me, since I do not gamble). Though she went on refusing she did not dismiss me and I harboured a growing hope.

Then of a sudden she began to wear costly jewels and close-cut shimmering silks, the skirts a mile wide; her hair dressed each morning in increasingly dashing styles. She drove a springy new carriage with four matched greys, paired footmen in pale green on the back. Trinkets, snuff boxes and gee-gaws appeared on every surface—these were also new; there were cascades of fresh flowers; her servants increased. I fell more hopelessly in love the clearer it became that I was losing her. She took to throwing dice, a taste acquired in Italy, and began living very fast, winning and losing with the predictability of a pendulum that always winds down to nothing, however great the swings. There was whispering about her—how much she cost—but no one could say for certain who was paying.

This unseen rival's identity eluded me. Out riding one morning, she became impatient, saying that I knew him well, and that she expected a proposal at any moment. Unable to reply, I got down and walked alongside, begging her to come away before it was too late, but she told me I was imagining things. Surely I knew, quoth she blithely, that he had risked his own life to save her husband?

My heart turned, as if his dagger-tip touched it.

I was on the point of disabusing her from this appalling mistake when she halted the carriage and leaned over, her fingers briefly touching my knuckles where they gripped the apron.

"Nothing will prevent me," she said, her eyes fixed on mine so that I could not drag myself away, but drowned in them: nothing would hold her back from having the life she wanted. He held it out. Her expression mocked me for being unable to do the same. *Was there anything further?*

Her gaze tore at me so hard it was impossible to breathe. She had to know that his story was untrue, but had grown too reckless to afford caring.

"Get back in and we will stay friends," she smiled, stroking the reins with a grey-gloved thumb.

Money was pouring through her hands from gambling. Her own funds were gone, but he showered her with more, spiralling amounts, for which she wrote IOUs by the handful, decorating them with flourishes, gay in the expectation of marriage. He owned her.

At last, instead of the proposal she counted on, the Earl made a different one. He called in the loan with a stark choice: ruin and disgrace, or a marriage of convenience (Much's convenience) to a drunken rake, another gambler, already in his debt. She took the latter, convinced that such an arrangement could not harm her, and that they would go on as before. But they did not.

The creature that Much had selected was worthless, petty and jealous. An officer, he was a mediocre horseman and a blaggard. Some cut her because of his irregular behaviour, while her lover continued pitiless, unconcerned by anything except his own pleasure. The officer she was now married to, once given the title of ownership, became as determined to have what was legally his as she was to prevent it. You will imagine the rest. Much was amused and spurred on by it. He was not a normal man—if proof was needed.

This second husband's leaving for war was the only good thing that happened.

I am no swordsman. If I had challenged Much, and died for her—the only possible outcome—would she have fared any better? My death could not possibly serve her, but living might yet, so I came home.

For more than twenty years I have not left this city, nor looked beyond my books. In answer to her rare letters, I offered what comfort I could, while he destroyed her, bit by bit. Her fault had been vanity—like so many—and she paid for it year after year.

When she grew older, he threatened to leave her penniless unless she procured the sort of perverse diversions he found stimulating. She sent her son abroad before doing as he bid. He had broken her. She needed to provide for her son, what else was there to do?

She and her whorehouse became notorious throughout London. Jocasta Danceacre lived at Hipp Street.

Tell me if you will honour our bargain.

~

July 20, 1784
Violet Denyss, XXXX Street, London!!!!
to Clio Denyss
The Rectory, W—
Tuesday

Darlingest, dear Clio, I have run away!

You must not tell anyone where I am, especially Mama and Papa, who would be very angry with you, and come straight here and bring me home.

I am not telling you where I have come to either, in case you cannot keep a secret, which you have never done in your life and I don't see how you can start now. I gave the housekeeper here my letter, which she said she was very pleased to send, and that she will look after all my letters if I give them straight to her, which will be a lot less bother for me, and she is sure that I shall get a great many in return.

It is so lucky to have somewhere this nice to stay in. London is much more exciting than the country! The houses are very big. This one has six floors counting the basement, with many rooms on each floor, and staircases front *and* back. There is lots of everything. My windows have curtains as well as shutters, and the furnishings are all new, of wood inlaid with patterns like boxes piled up on top of each other, or with flowers where the petals seem real, and with much more gold than I thought anyone had, but it seems that this is not so. I do not know where to start describing it, but it has all cost vast amounts of money, and unlike at home there is nothing with a hole or a glued-on piece.

The housekeeper—I will not tell you her name, but will call her Mrs B—says that even though it is lovely and expensive, and all from France, it is not as lovely and new as me and that is why it sets me off so well. I laughed when she said this but she said never laugh when someone pays you a compliment, in case they think you are laughing at them, which means that they will not do it again, and they might even become cross and punish you, but always smile with your mouth shut and curtsey.

I said that I had never had many compliments, and recently I had had quite the opposite. She looked sad, but then brightened up and declared that she thought I should get a great many compliments very soon if I did what I was told, and some of them would be the sort *that are worth their weight in gold*, that I would come to enjoy greatly.

I did not know what she meant, but she said I would soon enough and in the meantime we were going to go to a mantua-maker to have some modish clothes made, as those I have are perfectly good for the country, *but not for a sophisticated young lady!!!*

I cannot believe we thought that the most desirable thing on earth was a hand of whist in the afternoon and a dance with the Lampeters' cousins.

I am still very angry with Lord Frederick, altho' I am not sure why he was so angry with me. I have certainly never told lies in my life, nor put letters into strange men's pockets! I have not put letters into anyone's pockets, so why would one want to put them into the pockets of men such as Mr Coats?

I do not know why Lord Frederick said those things, but they were terrible mean, and made Papa unconscionable cross. He said I could never go to Mashing again or he would whip me, and then he would go and whip Lord Danceacre and Mr Coats (who is a Bart) into the bargain. But I should think, even though Papa *is* a Justice of the Peace, that he would not get much peace if he horsewhipped a

Bart. When I said this he raised his hand so I decided on the spot that I would run away. If I can't ever go to Mashing and see Freddy again, or help nice Mr Coats make the models for the new wing, or go and help Mr Tutton in the dairy when he needs me for the light paddle, I don't see that there is any future at home at all.

So you see I had no choice but to come to London.

I would not have been able to, with just my plate money, but when Mrs Fox's maid Victoire came to pick up her mistress's missing muff (when Mama and Papa were unfortunately out last week), I told her all my worries. She said I should not be concerned, because good things always happen to pretty girls, and circumstances had a way of changing much quicker than one thought. Then she gave me a guinea (!!!), that she said Mrs Fox would want me to have for looking after her muff so beautifully, and that I could pay it back when I had money of my own.

I was rather surprised that a servant knew a word like circumstances but Mrs Fox is a devilish superior sort of woman and I daresay her maid, who has a French accent, and so is a French maid, which is the best sort, is very *élevée* too.

July 26, 1784
Violet Denyss, XXXX Street, etc
to Clio Denyss
Monday

Hide this letter after you have read it, nb.

Clio, dear, I thought you might have answered my letter, that it wasn't much bother, but you were never good at writing, and besides I don't expect anything What-So-Ever has happened at home. I doubt that Mama and Papa have even noticed that I am gone, since they never pay me any attention! Have they?

So much has happened *here* that I do not know where to begin.

We were going to visit a mantua-maker, but then Mrs B said that I could just as easily be measured "at home" (of course that meant H— Street, not *our* home!) for my dresses, which was a grander way of doing it. She gave me a rather strange look when she said that and I realised that I must have missed a compliment and should have curtseyed, so I did and she said, that's better, and we were the best of friends again.

I would have liked to go out in the carriage but did not mention it again. Presently she knocked on the door of my room, which is on the fifth floor, or the fourth not counting the basement, and came straight in, although I had not answered. One of the undermaids came too, and a small lady I have not met before, whom I could scarcely look at she was so beautiful, with such jewels, and her hair like yellow mist curling round her head.

She was Mrs Salmon who I think must own the house, and she turned to Mrs B and said in a funny high voice, I see what you mean. Mrs B gave me her look to make me understand that I had been paid a compliment, although it certainly did not feel like one, so I curtseyed.

At that Mrs Salmon smiled and said that this girl would measure me, and also look after me *while I was having a holiday in the house.* She said that rather loud, as if the maid, who had her back to us, opening her work basket, might be deaf, and Mrs Salmon did not want to exclude her from the conversation. I asked what she meant, and she said that it was just a lovely visit, wasn't it, I could go home whenever I wanted? So I said, yes, but I didn't want to go home. Then she patted me and told me not to cry, and bid the maid take very good care of me. She suggested it would be a good thing to undress, which I felt shy about doing; but that is the proper way to get measured for fashionable clothes. Mrs Salmon then sat in a chair, with Mrs B standing next to her.

The girl took a long time turning me this way and that, while the two ladies stared to make me blush and decided what might suit me. They said that I would need bosom friends, which was most considerate, so I curtseyed again. Then I was allowed to put my old clothes on.

The dresses are done now, you would die with jealousy!!! They are the pinnacle of fashion, made of muslin, with sprigs embroidered on some, in colours, so I look like the mythical Goddess Euripides, in my opinion. There are sashes to match, and a jacket and cloak in very fine wool in a deep colour. You can see through the muslin, but Mrs Salmon says that that is all the rage, and besides, no one can see through *when it is on*, which does not really make sense. She said I looked *utterly ravishin'*.

I am going to practise droppin' my G's.

Then she told me that there are a few people coming to a party this evening, which I may watch for a while. Soon she will let me join in, for there is to be a Grecian Evening, and I am to have a lyre (without strings) and gilded sandals, and a headdress of bay leaves covered with yellow foil.

While I was waiting for my clothes last week, I had Dancing and Deportment. I think we were being taught wrong at home. You would be very surprised. Now, I have been shewn how to walk and sit and lie on a divan in the *French* way. Mrs Salmon has also done me the honour to teach me how to eat certain *French* dishes, although she says I have a natural charm that can scarce be improved upon, and will be a hit with the gentlemen!!! That made me blush very much and she said, "well done." She said I must be longing to meet some handsome gentleman, or perhaps she said gentlemen, it is hard to tell, the way she pronounces things—anyhow it was a pity I had been shut up in the country for so long, depriving so many of such a heart-lifting sight.

We have been out in a closed carriage, to the Park and Ranelagh and the Spring Gardens, and there was an outing on Sunday to a garden called the Jew's Harp. I walked with my maid and a footman and drank tea. I had to wear a close bonnet although it was not cold. I wanted to go to an exhibition at the Pantheon where there is a balloon big enough to hang a basket from and fly! But apparently, a girl can have too much excitement.

I dispute this. No one ever saw "dead of too much excitement" on a headstone.

There are always plenty of people in the house. I stay on the fourth floor, as I said. The maids' rooms are above mine. Mrs B has her study and bedroom on the ground floor, above the kitchens and pantry. The rooms on the first floor are very grand and panelled. I have not seen the rooms on the second and third, but they must be infinitely spectacular. My maid says there is a library and games room, and a stage in one of them, and some are covered in silk in wondrous colours. Mrs Salmon has her sitting room and bedroom there, and two of her sisters have just come to stay as well.

Another lady just arrived, a cousin by marriage who is of moderate height and perfectly Jet Black, also has rooms there.

I had not known Mrs Salmon had so many sisters or cousins, but am glad she is so well provided with relations, for Mrs B says that now there will be parties every night and I will be allowed to join in if I am popular at the Grecian Evening. I will have to hold poses, hanging in Balletic positions in front of a big light that is the moon, and stay very still. It is extremely difficult.

Don't you wish you were here!

Your elder sister—

July 23, 1784
Victoire
To Mrs Fox

Dear Madam,

Since you have asked me to be frank, I will come straight to the point. Martha is too high a risk. She has learnt everything I have taught her, but that is what bothers me. She is like a sponge, soaking it up, until you would think that if you gave her a good squeeze—as I have been tempted!—it would all gush out. But nothing comes. Wring her in a mangle and she will appear the other side dry as a bone. It goes in and it stays there. It isn't normal.

She is a secretive, scornful little Bitch, and to be honest I do not know if she can be controlled once she is out of our sight. I begin to wonder if she is cleverer than is good for her. She might go off like a rocket.

Another thing worried me, when I came back from staying with you at Salamander Row those two days, madam.

Martha wasn't in her room, although I had locked her in as usual. She must have escaped out the back. But it is a sheer drop! Unless she climbed up, to the Scribbler's rooms. There is a pipe; she might have done.

When she heard me calling, she comes sauntering down from upstairs, smooth as you like. I was too late to catch her at whatever she had been doing. I don't think it was right up at the top, unless she was just poking around. The couple that lost the baby two weeks ago have gone, and at present it is empty, although Mrs Sorrell says a gentleman has just taken them, but his arrival is delayed.

All the same, I locked Martha in and went up to look, in case Betty was entertaining the dishboy, which is a low habit they have got into. There was no one.

Martha isn't given to sitting on staircases. I am almost sure she was in with the Scribbler, although she faced me and said he was out, why didn't I go and knock if I was so hot about it, *lest my petticoat catch fire and I get singed.*

How can you talk to it! That is my perturbation. She can do a duchess if she wants, and then she goes and says something like that, out of spitefulness. I didn't show her what was in my heart, even though it was itching to come out of my hand.

Finding there was no more sport to be had, she calmed down in an instant, and asked if I would like her to make me a dish of tea, nice as anything. Then she turned back and laughed, saying I must be losing my facilities: I had forgotten to fasten the door, wasn't it time that I stopped locking her in, she was a grown woman, I should trust her. Trussed her, more like!

Could she be right? . . . madam, I am certain not.

She is a good seamstress. There is plenty of dress-making, she could stay here just doing that, and hire another girl to help. It would be easy to make something of it, given her talent. A kindness now would take her so by surprise, she might discover that she could succeed at legal endeavour.

And it would take a liability off our hands, for I do not trust her to be honest about anything she is set to, or to hold a secret unless it is in her own interest. The unruly spirit in her makes her unreliable and dangerous.

Forgive me for speaking truth, but rather now than later, if it is any help. I beg you tell me what is to be done, so that I may come and be in my proper place, with you.

Victoire

July 23, evening
Mrs Fox, Salamander Row
To Victoire, Warp Lane

Victoire,

You do right to have concerns about her. I agree that she has shown herself unpredictable as fire-works. Yet, in order to entrap Earl Much, just such an exceptional thing as Martha is needed, so far out of the ordinary sphere that he cannot judge it, so wayward that he can never anticipate it. Tedious though it makes her to manage, that unguageable nature of hers is precisely the quality I require as the means to humiliate him, so that he becomes ridiculous. Blinded with desire, he will not be able to see past our pretence of her being an untouched heiress, for she is dazzling, when she wishes to be. When he discovers that he has publicly betrothed himself to the gutter, a drain, a commmon whore who has been had by half the tradesmen hereabouts though not yet fifteen, he will writhe. All those once forced to humble themselves before him, afraid of his power, will laugh him into disgrace and exile.

Through long practice, he has made himself a connoisseur of *things* and believes himself an infallible judge of people, too. In that complacent smugness, we will have him.

Those whose pockets are deep enough, finding that humanity will jump for them, soon suffer the conceit of omniscience, confusing purchase with prescience. Earl Much is one. Years dedicated to congratulating himself on his deductions have blunted his judgment.

When beggars spur over a few of his tossed coins, or a crouching infant limps up his chimney and returns gasping for breath; if he sets off in closed carriage to the Park to relieve himself in a spent harlot, he clops gaily home, satisfied that mankind dangles at his fingertips. There is a room in his house with a wall of identical yellow cabinets with numbered slots, that you might think to put dishes between, where he keeps hundreds—thousands—of prints, collected over thirty years. I have watched him closely when he felt unobserved. Rifling with those boneless hands, scenting and savouring like a demented dog at truffles, until finally jabbing at a picture of some creature he says, *there you are, I have got you.*

His joy is not experience, but pigeon-holing, so that he can say *yes, yes, yes, just as I thought; exactly so.*

Only a fool would believe they had met Martha's type before. But so it will be with Earl Much when you bring *my distant cousin, our sweet young heiress, Amaranth,* here shortly. Try to make Martha remember her new name, teach her to write it if you can. God knows, short of calling her by her given one, Amaranth could scarce be closer.

The jade's mix of flash and fury; her readiness to reinvent herself after a fashion she rightly believes the world prices higher than her own; her tendency to go from obsession to indifference if she sees furtherance or favour in it, though familiar in Court upstarts, is rare in slatterns from nowhere. Other such women may exist—who can say?

Her greedy nothingness, combined with our supplying the polish she lacked and a deal more besides, make her devastating. What means does he have to navigate this unknown continent? He would be as likely to take up a pen and sketch, at a pass, all the inlets and rivers of New Scotland.

Take heart, Victoire. You are done, return to me. Martha is all she could be. You have made *pain raisin* out of a lump of unleaven; a few weeks longer would have turned her brioche. A little extra tutelage and she would be fit to take on those shallow box-doxies at the theatre, even as far as the Prince. Indeed, if she achieves Much, why should she then not do More?

I do not like to heap praise on you, lest you tumble into the trough of considering yourself indispensable. Nevertheless, on her surface you have effected miracles. He must not have the chance to plumb further until they are committed to marriage! Once she comes here, she must not be let out of sight.

Rehearse her in her story once more: that she spent a miserable childhood languishing abroad in poverty, undiscovered, through errors and a negligent stepmother. It does not matter that she can be gauche—one would not expect her previous life, as told, to have prepared her for this one. She will not want to recollect that dreadful time, nor he hear it, having a horror of the underclasses (unless they are under him) that is almost endearing.

Finish her wardrobe, letting her know that some of the things she thought for me are destined for her own use; it will grace her needle to believe that application now may improve her future. Go more gently than before. In order to play the part we have chosen for her to advantage, she must look forward to it.

I shall not expect you here until ten or more days have passed—surprise me, provoke him. Given what he will soon think he understands of *Amaranth*'s wealth and innocence, any inscrutable lapses in her behaviour can only add piquancy, that the sweet sauce of beauty turn irresistible.

Your mistress—

July 24, 1784
From the new owner of Hipp Street
Delivered by Mr Voster[I]
To Mrs Beddoes
Housekeeper

Madam,

I trust that you receive this letter safely, from the hand of my private secretary, Mr Voster. Respecting my insistence on anonymity, you know me only as your employer.

We have had no previous communication, which is the best way for our particular business. Allowing people to carry out the affairs for which they are suited in the manner they see fit is the surest route to profit.

Our present undertaking at Hipp Street, founded in pleasure and congenial company, cemented with the expertise of Mrs Salmon and yourself, must similarly accrue fame and fortune.

Good reports of Hipp Street are circulating. If conversations overheard in my club and elsewhere are to be believed, it is the talk

[I] Victoire

of the town, providing diversions so numerous as to astonish gentlemen of every inclination.

I am heartily satisfied, in all except one thing: do not grant further admittance to the individual called Urban Fine, Earl Much. His previous friendship with Mrs Salmon has come to my notice, rendering him an unfit patron of Hipp Street, on several counts. Should he be seen on the premises, it would be assumed that he is still that lady's master—indeed, must be chief of the entire affair.

Whilst I prefer to remain private, it is not my wish to have my thunder drummed by that gentleman! Next, piqued by Mrs Salmon's defection, he might become imperious, an embarrasment to himself and others, imparting an unseemly flavour to a place where pleasure, charm, good digestion and relaxation must never be disturbed. Third, if he should attempt to find solace in the company of other young women there, it would be an insult both to Mrs Salmon and those who look to her for moral guidance. Last, his fame as marksman and swordsman are such that the merest possibility of an outburst on my property would court tragedy.

Madam: reassuring you of my congratulations on your management, I insist on his immediate debarment. Inform me, through Mr Voster, if the Earl attempts any appearance in the environs of Hipp Street.

Your master—

July 30, 1784
Mrs Fox, Salamander Row
To Hubert van Essel, Amsterdam

Oh, really! If you believe me in such danger, clamber down off your high horse and make the journey to London. You say yourself that you have sat at the same desk for twenty years. Prise yourself off it.

What amusements can Amsterdam hold now I am no longer there? Whereas, there are sights aplenty here to please you.

Let me say at once how well these living accomodations suit me—so much so, that were there not other games afoot, I should easily be swayed to take up *permanent residence*—greatly pleasing the master of the house by it.

While I have no difficulty convincing myself that my charms are more than enough for any English man, other forces may have been at play to cause the sudden veer his attentions have taken towards me. For so it is: a triumph of ingenuity with which, being in possession of an half hour before a concert at Greenwich, with coloured water spouts, I will regale you.

The Earl is shocked to find himself forbidden entry at Hipp Street where, long habituated to being the master of its new incumbent Mrs Salmon, he naturally turns.

What reason he invents for being refused those fleshly portals (presumably on the orders of that lady) is impossible to imagine. But he is taking it badly. Deprived of Salmon's sparkling company and the lure of her pendant companions, he now bombards me with solicitude, being a man who defines himself through his subjugation of women. And I just as determined that he shall not have me!

The thought that I could be the very person responsible for his perplexity has not struck him, but in using the poison to effect the cure (an unpromising homeopathy) he may have embarked on a treatment that is far more potent than the one anticipated.

Every evening we go to the play or opera, then cards and suppers. Or dances, or ridottos, all in sumptuous style. He presents me as a woman of independent means, yet with an ambiguity that reflects well on him, but somehow tarnishes me.

The world is at his bidding; he is more puissant than the Pope. For one wrapped in the dusty work of collecting, it is astounding that when he issues the merest invitation everyone, from high-ranking government officials to the King's dwarf, is shoving and scuffling on the doorstop moments later. Each, I swear, terrified to death of what he can do if they do not. There is nothing he cannot buy, favour arrange—nor accident impel.

As long as he pursues me, everything is as a piece of theatre he has mounted solely for my benefit. But it is like a painting you once showed me, with a glass container and a tube, and a poor animal inside: at any moment, should I cease to interest him, he can stop the life-providing air and watch me writhe and die.

His open purse ensures my daily satisfaction in a fresh appearance—or I should long have run out of gowns. Every wish is supplied the moment it takes flight: if it could be done faster, it should. Glovemakers, tambourers, lacemakers, jewellers, tailors, fan-painters, purveyors of slippers, staymakers—all at my disposal, day and night. A hair out of place calls up a flurry so demented that you might think yourself in a snowstorm.

Victoire is not yet here, due to a feigned absence abroad. In fact, she is kept very busy posing both as my secretary, Mr Voster, making sure that Hipp Street runs smoothly and polishing our novice Martha, ready for hand-to-hand combat with the Earl.

But I do not lack for servants. Two maids and a footman are for my sole pleasure. I have to think up diversions once they have done their tasks twice-over. Which could have made me their slave, until I put the man, at least, to better uses. Beyond these three, there is an army of liveries so substantial that one sometimes mistakes the halls for fields of lavender. Then, Signor Gisbetti comes before ten to dress my hair, so that when Fine makes his morning call at noon, I receive him—only not, he makes plain, in the way he would wish.

Each day he arrives a little earlier, in a comic attempt to surprise me in *déshabillé.* I refuse to enter into this amateurism. If he would make a proper appointment, I could be in whatever delicious state takes his fancy. As long as he tries subterfuge, I am as determined to fox him as he is to foil me. Since when were intelligent women *surprised* from their garments? There is no female on earth who will not put off her paniers for a sum. But woe betide the man who tries to wrench them away! Then will lace rise up like steel cordons, and thistledown threads cut like knives.

As I continue to thwart him, the hotter his attentions become—and the more he masks them in public under glacial civility. When he hands me into a carriage it is with an hauteur that could easily be taken for distaste. But in his touch, tremulousness speaks. Anyone else would doubt what they were sure had passed. Should I look at him at a dinner, his eyes drill mine like the beads of a rat; yet if I glance covertly, he seems fully occupied by the ladies either side.

Ordinary women, lacking my perverted knowledge of your sex, do not survive him. He splits them as he sucks marrow, sharp teeth nipping and shredding, ignoring the tool put for that purpose in his haste to channel such sweet meats.

Now, after weeks of his incessant company, I agree with you: he is insatiable. Nor does his remarkable ugliness dampen his success. One watches bemused as married women who have caught no fish but their husbands and one or two amiable sprats (on account of which *hors d'oevre* they believe themselves *chef* of any man they meet) fall under his spell as on to a spit, basting themselves with blushes when his hand is suddenly not on the cloth. Then, in the thick part of night, lampless carriages take snuffed figures away.

He takes, he discards.

He is a factory of seduction.

All this comes dear, but how dear is impossible to guess. A stream of jewellers' boxes arrive: the maid tells me who supplies them, and oft-times what is inside. She would give herself for the smallest of them, not knowing that to fill a bored half hour he will soon have her anyway, before tossing her out on the street, like as not with an enduring memento.

But you must have no concerns for *my* safety. Whatever picture I paint of his punctilious despoilation, I count myself a breed apart. My security lies in having taken your challenge seriously from the first. You once joked that in Much I had met my match. It is the reverse: in me, he has met his.

The more I catalogue his ruses for throwing women on their backs, the more he bares his belly. He holds no horrors, his tactics are predictable—one could catch up a bludgeon and be praised for more finesse.

This holiday task you set suits me well, for I had begun to think that there was no occupation to be had in London. Alternately shut up reading lady novelists with Victoire, or incarcerated in a collapsing hovel in the countryside, meantime enduring the season's clod-hopping dissipations, my zest was pared to the bone. Much longer and I should have had to slink away to Manchester, or Liverpool—even the Virginias—rather than crawl defeated to Holland, as you would have me do.

Your dear Victoire, inoculated, through constant exposure to me against any ability to tolerate ordinariness, was showing sympathetic symptoms of degeneration, had boredom not turned her termagant, so she could have snipped out a petticoat just by talking to the cloth.

So, in this London society, where pattern-book gentility passes for intellect and the profile of a mule for superiority, we have as you know been helping an ignorant young woman, slut first and mantua-maker second, by showing her a way to escape an inevitable future of drunkenness, disease and death. She has learned those superficial refinements needful to a lady, with aptitude. Holding a conversation or a knife and fork: both are now within her grasp.

An accomplished seamstress, she has refashioned herself so well, that at close quarters you would call her Duchess. She can open a fan, dance moderately and look shocked at anything anyone says, unless they are above forty, in which case she smiles angelically.

For added charm we left her illiterate, rote-learning her a few sentences from the Bible that will get her in or out of trouble, depending how she uses them. In short, she is just the young heiress that Earl

Much has always longed to have in his clutches but never dreamed of finding.

I expect her any moment.

You know my motto:

SEMPER INFIDELIS.

Yours—

July 28, 1784
Frederick Danceacre, Mashing
To Mrs Fox, c/o Salamander Row

My dear Mrs Fox,

I learn with considerable astonishment that you have taken up residence in a house belonging to that . . . that man!

God's nightgown, why did you leave Mashing at such speed, madam? Why have I heard nothing from you all this time? Your scribbled note was deuced unsatisfying. What business could be so urgent that it took you from me to the dam' City?

Why stay under the roof of a man who surely means nothing to you, a dry old coot by all accounts, vain as a brace of peacock, only interested in things with a layer or two of dust on 'em so he can once more scrawl his name?

What does this mean, when everything I possess is at your disposal, in a part of the country you but weeks ago professed congenial? What of poor Coats, unable to come to any sensible decisions without your guidance? He laughs at every suggestion I make, although, dam'me, some are pretty good: turrets, monumental sphinxes, domes to outdo the Duomo . . . all out of the window. Now he threatens to desert me. Shortly I shall have to come to town myself, or be the only soul left in Suffolk.

There has been a dreadful to-do at the Rectory. The anguish of Parson Denyss's family must be seen to be comprehended. Violet, the eldest, who had the brief pleasure of knowing you, has gone missing—vanished from the face of the earth; none of her sisters knows anything about it. The mother is wasted to a baluster and pale to pity looking. The parson declares his daughter has been abducted by a tinker, but I say she's gone to spite him. He grounded her after some girlish nonsense, some romantic letters it seems she put in Coats' pocket. He had come back tired from a long absence and came down very hard on the poor mite. Tutton rided out daily in search of news, but it is thin on the ground, since the layabouts helping with the harvest will peddle any story you please for a gallon of beer. According to them she has been glimpsed on every road in every direction. The truth is that no one has seen her.

I am sure you will recall her as a pretty, ripe young thing, perhaps overly spirited and free with her opinion, so that she could make a fellow—only if he was inclined that way—a trifle overwhelmed. I am most anxious to discover that no harm has befallen her. Did she happen to mention any dissatisfaction with her life to you; or a beau whom her sisters may be too afraid to name? You befriended them; it may be that in a girlish confidence she said what nobody else heard?

It pains me to see my neighbours brought low, and I fear for the mother's life. If Mrs Denyss (who is in truth the man of the house, the parson being generally away) comes to harm, Justice Denyss will be as unable to carry out his circuit duties as he is to raise three girls unaided. The moral health of an entire county stands to suffer from this outrage, hence my plea. I have pledged myself to help them recover Violet.

I beg you, try to recall anything that may discover her and, God willing, before any real danger touch her.

Yours—

July 29, 1784
Mrs Fox, Salamander Row
To Frederick Danceacre

There are two subjects in your letter.

The first, the reason why I am here rather than there, is my business to know and certainly not yours to ask. The facts speak, there we must leave it. Mashing is delightful, I have no argument with it. Since you seem dissatisfied, let me repeat my unqualified thanks for your encompassing hospitality.

Whom I choose to stay with and why, is as closed to scrutiny as my reasons for having stayed with you are to Earl Much. Surely it behoves one gentleman to respect the guest of another, nor expose his motives to morbid cynosure? You and I must not exchange further words on this, lest we come to blows.

The second theme, the distressing disappearance of the eldest Denyss girl, Violet, is sorely troubling, particularly as you appear to be so fond of her.

I do not share your view of her being advanced and ripe. To my mind she was a shy, delicate thing, the image of her name. Blushing and uncertain, not near as forward as most girls that age. You ask if we had any privy conversations? Her family's despair lets me break the trust I swore to Violet as we walked in the garden one dusky evening, her pliant hand clutching mine. In that soft voice—so easily crushed!—she announced her intention to join a religious order. This aim struck me as fitting, and one to which she might quickly give substance.

Are there any cloisters in your neighbouring counties? Search them without delay.

Such sweetness and piety[1] are rarely combined in one so young. I daresay you are familiar with King Richard—I need not say more. If she has been abducted as you fear, things may not go well with her,

[1] Deliberately misquoted.

having no defence, save saintly piety, against the advances of enflamed males bent on her undoing.

I shall hasten to make enquiries, leaving no avenue unexplored, in an attempt to save that unprotected innocence (if it is still possible) and she not already lying forsaken in a sordid Bagnio, at the mercy of all comers, bruised and forgotten, fit only for the lunatic asylum, having had the purity crushed out of her.

I shall write again at news of anything that may speed her return to the bosom of her mournful family.

Trust me—

DELIVERED BY EARL MUCH'S SERVANT
August 1, 1784
Mrs Fox
To *Amaranth* Hublon
In her room, Salamander Row

Dear AMARANTH,

Welcome, blessed child, to the magnificent house of one of the greatest and kindest men on earth. When you feel sufficiently rested from *your trip from Dover,* send word by your maid that I may call on you.

I need not remind you of Earl Much's generosity in offering you a home here, with me; or wonder how it can ever be repaid. The following example suffices to represent it.

The day before yesterday, in talking to his lordship of this and that, I inadvertently referred to your charming letter announcing your arrival *at Dover* and departure for London, and your request for help finding temporary lodgings. His lordship insisted on examining it. I resisted, to no avail: he would tolerate no refusal, repeating his demand that I send someone to fetch it from my rooms at once. After some hesitation I confessed that the dear letter was even then in my pocket, since I was unable to be separated from such a precious communication for a single moment.

He was outraged that I had not shewn him immediately. "How long have you anguished over this, madam?" Gravely scanning your dear note, complimenting your hand under his breath, wondering if its owner could be a quarter as lovely as just one of its shapely curlicues.

His acuity is infallible: I had indeed agonised as he surmised, becoming quite unwell. I admitted that I had had your letter some while, debating how best to serve you without further trespass on his noble heart—he who has been the world to me! For, as I explained, one could not leave unaccompanied a young girl so pure and trusting, stranger to this city of adventurers lying in wait for an heiress to cheat of her fortune—or, worse, imprison in the despicable servitude that compels innocence first to corruption and thence unnatural appetite, leaving her no more than a broken husk! Pictures of depravity that made me tremble.

Before his insistence on reading your letter for himself, I had decided to return to my former modest lodgings, in order to provide you with that maternal care whose previous lack has blighted your happiness, without trespassing further on his generosity.

My scheme, extracted from me as agonisingly as a tooth, was not to be. I was unwilling, having already exposed your private correspondence to his gaze, to betray our intimacy further.

His response was unequivocal: it would be an unpardonable insult if you stayed outside his doors—more, that if you did not come *at once* he should hold me responsible—and I should know the shape of his fury!

Those words had no sooner flown his lips (and I as swiftly to his knees in my eagerness to sooth his burning wrath with my own—

which act I feel certain you will long to perform on your own account when you meet this Paragon, *but must not*), than, in due course, he raised me up and clapped his hands, calling for his man.

"Housekeeper . . . suite of chambers . . . linens, flowers, perfumed waters . . ." From where I stood trembling at my boldness at the window, I caught those phrases murmured with peerless knowledge of the female heart. The serving man took his instruction with an expression of awe and devotion, then left at a trot.

What blessing it is, dear AMARANTH, to be reunited with you. Bask without reserve in the cordiality of his lordship, your protector, and friend.

Your devoted confidante—

August 2, 1784
Mrs Fox
To Hubert van Essel

What are the expressions about a fool? A fool and his money is one, an old fool the other . . . why separate them? I assure you that both will soon be united in your erstwhile friend, Lord Much.

Already one hears the sound of your congratulations!

But let us not talk of you.

I had prepared the ground so thoroughly against *my distant cousin Amaranth*'s arrival that it was as if an entire batallion had swept along before, leaving the prize for the whistling standard bearer to canter past and catch up. I gravely handed Much's man a letter of greeting to deliver to Martha's room (all for his Lordship's benefit), extolling the handsome periwigged idiot twice that it was *for the young lady's eyes only, since it contained sentiments about his master that I should die rather than acknowledge.* Flirting and simpering the while, so that the dolt was on the point of attempting a liberty when (alas) a nearby door opened. Springing back, the conceited creature winked!

Those manoevres later proved tactically unnecessary, as Victoire has already had midnight confabulations with that particularly virile servant and learned that he passes everything to his master, however insignificant, on pain of death.

However, my literary dart's effect was better than imagined. When Amaranth was presented, refreshed from sleep and a slap, radiant in a simple muslin she had embroidered, instructed to give a courtesy at every sentence his Lordship spoke and a blush at every opportunity, he could have spared himself the use of a cravat with his own tongue.

Cousin Amaranth has been at Salamander Row a mere two days, and Lord M has already made an ass of himself, showering her with presents and attentions—which he now barely extends to me, except as a threadbare attempt to induce torpor regarding her honour. I might as well be ninety! Pah! As if I care what he wants to do with her! The moment he set eyes on her said enough. How deep the hook is in his throat! More of that by and by. Meanwhile, I pet and sigh over her as if she were my own calf, or made of spun sugar so she would melt with a lick. In truth, she is so—dewy—that it is tempting . . .

Were there so much as a shred of competitiveness or jealousy in my composition, I might have begun to feel that his treatment of *me,* that had only yesterday been so fulsome, was a shadow of his capabilities, insulting me with its dust-like paucity. The more one pursues this line of thought . . . Yes! Fury rises at his scandalous neglect, he treats me like a serf who is tossed a heel of bread from the scullery door.

At last, I am developing an appetite for his mortification quite separate from the tedious duty I owe you. He may discover himself struck down, not through the workmanlike fulfilment of a promise, but out of the far deadlier malevolence of a peevish woman.

For, however much I regret disappointing you, your long-winded tale of poor, tragic Jocasta Danceacre's suffering and fall from grace, her ludicrous inability to escape this buffoon's clutches, induced nothing in me but disgust. I told you that I needed a personal reason to strike him. Your notion of supplying it made me laugh for days. Nevertheless, I was still prepared to make the best of things, out of my enduring devotion for you.

But all that has suddenly changed—through my agency rather than yours. How can a Dutch philosopher—despite unexpected success at toppling a drunken sot into a canal (who was in all probability already planning a dip)—be competent to mastermind an affair of such feminine complexity? The part most restorative to my humour is that Martha, despite her cleverness, cannot really grasp what is going on, or what exceptional circumstances she has fetched up in. Thrown in so deep, the confused creature imagines all this to be perfectly normal—*and her due!*

Astonishing her is near impossible, she has taken it upon herself to be moved by nothing. Yesterday she mistook a coachman standing in the hall for a visitor, Duke Vespers, and formed her own conclusion as to the nobility of immobility which, Victoire informs me, she already practises whenever possible.

Earlier today, the Earl offered her a yellow diamond the size of a quail's egg and she declared the colour commonplace.

If only you had been there. We were in the basement of his house; an eery, vaulted expanse lighted with hundreds of tapers. We followed cautiously as he pointed his cane at bits of statues with legs and arms missing, or broken faces, culminating in a grimy white sarcophagus pilfered from a tomb. It was all to impress Martha, for I am a veteran of that particular tour, and was busy with my fan, trying to waft yawns out of the tittle-tattle reach of the candle flames.

As we approached the sarcophagus, strangely glowing from more candles set in its interior, Much tensed at being so close to Martha in the dark. In truth, as light caught her hair and ran along her cheekbones, she was a thousand times lovelier than the tag-ends of history he insisted boring us with.

We halted before the vast object. Much asked her how she liked it.

"*This?*"

She turned to me with an expression I should like to keep.

"Do the servants have to wash down here, in this dirty old thing?

"I hate bathing," she grimaced, as an afterthought.

A noise came from his throat, but he pulled himself together, patted his pockets and drew out the diamond, which sat blazing on his palm so that it took my breath away.

"Perhaps you prefer this?"

His voice was confident of success.

Plucking it from his hand, she turned it towards the candles lining the walls, so that it flashed and sparkled. Then, without any warning, gave it three hard cracks against the sarcophagus's flank, striking where carved kingly glyphs decorated the alabaster. Glittering chips flew left and right—altering the sex of the previous incumbent for ever.

After uttering her immortal line, she slipped the diamond into her reticule with *you could kill someone with that,* and walked out.

Because of this absurd demonstration, he is head over heels in love with her and has become her slave. Her insouciance has turned him putty, bearing the imprint of her feet; he has never seen anything like it, either in bravura or beauty. Though he moves in all society, there are no decent women left to advise him: he has abused most and the remainder are Whores. Even his recent mistress, Poppy Salmon, harpy and climber though she is, cannot match this spontaneous impudence.

Martha snuffles gifts like a rhinoceros, while the most lovesick cash-cow in Christendom is ready to saw his chest open for her—yet her only interest is in how many valuable objects she can acquire before the well dries up. It is delicious, you deprive yourself of a treat.

Should her novelty wear off, however, or she fail to give him *any* encouragement, even a smile, he may in time-honoured fashion leap the fence and take the prize, undoing all my work at a stroke.

A diplomatic visit at her levée tomorrow, when Victoire is by, is called for. We need to whip some sense into her charming head.

Excuse me, I am summoned to breakfast—

August 1, 1784
Dadson Darley, Mayfair
To Joshua Coats, Surveyor, Mashing

Coats, it's deuced awful to make a fellow put pen to paper, but that's what folly you have driven me to. I take no responsibility for the consequences, on my life I do not. Might turn out a proposal or a poem, out of my hands. Words back to front and upside down. Your fault.

The thing is this. I've come back brutal early from taking the waters at Bath after Nonce, one of the sharps at Whites, bumped into me at in the Assembly Rooms there. Got our weskits in quite a tangle, like two stags in a dingle, which he came out of rather badly snagged.

I was glad to see him. There is a limit to how much of that rusty stuff a man can drink without starting to flake. We went about together for a bit, stocking up on stockings, you might say, but there wasn't much doing. The frillier the filly the stouter the mater, have you noticed? Were both below par nursing our injured appearance, tailors in tow, when Nonce said he wanted to see what was going on at Hipp Street. So we packed the game in and shot back to town.

Didn't know what he meant about Hipp Street, I had thought the whole contraption was closed down when Mother Danceacre died, but it looks as if it's been taken up again in a bigger way by that dashed flash woman we saw at the sale—d'you recall? Well-pointed, in the front, took to her right off. Nonce says she's gone into partnership with General Beddoes and renovated the place. He says it is business as usual—roaring trade, i'fact. New acts and fresh girls; a sawcy Greek thing with lamps, and something called the Bed of Sultanas which sounds very fruity indeed, although word is there is only one sultana and an awful lot of mirrors.

I know you never paid much attention to that sort of outfit, but buildings are a dry biscuit to spend your life on, and since Hipp Street is parked right next to that square you've rather given up on, oughtn't you come and look at it? Odds sir, before you know it they will have built over it. Never seen such a fashion for bricks. When a fellow dines now it is the only talk, courses of mortar instead of nourishment, until I could offer a duel rather than stomach any more. Might dash off an operetta—*Brickoletto,* or somesuch—ought to set the house afire.

The minute you arrive we will winkle Black out of his damn attic, where he has got a sight too dramatic. He has been making more of a tomfool of himself than usual, badgering every woman in London to be an angel for his paintings, but they all refuse, Mrs Fox among 'em. He can't see where he is going wrong, got himself very low.

Talking of that Fox lady, she's been given a house by Earl Much, provoking a great deal of speculation, none of it flattering to a lady. I had rather got the notion that Danceacre was keen, what?—can't fathom it, brain too feeble.

Dash it man, come back at once, London's a mystery without you to measure it—I've no leisure without your wit.

What d'you say?

DD

July 28, 1784
Sarah Beddoes, Hipp Street
Given to Mr Voster
For the attention of the proprietor

Sir,

You have required an account of how we fare, which I am sending as you requested, through your agent, Mr Voster.

Upon recently receiving your order to bar Earl Much from Hipp Street, I found myself sorely tried, debating how to carry out your wishes in a manner that would reflect the gentleman's place in society, and that you would approve.

I sought the way least like to provoke unforseen difficulties—on which I would not dare proffer opinion, had you not requested it *if occasion merited.* You mentioned my age and experience. But by what right does a housekeeper pretend to know how to prevent consequences that the wisest men would not attempt? You have travelled the world and know human nature; I have never left this city. But, since I have been told that you are a stranger to England, here is information you may not know.

I will be frank. Your instruction to bar Lord Much is founded on his previous association with my mistress. However, his Lordship had been a visitor at this house long before. He was an intimate of my first mistress, Lady Danceacre, and so a familiar figure. Her Ladyship's entertainments were renowned. Lord Much was so often here that he might have been a member of the family. As housekeeper I could not avoid knowing him, nor him me. He treated me as if I was the head of his own household. Although I owe him no feisance—being wholeheartedly in your service—I foresaw that if I presented your request in person, he might challenge or refuse me. My knowledge of his superiority of station and distinction of intellect, persuaded me that I should then need assistance of the male servants, with who knows what consequences, given his Lordship's skill with a sword?

Therefore, I laid the matter before Mrs Salmon, my new mistress, since her knowledge of the Earl (begging your pardon, sir) must outstrip that of any among us. I delayed for several days, lest she disputed the correctness of my decision and ordered me to take another path—hard to perform, should I be sent in opposing directions by two masters! To my admitted surprise, madam was in immediate agreement and mocked my hesitation in what she called the only course, agreeing with you in every particular.

Yesterday a letter was sent to his Lordship, intimating your honour's wishes and our intention to acquiesce in them.

We have instructed the doormen accordingly.

Your servant,
Sarah Beddoes, Housekeeper

July 30, 1784
Poppy Salmon, Hipp Street
To Earl Much
Salamander Row

Sir,

I daresay you have had Beddoes's delicious letter by now, turning you off from Hipp Street?

How does it feel to be given marching orders *by a housekeeper*? *My* housekeeper, come to that—who used to bow and scrape when you came here to humiliate her mistress and, once, mine. Thinking that when Lady Danceacre wasn't looking you would get fancy with me into the bargain.

How the tables have turned! Look what you get for not buying me this house when I begged you to, when she died. See the cost of hesitation!

London is laughing over the joke of you skulking like a purple fog round Mayfair. I hear that drawings have been pinned up in all the coffee houses from here to Cheapside: are they witty enough for your collection? The artist captures you well. Some are coloured—that must have cost. Rumour has it that they are by an American painter, who has got your shrivelled arse and bandy legs, scuttling away from my entrance in a most remarkable way. Or perhaps it is not you but someone very similar. All men look alike in retreat. These fine engravings bear the legend *Crepuscular Snivel-Git Deprived of Tit.* Vastly amusing, sir. Only you can decide if it is overly flattering. They are blowing in every gutter, it is not difficult to come by one.

Should you attempt to pay a call at my establishment to discuss it, I must dissuade you: every manservant is primed to defend me to the last drop. You are proud of your sword, but how keen can it stay against twenty blades, each half your age? Remember too that it is neither I nor Beddoes who forbid you Hipp Street, but our new benefactor, who has this one inflexible condition, which we have agreed. For, without the (predictable) demands of your company, I now enjoy a life of ease and pleasure.

Do you remember the first time we met: here, in this very house—how long ago was that? I was only just arrived from the Surrey countryside to become maidservant to Lady Danceacre, and was still finding my bearings. Her Ladyship showed such kindness that I was puzzled, suspecting it was some trick. Though I had been raised fairly, there was nothing that could be called indulgence. Her Ladyship's gentleness, as well as making me presents of her dresses, made the other servants resentful. I was wary, believing that she must plan to accuse me of theft and have me thrown in gaol! She did not know the effect her generosity had, God bless her.

The day *our* paths crossed, the other maids had had me in tears for a week with their spitefulness. It was in that state of misery and rebellion that you scented me out, whiskers a-twitch.

You gave me the shivers, my Lord, from when I first saw you. It was on the stairs, from the second floor down to the library, and you came swaggering up as if you owned the place. I didn't like your look or the way you stared, fixing me like a cobra. I tried to pass, but you got hold of my arm, spoiling the silk, trapping me against the iron rails. For a moment I feared you intended to snap me in two and tumble me over. I near fainted from fear, with no soul nearby, too scared to call out. I shall never forget what insults you offered under your breath as we struggled, or how you laughed an inch from my face. Nor your other hand.

You kept on at me like that for a month, until at last you found me alone one day, in a part of the house where you had no right to be. Once ruined, what was the point afterwards in resisting? You made it clear that if I did not accept your terms you would kill me, which I heartily believed.

I do not deny liking the presents you gave me, or that having Marylebone Park for my own was worth it. Diamonds look well on fine women, and I had no more inclination for being a servant then than now! But how wearisome you became.

It is better being my own mistress to being yours. When this house came to auction, you did nothing, however hard I pleaded for it. It is the way of the world, sir, for women like me—best bid gets all.

You made me what I am, just as you did Lady Danceacre, who never would have done those things if you hadn't got her so fast in debt she had nowhere to turn. She was not like me, not at all. But scum like you wouldn't know the difference.

It took me a long time to find out what you did to her—oh, but I did! The lies you told me about her, to turn me against her, when she was a saint and you the Devil. May you swing or burn for it—what do I care? I regret nothing, except the pain I caused her. I owe nothing, neither. I rendered account with you daily—twice daily, have the grace to recall.

If God allows me one favour in my ungodly state, it is that I will not set eyes on your ugly countenance again until we meet in Hell. Then do what you like—if you find me before the Devil claws you to ribbons.

This is how hard I have become. Show your face here and take the consequences. I wish you would. The pity of it is that we have so many lovely young women now, even your Lordship would be so sated by their cunning enthusiasms, they might even prove the death of you.

Let me repeat my new master's request: do not call here.

August 4, 1784
Hubert van Essel, Amsterdam
To Mrs Fox, Salamander Row

Dear Mrs Fox,

Your last letter left me shaking with anxiety for the danger to which you subject yourself. Where shall I begin denouncing the foolhardy course on which you have embarked?

I admit that when I asked you to destroy Urban Fine, I had no plan of how you might do so, trusting your previous success at inadvertently ruining or killing people to carry this fresh challenge with grace and safety. Or was it merely an outburst from an embittered man who has long lost any sense of his stupidity? Why did I involve you in revenge grown cold, against an intended victim who, after so many years, must be oblivious? You delivered the *Curiosities* to him—that should have been enough.

The more I reflect on my spontaneous challenge, the clearer my folly becomes.

Not in asking—although that was great—but in letting you take me seriously. I had only imagined that you would, in some way, confront him. But I should have known you better! Why would you risk your own skin when you could throw someone else to the lion?

When the new day has begun by the clock and the rest of the household sleeps its piety, when I have reached the end of my endurance for study, I reread your letters, longing to have you by me to give your own account, or begin a better one. Reading of your making light of the Earl earns both my fear and admiration at the end of a long day, when I hide in my study to avoid Albrecht's puerile inquisition into the progress of what he sees as his inheritance.

Your spirited jousting with that foul nobleman is the only sort of nobility I can admire but which, in its contempt for consequences, marks you out as one of a dying breed.

For, though you are the most scheming, worthless, contemptible woman, my city suffers now that you are not in it. The water is no longer refreshing nor the breezes cool; the bright colours of the houses dim, and the canals seethe like lead.

It could be my eyes. I am having new spectacle lenses ground, having conducted experiments that prove that the ball of my eye has become flatter, and so less able to conjoin God's rays as well as hitherto. I do not yet comprehend how this can be, but will embark on a series of dissections, once a fresh body whose eye-orbs have not yet dried out can be found.

Last week, possessed by thoughts of you, I had my watchman open your house, to check that nothing needed attention, neither from moth nor wet. In the attic was that absurd dress, in a trunk. I laid it on a low stool, running my hand across the pearls (never dared when you were in it). This fantasy lasted until the light began to fade, when I shut it up again with lavender, and had the house sealed once more.

While sitting there regarding it, I conjured you not only as the approximation of a queen, but as a bride—albeit too heavily garnished for my taste. I reproached myself, since at fifty years it would be more decorous (as you do not hesitate to point out!) to imagine a shroud as companion. The picture held stubborn all the way to my nephew's house. Helpless to shake free of you, I collided with couples idling in the fine evening air.

Approaching Albrecht's, I could hear Joachim calling his sister, Hesper, a Belgian clog—for which he was pinched and began a determined shrieking. At that I debated returning to my own roof.

But my life is now so linked to yours that I am unwilling to go home unless you are there. Which sentimentality you cruelly anticipate in your last letter, with that barb about the Virginias.

Most foolish of women! Beware voicing those notions, even in sport, lest they take root and direct your actions. If you pursue your current course, the possibility of your being sent as a criminal to those inhospitable climes is closer than you imagine. I know something of English law. It is little different from our own, except more savage. Do you know you could be deported for stealing a single spoon? You, who never knew how many there were in your household.

Or even hanged? Do you have the slightest idea what the punishment is for procuring, let alone for murder, or attempted murder?

If you do not take care, YOU WILL BURN. Listen well. Should this ill-conceived plan of conning the Earl with a Harlot-bride—if such a ramshackle plot be glorified by the name—backfire, I shall never see you again, while your last prospect will be the black nails of the bagman's hands as he steadies you for the swing.

For the love of God, renounce your *holiday task* before it is too late. I curse myself for an idle suggestion that now mortally imperils you.

Give it up, return to me.

It is no longer a diversion.

Part Four

August 8, 1784
Mrs Fox, Salamander Row
To Hubert van Essel

My dear sir,

Marriage?

Can I have understood you right? Do you cherish a growing inclination towards me?

Surely those eloquent concerns for my safety were no more than a selfish wish to insure your old age against loneliness? Which at present there is no time to discuss, since events these past days have moved so swiftly that in your feeble state you would be unable to keep up. If you are fearful of a brittle twig like Much, and vastly under-estimate *my* abilities, to which slur I take exception, then put yourself to bed in a fur nightcap with a dish of posset and sip experience circumspect from writing paper.

Victoire has just run in, cap sideways, a look in her eyes that can only be described as mad—I will continue when I have found out what trivial matter has discomposed her to this unseemly degree. I dare say it is something to do with our hot-house experiment, Amaranth-Martha.

Continued two hours later

Good God.

Martha has gone!

Not so much as a note! (But then, I forget, she cannot write.) Our plan is turned to shreds at one pass, on account of an illiterate cheating bitch. The orchid has walked, there is no denying it—and to Marylebone Park, to the house that was only recently Poppy Salmon's, where the warm imprint of one whore's backside will now be filled by another. I begin to think myself the only Harlot in London capable of making my own bed.

Victoire has been prostrate this past hour, on the verge of drinking a phial of volatile to steady her breathing—which would have become *so* steady, had I not stopped her, that she would never have had occasion for its services again.

How can it be that a not-yet fifteen-year-old novitiate whore, indifferent to any finesse, a jobbing piece of fluff with nothing more than scrim between her dirty ears, can outwit a woman near twice her age, who has granted harbour to ships of every state, Doges and Dukes among them!

I thought we had been progressing very well. The Earl was ensnared by her to such a degree that he would have believed her the Prince of Wales if I had said so, and was obviously on the verge of proposing. He was blind to all her failings, although I anticipated discovery on any number of counts. Her inability to read was proving the most awkward obstacle; even my ingenuity could not have supplied a bulwark against its exposure much longer.

On her third day in the house (as instructed) she declared a keen interest in his library. At which any *gentleman* would have bestowed her the run of it and left matters there, where they generally rest between so-minded men and women, both sides content in the suggestion of cultivated habits and free to enjoy less ambitious ones, for example, those that use only candles as props.

Not a bit of it! While I admit that she did not noticeably give off Odour of Scholar, nevertheless, the alacrity with which he whisked her toward the belly of his octagonal masterpiece, with its shelves nine rows high and gilded windows to rival Venice or Buckingham House, could have been missed in the beat of an eye. Gravely concerned that he would open any book at random and demand the poetry of a paragraph from her rosy lips—nay, a sentence—I sent Victoire in pursuit at a brisk trot, while I idled at the rear. We arrived just in time to observe Much volunteering to thrust Martha up one of the dainty ladders, so that she could admire what was on his top shelf while he took stock of her bottom one.

I called an immediate halt to that activity, somewhere in the middle, gently reminding Martha of *her fear of heights,* while tenderly guiding her little grass-green and pink slipper out of Much's grip to the safer territory of parquet, observing that we should limit our amusements to the few appropriate works I would select, since she was not of an age to make a beneficial choice herself.

While counselling her thus, tugging her torpid carcass towards a row of improving tracts, attempting to keep between the pair of them and yet constantly discovering that he had slipped soundless to the other side, I caught a look that passed from her to him, that said plain as glass, *yes we will have private conversations, do thou rely on it.* Tho' not able to write with quill, her winks and dimples rival Shakespeare. Just one among many examples too tedious to recount, but illustrating the same principle: reliable endings will always be thwarted if the actors read a different script from the author.

Her audacity not only caught me off balance, but threatens to scupper my plan at a blow. If he realises that he can get what he wants without signing a contract, that is the end of the matter. How can she be so stupid? He would cede his life to her at this moment, so great is his lust.

I freely admit that I did not think Martha sufficiently ingenious, or hideously cretinous, for *such* a destructive act, that does her no more good than it does us. Before coming here, she was following Victoire well—albeit briefly distracted by the painter, Nathan Black. The ease with which that fixation was quashed, by explaining that Black has not a penny and lives in one cold room, with no maid-servant to rinse his slops except his current love, flattered us. Having heard his circumstances so nicely put, Martha agreed that returning to *that way of life* with no recompense bar being plastered angelically twenty feet above the faithful, did not compare with the lustrous future we held out, in which, in particular, the word *Countess* shone.

I demanded the observation of one stricture alone in return for our solicitude towards her glittering future: unavailability. She seemed to understand, and agreed. An untouched young woman, close-hemmed as a pearl, is the only desirable object to a man who had spent his life having anything when, where and how he chooses—as you, of all men, know. I was sure she would comply, lured by the limitless richness of the prize.

What a fool I was!

That sort of tart considers saying no for five minutes proof of a binding engagement. The notion of being restrained is unknown to her, except as something to evade at any cost. Indeed, her experiences of it, far from being philosophical, have been mixed with cruelty, violence and the prospect of prison—from which only cunning kept her. *Knowing* her whore-ridden past, why did I not take fuller account of it? For, though my own life has been dedicated to what amounts to the same business, whoring from choice is not the same as acting from necessity. What I did for amusement, Martha did to eat. Accustomed from childhood to make her way unaided, going from one cull to the next, like stepping stones, why would she not continue? My control irked her, she did not trust me to provide for her as well as experience told her she could for herself.

In which she was right, for had our plan continued, her reacquaintance with either the gutter or the Fleet would have been swift, her only title that of *felon,* her scutcheon a portcullis.

It is a mystery how she got wind of the truth of her prospects—although doing so proves wit. Somehow she must have slipped our attention long enough for Much to make a bid.

Which he would have done first, I daresay, in writing. Then, surprised (but also excited) by her lack of reply, he must have stalked her—at last, triumphantly insinuating his narrow taffeta frame against her in a perfumed corner, that repulsive pallid hand gliding up her arm, as it has with so many. His fetid breath tantalising her, describing how he would set her up in a house beyond my reach, surrounded by servants, so that she could be her own mistress and do as she pleased, rise when she liked, eat and drink what she wished, choose her carriage, drip with diamonds. Swallowing the bait at one gulp she would have given him everything. How many times he must already have had it, since that bargain was struck! If, after taking his fill of her, he discovers what a common Harlot she really is, with no substance to offer him challenge, he will either throw her back broken on the street, or kill her . . .

Or me . . .

But then he may not, since men's capacity for self-delusion is equalled only by their appetite for self-indulgence, of which his is so bloated that we may yet survive long enough to get away.

It might even be, when Martha learns that she has been shoehorned into a second-hand, second-rate berth, scarce cold from the last bed-warmer, that she seeks revenge of her own accord and decides to kill him herself, doing my job for me in the manner of a mercenary . . . Whatever the outcome, she is gone from my reach.

My own future can wait until this letter to you is finished—see how low I place *my* safety, when set against your pleasure! Note how little fear the Earl inspires in *me.*

Now I think more clearly, having got his way so easily with *Amaranth,* why do you imagine he would turn against the provident hand that supplied her? The more one considers it, *I* am the one tricked by an adventuress posing as a relation to trade on my maternal heart—for which imposture she should suffer. *I* am the one desirous of explanations and redress, in need of succour and easement.

This is the line I shall take.

In fact, having snuffled up such a delicious *bonne-bouche* or *saltim-bocca,* without having to pay a penny, copious gratitude should flow my way. Certainly a carriage, perhaps the outright gift of this house; who knows the limit of his purse? After all, it may be more rewarding to bleed him dry.

Thus, while your romantic turn sways your judgment, turning you soft—which one must urge against—your wish for my withdrawal from this sport may soon be realised, now my Queen has flounced off the board. But do not think I shall gallop for port this instant. That little cat's interference has angered me and only added to unfinished business.

You know how Much's total neglect of me in pursuit of Martha had already turned me less than benevolent. Victoire had been right, the girl *was* too unpredictable and has, in my perceptive servant's phrase, *gone off like fireworks.* Or I am losing my touch and the world begins to move beyond my sway, while younger women, even ones this talentless, prick out the pattern that takes the prize . . . but not yet.

I gave you my word to destroy him, and so I shall—unless, in a unique display of humour, he destroys me first.

Diligent, as ever.

Your—

PS: During our visit to the library, when he could spare a moment from salivating over Miss Mayhem, the Earl, leaning against a case of books and appearing somewhat dizzy, remarked that two evenings ago, he had opened the *Curiosities.* He said he had spent hours *poring over them* each day since. And had woken, he said, still under their influence, as if they had taken an insidious hold of him.

Pronouncing which, I swear his red tongue flickered. What is in that small volume that you were so determined to acquaint him with, yet to withhold from me?

August 7, 1784
Violet Denyss, H— Street
To Clio Denyss,
The Rectory, W—, Suffolk
11 AM

Darling Clio,

It is no good, I simply cannot wait a moment longer before telling you my news. My maid can do my hair later. I don't care what Mrs B says about always looking one's best as one never knows who might walk through the door, her constant interferences are tiring.

She is merely the housekeeper!

Last night—at last!!!—after lifetimes, centuries, I swear, Clio, of *agony* . . . at last it was the Grecian Evening that my costume has been made for, with the golden sandals, and the wreath of acanthus that I made by myself (out of bay leaves), fastened with a bit of ribbon at the back, trailing among my hair which had been in papers and hot rods that were quite painful.

All Mrs Salmon's relations had spent the morning decorating the theatre—there was a lot of banging. There were clouds and gold and silver cloths hung very artfully from sticks and hooks, and layers of thin blue silk with stars that wafted.

A carpenter had made a great rock and some bushes, and a contraption above with a sort of rope harness on it, that was for me! Mrs Salmon decided on reflection that it would be more spectacular if, instead of just standing still on one leg in front of the moon (surrounded by twinkling stars held by other girls wearing dark azure to represent the heavenly firmament, or the Milky Way, Mrs Salmon could not decide which and said it *really* did not matter), it would be more dramatic if I was lowered *as if from the ethereal heavens.* I was pleased about that altho' still concerned about what could be seen through my chiton as I came down from the ethereal heavens and hovered in front of the big lamp with greased paper that smelled and started to smoke when it got hot, not to mention that the stage was raised up so that everyone would be looking at me practically from underneath. But at this Mrs Salmon became rather peremptory, asking me if I was an Architect all of a sudden, or a Friend to Geometry; and added that she had told me once and never expected to tell me again about anything, ever.

Then, just as I thought she must be very cross indeed and began to feel alarm, she hugged me close and kissed me on the lips in a way Mama never does, and said I must stop worrying now, as my life was soon going to change, and we would all have so much fun afterwards!

Can you imagine the bliss? Aren't you just dying to come too?

Anway, soon it was time. I had been dressed for ages and was sitting on the bed, too excited to feel sleepy, waiting to be fetched. I had pulled the shutters open a crack (though they had told me not to) and saw all the carriages coming, and chairs, with some on foot. That had been going on for several hours, there must have been hundreds of people. It was past midnight and the hubbub from downstairs, shrieks and laughter, was something you would never believe, as well as people chasing each other up the stairs and many others laughing and shouting. I wanted to open the door, but Mrs B had locked it from the outside to protect me. Goodness knows from what!

When she fetched me down, the floor below, that has the theatre, was full. I have never seen so many in one place altogether, making a vast amount of noise. There had been dancing and eating and drinking, and much merriment. The rooms shone with a thousand candles. Someone gave me a glass of wine (that I did not ask for), which I was told to drink straightaway and have another, since it was so hot! The room was packed; many gentlemen and very few ladies, including all Mrs Salmon's cousins. Most of the women were sitting on gentlemen's laps for lack of chairs, quite different from the rectory, but everyone happy and smiling and stroking me as we went past, having the nicest possible time.

I was to be part of the Grand Finale, after which, Mrs B said, I would go back to bed and no nonsense, *as it would make me much more appealing*—which I did not understand, for in my estimation I was the apogee of appealing already—and it turns out that I was not the only one with that thought, as I shall explain.

Everyone was full of delight and several of the gentlemen tried to engage me in what I knew would be interesting conversation, but Mrs B had my arm and marched me through the whole length of the rooms without stopping, *to whet their appetite*—for the performance, she said, when I asked.

As we approached the centre of the room it was fuller and fuller and harder and harder to move, what with everyone drinking champagne out of glasses with hollow stems, laughing. Right in the middle, near where Mrs Salmon stood in a bright dress with feathers in her hair, smothered in jewels, surrounded by at least ten men, we came to a definite impasse and had to excuse ourselves to get past a pair of gentlemen who had their backs turned, under the biggest of the three chandeliers (turquoise and white, sparkling like anything). How pretty the glass was, like bunches of grapes and blue-birds. One of the men was dressed like a zebra. Swear, Clio, cross my arms and feet and die, I have never seen anything to equal it and thought he must be part of the entertainments! They both turned round when Mrs B patted the striped one quite firmly on the shoulder. The Zebra had an orange waistcoat with the glass buttons shaped like zebra heads, and a green eyeglass, and his hair had been pulled in three directions, like a tricorn. He gawped at me as if *I* was the odd one!

I think not.

But even though Mrs B was trying to make them stand aside for us to pass, they did not move. The other man was taller, and thin, as if his clothes might have been made for someone else, head to toe in black, with linen that did not look quite clean. His hair curled on his shoulder and his eyes were blacker than his suit, but as if they were on fire, like coals, with a sort of hot intenseness like a cat. They glittered, he glittered. Just as he was about to say something, Mrs B pushed him very rudely saying *enough of your sauce, you couldn't afford it,* and put her hand in my back, hard, so I could not look round, which I wanted to.

Once we reached the stage, everything happened very fast. I forgot about the man with long hair, as I was being told what to do and not to make a mistake or I might catch fire. There were fanfares, and music played by young women in garments that only covered one side of their body. Leaving the other (you know what I mean) utterly uncovered to the general gaze, which made me blush—their knees naked too! Other women wore similar garments, of various hues, and the women *themselves* were different colours, which would most certainly be a novelty in Suffolk. The carpenter strapped me into my harness on a narrow platform at the top of a flight of wobbling steps he had put up that morning. A heavy draped cloth, painted like clouds, separated us from the main part of the room, where you could hear the assembly gathering closer and closer. It was very hot. Then there was a much bigger fanfare and the Titanic Clash of Symbols.

Without warning everything went dark, with a strong smell of snuffing. A few pinpricks started up from the girls in dark blue, weaving to and fro with tapers, crystals on the hems of their dresses and scattered in their hair. Then, wavering notes came from three flutes. I was made to jump off, and was lowered slowly towards the candles some way below, trying to balance in the ropes and keep my skirts together, which was difficult as the silk kept sliding apart, but I couldn't let go for fear of falling.

I kept smiling just as Mrs B had said that all proper actresses do, while the women danced in front of the pink hangings. It was as quiet as if everyone was holding their breath, although right at the front someone made a sort of neighing giggle and was straightaway shushed.

It was a relief that the audience was in darkness, for if I could not see them they could not see me. There were many voices and then there was an *Oh* when I came down in a sort of rush, which meant that they *could* see me, after all; my white dress shining in the light of the tapers. I felt a surge of pride that my gold sandals and lyre must look pretty, then started to blush again, and then the ropes jerked without warning, which really hurt, bringing me to a stop, twisting in darkness.

Suddenly, the lamp was lit and blazed from behind the circle of oiled paper. The heat was very great, but I tried not to worry, holding my arms out and moving my legs, although my costume was a trial. I was supposed to be flying, so did my best. A tremendous uproar started, everyone shouting while the star-girls danced quite sulkily to and fro, slapping at my toes with the beaded edges of their pink clouds. The Zebra was in the front row with his mouth open, and next to him his friend, who just stared and stared, and I stared back and then . . . then Clio, something so awful happened that I blush too much to recount, my chiton—and the curtain was brought down very abruptly, and I was jerked up, and sent to bed by a back way.

A letter has just been brought in by Mrs B's maid, who says she must dress my hair without further dispute, on Mrs B's particular orders. She also told me that I am to rest today, since there will be some callers tomorrow evening, or the next, who after last night are *most anxious to make my closer acquaintance.* It seems that I am a Hit! The emphatic way she said it made me think of that bit in *Hamlet* and I couldn't repress a giggle. She looked sullen then, that I am getting so much attention until a sly look took hold of her, as if she knew something I did not—which is really most unlikely!

"You will need to conserve your strength," she smirked, "for when they see you, the *gentlemen* will want to stay up all night."

You could have wiped her arch look off her crooked face with her apron. Who cares about some boring old men playing cards?

I hope the letter is from the man in black!

In haste,

Your loving elder sister—

PS I have given this letter to *my* maid to post, as I really do not see why Mrs B needs to meddle in *all* my affairs! If you write back, address it to the under-ladies' maid, Sally. She will see that I get it; her mother is in a sort of hospital called the Magdalen and takes in sewing. Sally is grateful for the pennies and will not tell a soul. She is younger than you and dislikes Mrs B very much.

August 6, 1784
Nathan Black
To Joshua Coats, Mashing, Suffolk

Coats,

God dammit. Darley has already told you to dig yourself out of the vegetable patch before you take root and come back to where your proper civic work moulders. We still have to get up the subscription for the King's statue in your square. But no, there you stay, flunkey to that monkey Danceacre, twiddling with the most spectacular ten-inch folly the world has ever known. Why? Let me assure you it will never be built, however tenderly you turret it.

What in the name of civilization are you doing? Danceacre has less notion of employing you the right way than of buttoning his breeches. He only asked you down there because Mrs Fox suggested it, and where is she now? Bolted long since! Given the pair of you the brush-off. Why persist?

He is a buffoon. I cannot believe you have not heard his story; even so, here it is.

Danceacre is a dilettante of an order that turns Darley Dominican. Years cavorting round Europe, leaving a trail of b—ds, doing his best to echo the fact that his mother was spending her declining years running a knocking shop. The moment Lady D died, he gave the housekeeper powers to sell Hipp Street. Consumed by the latest fancy, London bored him, he hankered to make mud pies in the country. His head had been turned by all those aerated fellows on the Tour who wear sack-cloth and spout about how healthy it is to raise children running around naked in a hovel (rich as Croesus every one and as half-baked as one another; they cannot poach an egg but they can addle their own brains). Just a craze, but they think they are being revolutionary.

It won't last. Why would anyone turn a grand old house that has stood since Elizabeth into a modern villa and live making curds? Before you know it he will be back in town, all *your* designs parching to tinder on the table. Give up! Unless there is something else—or *some one*—keeping you? I cannot imagine what sort of rustic petticoat you might have unearthed, woven from wattle and wood-eyes; but the ways of Albion daily humble me.

Another mess of Frederick D's is Hipp Street. His housekeeper Beddoes sold it as instructed to an unidentified Maecenas, on whose mysterious behalf it is run by *Madam* Salmon, the one who recently flit her own *Bolt-Hole* in Marylebone Park, where she had been kept by that slimy purple thing, Much. The housekeeper still manages Hipp Street, so stands to make a handsome profit. Some say she cut the lawyers in—they are Much's Wigs too, take note.

Mayhap they are all in it together, for Urban Fine is a nasty concoction. The more one sees and smells him, the more one detests him; rotten to the core of that wormy frame. If you wished to illustrate what stands between your world and mine, he is it—the entire *old world* clinging to a rackety set of syphilitic bones. He is dirty, for all his money; I can't see what women find attractive. But if you ask me he turns them rotten too, in one side, out the other, pop! leaving a trail of slime. The man is a maggot.

To return to Mrs Fox . . . what has become of her? *We* never see her, since she took to Earl Much's *exalted company.* She would not give him good day if he could not afford to bathe in attar—and, God's breath, if only he would; he stinks so high that embalming is the only thing to improve it. Mark my words, that association will kill her if she does not take care, he will suck her dry and suffocate her.

Here's a prime example of his vileness. I would not dream of saying this in front of Danceacre, but rumours have started up about his mother. Spreading like wild fire. That Much compelled her to Harlotry, had her over a barrel: a forced marriage and something to do with gambling debts . . . and a great deal more astonishing besides. No one could ever figure her for a born Whore, and it seems they were right. Darley is your man if you are interested in detail. This is a fragment of what he told me last night, and my stomach is already rennet.

The tale is flying all round the clubs: Lloyds, everywhere. I went to sort out my water yesterday and a couple of fellows were discussing it, very animated. Seems Lord Putrid has some *exceptional habits.* Not only Lady D: smart money says that he also queered Poppy Salmon when she was a mere maidservant in old Lady D's household. Look at *her* now. Flagrant. Hipp Street is a disgrace. If that was not enough, I caught the tattlers whispering something else, about a fresh adventure he's just started, with a very young heiress who is believed to be some relation of Mrs Fox . . . but when they found themselves overheard, they stopped.

Mrs F ought to watch her step, however sure she is of it. I would hate to hear any of those words attach themselves to her, for they are damned difficult for a lady to shake off, once stuck. Living in a house that belongs to him does her reputation no good, whether or not he is in it. Once the chatter starts it goes to and fro like a clapper, the devil to stop the racket.

General Beddoes and Mrs Salmon are running Hipp Street as a gimcrack circus—*entertainments* every night—shocking exhibitions. It would be closed down if the beadles weren't wedged in ringside seats guzzling claret. Salmon is shrewd and turns all the tricks that that Purple Pimp taught her, and those of her own besides. He made Hipp Street a slop-shop in the first place; doubtless he is dabbling in it still. Plenty are calling him the owner, and unless someone can put a better name to the mystery, I am inclined to agree.

Joshua, how can you stay away? Darley complains that a letter he sent you has gone unanswered. He is so enraged that he has become indifferent to dressing—which is the first and last sign of lunacy in his case—positive morbidity. When he does hurl on a few items for modesty, he is so distracted that every part of the get-up belongs to a different outfit—making him the most exorbitant scarecrow in Saint James's. You should have seen him yesterday! Since you will not listen to *him* (in truth, few do) you may be persuaded to cock an ear in my direction.

You *must* come at once. If gossip does not persuade you, then do it because I urgently need your advice.

Last night I met a *divinity,* but in inauspicious circumstances—at Hipp Street. She is the one that disproves the rule, so different from the rest that I have kicked out my model—who anyway looked like the underbelly of a horse—which I was trying not to dwell on, since everyone has turned me down for this damn painting and the Commissioners grow daily more vociferous. Those preachers perk up when they think their chalice is verging on half-empty. I have told them to keep their surplices on. I take pride in my work. Great Art doesn't happen overnight—or, at least, that is what I thought until yesterday evening, when the greatest art ever seen was dangled in front of my nose.

This girl—God bless her, whatever her name is—is the only one who will do. She is the embodiment of everything, her face and figure without blemish, the picture of uncorrupted innocence. Yet she is nobody. Nothing, worthless, worse than nothing, the sum of nothing—a Harlot! Practised at every trick since she could open her mouth and flex her fingers; scheming, cheating, crooked . . . dammit, I see nothing else wherever I look. I am undone, in love! So help me, even though I detest this country, she is the holy grail, a second Eve. Patent and bottle her—if you do not, I shall.

We met—if stellar explosions go by that term—at Hipp Street; at its Grecian Evening that Darley had seen announced in *The Times* and dragged me along to as a makeweight. My angel was the last of a series of awful tableaux, before laurel wreaths were torn off and the evening turned to flagrant debauch: nymphs and satyrs chasing each other up and down the stair-cases dodging frightened animals, things passing in some of the rooms involving statuary that beggar even my power to describe. I caught sight of that parson, the one who had been at Drury Lane the night of the fight, dressed as an old Faun with his furs agape, in a side room with two girls in his lap, but he didn't know me.

My Goddess was kitted out as a tawdry nymph doubling as a sacrificial lamb, an innocent effect until her robe fell off. The perfection of her figure made me determine to rescue her. Even if she proves worthless—for in these places, the most innocent invariably prove the most corrupt—I am sleepless and unable to lift a brush, until I see her. My life is at a standstill. I have just sent a letter to try for an interview.

Should this sublime creature have a name, it is one the world can never have heard, for certainly she is not of it. But I will glorify it! I *will* paint her! I may even marry her, though you call me a fool; but more fool if I do not. Dadson tells me to stump up a handful of guineas and have her *like everyone else*—over which low estimation of love we came to blows. He is a bigger idiot than Danceacre.

You possess the one sane head among us, but you will soon lose it, doodling for that nincompoop. Come and advise me, I beg, or I will not be held accountable for my actions!

Nathan Black

5 AM
August 7, 1784
Nathan Black
To Miss X, Glorious Nymph with the Golden Lyre,
Hipp Street, Mayfair
(fan-shaped)

Madam,

Sleep had deserted me. Words fail me.

Nevertheless I will try.

I speak as a native American, a country whose grandeur makes England look like the side of a dish; and as a painter, daily surrounded by the finest faces in the land. But last night, dragged to the so-called Grecian Evening at Hipp Street, which tawdry prospect filled me with horror, I was eclipsed by a sight that turned my elevated principles to ashes.

Mayfair is become Paradise! For it houses—you, madam!

The moment you appeared, light flaring round you like the Apocalypse, I knew I must paint you before a day passes, before another breath leaves my body, or your angelic countenance alters by the quality of one second. Oh! That I could have you here! I burn to draw you, to immortalise you for the panels of the church I am working on. . . .[1] I never thought that it would be such a place as Hipp Street that held my angel, but so it proves, just as Tintoretto's Magdalene shines out from the shadow of the cross. How I envy those men who have already clasped you to their bosom!

My companion, at whose insistence I came (most unwillingly), swears you for his new heroine—the prettiest thing in all London, he says, prettier than any picture. High praise, if only the glorious task of painting such a picture should fall to me! I cannot pay as handsomely as those cursed gentlemen who have already had the pleasure to know you—but hope that the prospect of immortality will be a greater reward.

Waiting your reply, on which all my future happiness (and that of the world) depends—

Nathan Black

Midnight, August 8, 1784
Joshua Coats, Mashing
to Miss Clio Denyss,
the Rectory, W—, Suffolk

Dear Miss Denyss,

Profoundly aware as I am of your mother's continuing anguish at the disappearance of your elder sister Violet (altho, I am sure, shortly all will be explained and she restored, full of amusing escapades), I would do nothing to cause your family further distress.

[1] A great deal more of the same follows and has not been included.

Therefore I struggled before writing to you in whom youth and purity combine so perfectly that God alone may determine where one ends and the other begins. But your expression of dismay this afternoon, on hearing my intent to leave Mashing and so—ah, unwillingly—give up the delight of your company, moved me. After solitary debate, dear Miss Denyss, I am persuaded to reveal my reason for leaving.

Had I dared think that my announcement could have the effect it did, I should never have had the courage to utter a sound; but merely quit the county and slunk away, cursing myself for a coward. Yes, coward! For the hint of shadow crossing your pale brow was a death-blow, against which an eternity of torment with red hot dividers would be nothing. How could I then tell you my reason, involving as it does the depravations of the wider world, from which you should ever be shielded?

Only when you rained scorn upon me and accused me of *tiring of you*, of *leaving on an ignoble pretext* rather than *spend one further minute in your company*, did I dare entertain the hope that sprang from your scolding! As if one could ever tire of someone so perfectly good, wise beyond their years, considerate and trustworthy. Our friendship is young, Miss Denyss, yet it bestows pleasure beyond its scope. Your intellect; your discernment; your reasoned observations on all matters, would impress the harshest critic. Each visit to your family has left me refreshed, by your conversation and your grasp of things generally ascribed to the world of men. How can such sagacity occupy such a small frame?

Alas, the world is different in its parts.

If it ease your mind to understand my need to leave at once, if you would know why something of the gravest import—the health and happiness of a valued friend—drags me from even one *second* of your company, then read on. Should my words strike too harshly, put away the paper—merely trust that things cannot be otherwise.

The friend who takes me from you is a hot-tempered genius from

Boston, a painter, scarce twenty-three years old, like to become a Royal Academician—the highest honour our King bestows.

Yet (which is the scourge of all of his temperament), he is prey to strong fancies, calling on them to to fuel his work—which powerful imaginings ever threaten to capsize that prized reason that you and I value above all things, bar familial duty. Thus, in allowing himself to be constantly urged by new experiences; tugged from one throe to another in unceasing exploration; willfully seeking sensations—thus it is that he has exposed himself to that which threatens his undoing and endangers his life—*the appalling error of falling in love with a despicable Harpy, a diseased thing of no moral worth, one who earns her living by feeding off others!* A young woman so unrelated to you that I shrink to mention her in the same sentence.

But, so it is. He met this Gorgon, who by God's light is undoubtedly a malformed, evil monstrosity—at a so-called Grecian Evening, at a house of ill-repute. Painted in false colours, indecent in a transparent garment, the shallow strumpet lured and corrupted him, using the panoply of her vile arts to ensnare him, having herself lowered half-naked (I tremble to mention it) before an assembly of a hundred men, before whose eager eyes she allowed herself to be undressed as many times.

He is in thrall, dearest Clio—he even believes himself to be *in love!* I cannot vouch for what idiocy he will commit if a sane person does not take swift action. Now you understand my need to go to town at once and rescue him from this speculating temptress, in whose veins runs disease, whose ambition is to spend his money, dissipate his health and erase his good name.

I leave at first light, madam. I will take the liberty of writing you from London.

Sincerely,
Joshua Coats

MOST URGENT By courier
August 9, 1784
Clio Denyss (*at Mashing*)
To Joshua Coats, Conduit Street

Great Heavens, Mr Coats, I die!

Good sir, I cannot breathe. I beseech you, in the name of all that is honourable, If you wish to see me alive again, if you have any pity, save me.

I tried to reach you before you quit Mashing, but it was too late. This letter comes by the kindness of Lord Danceacre, whose messenger set out at a gallop six precious hours after you left for London. His Lordship has himself already long gone. I am at Mashing under doctor's orders, brought low by events, under instructions not to move until tomorrow—which my mother, unable to rise from her own bed, is in no fit state to dispute. I feel so helpless, so alone!

How full of joy life was yesterday. I opened your precious letter on my favourite window-seat, that gives across the park towards the spinney, beyond which is Lord Danceacre's estate and all its happy associations. The leaves were gay flecks on the grass. I began to devour the paper you so recently touched, with the vanity of any young woman for whom admiration is a caress, in a haze of greedy guilt at your undeserved praise. Whatever was of such import to snatch you from me, your esteem made me feel delight, at your solicitude, and insistence on shielding me from harm.

Thus cocooned, intrigued by your friend's having become embroiled with a deceitful cocotte whom, by her shamelessness, carried every ounce of blame for his entrapment, I read on. Your contempt for her made my own value increase—as you intended—and, guided thus by you (as I would be in all things), I felt nothing but scorn for the erring Sybil, wilful stranger to modesty, for whom there is no hope; to whom, having chosen a life of degradation, heaven rests forever barred. Your strenuous hatred of this *"creature"* who threatens your friend—nay, all mankind—was very real. Under my breath *I congratulated you* for putting another man's cares before your own—and mine—in the struggle of the moral-minded against profligacy! Then, carefree and at ease, proud of *my* difference from such a wasted life, I turned the page.

And O! Good God, sir! How can this vile falsehood be?

It is no foul-fevered strumpet you describe, but my beloved sister! There can be no doubt that it is she—that the most terrible fate has befallen her! What can have become her in this short time? What desperate criminals have perverted her? Is she held against her will, imprisoned? Dear God, is she held under duress?

I enclose a letter received yesterday from Violet's own hand,[1] from which I had not—no one could have—understood the gravity of her situation. No, I am quite sure I could not . . . nor, I shiver from fear saying it, does she! In the name of goodness, what manner of place is she in?

Help her and help me, you must, I implore you.

I writhe in anguish that I obeyed her commands not to tell our parents what little I knew, thinking her happy and safe, since her letters were full of high-spirited joy and ease. My elder, my superior, she enjoined me to secrecy. I obeyed.

What must be done? My mother already suffers so much that she has locked herself in her room, neither eating nor speaking. This grief will kill her—and my father is still away on business. Surely it would be wrong to endanger my mother's life with this fresh tragedy when she is so frail?

[1] Letter dated August 7, Violet to Clio Denyss

What will they do to me—but that is nothing compared with . . . Ah, I deserve to be punished, whipped . . . I do not know what to do . . . I beseech you, find Violet and save her. I weep, it is impossible to think—*what have I done?* If only I had betrayed her trust and shown my parents her letters . . . but she swore me to silence!

Help Violet, Mr Coats, before she is lost forever, becoming that thing you so despise. Waste not a moment: each particle of a *second* might contain her life and honour. You are her only hope. Do all in your power—which I know is great; but dread that the forces of evil may prove greater.

Send note by the messenger when you get this.

Your despairing friend,
Clytemnestra Denyss

BY URGENT MESSENGER
August 9, 1784
Frederick Danceacre, Mashing,
To Mrs Fox, Salamander Row

Dear Mrs Fox,

Just had the damndest visit from Clytemnestra Denyss, Violet Denyss's younger sister, Clio, what, gibbering for Coats. Incoherent, came racing through the fields half dressed, hair down, skirts black with dew. Saw her from the gun room, tearing across from the spinney, making a trail clear through the field like a snail. Thought she was a wild creature! Behaved like a mad thing, wouldn't stop for breath. Almost took a pot at her, could have been rabid. Brought her in, whereupon she began tugging at my coat sleeve for dear life. Let me tell you I stowed the gun I was cleaning on a high shelf straight off! Guessed right away that something must be up.

It looks as if there has been some hoo-ha: could not make out a word for a while and made her drink a stirrup of brandy. When she became calmer I sat her down and parked alongside and told her to let me know what the matter was, in her own time; female nonsense, couldn't be all that bad.

Blast me down a barrel when she opens her mouth! As far as anyone can tell from Clio's ravings, her sister Violet has been found. Although after a third cup she was so agitated, i'fact close to delirious, that it was hard to be certain. Something about Mr Coats and a letter and a Greek nymph. When she said *Mr Coats* she went soft, which would not advance the tale at all. So I tan-tivvied her, and she fell quiet, plucking her skirts as if preparing to howl.

Then, instead, she looked me straight in the face like a man and declared clear as anything, "My sister is in trouble, sir. I must speak with Mr Coats. At once." Fixing me like a gimlet.

It has got to be some sort of terrible muddle—no sense to be made at all. I couldn't get any further information from Clio: the moment she learned that she had missed Coats by three full hours, she fainted clean across my lap.

Tutton was fiddling on the terrace, so I handed her over to him. Deuced useful fellow, always nearby when you need him. He catched her up and off they went to the housekeeper, while I sent a note to Mrs Denyss.

Since Justice Denyss is detained in the North, I am proceeding to town at once. Don't want to lose time waiting for Miss Denyss to wake up and go through all that what-for again: upsetting; wailing, what. Thought it best to get on. I will call on you if I may when I arrive, if it ain't a trespass—the assistance of a lady sympathetic to the family—excellent good thing, time of need, so forth. You'll find me care of Coats, Conduit Street.

Dark shutters. Very modern.

Pray that matters are not so bad as I fear.

Yours as ever,
Danceacre

August 9, 1784
Mrs Fox, Salamander Row
To Hubert van Essel, Amsterdam

Are you better yet? Shake off your torpor, here is today's dose. Chew it well, for it is strong meat that will likely have you back in bed before you turn the page.

I have frequently observed how, when one ambition falls short of its aim, another fills the space. Nature abhors a void, is that not what you once lectured me?

On the heels of the discovery of wretched Martha's perfidy (even her name is painful to pronounce), putting Much's excision from the world's flesh temporarily into abeyance, came news that the eldest Denyss girl, Violet, is performing over the odds and ruining herself at full tilt practically unaided: from schoolgirl to slattern in a matter of weeks. It is most diverting and proves the power that *Natural Selection*—by which I mean, choosing those skills that life offers with open hands—is more potent than those crusty little volumes you insist on piling around you and sending to other people; that you say are freedom, but which, I tell you, are a cage, and you a willing bird . . .

Ah! as always, you always bring my attention round to you . . . through God knows what black arts.

But my own tale is a great deal more exciting, as you will shortly agree, even though by so doing, you cast yourself in a dull light.

Violet first thrust herself to my attention when I was visiting Mashing. She found it amusing to twit me over my friendship with Danceacre, with whom she was clearly besotted, and about whom she made the astonishing declaration that she had *prior claim*—as if seeing off a rival of equal standing! Which jest, in some moods, one would have laughed off as schoolroom ribbing, but in others, take singular and potent aversion to. Sadly for Violet, it was the latter.

Thus simply are our futures decided: a smile here, a frown there; a glorious peerage, an embowelling.

A simple country girl (father parson and Justice of the Peace), Violet had been rubbing along well enough towards her unexalted future as some clump-footed farmer's wife, making rhubarb custards and flannelette petticoats weighed down by blotched Greek and Latin epithets in cross-stitch, when Lord Danceacre returned unexpectedly from abroad and decided on a whim to settle at Mashing, rather than the more *liberal* Hipp Street. Little effort conjures the fevered speculation that the news threw the County roundabout into; but especially at the rectory, with its three girls between thirteen and sixteen, the eldest of whom could barely read when his Lordship went abroad, and whose only amusement was a weekly card party with her dismal cousins.

You will be the first to agree that mine is a nature rarely roused to aversion or revenge, particularly against younger women.

Violet Denyss was a special case.

Having achieved the astonishing feat, for a lumpen peasant, of *gaining* my interest with her absurd claim to Danceacre, she might, even at that reckless moment, have speedily disengaged it with a weeping apology. Which escape route did not cross a mind already fixed on a fantastic course that included her neighbourly noble as a life-long dance partner.

She made the fact that she chafed at the rectory as clear as only disenchanted youth can; that she considered herself superior to and was exhausted by her sisters' babyish demands, longing to stretch her wings wider—in short, she was everything that a perfectly healthy young woman, with every promise of a bright future, should be.

But, since she had impaled herself on my notice, I decided to take an active rather than a passive interest, and try the experiment of seeing how little aid was needed to launch her on her chosen path. It struck me that it would put her out more mightily if I let her be, than if I gave her the tiny particle of assistance she craved. At which point, you may wonder why I did not take that course, of thwarting her by doing nothing, rather than stepping forward helpfully with the key she lacked.

Generosity won out.

However much her malformed insults had irritated me, however attractive it was to sit back and neglect her . . . in the end, the delight of helping a young girl realise her ambition proved irresistible. And required so little effort! Less than aimlessly skimming a touchpaper with a glowing taper; a hint so subtle that one might never afterwards be certain . . . since there is always the question of spontaneous combustion. My involvement has been so slight that no one will have detected it, her being so hot that it is almost certain she set herself aflame.

If I recall correctly, at about the same time, Victoire gave Miss Denyss a small reward for her diligent care of one of my muffs, or stoles (I forget which); but I am almost sure that Victoire did one day observe, while dressing me, that she had given Violet a few pennies. I remember my surprise at such largesse *from her own purse,* for I am sorry to say that Victoire is extremely parsimonious. Yet, so zealous is she in everything that affects *me,* that she must have considered that the girl's care of my possessions merited notice.

What the spoiled child did with that small sum is her own concern. In the event, it seems that she may not have used it wisely. Hardly a fault that can be lain at my door! Where were her parents when she ran away? Where in particular was *her father*?

Violet had been *burning* to discover her womanhood, for which her first choice of helpmeet was, quite properly, Danceacre. Whom among us does not applaud ambition? There is not doubt that he is well-made and handsome, even before the estate and title and numerous holdings are computed. He was certainly adequate to the task and even appeared to have taken cursory note of her.

It goes without saying that Violet and he were not suited. Her impoverished outlook, her sloppy bookishness, were feeble match for his wealth, nobility and urbanity. Which straightforward fact I tried to explain to her, gently pointing out that no one likes to make a fool of themselves. My kind attempts to guide her in the direction of Mr Tutton (a passable man of not inconsiderable means, keen to help her fly the nest—at least, as far as his own), met with vigorously expressed scorn.

At that time I noticed that Violet, in common with any female animal in heat, while sighing at Danceacre, also let her eyes drift toward Mr Coats. Before we knew where we were she was up at dawn in the model room, holding scalpels and pencils with the dedication of the Surgeon General's servant at a dissection. With a flash of genius I saw how it would be a crime to restrict her choice of mate to just *three* eligible bachelors. So I hit on the charming idea of giving her the run of an entire city. At our very first meeting she had asked me to *help her come out*—why not do so spectacularly?

Thus, by logical and fast progression, Violet shortly found herself in a very smart whorehouse, better than any she was entitled to, more Golden Square than Grope Cunt Lane, being prepared for experiences that one may safely say were outside the scope of her upbringing.

Alas, her career has taken a turn so sudden that even I was as unprepared for the rapidity of her ascension as one would be to glance out of a cottage window and see a comet perching on the garden fence.

It would appear that, during a fleeting appearance in a tableau at an evening held by Poppy Salmon, Violet made a sensational impression on half the gentlemen in London. In a transparent gown designed under the goatish eye of Mrs Beddoes (unless it was one of that Ancient's own night-dresses), the garment fell off as Violet dangled on a gilded rope, causing something just short of a stampede. She was hurried to safety by a back way.

The scale of this triumph led Poppy Salmon to the novel idea of selling Violet to the highest bidder. Thus, while the innocent flower was snoring in her bed, the guests leaving Salmon's premises were discretely advised that bidding by promissory note would take place throughout the next day or so—*for the opportunity to be the first to make the young nymph's closer acquaintance.*

No one has ever heard of such an audacious idea. Despite irritation that it came from the fluffed-out head of that pixie, nevertheless I feel a sort of pride. It is, after all, *my* creature being so singled out for special favour; the talk, I promise you, of the entire town.

The winner of the prize (which is supposed to be enjoyed this very evening) remains a closely guarded secret. Even Victoire, dainty boots stabled under the kitchen table at Hipp Street where she flirts as Mr Voster, while the cook regales her with hare pie and port-wine, cannot discover the beneficiary-in-waiting.

Salmon and Beddoes's greed in wringing every advantage from the affair has brought a city already a-quiver with expectation to a standstill. Every newspaper is poised, having made large bids under clandestine cover, hoping to secure the story by fair means or foul. Meanwhile, Victoire tells me that Violet stays in her room, reading and stuffing herself with cinammon milk, delights she believes to be recompense for her performance rather than preparation for sacrifice. While she yawns and gawps out of the window, oblivious to her fate, how quickly the experience she once yearned for rushes to meet her.

Are you yet living? Long silence does not suit you. While I agree that you can have no news in comparison with mine, even so, it would please me *to be allowed to share the crumbs.*

Yours in expectation—

August 10, 1784
Nathan Black, the Strand
To Joshua Coats, Conduit Street

What in God's name do you mean, sir, that my beloved Violet is safe under your roof, but that I cannot visit her?[1]

Must I call you out to get an audience with the woman I adore? Whom, you will recall, I brought to your attention in the first place? Pray, what is she to you that you keep her imprisoned? She demands to see me! I shall prove it.

Yesterday I went to Hipp Street at eight in the evening, having received a note[2] from my blissful, beloved Violet—as I now thrill to call her, granting me leave to call on her; but to go to the area and ask for a particular maid, as my angel was not sure how amiable the household was to her having visitors without the agreement of the housekeeper or the whoremistress.

You may be certain that I did not like the flavour of that, being a restriction of liberty by those placed in false authority, against which America succesfully rebelled, as should all nations.

I stepped over to the house at the appointed time. The sky was very overcast. It was already dark and becoming cold, and had been since I arrived an hour earlier, time spent walking across the end of the

[1] The letter he refers to from Coats refuses Black permission to visit Violet at Coats's house.

[2] Too dull to print.

street, winding my clock and looking at the windows for any glimpse of movement—of her! But the house was quiet, its shutters closed.

The fateful minute found me on the skullery step, fist raised to the door. But, before I could touch it her maid, Sally (who is not above fifteen), flung it open as if she had stood awaiting my knock for quite some time. Face pale, she glanced around as she spoke, evidently afraid of being discovered. "We may not be above a moment, sir!" Speaking quick she took hold of my arm and drew me closer, pinning me to the door-frame, making us less visible should anyone come out of the front portal, massive above.

"Pray milord, I beg you, keep your voice low."

"I am not a milord," I exclaimed, forgetting her injunction to silence in my urgency to approach my Love, at which Sally looked grievously alarmed. She quaked with fear.

"Come," I said, "Sally, is it not? Take me at once to your mistress, and mine; or point the way, and then you shall be quit of me, and no blame attach itself to you."

Trying to calm her with the reasonableness of my tone—which I was far from feeling—at the same time I prised a shilling from my waistcoat, which was difficult in our proximity, and held it before her eyes. At which, instead of siezing it, she burst into tears, half lying on my breast, sobbing.

At other times, this unforseen event was one that I should have made swift use of, given the concealment we were in and the pliant youth of the girl, but my amorous inclination was firmly elsewhere. I offered my handkerchief, demanding what could have upset her—wondering too why she kept me from my love, and if this was some mischievous tactic. Those doubts shame me now, knowing what risk Sally took in bringing Violet's letter, for which she could have been discharged; but once one begins subterfuge, mysteries leap out at every turn. I was close to tears myself.

"Do not be afraid," said I, "but tell me what is the matter, and we will make everything alright."

My gentleness brought on even more noisy sobbing and nose-blowing. Luck had it that the street was empty and the kitchen in darkness, save one candle on the table, or we should most certainly have been discovered. Gripping her tight, I admonished her to control herself and answer as directed. "Is it your mistress?" I demanded, shaking her harder. "Has something befallen her?"

Sally looked quite wild, then took a breath. "Oh, sir, she is gone!" she burst out, forgetting her own plea for temperance and continuing in a high-pitched wail, "a half-hour ago, they came and took her!"

I could not believe what I had just heard. "Who?" I demanded, trying to see if she told truth, knowing that she did. "Who took her?"

"Noble gentlemens," Sally snuffled, "two, what came into the house with the elderly gentleman. Strode in like avengeful angels."

"What? What elderly gentleman?" I was perplexed; for in Sally's wish to be disburdened of her tale she was speaking too fast and low. It was impossible to make sense of half her words, while those that were clear meant little, except that a mysterious elderly gentleman was somehow crucial to the fate of my beloved.

"He was the gentleman who won—" Sally stopped very abruptly as if she had swallowed her own tongue, glancing at me and then looking away.

"Sally!" I commanded, with a violent shake from which any pretence at kindness had evaporated. "Do not break off now."

"The gentleman who won the . . ." She faltered again and then squealed in a rush of unpent discomfort, "the gentleman who had *an appointment* to call on Miss Violet, sir. He arrived at about five of the clock, sir. He was shown up by Mrs Salmon herself, as if he was the King of Sheba. I seen him come in, but thought nothing of it, not knowing then that it was *Miss Violet* he was come to see."

Her account was causing me profound agitation. Without intending it I squeezed her so hard that she shook free and put the table between us. "Quite a number of gentlemen call here, sir, there was nothing unusual in it, except perhaps in Mrs Salmon herself showing him up . . . I don't know. I had duties in another part of the house.

"At about half past six, I had just come up with a tray that I was to take to the library, for a card party. It was heavy and there was no one to help me get through the door into the hall. I was stuck there on the top step when there was a great pounding at the front door—like someone wrenching the knocker off, an awful noise, worse than the devil in thunderbolts; it must of rang through the house, *Bang Bang Bang!*

"I wanted to cover my ears, but could not on account of the tray, so I tucked myself back into the shadows and peeped through a crack that I held open with my shoulder.

"At that din, Mrs Beddoes herself come out of her office, making a sign to the doorman, who had declined to open, to investigate. The door was duly pulled wide and the two young gentlesirs strode in wearing dark clothes, one tall and the other one shorter. Behind them came what I felt certain was the older gentleman that had come earlier, that I had supposed was still in the house, but must of gone out when I was below stairs. He was wrapped to his boots in a cloak with collars that was too big for him, hat pulled down like a coach man—except he wasn't no coach man. I'm good with people, I knew it for him from the way he held himself. The moment he began to walk proved it.

"Mrs Beddoes had not noticed him, being so taken up by the angry look of the young sirs. Besides, he hung back, as if he wanted it so, and melted against the wall. She come towards the other two, and you could tell she was very put out. She accosted them in a loud voice, asking *what they thought they was doing there at that time of day?*

"The shorter one, who had been taking off his glove, examining the tips, moved very suddenly and hit her slap across the face with his bare hand, on which there were several rings. One way then the other. 'Ask again, madam, most willingly!' he declared. Then he stepped back and started calmly pulling his glove back on."

"Then what?"

"Mrs Beddoes clapped her hands to her bloody nose and bellowed for help. Meanwhile, the older gentleman had skirted round the walls and was going up the stairs as if he would not be turned back. Just as I noticed him, so did Mrs B and the footmen: he moved soft, but fast too.

"The taller of the pair of gentlemen now stepped very close to Mrs Beddoes, and said something."

"*What?*" Had I asked Sally for the crown I could not have got a more withering look.

"Oh, sir! I could not of gone no nearer! Footmen was running from all ways . . . I could not begin to guess. Then he bent his head right down to her ear and whispered something else, pointing at the old man who was now on the landing, where footmen were just about to handle him.

"Mrs Beddoes looked from one to the other, and went white as her lappets. Whiter, so they looked grey all of a sudden. She seemed about to lose her footing. Blood was trickling down the side of her mouth from a cut on one side of her nose. She called out *stop* in such a horrible voice that everyone stood glued to their spot and the old gentleman moved beyond the touch of the footmen as if walking in a field of statues.

"Then she went quietly into her room, closing the door. That was that. A footman caught sight of me and said what did I think I was doing. So I brought my tray back down.

"Next thing, there were sounds on the stoop. Out of the window I saw them three dark figures put Miss Violet in a carriage, so swaddled in the old gentleman's cloak that you couldn't see her face, but I knew it was my mistress. They handled her very quick, and were off.

"Then I battened the shutters, and have been waiting for you to come ever since, sir."

Coats, you must see that you have no right to keep me longer in the dark! You must tell me what you know, to clear up this horrible mystery. I require an explanation of your unfathomable behaviour.

At the least, tell Violet of my anxiety to see her, that I am consumed by concern for her wellbeing and insist on hearing from her own lips how she fares. If you cannot give her this enclosed note,[1] at least have the courtesy to tell her what I have said, and let me know her answer.

Be reasonable, sir! I call you my friend. Keep me in ignorance and there is no choice but to question whether *your* involvement with Violet is more than it should be.

Black

August 4, 1784
John Verney
Treddle Hall, Lancashire
To Hubert van Essel
Amsterdam

Dear Doctor van Essel,

I believe that you will remember the brother of Jocasta Verney, despite the years that have passed since we said good-bye in a coach yard, one wet dawn.

If it were as a doctor of medicine I could write to you now, there should be better chance of my living a while longer. As things stand, my costly quacks tell me I have a few weeks left, less if lucky: a rich man rotting in a fine bed, with scented sheets fit for a harlot. There

[1] Predictable breast-beating. Not included.

are factories and canals, even a town named after me—yet no son or daughter to pass it to and only my sorry flesh to discomfort me for all those wasted years.

They tell me I am cankered to the marrow.

It may be that a life of bitter thoughts, reflecting on the waste of my sister's life and of your love; on the lack of children, or youth spun out in cloth bales—having consumed my spirit, then turned to my body and began gnawing that. They say I am *eaten from within.*

Why pay for such a diagnosis? I have dismissed them. My household staff serve me well enough, we drink together to ease the pain (theirs too, for they are as kindly disposed to me as I to them). Laudanum does the rest.

I have prayed that you hold our former friendship in some of the esteem in which I always have. Few men have your nobility, as my sister knew full well.

It may surprise you to learn that until her death, Jocasta's rare letters spoke of you with admiration and regret. I wish that things had been different and she had become your wife, rather than suffer the dreadful fate that was dealt her.

Do you recall that last time we met, so many years ago? I still see you springing up on the London Stage. Dear Doctor. The hopes that you failed to conceal, your trembling impatience to reach London and my beloved sister. My heart went with you on that hopeless journey, and has travelled with you yet.

I loved Jocasta as dearly as any brother can and confess to you on my death bed, what could not then be said: you were the only one who could have saved her, had salvation been possible. But she had gone too far on the path to damnation—much further than you knew. Earl Much, the devil pitted against her, was too strong. I have tortured myself arguing whether, had you known all then, it might have changed the balance of events?

Continued two days later

You and I are both men of our word. Jocasta swore me to secrecy, so I swore. I was more easily persuaded in those days. But I will not take her secret to the grave, since there is another life at stake. If anything can be done, any evil repaired or just revenge taken, now is the time—when shortly I shall have eternity to defend the action.

You are a scholar, so no dissimulation follows.

When you and I met, in Lancashire—where I found you, patiently waiting in that inn—my sister had just given birth in London, to a baby girl.

Before assisting her, I demanded the name of the father. After days of sullen refusal she told me that the infant was the daughter of an Earl Much, who, it seems, somehow persuaded her to lie with him when in fresh widowhood, a mere day after her husband's death. I refused to hear any details of such a disgraceful passage, although I could see that she wished to say more, presumably in an attempt to extenuate her crime. *The day after her husband died!* Her cupidity shamed me. My ears were shut!

However, she asked my help for the final weeks before the birth, and I agreed. Our parents believed me on mill business. Half their fortune was lost through that subterfuge. I cared little—they dared not cut *me* off for it, as they had her. There was no one to oil their pitiless engine if they did.

As with everything in our family, loss—of money, of their only daughter—was never spoken of again.

At the moment of her daughter's birth, that should have been the happiest of her life, Jocasta covered her face, and told me to name *it.* I held the baby, marked by her father's evil, long enough to give her the name Persephone. She was very small. Jocasta would not look at the infant, who was sent that evening to a wet-nurse in Kingston.

I do not know where Kingston is, or the name of the woman who took Persephone in, nor how they fared. Nor what name she may later have been given, or if she even lives. In all my sister's letters—until the very last one—Persephone was never mentioned.

Jocasta did however declare that she would provide for her daughter herself. She intended to marry the father, although she claimed she detested him.

But he never knew about the child. When he failed to propose—something I still believe Jocasta could have made him do, by telling him that simple fact—she set her teeth and took instead the repulsive life he inflicted on her.

It is beyond my ailing powers to guess if you know any part of this story. Breaking the promise made to my sister troubles me less than that there may be a woman, now full-grown, as entitled—more entitled!—than any being on earth to benefit from my fortune; who may, for aught I know, be in desperate need. Pain though it is in principle to bequeath anything to a bastard of Much, this person, if living, is my sister's child and my niece.

The address of my London lawyers is enclosed. As a final act of kindness to Jocasta's memory—and I hope to mine—be my conscience and judge. Seek this person out, whether she is in need or want; whether she favours my sister's goodness or the evil of her father. Judge whether she is worthy of a third of my wealth. The second part comes to you. Should Persephone be dead, or comfortably provided, or rotten, her share defaults to you to support your studies, and for a foundation. Even if you decide to do nothing at all, it is the same.

Jocasta also left a son, Lord Frederick. According to my lawyers' report he inherited his mother's wealth and looks in equal measure with his father Danceacre's title and vacuity. He is well provided for. Even so, the third part of my estate is his.

I have so pondered these matters, having nothing else to occupy my mind, that the papers are thorough to the last degree. My lawyers are primed to do your bidding in all things. I know you will undertake this task with probity. With this letter, any decision you make in these matters become binding.

One last thing: the infant bore a tiny mark, delicate as a petal, far behind her left ear. I doubt that any living soul knows of it.

Your lifelong friend,
John Verney
Witnessed by Archimbold Battle, servant

By runner
August 10, 1784
Frederick Danceacre
To Mrs Fox

Dearest Madam,

Your help and confidence is most urgently required to prevent what is, without doubt, already scandalous escalating into something far worse, that will destroy a family known to you.

There is no time to write—let me trespass on your patience only long enough to reiterate my request to call on you, once I am arrived in London. Although eager to admire your inestimable qualities, that indulgence does not inform this plea. Rather, it lies in begging your noble-hearted wisdom in the service of a family now fallen into difficulties so dire that they even perplex an eternal optimist. It were best not to commit such matters to paper. I shall present myself a half-hour after you receive this—unless your servant tells my fellow no.

Your friend,
Frederick Danceacre

August 10, 1784
Mrs Fox, Salamander Row
To Hubert van Essel

Astonishment follows on the heels of amazement, so many barkings and scrapings of shocked shins that one cannot take a step without tripping over a fresh revelation. I swear that when you read this you will board the first vessel. Why wait till the end? Come and enjoy the best seat in the house! Pack your bags!

First, the girl Violet—whom we left stuffing herself in preparation for being [s. . . . .d][1] herself, who was to be sacrificed to the highest bidder. The hour of accounting came at last. I got this tale with great difficulty from a reliable gossip. Let me set the scene.

Above stairs:

Violet. Replete, lolling unlaced and undressed, slumbering on march-pane and sweet wine, and God knows what-else that had been slipped into her glass.

In the grand hall below:

The holder of the winning ticket is met by no less a figure than Mrs Salmon, gleefully rubbing her hands along her transparent sides in knowledge of the money just transferred from the gentleman's bulging pocket to her reticule, thence to Mrs Beddoes's waiting apron; a spectacular sum that must, from the rumours scorching town, be around two hundred guineas—more than Kitty Fischer ever dreamed of, and part of a speculation that must have minted them thousands.

The victorious conqueror-to-be had long said farewell to middle age. He was balding, with a straggle of whitish whiskers and a waist-

[1] A word has been cut out.

coat straining from button to button, a size too small. A parson, no less, that should know better, already intimate with the charms of Salmon and her circle at Marylebone Park; one of that Harpy's company at Drury Lane the night I suffered in the opposite box, as I have already told you, though I was so taken up with Mrs Salmon that I paid him no attention. Apparently a seasoned libertine who cuckolds his innocent family into believing him on charitable trips giving succour at the Magdalens, while instead he tastes one Harlot after another, possessing both insatiable venality, and a big enough dose of the clap to applaud himself at every step. This *gentleman,* then, gleaming with perspiration at the thought of his purchase, and at its price (enough to bankrupt a lesser man and very like to rock him), trotted behind Salmon's indecently trembling rear. She meanwhile talks at him over her shoulder, of the *sweetness* he was shortly to encounter, the *untried innocence* lying above, all unknowing, *waiting to perform his pleasure.*

With the real art of the procuress, she incited him so much that a glimpse of his quarry would be enough to set him off: that true cullster's skill—of cunning conversation—that distinguishes a great courtesan from a cheap trick, although I am loath to pay her compliment. With a final finesse, she led him into a gilded anteroom on the fourth floor, where two young women in Persian undress were playing at a board game, who plied him with champagne and tantalised him further, before showing him to his purchase.

This man was in the highest possible state of expectation for, although he had been present at the Grecian Evening, he had spent it pleasing himself in a similar side room to that he was now in, thus missing the famous tableau, only snatching a glimpse of Violet's naked back as she was bundled off through the fog from cigars and extinguished candles, from the end of the packed room. Yet what he had seen (or what he could not)—coupled with the pungent atmosphere and riotous cat-calls—determined him to possess what the rest of London desired.

Salmon assured him that he would find the maiden alone, sleeping, in darkness; and that he should be left to toy with her for as long as he wished, doing as he pleased, there being no bar, at such a price, imposed on his conduct—*not unless he killed her.* Even if he did, the Witch tittered, they would throw in another to take her place.

Scarce able to breathe at the picture of criminal indulgence painted by that vicious harridan, he panted into his second glass of wine. Some time later, she points out a door draped with a gay curtain; hands him a key; and watches him creep into the darkness, whence there is no sound but the breathing of a sleeping, half-drugged girl; hears him turn the lock in preparation for his business and then scampers to another part of the house to help her colourful *sister* entertain a large party of soldiers who *are looking for a skirmish in exotic parts.*

Downstairs:

Mrs Beddoes receives an unannounced call in her study from my *Mr Voster,* in the charming company of two burly bullies hired from the very house in Frying Pan Alley that Martha once made the mistake of visiting. These men, twice Victoire's size, armed to the teeth but nicely dressed (given the nature of their call), were let in without question by the doormen, since Mr Voster comes and goes as he pleases.

In my capacity as *landlord,* (an occupation I wear very light, exacting scarce any demands)—except a fair share of profits—it had been disappointing not to be told of the sale of Violet, and invited to share in the happy prize. I daresay both Mrs Beddoes and Mrs Salmon forgot, in the excited rush of organising it, and were planning to surprise me with my good fortune later.

Victoire, however, having spent the previous evening closeted with the lovesick cook, practising the sorts of arts that could get her hanged, got wind of the affair and alerted me to the fact that large sums of money would be coming into Hipp Street and, as she shrewdly observed, would not stay long before going out again.

Further, having heard of the party of soldiers due the next evening, she was certain that any monies would be kept in the only safe place in the house, as far as possible from prying bayonets. This was a panel in Mrs Beddoes's room, so skilfully fitted that it could not be discovered by observation. French work, Victoire told me proudly, fitted by a local *Ebeniste* for the first Lord Danceacre to hide his gambling money.

Thus, Victoire and her friends surprised Mrs Beddoes ensconced with a bottle of Madeira, going through some papers. On being confronted, the noble lady professed seamless innocence about any money, patted her cap-laces, and recommended Mr Voster to come back the next day to discuss it with Mrs Salmon, *who was not then in the house.* At which she gave a strong indication of considering the interview over.

"But my business is with you, ma'am," Victoire let her know with a bow, "so your mistress's whereabouts, though always of interest"—bowing again—"even if she prove after all to be in the house *entertaining a cadre of soldiers!*"—at which Victoire laughed merrily—"is of no consequence. Therefore I will stay."

Voster-Victoire then threw out his-her coat skirts and took the chair by the fire to roast his finely turned shanks, opposite Mrs Beddoes, hand resting lightly on his cane as if it might hide a sword, while the implacable bullies stood by the door as if they nailed it shut.

At the remark about the soldiers Mrs Beddoes blenched, but quickly collected herself and asked if Mr Voster cared for a glass of wine?

Victoire ignored that request to repeat her own, recommending Mrs Beddoes to think whether she had forgotten anything that she would now like to impart? *Which would not go against her but, on the contrary, do her a great deal of good.*

Victoire told me afterwards how, backed into such a dangerous position, Mrs Beddoes stood her ground. It is impossible to guess what she thought, except that she may have planned to run off with the money that very night, and was defending her future like an enraged badger. Or that she trusted to its concealment, which is the more likely.

Alas for Mrs Beddoes, at a sign from Victoire, one bully pinned the housekeeper into her chair, his enormous hand over her mouth and nose, which he quickly replaced with a tight cloth; while the other, rather than bothering with fancy fittings, wrenched open the entire panel, from whose interior he removed a stout iron box that he set on the table next to Mrs Beddoes. Victoire suggested that if Mrs B cared to open it without delay, she would be left a quarter of its contents and none to say contrariwise; but if she refused, they would simply take the locked box and bid her good evening, wishing that she had been more helpful *while still able.*

Moments later the party was gone—without the box.

Are you packed? My tale is not yet ended. So, Victoire left the housekeeper tied to her chair but otherwise unscathed, eyes fixed on a still-substantial pile of money that had been honourably left in the open box next to her, wondering what lies she could tell to keep it, and working her hands loose of their imprisonment.

Just after the door closed behind Victoire and her *gallants,* the elderly gentleman came slowly down the great stairs. Unescorted, gripping the rail, his perspiring face grey. He could not have been with Violet more than a few minutes and now left without notice, wearing the most peculiar expression.

I learnt all this from the head doorman Sibbald, a spy in my pay, one of Frederick Danceacre's servants who stayed on in the new household, who has been a constant source of information. A man who misses nothing, despite his squint (I vouch because of it), of whose role even Victoire is unaware. He could not inform me of the man's name, having seen him only once, at the Grecian evening, wearing skins, when he considered him to be beneath particular note.

Wrongly, it turns out.

But, as Sibbald now sent a runner to tell me, if that man was not on the point of death from illness, he was suffering a shock that was likely to kill him as quick, for Sibbald had never seen such a dreadful countenance, or one that had aged twenty years in half an hour. It was, he said, as if the fellow had teetered on the abyss of Hell itself, and on looking into its depth, seen a mirror image beckoning him to leap in—

Hold, sir, an urgent note has been brought by a waiting feathercap.[1] I will let you know more as quick as I know it myself.

Your loving—and lonely—friend—

[Forwarded to London from Mashing]
August 7, 1784
Archimbold Battle
Treddle Hall
To Frederick Lord Danceacre

My Lord Danceacre, Sir,

If it please you, my late beloved master, John Verney Esquire of Treddle Hall, asked me to dispatch the enclosed to your Lordship in the event of his death.

He was the best of men, sir!

I cannot write more.

Arch. Battle
Servant

[1] From Frederick Danceacre.

[Enclosed with the above]
Undated
John Verney
Treddle Hall, Lancashire
To Frederick Danceacre

Dear nephew,

For so you are, although we have never met.

Our family has been riven by disappointments and misunderstandings, and so it continues, as if cursed. I doubt that my sister Jocasta ever mentioned me to you. When you read the following words about your mother, I will be dead.

Your mother was the most beautiful of women, with a sweet disposition. Yet, too, headstrong and vain, as most lovely young women are. Do we not encourage them?

In youth, on her travels (on which I accompanied her, since she flew in the face of our parents' wishes) she was always the centre of attention. Exhilarated though she was by such admiration, it led to folly and misery. Her first marriage (of which you may not even be aware) ended in abrupt widowhood when, I have it on good authority, her husband died in a brutal accident.

She lost your own father, as you know, to the French.

My concern is not with that, but to assure you of the constancy and love of that dear woman; to dissolve misapprehensions you may harbour towards her and reveal what I believe you will be most keen to learn.

It pains me to speak so levelly of one whom I have mourned bitterly for years—even while she was still living. I do so entirely for your sake.

You think that she acted cruelly, sending you abroad on what must have seemed exile, to free her to lead a degenerate and immoral life. Is this not the case? Are those not the festering imaginings that poisoned you against her?

They are wrong. A painting of you as a very young man hung at Hipp Street. It is in front of me now; my agent acquired it at the auction. You have her colouring. This fine work was ordered by your mother a full two years after you left for Rome. It was made from some earlier sketches. She took great pains and very great expense over the likeness with Mr Gainsborough, as I recall from a letter at the time. She could not live without something to remember you by. You were life itself to her. Her own life horrified her, doubly so when the one thing she loved without reserve—you, sir—was gone.

Continued a day later

Following the death of her first husband, and before her marriage to your father, your mother was somehow ensnared by a nobleman, so immoral that honest people do not speak his name. Moreover—a trust only broken now, on my deathbed—she had a daughter by him, to which event I bear witness. There is no shred of doubt, Lord Danceacre, that before you were born, your mother gave birth to what, if she lives, is your sister.

I cannot keep silence any longer. I baptised her . . . Persephone . . . as well as could be done in secrecy. Your mother refused to look upon or touch her. She went to a wet nurse at Kingston.

Whatever the faults of the father, surely the child was innocent? Yet, even if that were so, I fear that the utter lack of maternal attention will have had a profound effect on Persephone, should she be living. Cruel, unnatural behaviour! I have stayed my tongue for a quarter-century. There. It is done. It can make no difference; I daresay your sister is long dead.

No papers record her. For all legal purposes, as with so many of lowlier birth, she does not exist. Without doubt she will have adopted a false name and a new identity; she may have gone abroad. There is nothing more to help you find her, except a tiny mark like a petal behind her ear, which must be there still. The same, only coarser, is on her father's hand.

I believe he knows none of this. As with all violent men, the outcome of his actions does not concern him. Like a tidal wave he surges on, unable to turn back to the splintered fragments and wrecked lives scattered behind. Perhaps your mother understood it for, with the mix of pride and shame that characterised her, she suffered his indignities, rather than admit the one thing that might—were he human—have tempered his extremities.

Let me repeat: you were not sent abroad to facilitate her pleasures, which I believe is your wrongful opinion. It was done so that you would not be marked by the man who cuckolded your father and forced your mother into depravity, nor witness her suffering at his hands.

Frederick, I have burnt all her letters. But know this: tears were on every one. Yours was a noble mother who sent away first her daughter, then her son, to protect them.

I have always been a coward. Eventually our parents discovered that I had spent months in London, which neglect lost a great part of their fortune. Had I made any further move towards helping your mother, they might have cut me off.

So, I sacrificed her, so that one day I might help her children. Both you and your sister—whom I refuse to believe dead—stand to inherit fortunes. *You* are already wealthy. No provision was made for her. My executor will contact you and be as a father to you. Trust him.

Meanwhile, find Persephone and make what amends you see fit. Punish the man who disgraced your mother, help me strike him from the grave. Correct these wrongs as best you can.

Dear nephew, I believe you would rather know, than live deceived.

May God go with you.

Your loving uncle,
John Verney

Part Five

August 13, 1784
Mrs Fox
To Hubert van Essel
Amsterdam

Shortly after my last letter to you had been dispatched, Lord Danceacre came to see me, in extreme agitation. I allowed him to be shown up, his curses audible as he took the stairs two at a time. The stone rang under his spurs, a militant note that curdled my blood even before he burst in, knocking my maidservant sideways as she strove to announce him before he announced himself.

"You cannot stay in this revolting place a moment longer, madam," he shouted, rushing to where I had half-risen to greet him and siezing me so violently that I was thrown against his breast, our breaths intermingling.

"This monstrous man! This—this—" Releasing me as abruptly, he strode about the room, swiping at objects with his hat as if it was a sword.

"Whatever can be the matter, sir!" I cried out, making myself comfortable in a welcoming attitude, hoping he might profit from example. "Calm yourself and explain this violent intrusion, before I am compelled to call for help!"

He was some ten paces away, heading towards a large and valuable figure on a yellow plinth. At the authority of my tone he stopped in mid-lunge and came about, face heliotrope, a poem of perturbation.

"For God's sake, madam, forgive me," says he, clasping his forehead in a gesture that made me smile at the pleats of my fan, "I forget myself in anger and scarce know where to begin!"

While he was turning horizontal cartwheels I signed for the maid to leave glasses and strong wine, before closing the great gilded doors.

I offered Danceacre a glass, which, however hot his mood, he was in no position to decline. He hurled himself beside me on the yellow silk, long legs thrust out, neglectful of how his spurs gashed the inlaid floor and scored up woody fronds like petrified fern.

"*Dearest* sir," I murmured, "surely whatever it is cannot be near as bad as you make out. Tell me everything, omit no detail, let me be judge."

After momentary hesitation he recounted the following tale. That Violet Denyss's father had narrowly saved her from prostitution under the roof of Poppy Salmon, who had pimped her and must die—*and by God he would wring that bitch's neck and whoever had aided her in her devilish work, snapping their heads off like a row of pullets;* that he had learned that his mother had been ruined by the man in whose house we now sat (at which remembrance he swore profanities and swallowed a third glass, while I hastily poured again, steadying his hand with mine); and that—whereupon his face turned apoplectic and his eyes gleamed—he had learned that he had a sister, thrust on his mother by this same Earl whom he intended to challenge at once and disembowel at the first pass.

Tears of rage sprang into Danceacre's eyes. He hurled himself upon me, berating the gods for his misfortune, begging me to explain why he had been so singled out and where should he find any ease?

Let me spare you the tedium of the next.

In short, I hit upon a means to calm him. In due course we were able to resume reasonable conversation.

It would avail him nothing to seek out Earl Much that night, I advised, for he was not at home, having taken up residence at Marylebone Park with his *heiress.* Indeed, liveries had been observed two days before, loading a carriage with coroneted trunks. I bespoke his Lordship to ponder the fact that Earl Much is considered the finest swordsman in London and perchance England, so that, however angry Danceacre was, the likelihood of killing his adversary *at a stroke* was slight.

Ignoring his expression I went on, "why allow *yourself* to be killed, thus putting you in no position to aid your sister?

"Were it not better to find her, before pitting yourself against this worthless villain—her father even so, do not forget, whose death at your hands cannot recommend you to her!" Which last appeal—to common sense—had some effect.

Doubtful as it is that the woman can be alive, or he able to find her, I did not add my reservations to his already burdened heart.

Before quitting Much's house (a course Danceacre now insists I also take, and without delay), he begged my assistance, adding a solemn vow that he intends nothing rash. In return he extracted my *own* solemn promise to identify those responsible for Miss Denyss's foray into harlotry and to bring such persons to justice.

The impossibility of doing which, a glance in a mirror in the middle of our parting embrace confirmed.

Nonetheless I remain,

Yours—

August 13, 1784
Justice Denyss, Mount Street
To Mrs Hannah Denyss,
The Rectory,
W—, County of Suffolk

My dear wife, dearest Hannah,

Prepare to rejoice, Violet is safe! Since every unknowing moment torments you, receive these tidings without delay. The courier stands impatient beside me with his bag, to bring you news that must gladden your heart.

A few days ago, my urgent duties in Coventry being curtailed, more pressing business brought me to London—an unwelcome addition to other pastoral cares. But it was by the Grace of Him who is all-knowing! Not long after my arrival, the news we have scarce dared hope for, came.

In brief: Violet is well. Though shaken, she is unharmed. Worry no longer. Nothing has befallen her that solitary contemplation will not heal. She is still worthy of our love and the approbation of society. Once she has rested from her adventures, we will return to you.

Look to your own health, too long neglected through concern for your child. Believe yourself truly free of the anxieties that have brought your generous heart low. Relinquish your sick-bed, and when Violet returns to your breast, welcome her as a prodigal.

Whatever rumours seep to that beloved county, be indifferent, for they are lies. Malicious tongues spread lascivious stories, the corrupt spring that drives the moral turpitude of the ungodly. It will be said that Violet was taken into a house of ill-repute and prepared to become that thing whose name I cannot mention. Cheap, untruthful stories, familiar from every peddler that shuffles through the gate, or the village gossips, the fables of impoverished minds.

Discount them, Hannah, every one, for all are without foundation. You are the good wife of a man of the cloth and powerful man of the law. Our prosperity arouses covetousness, while our godliness, like that of the Lord, is subject to scrutiny. These events are a test from which you will emerge stronger.

And yet . . . what agony must I thrust upon you, scarce risen from your bed . . . ah, it is no use, it can no longer be concealed!

Violet has been snatched from a disaster worse than death. But, I implore you to believe, *snatched in time.*

As her father, whose only crime is to love her above her other sisters, since she is first-born and closest, had God so willed, to being my only son; and as her pastor, I alone shoulder the blame for the sins of men, that almost cast her beyond redemption.

Violet came close to the worst, but for a marvel: to me fell the opportunity to save her, plucking her from the very jaws of oblivion!

One must consider this a singular blessing. With my bare hands I fought off those who sought her destruction, carrying her to safety as if I was Abraham. She need not be outcast, she is our daughter yet, and your spouse is twice-blessed, having been chosen as the instrument of her salvation.

So, Hannah, compose yourself. Tell Clytemnestra the happy news without delay. Let her read my words and be guided as if by a sermon, for there is nothing here that cannot be beneficial to her, as precept, and timely warning of the dangers waiting to ensnare disobedient young women. Being the closest to Violet, Clio will have suffered most. Looking up to her sister, in possession of a more sober disposition, Clio may believe that she bears some responsibility for the other's actions, or chide herself that she played no part in her rescue.

I exculpate her from those infantile sensations of shame and guilt. She need not fear punishment; we will forgive and embrace her wholeheartedly. This is no time for recrimination. By the grace of God guiding my actions, our eldest is saved: it is a miracle.

I do not know how much longer we will be detained. Once Violet and I have returned we shall never set foot in the carnal city again, but stay in Suffolk, proud in adversity, united in faith.

Before God,
Your husband,
Rev Robert Denyss

August 13, 1784
Frederick Danceacre
c/o Dadson Darley,
Bond Street,
To Mrs Fox
Salamander Row

Dear Mrs Fox,

After last night . . . my gratitude is boundless. You are a woman above others, peerless, adorable. Visions of my unexpected good fortune recede in a delicious haze . . . how long must I wait before you remind me of it? Name the hour of my happiness and I shall be there, not a second after!

Meanwhile, forgive my having been overwhelmed by a murderous urge to root out wickedness and destroy the man responsible for my mother's downfall and sister's shameful birth. The mere thought of his ownership poisoned the place we were in. But for you, I would have razed his house and possessions to the ground. A duel is too quick! He and all connected to him must burn, the vile discoloured ashes ground in the dirt. So prominent, so rotten. Is this what civilisation falls prey to?

Yet, as in all things, you are right: your judgment so refined that it is as if you possess a sixth, a seventh sense! Yes, rather than grasping the nearest weapon, he must be brought to justice. Your wisdom has saved me from regrettable actions. His sins are so deep that they will neither dissipate nor leave him. His punishment can wait a little longer.

More urgent is whether my half-sister can be restored to me and acquainted with her fortune. Though trembling at what her circumstances may prove, the happiness that must soon be hers outruns those fears.

What is she like, where living? Does she resemble me? Is her voice sweet, her appearance modest?

Last night, after unwillingly quitting you, sleep an impossibility, I walked the streets, searching for her in my mind. From a shadowy figure (to which I gave something of your slender stature), little by little she stepped forwards. You advised caution in any estimation of her, since she may have suffered hardship, even penury. Who knows what station of life holds her?

As the hours chimed towards dawn and the deserted streets unrolled and passed, first black then grey, rain wetting my clothes, I persisted. By sunrise, when I was exhausted, she had become real. A governess, or a companion in a family of middling means. Neat, gently spoken, brown-haired and brown-eyed, beloved of children, retiring in thought, of lucid outlook. Not married, having an unworldly disposition—long-lost, saintly sister! What impatience in embracing her who has been too long outcast by the accident of her birth.

Ah, Mrs Fox . . . your generosity, your giving nature, have made me think only of myself and stray from the most urgent question. How hard it is, not to put one's own concerns before those of others. How selfish you must think me—you, the embodiment of selflessness, motivated only by the happiness of others.

Joshua Coats called at Bond Street this morning while Darley and I were at breakfast. Violet Denyss is being cared for in his house, hidden away from the gossips and journalists, who, familiar with the goings on at Hipp Street, had somehow got a whiff of her flight—most likely from a servant. Several of those jackals, scenting a shocking scandal, had camped in the street outside Coats's house and mobbed him as he ventured forth this morning, demanding to know if Violet was within. He fobbed them off, since Violet's future depends on the matter being forgotten as quickly as possible. In fact, Coats's housekeeper, his old nurse Mrs Coke, tends the girl and believes she will soon be fit to be questioned, although at present she has a fever and her mind wanders.

We made Coats sit and drink some coffee with us, persuading him to reveal all he knew of the scandalous affair.

When Justice Denyss found Violet, it seems that she was locked in a room, drugged. By all accounts, he broke down the door, using superhuman strength and at great risk to himself. He is her saviour—although his account is modest, as befits a preacher. Coats had to drag even these heroic details from him.

Once, by what miracle, he had found her, Denyss had to leave her again to go in search of help, which God provided coming down the street at that very moment, in the shape of Darley and Coats himself, who were both on their way to Hipp Street after Violet's sister Clio had sounded the alarm.

Joshua says that Denyss looked as crazed and wild-eyed as if the flames of hell were racing after him, and that if they had not catched hold of him, they really believe he would have bolted straight past! But then the parson is short-sighted. As soon as he came to his senses he enlisted my friends' help.

Inside Hipp Street, they restrained Mrs Beddoes, while Denyss went upstairs once more, apparently getting so badly bruised fighting those barring his way, that he refuses to see anyone until his appearance is *less appalling to the ill-prepared.* A further mark of a saintly disposition.

The horror of finding one's daughter in such a place! What can have passed through his mind when he entered the room in which she lay, insensible, in debauched undress? So different from the sweet young girl he remembers that he swears he hardly recognised her! She will rush to thank him when next they meet.

What might have become of her otherwise is too dreadful to contemplate. Abused, disgraced, family ruined and sisters' prospects destroyed—for so it would be, and still will, if this scandal becomes public.

At present, Violet remains hidden from vulgar attention, otherwise her reputation would soon be as tarnished as if she had committed the sin from which she was saved.

After a few days, a warrant will be issued against Salmon and Beddoes. Their crime is unthinkable: Violet's innocence had been sold to the highest bidder (whose identity still remains unknown). It is such an irrefutable example of procuring and prostitution that that Bitch Salmon and her accomplices will be hanged with all speed. There can be no mercy for such perverted creatures, or for those who abetted them. Alas, though Violet's father is a Justice of the Peace, he points out that London is not his jurisdiction, so his hands are tied.

Nor, he says, would he be able to set eyes on Mrs Salmon without destroying her, before (as he does not doubt would be the case) she could utter a single lying word.

Violet herself is dashed low, still not out of danger. She has a high fever, moaning and ranting, and is given salts and laudanum by turns. Coats has not dared enter her chamber since bringing her there, lest, in her confused state, the mere sight of a man throws her down further. It is the housekeeper's opinion that isolating Violet does little good and that she should be properly examined. But Justice Denyss insisted that no doctor be summoned—which, I admit, took me aback. He declares there to be nothing wrong with *his daughter* that rest will not cure. A father may not be gainsaid in a matter of such delicacy.

Dearest madam, if only you would go and cast your eyes over her to see how she does, Coats would be grateful of feminine intuition. Clio cannot make the journey to town unescorted and besides, her mother, terrified of losing another daughter, refuses to let her out of her sight. (Although since Coats and the younger Miss Denyss have been writing to each other thrice daily, by the time they marry there will be nothing left to say.)

But there is a great deal that I would say to *you* madam, in a privy conversation. I will call this evening, to convince you of the estimation in which I hold you, by whatever means you allow, until you beg me stop.

In anticipation—

August 17, 1784
Violet Denyss, c/o Joshua Coats,
Conduit Street,
To Mrs Fox,
Salamander Row

Dearest Mrs Fox,

Thank you for coming to see me this morning! What a lovely unlooked-for surprise!

When I awoke to the sound of footsteps in the courtyard outside my chamber, I freely admit to being more than a trifle alarmed.

It is easy to sleep a great deal here and I must have been dozing before you knocked on the shutters, having the strangest dream about my father; which dream made me uneasy and glad of your intervention.

Yesterday, when you sent Victoire with sweet-meats and the basket of novel pink and red flowers—*Fewshers?*— it was most kind. Victoire and Mrs Coke spent a great deal of time gossiping in the housekeeper's room, so much so that Mrs Coke nearly forgot to bring my chocolate, until Victoire sent her up while she waited below, saying it would be wrong of her to parade through Mr Coats's house when he was not in it. After those kindnesses, there was no reason to expect anything further, but when Victoire had gone, how my heart sank at the prospect of another day of solitude!

It was such a clever idea of yours to come in through the courtyard at the back! And I agree with you, how surprising that the gate was open, when one really would have expected it to be locked. Only someone as kind as you would come all that way across town just to try it, for my sake.

Since being brought here, no one else has visited. I have been shut up as if I was ill, or in disgrace. It seems that I *must* have done something wrong, although I cannot begin to understand what, and keep bursting into tears. The feeling of being in trouble lies so heavy when one doesn't know why. The housekeeper brings me soup and delicious little jellies, calling me *poor lamb* and crying herself, so that we both eat something for consolation.

You say that it is best to keep your visit secret until the fuss has died down. Why has there been such a fuss? Can it really be true that I have been delirious for days? Mrs Coke says she tied me to the bed in case of harm, and that I shouted things *scandalous to her ears.* She will not repeat them, just muttering *best forgotten* and *no wonder,* and making me eat. I cannot remember any of that.

Something happened . . . but what? Trying to remember makes me get a headache, so I give up. Nor can I recall my father rescuing me—which did happen, did it not?

I remember that Mr Black was going to call at Hipp Street. That part is clear. It was all arranged between us. He is so handsome, I was longing to see him. Then shortly before he was due, Mrs Beddoes came in with wine, which I drank, as the expectation of seeing Mr Black made me nervous. I was debating how to get rid of her, because she had made her contempt for him very plain; but she made herself comfortable on a divan and offered me another glass, winking repulsively, so I drank it to speed her leaving. That is the last thing I remember.

It mystifies me how it came to be my father who found me, rather than Mr Black, who would in honesty be a great deal nicer to be carried out of danger by. An entire piece of my memory has vanished. The next thing I recall is Mr Coats, patting my hand, looking as if he was searching for something in my face that would not be found. We were in this room. He became uneasy, then left and has not come back since. He is nicer than when he was at Lord Danceacre's, especially as he said that he no longer believes I put letters in his pocket, and *whoever did created a great deal of mischief and has much to answer for.* Do you think it might have been one of the servants? Or Mr Tutton, whom I rather think saw Mr Coats as his rival?

Staying in bed has gone on forever and is too annoying! I shall die! No one has explained why I am kept prisoner, so it was kind of you to try. I have thought over every word you said. There were one or two things that confuse me, even though they made sense at the time.

I was puzzled by your opinion that I had expressed a falsehood about Victoire's having given me a guinea to come to London. Of course I may not dispute with you over your maid, you know best what money is at her disposal, and you declared it quite impossible for her to have possessed such a large amount. You seemed angry—but I swear, Mrs Fox, it was never my intention to suggest that Victoire had *stolen* the guinea! When you said she would be tried and hanged if the accusation was ever repeated, and only me to blame for her death . . . I have hardly slept. How could I have made such a mistake? But I could not live if I killed Victoire, so I promise not to say anything, except that I found the money in the lane when I was out walking.

Next, you made me wonder if it might have been my acting, at Hipp Street, that caused such a commotion—because actresses are not received? That is certainly the view of Papa, who says actresses are vermin, no better than Wh—, at which mama looks up, and he does not finish. But you say that our future King lives with an actress *as he would his wife*—so a Wh— may one day become Queen? And playwrights like Mr Sheridan move in the highest circles. So how can it have been wrong to act for a few minutes? Moreover, *what I was doing could not even be called acting*—was that not your stated opinion?

You were very kind to declare that there appears to have been an honest muddle, that I fell in with a bad lot after reading the newspaper cutting someone sent me. If, as you say, Victoire really might be blamed for that too, then no, of course it would not hurt me to pretend that I learned about Hipp Street from one of Papa's papers at the rectory.

If only, when all the fuss *has* died down, might I be allowed to stay in London? Until I was brought to kind Mr Coats's house, I was having such fun. The country is so dull! Why must my father take me back? Though it sounds disloyal to speak so, it cannot be helped.

If I do all you suggest, will you really get a note to Mr Black? What joy! If being grown-up means having true, kind friends like you, then I am the most fortunate girl in the world. All this will have been worth it, just to see him; for I verily believe ma'am, even though everyone thinks me foolish and childish, that there is no person on earth dearer than he. Even if I am most severely punished for running away, not even death can change my love for him.

Your adoring friend,
Violet Denyss

August 17, 1784
Violet Denyss,
Conduit Street
To Nathan Black,
The Strand

Sir,

A very dear friend—the only one who remains steadfast in my Hour of Need, but who has sworn me not to reveal her identity—but a more elegant or compassionate soul never existed—will see that you get this, out of pure friendship for me.

I am suffering anguish: is it possible that you can have forgotten me so soon? Ah, do not punish me more than others already have! Am I deserted? I begin to believe you must have forsaken me.

My kindly friend declares that you must have heard of my arrival here, so I should not bother you with it again. I only mention it, because it was while waiting for you that everything went from my mind. The next thing was waking up in bed, without my clothes or shoes! The housemaids whisper when they think I sleep, which is more than intolerable.

I cannot be certain whether you came to see me at Hipp Street or not, since part of my memory has gone, as I just said—or perhaps I am forgetting again. Mrs —x says not to try to force my brain, as it is rather weak. Did you? Will you come and see me now? It is lonely without a friendly face, especially yours.

My father, Reverend Robert Denyss, will take me home soon, to stop my running away again. Oh, how will you be able to paint me once they put me under lock and key? One should not despair . . . but, in truth, how can it be done? At last there is something for me to do in life that is worth doing, but it is going to be taken from me.

Please find a way to send word before then? Mr Coats goes out in the morning between eight and ten of the clock, should that be of any help, and I have asked for my chocolate not to be brought before ten thirty, in order to rest . . .

If you care even a particle of what you once swore you did, find a way to send a message. I am nothing without you.

Your loving and unhappy friend—

August 20, 1784
Joshua Coats,
Conduit Street
To Dadson Darley,
Bond Street

Never in a thousand years, Dads, did I expect to witness what met me this morning, on my way to bespeak a dozen white waistcoats in Jermyn Street.

Pursuing that business, I had the unlooked-for pleasure of running into Parson Denyss, who seemed greatly recovered, and explained that he was taking hesitant steps outdoors, finally feeling well enough to sample the air for the very first time since his heroics at Hipp Street. His health was evidently not yet *entirely* restored, as he was leaning closely on a woman of festive appearance, whom he introduced as his nurse and who interjected, in an accent I could not recognise, *human crutch, more like.* At which the parson reminded her of some urgent commissions, and she took her leave.

Mightily worried that Denyss, who had turned pale, resting a hand against the window of a shop to steady himself, would have difficulty walking without her—and realising that two events could happily be combined—I cut short my own affairs and invited him to stroll back to Conduit Street, letting me take the place of the professional young woman as best I could.

What profound contemplation shone from that good man's countenance in anticipation of visiting his daughter, whose recovery has been so remarkable these past couple of days that the restorative power of jellies had impressed even Mrs Coke.

"Come sir," quoth I, my breast surging with pleasure at the imminent reunion of the lucky pair. "Let us surprise Violet and tell her that she may begin planning a triumphant return to her family, accompanied by him whom she must long to see above all others!" At which I glanced sideways, certain of catching a smile of pleasure breaking involuntarily from that goodly frame.

Yet Denyss, doubtless remembering his *gravitas,* not only as *parson* but as *Justice of the Peace,* curbed his enthusiasm even more than one would expect and attempted to dissuade me, arguing that the shock to Violet of seeing him, unannounced, could plunge her into an irreversible decline.

"Nonsense," I declared robustly, recognising the delicacy of his concern but refusing to fall in with it. "Although your reticence is noble, would you deprive her of the opportunity to prostrate herself in joyous gratitude before you?"

My argument had an effect, for Denyss made no subsequent attempt at conversation.

We went the short distance slowly and in silence; he surely composing his opening remark—perhaps a blessing of some sort—as she cried out for joy at seeing him. My own thoughts tended to how gravely I had misjudged poor Violet, led to the brink of Harlotry by those for whom a warrant is now out.

Hipp Street has been shut up by the Westminster beadles, an armed watch set on the door, and the few occupants who had not already run away (those with nowhere else to go) carted off for questioning. Salmon and Beddoes have fled with a fortune, after emptying the strong box and leaving a gaping hole in the wall. Their crime is so serious that there are printed bills at street corners and every public place announcing a vast sum in gold (bonded by Danceacre) for information leading to their arrest. In these circumstances, their capture must be swift.

Thank heavens for Violet's sister Clio, who challenged my belief that any acquaintance of Black's formed in a stew could only be a worthless trollope! Had that dear girl not mounted an indignant defence of her sister's virtue, you and I would not have been on our way there at the very moment that Parson Denyss came flying out of that despicable warren! D'you recall the awful look on his face? Timing, Darley, is all. As a gambling man you know it. Moments later and we should have missed him, without whom we might not have found Violet in time.

I considered, too, how, just as I had cast slurs on Violet before meeting her (on the plain grounds of her being inside that foul place), I had also maligned Black on a similar principle, when in fact he had had the discernment to choose the sister of my beloved Clio as his Love! Artists are easily accused of depravity and unnatural vices, yet Black would no more lay an intemperate finger on Violet than would her own father.

At that moment, each brimming with his thoughts, Denyss and I arrived at Conduit Street. We went directly to Violet's chamber. Her room is in the quiet part at the back, looking onto a small courtyard. Making sign to the parson to hush, I turned the key softly and threw open the door, stepping back so that Violet's father might surprise her without ado.

An awful cry came from inside! At which Denyss, staggering forwards and blocking the way, making it impossible to see past him, howled in rage.

Still held back, I cursed myself bitterly that he had been right: the sudden shock of seeing her saviour was too much for his daughter to bear. Violet's horrid yelping was that of a tortured animal. As Denyss's cloth shoulders shoved ahead into the room, it took a moment before there was a chance to glance round him.

The sight that met my gaze was not, I admit, the one anticipated. The young woman was engaged in the act of entertaining Nathan Black. Who, risen up in a condition to which words cannot begin to do justice, stared wide-eyed at Parson Denyss.

"Before God, I will kill you, you blaggard, sir!" Violet's father screeched, discovering a mobility he had not formerly possessed and rushing towards the young man like a bullock in its final charge. "What manner of monster—"

Nathan Black had meanwhile had the grace to spring away from Miss Denyss, who was busily burrowing under the bed covers (whilst still peeping out just enough to witness her Adonis torn limb from limb).

Yet Black, instead of squaring up manfully for a thrashing (or, more sensibly, putting the bed between the pair of them—a manoevre I admit to favouring, in the circumstances)—having taken very careful stock through narrowing eyes of Denyss's enraged, squat figure hurtling in his direction, slowly straightened up to his full height.

"You dare speak of assault *to me? You* accuse *me*?"

While Black's eyes glittered in an increasingly dangerous way, an expression of contempt came into his face that turned it first red, then pure white with anger. "Not a pace further, you unspeakable old goat," he went on, "unless you would have me explain myself to your daughter?"

Eyes aflame, undressed hair tumbling round his head, indifferent to the astonishing picture he presented, Black towered over his would-be assailant—an impression of hawk confronting toad to which Violet, gazing rapt from the tousled bed, was by no means insensible.

After a pause to make an agreeable bow in my direction, Black fixed his scornful eyes once more on the parson, who stood rooted to the spot.

"Yes," the young man continued, "yes, indeed, I know your face well, sir, as does most of *Drury Lane* and the darker purlieus of *Mayfair.*

"If you are the father of this young woman, he who calls himself *her saviour*"—at which Black took a bare-footed pace towards Denyss in such a muscular way that he might have been Ajax, armed to the hilt—"then you will do me the honour to step outside." Catching up his shirt, Black motioned the older man ahead.

Unable to grasp what was going on in my own house, and certain that in the astounding circumstances a small further breach of propriety would be overlooked (in truth, feeling somewhat confused), I sat down on the bed. Quite unabashed, locks tumbling on her shoulders, Violet handed me a letter just come from Clio, which Black had already seen. In which, my satirical beloved had copied parts of a letter from the girls' father to their mother, given to Clio *for moral guidance,* that was full of impious and arrogant claims made by the Reverend, including the absurd one of being Abraham. With Violet casting mischievous glances at me while I read it, we awaited the warriors' return.

At last the door opened. Parson Denyss, who had aged ten years in as many minutes, came in first. Clearing his throat and wearing the dam'dest expression he addressed Violet.

"This—*young man*"—Denyss paused and swallowed, darting a hopeful glance first at me and then at the French door, before scowling unwillingly at Nathan Black—"has just asked my permission for your hand.

"Which—I—have—granted." He wiped his mouth.

Violet stared, from her father to me and then at Black, a vision of lovely incomprehension, as the parson began again.

"If—you—wish it?" he shook out at last, with difficulty.

His daughter's eyes, gleaming from the lace of the bedlinens, continued gawping in astonishment. But Black appeared unmoved, and coughed.

"With your unreserved blessing?" He demanded sullenly.

"Yes, yes, *with my blessing,*" ground out the other even more sullenly.

"And," Black pursued, mercilessly, "with immediate effect, to which Coats is witness?"

This last edict was too much for the parson. Muttering *yes* in a voice stilted by fury, Denyss pushed past me and left the room.

Suddenly noticing the blissful expressions of the lovers, I made some excuse and proposed to return in half an hour, so that we might all breakfast together in more predictable surroundings.

Outside Violet's room I leaned against the door. It was hard to tell if those events had taken place, or were part of a dream; a decision not aided by Mrs Coke's appearing from the far end of the hall, wearing a fashionable sprigged dress that revealed her bosom and balancing a tray with a fat silver jug steaming out the agreeable smell of chocolate, *and two bowls.* Damned if I understand head or tail of what goes on under my own roof.

One likes to think, Darley, that one is able, in these modern times, to overlook certain irregularities. The way in which Black came to be in Violet's room *at all* springs to mind, since Mrs Coke says that none of the staff had let him in and that the gate to the courtyard is always locked, swearing most energetically that the key has not moved from its usual place in her office these past months, and that *no one could no more get past her for it than Cerberus would eat his puppies.*

A more honest woman never lived.

However, as my future happiness involves Violet's sister, it is my duty to ensure that further scandal does not touch her or any member of her family. To this end I attempted to question Black, who furiously challenged me to dispute him, threatening to call me out if I wanted to know what he had said *in private* to Parson Denyss, and that if I compelled him to tell me, he would be obliged to kill me.

Utterly harmless fellow, of course, has no idea of either sword or pistol. He would have to paint me to death. But his repeated swearing that Denyss is the worst type of Lothario, whom, had he not worn the cloth, Black would strangle or stamp underfoot, did not fill one with confidence. Indeed, growing concern about that and certain other accusations, monstrous between a father and daughter (if I understood Black's inferences), prompted me to go at once to Denyss's lodgings, to demand an explanation for the noxious charges.

My nervousness increased the nearer I got to Mount Street, where the parson had rooms. I hoped that, after swiftly clearing things up and proving Black wrong, we might discuss the best way of broaching the forthcoming marriage to Violet's mother.

But Denyss was not there. *Upped and Gawn,* according to the landlady; cleared out in a hired carriage in the company of a red-cheeked woman he claimed was his daughter but whom, the landlady hinted, *was one of them as is everyone's daughter, as care to pay for it.*

Queerest behaviour, Dads! Damned if I know how to square *that* with the Reverend's wife. Begin to wish I had never got involved with the whole crew—except Clio, of course.

Your friend,
Joshua Coats

August 21, 1784
Mrs Fox,
Salamander Row
To Joshua Coats
Conduit Street

My dear Mr Coats,

I have been amazed to learn, in a poorly penned note from Violet Denyss, of her intended marriage to Mr Black! What an unlooked-for outcome to a desperate situation! One where, only recently, there appeared no avenue that did not lead to blight and desert. Happy nuptials, decided at your house, I understand, with the blessing of her father. How swiftly the most hopeless matters improve from one day to the next!

When I last saw that dear young *woman*—for it is as a woman that we must now refer to her—none of this had taken place. It was early summer, she was chasing her sisters round a fountain at Mashing. I recall thinking what a fine bride she might make for Lord Danceacre, with a little finishing—for one must always put the happiness of others before one's own—particularly that of innocent young girls.

The notion of marriage was further then from Violet's still child-like mind than what ribbon to wear.

In the current circumstances, Mr Black is certainly a reasonable connection—for who knows, one day he may even climb out of ignominy to make something of his painting; and artists are no longer entirely despised. Nevertheless, it must be a bitter disappointment to her mother, to see the prospect of land and a title only two miles beyond her windows, that had seemed in her grasp, crushed. One hopes that the *speed* of the engagement does not throw that worthy woman back on to her sick bed, never to rise again.

Dear Mr Coats, congratulations on your discovery and rescue of Violet, in which you played the largest part; and in offering her protection without hesitation. Think of how her reputation might have suffered had you not taken her in! Yet too, how easily her presence in your house could have led to nasty slanders too damaging ever to shake off!

From the beginning of this scandal, Lord Danceacre sought my help: yes, from the second he heard of Violet's turning runaway. He had grown so fond of that quaint family that he considered the Denyss girls as his sisters—until now, naturally, when such a notion is forever dashed.

Before the news of Violet's adventure, one had no inkling that her sweet demeanour covered such a rebellious spirit, so versed in subterfuge that she could find a way to London without her parents' knowledge or consent. Scarcely the act of a guileless child!

Now that she is found, one may ask who put the idea of such a dangerous escapade into her head? It is imperative that the person who led her into such folly is prevented from doing such a thing again!

I hesitate to mention the amount of time she spent in the creamery at Mashing with Lord Danceacre's agent, Tutton, while you were busy with his Lordship designing the new wing and chapel. Mr Tutton *seemed* hardworking, building himself a house on Lord Danceacre's land, when not occupied with the comfort of the dairy maids. The trust that Tutton enjoyed, first from Lady Danceacre and then his Lordship, gave him great freedom on the estate—and elsewhere. He was *cosmopolitan* beyond what one expects on a farm, and did frequently come up to town . . . But it is not for me to pursue this line of thought. Nor, as a stranger to country ways, would I know where to begin.

For my own part, once Lord Danceacre had enlisted me to help finding Violet, I put my personal concerns aside to make enquiries: always speaking low, since the loss of honour in a daughter of good family—especially the eldest—casts a pall over the chances of the others. A slip by the eldest leaves a taint, and no gentleman will touch the rest for fear of being sullied. In a family such as Justice Denyss's, where learning and honour took the place of financial security, this whole affair had to be, and still must be, kept quiet—in particular, the haste of Violet's approaching marriage, which so often points to reasons other than pangs of immortal love.

That the next girl, Clio—who is dreadfully plain—will be fatally disadvantaged by her sister's behaviour, there is no doubt. The world will see to it. Her future is dashed, she will never find a husband. However we scorn these outdated rituals, there is no denying their effect.

In light of the above, you will agree that my enquiries on Lord Danceacre's behalf were done with such careful circumspection that, to the general view, it must seem as if none was made at all.

What is divulged here regarding Tutton is for your eyes only, for Lord Danceacre, the most generous and forgiving man alive, without an atom of revengefulness in his nature, might look askance should such an idea be proposed *by a mere woman*—particularly one as unworldly as I. If you agree with me, I beg you to put the idea forward as your own.

Only after much agonising have I overcome my shrinking feminine cowardice, forcing myself forward in the world of men. Should these feeble thoughts be of any use, sir, then,

I remain,
Yours—

September 6, 1784
Frederick Danceacre
London Inn, Kingston,
To Hubert van Essel,
Amsterdam

Dearest Doctor van Essel,

Since first reading my uncle John Verney's letter (a relative of whom I had no previous awareness, and now can never know), I have had only momentary peace.

Your own letter,[I] declaring your benevolent interest in my family, has been balm to my soul. That a man of your wisdom (though as yet unmet) cherished my mother, confirms noble inclinations in her that the cruel world ignored. Before, it was impossible to judge whether the suffering she endured at the hand of that monster Earl Much was no less than her due for a life of degeneracy. Now it is clear that she must be avenged, mercilessly, without recourse to law. As soon as my sister, whose estate you have spoken for, is safe, Earl Much will meet his maker: no sooner is she found, than my sword shall find his heart. It cannot be helped that my sister will lose her father: he has been lost to her since birth.

Before his death, my uncle Verney sent me as full account as he was able of Persephone's birth, which is all there is to help find her. His letter to you, a copy of which you were generous enough to send, tallies with mine, eradicating doubts that his words might have been fabricated, through jealousy or rivalry . . . who knows what. It does me no credit to have had these doubts: but who, reeling from similar shocking revelations, would not question the motive of whoever made them?

Sir, I have been fortunate in life, having youth, money and possessions, but am neither rational nor well-schooled. My father was by all accounts a spineless, unsuccessful gambler, whom none but creditors and card-sharps missed when he was cut down in France. My mother—albeit counter to her nature—was a frank Whore.

With such parents, what surprise that my youth was given over to dissipation? My chief lesson was that a handful of words in any language, if backed by a fortune, offer a univeral route to gratification. With such a bastard upbringing, I have always trusted in the hand dealt by Fortune, rather than selecting a better one.

This unexpected business is not one I should have picked. Nevertheless, following the principle that has guided my life, the game is

[I] Not included: written by van Essel to Frederick, after van Essel received John Verney's letter.

dealt and will be played to the end—until my sister is found and Earl Much lies dying or dead.

You expressed the opinion that if only I would stay my hand a while, you would *undoubtedly kill him.* With respect, Doctor van Essel, do not delude yourself. You cannot harm him, you are too old for fighting. But I am not. Pardon the truth. Nothing will dissuade me from prodding him sharply into the grave once I get back to town, which prospect has urged me to make every effort to discover Persephone as quickly as possible.

Two weeks ago, on a hired gas-bag masquerading as a horse, I came here, to Kingston, a market town on the river, with nothing besides a square, some old buildings, and an ill-appointed, dirty inn. It was your good suggestion to represent myself as Tutton my estate manager's invented *assistant.* Dressed the part, I named myself Vernish (under which you may find me). This wisdom has already served. No sooner had I arrived than a farm-hand from the West Country fell in with me, who, but for your advice, could have jeopardised my quest. He offered himself for hire, demanding so many particulars of the running of the estate that it was tempting to declare my true identity just to be rid of him. He has now left, disgusted by Mashing's poor wages.

I began my enquiries. Since the commonality rarely travel beyond their birth-place, I asked after wet-nurses, surgeons, tooth-pullers and quacks; for details of every midwife, innkeeper, brothel-keeper and school-teacher . . . all to no avail. Announcing that I was searching for my sister, I gave her name and small coin, so as not to attract fortune hunters—for which once more thanks, since it has always been my inclination to throw money into the air and wait to see who catches it.

The local magistrate, church, coroner, paupers' yard . . . nothing has escaped my attention. But no one recalls such a child entering the parish. Was she forced to leave, or did she die of a childhood disease? Even her birthmark has not impressed a soul.

Then, yesterday, came news of a woman who took in laundry and sewing, but had once been a wet-nurse. This Mrs Fisher died ten years ago, after which her daughter Sophy left town. The old chandler who recalled them said that Sophy had disappeared *as if from one from one moment to the next.* He gave me the name of their street—but to no avail. All who might have known them have died or gone. Blank faces. How unremarkable they must have been, like all of their kind: the daughter rarely outdoors, the mother uneducated. Unendurable monotony, the lives of the poor! Trudging from one day to the next, without relief or hope . . . why do they not do away with themselves, or drop dead, disgusted by their dreary lot? Surely this peasant is not my sister? Can she even read or write?

I shall persevere a week more before quitting a fruitless search. Then dispatch that tyrannical insult to humanity without further delay. If God will not uncover Persephone, it still signs a death-warrant for Much.

Your servant,
Frederick Danceacre

September 14, 1784
Mrs Fox
To Hubert van Essel
Amsterdam

Dearest Doctor,

What, in the name of Philosophy, are you doing? Why have you not answered my letters? Goodness, smell the air! Open your eyes and put up your books! Does nothing concerning the living move you anymore? Or—which I suspect has long been the case—perhaps you are dead yourself.

Once, you made my heart beat: now, hearing nothing from you drives more than distance between us. Jump out of that paper coffin and feel this jolt, as if the whore herself rode you: the procuress Salmon has exchanged the comfort of Hipp Street for the luxury of Newgate!

Poppy Salmon and Mrs Beddoes, after spending weeks pent up impersonating Sisters of Mercy in Cock Street (a godforsaken part of town near Smithfield, full of reprobates and murderers), made their bid for freedom. As the light began to fade they headed north, with no luggage except a small leathern bag carried by Beddoes, to join a coach party at the Angel.

Ambling along, nodding blasphemous blessings right and left, dodging the hurtle of trade to pick a way through the fatty slime of scrapings and sludge, they had turned into Giltspur Street and were passing through the thickest part of the yards. Suddenly overcome by gore and entrails, Mrs Salmon loosened her wimple to vomit into an overflowing vat of hoofs, at which unusual activity she was observed, wiping her pretty mouth free of spittle—since, too vain to sully her linen, she had pulled the veiling clear. Her face had been fairly drawn on the bills offering Danceacre's reward, one of which was pasted to the other side of the barrel in which she relieved herself.

A cry belted out from a steward: *Stop! There go the trollopes what's worth a Mint!,* at which even the butchers threw down their saws to give chase.

The two women, grasping what danger they were in, hauled up their skirts without regard to modesty (which came naturally) and legged it into St John Street, to meet head-on a herd of amber cattle being whipped towards the slaughter-house. Salmon, the younger and more nimble, at the fear of the place roaring down, of nearby Newgate and Bridewell, of the stink of blood and mounting uproar as dripping hands grabbed from every side, darted through a gap between the flanks of the uneasy rushing beasts and the side of the street. Forging into a sort of alley, lath this way, heaving leather that, she cried out for the other woman to follow.

Which Beddoes, struggling to keep the bag under her arm, did, only to be knocked spinning by one rushing cow and caught up between the haunches of two more. In an eye-blink, her cheating garments twisting on her, she was thrown down, rolled over and broken to a pulp by enraged cattle in full stampede, so that had it been boiled out of her, her skeleton would have been fit for a rattle.

Meanwhile, thoroughly terrified and scarce able to breathe, unaware of the fate of her accomplice and still bawling *come on* over her shoulder, Mrs Salmon staggered into Eagle Lane and fell into the arms of three constables—a needful quantity to restrain one so apt at handling your sex.

Temporarily deprived of its reward, the mob's outcry grew. Before the Whore knew it, and indefensible against the bloodthirsty crowd, she was siezed and stript naked. Her lying habit was smeared with render in front of her trembling body and set ablaze. Derided and spat on, the jeering crowd invited her to step into the flames for one last hot f— . . . saving the city a deal of expense in faggots into the bargain.

Although they had stood back so far, the constables now recognised that their charge was at risk of fatal violence from the inflamed mob and set about all and sundry with their sticks, before bundling Salmon to Newgate in that insulting condition. Where she lies, badly bruised, without hope of clemency, to wait arraignment and trial.

In the meantime—if that is not enough excitement to get you here—try this. While the manner (rather than the fact—as I shall shortly explain) of Poppy Salmon's death remains to be decided, the eldest Denyss girl has trounced the pair of them!

Two days ago, on the morning of her elder sister Violet's wedding to the American Nathan Black, Clytemnestra Denyss (who had come to help) went into Violet's bedroom at their lodgings. The bride, who had been unable to sleep, was already perfectly dressed and coiffed, ready for the church, down to the last bit of Paris ribbon.

Alas, though.

Violet was dangling from a stout joist.

Lit from behind by the strengthening sun, she re-enacted her brief moment of fame at Hipp Street.

News of Miss Denyss's impromptu last act flew across town faster than the Fire, leaping from mouth to mouth as if the vents of hell spat spit and blood. Which casts doubt on the need for newspapers, when information flashes through the ether like a lightning strike.

It must have gone down particularly badly in Newgate, where Poppy Salmon, who will hear of it, will now be charged not only with procuring and pandering, but murder too—for how otherwise should that innocent child have come to be climbing on to a chair on the dawn of her wedding day? Who but Salmon to shoulder the blame?

Poor sweet Violet had been plagued by a recurring dream, whose end eluded her, and which had been provoking great distress. Stirred to mental agility on the morning of her nuptials, she had sat suddenly upright in bed. As the sun sharpened a nearby spire she suffered the return of the lost vision—*of her father entering her room at Hipp Street!* Before launching herself from the beam she left a note, hinting at something so dreadful she could not quite express it.

Such delicacy is not allowed the dead. The awful gaps in Violet's tale have been eagerly supplied by all who hear whisper of it; a story that tumbles like weed through tap-room and club, faster and faster.

An order has gone out for Denyss's arrest. If found, he will be shredded standing, so fierce is the universal disgust at his crime—if indeed he committed one, for Violet's note could certainly be considered ambiguous, should anyone care for the truth, or give a toss for clemency.

Besides, it is likely that this oily despoiler, her father, has cheated capture, being hardened and alert to trouble. He is believed to have boarded a Wherry for the Continent, in the company of the cheap woman that his former landlady called *a rough bitch of a trull, what spoke Foreign.*

Violet also left a note for her intended husband, Nathan Black, which Clio managed to give to a messenger before collapsing under the unscratched soles of her sister's gently hovering bridal slippers.

At present, no one knows the painter's whereabouts.

Continued

Yesterday, by utter chance finding myself in David Street, I called on Mr Coats, who was very overwrought.

Violet's note to Nathan Black had arrived when Coats and Darley were helping him put the final touches to his own wedding clothes. Which is the last time anyone saw him. It is certain he has gone to destroy the parson without regard to process of law, since he holds English justice in voluble contempt.

Coats described how Black's skin, as he read his dead bride's letter, grew so dark with blood that they feared a fit. The unhappy young man tugged his hair until hanks flew right and left, then started tearing at his garments, at last siezing a mallet and hurling it at a canvas of Violet as an angel, that rested against the wall, ready for mounting in the nearby Church. Having knocked it off the support with that one flying blow, Black began trampling it, destroying the only fruit of his brief happiness, before bursting into livid tears.

His friends pulled him away and attempted to calm him. But learned instead, between Black's violent paroxysms of rage, that Parson Denyss was the very same man the painter had once pointed out to me at the theatre sitting with Mrs Salmon, so well-disguised in a fashionable perruke and flashy clothes that no one but his own mother would know him! In another cheating guise he had also been a regular customer at Marylebone Park when Poppy Salmon ran it.

While his wife believed him on God's work with fallen women, chameleon Denyss had been adding to their woes.

Black had also seen him (dressed as a goat) at Hipp Street, the night that Violet made her stage debut and had believed that this shocking fact alone had made Denyss agree to the marriage. Only when he read his almost-wife's note, did Black learn that it was the parson who had made the highest bid and won the ticket to seduce his own daughter.

For his own part, Parson Denyss, with the over-ripe guilt of all cowards, thought Black knew everything—some of which, as Violet's letter now implied, was a grave offence.

Anguish at what Violet had suffered drove Black into a mood so incontrovertible that Coats and Darley released him. Rushing from them he plunged down the stairs, shouting at the top of his lungs that *he would bathe in that devil's blood!*

You can imagine how reduced Mr Coats has been by this affair. Unlike Mr Darley, who still behaves as if the entire thing might yet turn out a jolly jape, Coats has become *very analytical indeed.*

When I was shown into his library he was going to and fro in a figured Banyan, wholly indifferent to his surroundings. Paying lip-service to formality, he rounded on me: "How can such a Godly man have got so deep in this terrible affair? How came his daughter to be in that awful place, to let it happen? Could what you said of Danceacre's agent Tutton be true? In the name of God he will swing for it, if so it proves. I do not understand—"

He broke off and continued savage cursing for some moments, occasionally glancing at me with a peculiar expression. After which he fell to groaning, biting his fingers and staring out of the window.

It strikes me that everyone is beginning to call down the full force of the law with startling frequency and vehemence, and very little regard for who had deserved what. Such a growing witch-hunt runs the risk of all manner of small fry being scooped unfairly into the net.

You will agree that I have had no part in any of these matters, having always been something of an *impartial observer.* Indeed, my support and confidence has been of great help in numerous directions. However, when men are roused to indignation, determined to find a focus for their wrath, accurate judgment flies out of the window. Watching Coats gnaw his slender fingers, I mused whether anything could be wrongfully laid at my door.

Had Violet ever confided to Clio that Victoire gave her money and told her the way to get to London? Would anyone ever wonder at the similarity of stature between *Mr Voster* and *Victoire*? Might Poppy Salmon, foolish though she is, begin to think harder than she ever had in her life, with that sudden intelligence that a sentence of death provokes in even the dullest intellect?

How astonishing that such a parcel of trouble should be set off by Violet Denyss! The girl was merely a cursory amusement, an entrée! I should have drowned her in the pond when I had the opportunity, rather than attempt to help her better herself.

While the untimely death of any young woman is a blow to society, it is unclear why the death of *that* one affects Mr Coats so tragically. After all, she was not promised to him, nor was she notable in looks, wealth or wit. She could not act. The only superb thing about her was her inspired death.

Coats's seemingly *noble misery* is to do with *him* not *her.* In short, he wonders how fresh scandal may affect his marriage to her sister Clio, doubtless recalling my prophetic words on that score—which experience has taught me not to repeat.

Putting pride at my perception aside, I soothed him, debating whether to use the technique that was so effective with Lord Danceacre—always superior to words or gestures in comforting distraught men or distracting other ones. But since Coats has a Puritanical bent, I merely touched his arm, judging (from the way he snatched it out of reach) that any further attempt at intimacy might be misguided. Moreover, his intended bride was in the house.

Clytemnestra Denyss has suffered unlooked-for excitements for one so dreary. Rapidly deprived first of her father and now her sister, while her mother's life shivers in the balance, only her little sister Nettie currently stays blissfully unscathed.

After her faint, Clio was overtaken by delirium. At Mr Coats's instruction she was brought to Conduit Street where, like her tragic sister before her, she was put in the care of Mrs Coke, even in the same room that had been her fated sister's. On the way to Mr Coats's library, I noticed that the housekeeper had resumed her dingy clothes—as if the dead girl could be expected to care one way or the other whether she re-adopted her ancient garments or continued racing around in the height of French fashion! No stretch of the imagination could conceive that the recent display of Mrs Coke's withered charms could have contributed to a general decline in morality, or to Violet's death—even though, like all women, she appeared to think otherwise, fixing me, from the enveloping gloom of her dismal sooty garments, with a very smug nod.

Complimenting that lady on her nice sensibility, I backed it with two guinea *for the shock.*

"Is it wise," I later probed Mr Coats, moved by a genuine interest in human nature (an insidious habit, caught from you!), "to have the girl put in the same room that her dead sister occupied?"

He gave me a strange, questing look, before rebuking, *not dead at the time,* then went on, "There is nothing in this house that can harm her. I am not superstitious, dear lady; nor is Clytemnestra. But you will do me the singular favour of not mentioning that again, while she remains in her vulnerable state."

Such tactlessness at implying the possibility earned him a sharp look.

Might Mr Coats be more intelligent than previously supposed?

Dwelling on that, I took leave, pressing a token into his hand, *to give to Clio when he thought fit.* A mere bauble, a geegaw: a row of fine matched pearls (with the name of a dead sailor on each one, and the only string that had not been stolen from me), to console her for her sister's hasty demise. They had been my wedding gift for Violet Denyss, but, since I had been put under orders not to distress Clio, that small fact did not now seem worth remarking.

Lord Danceacre has spent a great deal of time away from town, first at Kingston, thence to long-neglected Mashing, and the Rectory. Mrs Salmon's capture has brought him flying back to town at once. He intends going to Newgate this afternoon to question the procuress, and requests an interview with me this evening—which I will not grant until he has seen her and has something interesting to say. All this, in a hasty note,[I] has been my first news since he began his foolish mission to track down his sister.

Victoire and I are moving back to Warp Lane, since Danceacre refuses to set foot on Much's property again except to kill him, and is highly agitated by my perceived connection with that gentleman—whatever protestations of indifference I make. I have agreed to his demand, only because it would look particular if I did not, and one becomes innocent—or guilty—by acting as much.

When Danceacre visits tonight, excited by the *gaol bird*—there being nothing more invigorating to a normal man than the sight of a Whore sentenced to death—and further inspired by our separation, he is bound to wish to repeat the liberties that Salamander Row began, reminding himself, in the act of doing so, how my presence is balm to him, how indispensible I have become.

I will write again only if you give the smallest sign that my words do not vanish like chaff in the cold air . . .

Your erstwhile friend—

[I] Not included.

September 18, 1784
Hubert van Essel
To Mrs Fox,
Salamander Row

Exasperating woman, what sort of sign do you require?

Shall I come and write your name in blood, or wait until someone else does? For madam, believe me, that moment is fast approaching.

You taunt me with my silence. I castigate you for your noisesome evidence! Can you not see the shadows gathering? How can a woman so clever be so purblind? The noose dangles inches from your lovely head while you blithely boast your conquests—as if I could have the slightest appetite anymore in either them or you. But you are so caught up in self-congratulation that you do not understand how a diet of wickedness has shrunk my stomach. Yet . . . yet, I will save you from yourself if it can be done, for it is my belief that you have only lived according to your nature, as others do; in which warped existence I have been complicit, by attending to your nonsense, tacitly spurring you on.

There is more trouble close at hand than even you can manage.

I had my own investigations made at Kingston while Danceacre fumbled his. How easy it is to see that he is the son of his wastrel father! He could not find his own hands if his sleeves did not point the way.

My own paid man was that very same *labourer* who asked Danceacre for employment, and whose report now lies before me. While Frederick flailed from pillar to post, in one case given information so laughably false that it was a miracle he did not understand it, my agent took only a week to discover Persephone's whereabouts. A child could have done so—you, certainly, would have (habit makes me strive to compliment you even now).

Though I kept Danceacre occupied in Kingston longer than he intended, giving me time to pursue my own investigations without him stumbling across them, all has proved futile, as you will shortly discover.

So let us return to you, madam, and the grave danger you have put yourself in.

Do not look for the first blow from any expected quarter; certainly not from Urban Fine—even though you appear to have committed the unforgivably dangerous error of neglecting both him and the brazen tart you foisted on his attention. It may be possible to shut our eyes in one direction and survive, but to give up every sense and still expect to stay alive, betokens rashness bordering on suicidal.

Fortunately for you, my mole has not been idle. Since his outing in Kingston scarcely stretched his legs, I turned him elsewhere—to be exact, following *your* business, with the view of snatching you from the hangman's foul breath by the scruff, if there was the slightest chance of it. It is proving an increasingly difficult task!

Yes, Much has discovered your attempt to fob him off with a trumpery heiress: which in ordinary circumstances would be reason enough to have you killed. However, since she sprang into his lap long before he was tempted to marry her, he never made himself ridiculous. You did him a service—as an unpaid pimp. The provenance of his Harpy matters not one whit to Earl Much, so long as she performs to his perverse taste. If she ceases pleasing him, it is her he will get rid of, not you.

Through no talent of yours, the tricks the seamstress Martha already knew outweighed those with which you imbued her, handsome addition though yours were. Therefore, far from damaging him (as you promised me), you have added to him! Were he really looking for a wife, he would find it hard to do better than promote this creature to the title, whose dexterity with her fingers is reputed to be pleasing in every sense. Who knows, he might reward you for the introduction yet.

My spy has gleaned other news regarding the Earl. He is suffering from a mysterious, sapping malaise, that increasingly lays him low and dulls his instinct for violence. He staggers, becoming green and breathless, for no reason. You would do well to pray that this sickness lasts, for he could still decide to snuff you on a whim: it would be so easily done, he owns the magistrates in several wards. Or he might exact *other payments* from you, in reprisal, or merely sadistic pleasure. If he knew even half your enterprises, he would find you diverting. You are more alike than you realise, as unprincipled and careless as each other. Upon reflection, it seems to me that you could not have destroyed him if you tried—unless you enjoy raising your fist to the mirror?

Ah, but madam. The blood of the Denyss girl has penetrated your skin, marking it. Beware of those able to look past that pure white carapace, who see death in your red lips. Have you no remorse for the waste of her, or the misery of her lover? Are you so entirely careless of the consequences? Are you unmoved as stone if Poppy Salmon hangs because of you, for your amusement?

Watching this approaching storm from such a distance, with your unforgettable figure at its centre, makes me increasing anxious.

Just one word from you now will bring me to London—if it is not already too late.

Yours—

6 PM
September 21, 1784
Mrs Fox,
Warp Lane
To Hubert van Essel
Amsterdam

Who knows when—or if—your answer will arrive, or if you will even write again. These intolerable delays strangle us.

Were you here we could have a conversation. As it is, everything is cold meat before we taste it. However, since you are not and I must make the best of what there is, stay in my company until Danceacre comes; for this place makes me uneasy in a way it never did before. I had forgotten how cold Warp Lane is!

I sent Victoire ahead two days ago with my trunks, to open and air our apartment, while I followed later. Despite freezing rain, the streets were thronging with filthy men and women jostling at my chair, however hard the link beat them back with his stave.

Agreeing to Danceacre's insistence on leaving Salamander Row for this foul place, simply to assuage his fury at Much, is a hellish bargain; but I will find a way to torment him in return. Besides, it is worth humouring him if it means being the first to hear a description of Mrs Salmon's *new establishment,* surrounded by far more women than she ever was at Marylebone Park or Hipp Street! All the comforts of rotten straw and a flea-bitten dress. Her puffed-up muslins and airs and paste avail her nothing now!

She has been arraigned on a charge of aggravated procuring and prostitution, and tomorrow goes before a Grand Jury. If the outcome is not death there will have been a miscarriage. Since I came to this mildewed country, whose cold slips between one's garments like the hand of a fishmonger, nothing has endeared it so much to me. Once Salmon has been hanged, Violet's brief excursion into adulthood will be forgotten. So much noise over so little, hushed at last.

Warp Lane has not improved since we were last here, nor have our rooms been aired. Damp comes through cracks in the windows and the walls feel as if they have the plague, or creatures slithered up and down inside. I had forgotten the rustles and creaks! How like an invalid this house is, skin mouldy, innards rotten! There is a nauseating smell, as if the building is dying, brick by brick, watching the living with evil eyes. The fire Victoire laid this morning scarce flickers . . .

. . . . I will write more tomorrow, when Danceacre has been and gone, for you must be as keen as I to know how that Trollopy looks among her natural Sisters, or how brave she can be, walking towards inevitable death.

Continued 11 PM

An insulting note arrived from Lord Danceacre an hour ago, excusing himself from our appointment, saying that he had been *unexpectedly detained on urgent business, but that if I would honour him by waiting, he should call on me at the first opportunity; until which happy time, regretfully, etc and etc*—

Urgent business! *Regretfully!* What could be more urgent that an appointment with me? What need or use do I have for his deceitful blandishments?

He cannot fool me, nor persuade me to rest content at being levered out of a very comfortable house to sit in a wet shed with Victoire for nothing! What happened at Newgate? There the answer lies.

Yet, even in my blackest humour, I am certain that that Whore could say nothing to implicate me in Violet's downfall, not one word. Her wit is sharp, but aimless, as far as I am concerned . . . No . . . it is some misguided whim! Heavens, how Danceacre is drawing up an account to be settled!

Victoire and I have spent the evening waiting for him in this creaking claphouse, huddled together on the bed for warmth, with the Scribbler shuffling and scraping over our heads, and all to humour Danceacre's indulgence! His behaviour is in very poor taste.

I have ordered a chair to go back to Salamander Row, where he may visit—or not. A matter of utter indifference. However Victoire, having unpacked, refuses to move again. She may stay and die in this infested hovel for all I care.

What interest is Danceacre's conversation to me? I can make my own enquiries regarding the comforts of Newgate—indeed, now heartily wish I had bethought it earlier.

How wrong it proves to have indulged him in a momentary weakness. He has taken that single kind act of feminine generosity as an admittal of eternal fealty! He supposes me at his beck and call.

My *Lord and Master* must learn otherwise.

Yours—

September 19, 1784
Nathan Black
To Joshua Coats, Bart
Conduit Street

Coats,

I have found that worm, Denyss.

Two days ago I tracked him and the Flemish Harlot to Harwich. The weather has been so bad that no craft were putting out, which was the parson's misfortune, although he was unaware of any pursuit and the pair were taking their ease. Denyss had not heard about Violet's— Violet's— . . . I cannot bring myself to speak the word. He does not even know there is a warrant out against him.

But you must have it stopped at once! Let me explain.

I came upon Denyss and his Trull in the early morning, at the inn where, along with other passengers, they were waiting for the wind to die down. He was breakfasting alone in a pair of fine rooms on a sumptuous repast, in a night-gown. I had not eaten for a day; his carefree enjoyment was reason enough to destroy him.

Why parly with the Devil, bent over his pewter as if blessing it? I prepared to shoot without warning, from the doorway.

But at the hammer-cock he looked up, terror taking him that I was not his iniquitous Harlot, and that lead would shortly replace the lust oiling his belly.

At that decisive moment, someone grabbed my arm from behind and the pistol went off, making a hole in the wall above Denyss's head. The Whore had clamped herself growling on to my arm where she clung like a spotted dog, without care for her safety, while I tried to batter her off. Side to side we went in a demented tug of war. But my argument was not with her, and shortly her loud sobbing and pleading brought me to my senses.

Waving her back and insisting that I should attempt no further harm, I strode into the room, where Denyss, crouched in the far corner, was so pitiful that my mood changed at once from anger to scorn.

"*Your daughter is dead!*" I shouted out without pause for breath, wishing to see him suffer and approaching with a mind to give him a good kicking.

Ignoring his gasp of horror, or how he clasped his flabby mouth as if it might fall off, I went on, "But for the misguided tenacity of *this—thing*" (indicating his Trick), "so would you be! How do you answer, sir!"

Before he had a chance to speak—and in truth he was so shocked that I doubted his ability—the woman flung herself between us, hands on hips, her painted face flaming in her paramour's defence. There were three fine rows of pearls round her neck, that all but disappeared among the crags of her bosom, reappearing at each pant with mysterious glimmers.

"You are all mistake!" She cried, seraphimous, "your argument is not with he." Though her command of English was lacking, her meaning was clear. She glanced back to Denyss, as if to say *do not try to stop me.*

"He is as weak for womens as any, but he is no Murdering. What it must be you think he has done, he did not know. He has suffered games of others as much as her.

"Look here." Proffering a tight-folded paper that she drew from the seamy gap between her cantilevered breasts she went on, "Before further violencing, judge yourself." She then offered me to sit, in a tone so commanding that I did as bid.

The paper had been closed for a long time, being worn at the edges and pressed sharp. Sweat had left it damp. Little bigger than my thumb, it had been folded six times. Opened with difficulty, it was just under two hands. A puncture showed where the frail thing must have been nailed up and, by all appearances, ripped down again. Since it was written in French, of which I have only a little, I studied in perplexity until, arriving at the meaning of a few words, my heart began to pound.

Then, at my expression, the Harlot declaimed the words from memory, in slow English, without moving from her place where she sat on the floor, her arm round Violet's quivering father.

Madam
You are to blame for
the ruin of an innocent girl,
the corruption and death of a wife,
and the slaying of your own lover.
My freedom is forfeit because of you.
Those who live by the sword—
I will see you burn in hell.

As the first horrid phrases left her mouth I sprang up.

"Who talks of Violet thus familiarly?" I demanded of Denyss. "Who are these other unfortunate people? Tell me, in the name of God, what is this paper, how came this Harpy by it, and whom does it address?"

It flashed into my mind to destroy the worthless couple there and then, without further preamble, and let them rot! But, through neglecting to recharge it, my pistol was now unloaded.

The Whore did not answer, but Denyss rose warily and seated himself across the table from me, fiddling with his abandoned chocolate bowl.

"It is not—Violet—that is talked of." He licked his lower lip, placing one hand flat across the other, in a futile attempt to stop its trembling.

"Though it might as well be. That bill in your hand is old. It talks of someone else, from some years ago, in Paris."

He waited, to see whether I might lash out again, before going on.

"It was a terrible scandal. A woman whose chief amusement was the corruption of innocent lives. She and her paramour, as a game, preyed on a young virgin and a devout wife, destroying the virtue of both and sucking others to destruction into the bargain. It was widely discussed in church circles at the time. The depth of the woman's depravity caused a great deal of alarm. I paid close attention, and am certain that the person who did those dreadful things is to blame for what has happened now."

"But how could such a monster—" I began.

"She escaped punishment," he went on. "It was said that she fled to Holland. Perhaps someone routed her from there. It is very clear from that note that there were those who would not rest until she was destroyed."

In late spring, Denyss continued, he had been travelling with the orange-haired woman, while supposedly on episcopal duties with the fallen in Holland. On the way back from Rotterdam to London they had met two French travellers, a lady and her servant. *Very incognito,* interposed the Whore; but still giving themselves a great many airs, which had infuriated her. The two women had said that they came from Amsterdam.

"What were their names?" I cried.

"The lady carefully to given nothing," said the Harlot, fingering her pearls, "but I can tell you her face as if it mine, even though she covered. Very beauty. Once she call her maid *Victoire.* They running away from something, carry hardly no baggages. That's why they were using the long way, from Rotterdam, if you wilfulled to know."

"Money?"

"No. Money, sir, no, none . . . a few piastres." The Harlot did not even blush: "The lady's purse, it fell from her pocket," she continued, blithely indifferent to such a blatant declaration of theft when I had a pistol and could point her in the direction of a gibbet in no time at all. "In the one side there was a secret place, with papers and letters and bills of lad—" She paused and, unthinking, again touched her fine necklace, "—with *letters,* and that paper you hold."

The letters were introductions, she continued, which she had not been interested in. She said she had thrown them away, only keeping the handbill, *in case it was of any use later.* She meant for blackmail, which I did not pursue, understanding, as did they, that any profit it might have brought must now be bartered for their lives, if Parson Denyss hoped for freedom.

I asked if she remembered any names from any of the papers she had destroyed, to which she shook her head; but then Denyss whispered rapidly in her ear, pressing the heel of his hand several times flat against his chest and giving her a look, after which she thought better and told me there was one.

Lady Danceacre, Hipp Street.

Coats, I am on my way back to town, leaving the parson and his moll behind. I have no appetite left for his utter destruction. It is better that he lives to contemplate his wickedness year after year, in exile. Nor, after further discussion out of the hearing of the whore, do I believe him to be as guilty as first supposed. His suffering, knowing that his eldest daughter is dead, is complete. Let them never set foot on these shores again. Nothing can bring my beloved girl back.

My business now is with a woman whose time on earth has run out. If you see me again, Violet will have been avenged and her murderer breathe no more.

Have the warrant for Denyss called off without delay.

Nathan Black

September 21, 1784
Frederick Danceacre
To Hubert van Essel

Dear Sir,

I am distraught, and there is no one else in whom to confide the awful events that have befallen me.

This afternoon found me at Newgate, to visit Poppy Salmon, the creature who recently ran that ill-fated nest (once my mother's house, where I was born!) where Violet was lured to her downfall.

The criminal had already languished in the prison's irksome precinct for five days waiting for the Sessions, and appears before the Grand Jury in the morning. If it finds against her she will go to trial and face Death for her part in Violet's, one life for the other. She will be ordered to await the hangman's pleasure, which she will gratify alone, since her accomplice was prematurely snatched from Justice.

I had only met the dissolute creature once, six months ago, got up in the height of fashion and heaped with diamonds, openly parading her trade. Some years before, she had been my mother's maid—which I dare say is how she came to set her sights on the house.

I confess that the story of this unnatural female (to whom, because of her association with my mother, I felt a sort of connection) intrigued me. How difficult would it be to spot her?

Even at a considerable distance, among seething women catcalling and fighting and wailing repulsively, better covered by vermin than rags, without her former glitter, I knew her. An unwarranted pride of carriage marked her out, she held her head higher than those nearby. Yet with no just reason, being so much worse! *They* had been driven to their crimes by necessity, while she spurned goodness for a felon's path, destroying a young girl and perpetuating evil—her sole ambition—like a man-eating plant that propagates itself.

The thronging hags, stinking of pus and excrement, in clothes so smeared that it was no longer possible to guess the colour, drew back from where Mrs Salmon waited. We had been granted ten minutes' conversing in a corner of that desperate place, in view of a warder who was throwing dice with the Chaplain and Keeper, all of them drinking heartily from two large jugs, a substantial leg of mutton that had been stript to the bone lying in the foul straw at their feet.

I was determined to discover who had influenced Violet to go to Hipp Street. What difference would it make to Salmon to tell me what she knew? In return I would promise to present a disposition to the Grand Jury, that the older woman, Beddoes, was wholly to blame for Violet's corruption and downfall. Which was false, and must surely be thrown out by any jury concerned to make the slightest search for truth: for Salmon was a hardened criminal, Beddoes merely a housekeeper set adrift by my not retaining her, who had turned to wickedness rather than face pauperdom. However, since that lady's mouth was too stuffed with earth to object, I offered her up without hesitation.

Mrs Salmon sat down opposite, where I gestured. She was smaller than I remembered, wrapped in a cloak that was not hers, uncurled hair scattered at her neck, rouge like the nap of inferior velvet on her dry cheek. She had been badly handled; bruises marked her hands and front and one of her eyes was blacked, the stain spreading across her nose.

"You have been harshly treated," I observed, surprised at not feeling greater repugnance and not knowing where to begin, now that we were sat together with so little time to spare.

"*That* is nothing," Salmon fluted arrogantly in her remarkable voice. "If you want to see something, look at this, *your Lordship.*"

Without warning she threw herself forwards, so that she was stretched across the table between us. The ends of her yellow hair touched my wrist with a shock. She lay utterly still for a second, face pressed into the splintering wood as if to say, *what do I care, I shall soon be dust;* then swept handfuls of hair aside, to show where a vicious, vertical gash scabbed the strands into thick tar.

But all I noticed, almost hidden by clots of blood, was the tiny blemish like a heart, tucked just behind her ear.

It was as if she stayed there motionless forever, although it was only a moment before she drew back to stare at me accusingly, eyes sharp with loathing. *This is of your doing,* they said, *you and those of your kind.*

I do not know what colour her eyes are—I could hardly see. But I pursued my questions, impervious to her answers, being then good for nothing. How I longed to examine the mark, once more concealed by her hair, in case it proved some trick of the light or was a strange counterfeit!

Not knowing what ran through my mind like the hammering toll of a bell—the certainty that here was my own sister, callous, charged with death; thoughts that blinded me to reason like a black torrent—she answered everything in the same dreary tone, as if indifferent to her impending trial and the certainty of its outcome.

All she knew, she repeated, was that whoever had bought Hipp Street always sent a man called Mr Voster to collect the money. He was slight and effeminate, so she did not take further notice: Mrs Beddoes dealt with him. Salmon said that she had been pleased enough not to answer any longer to Urban Fine—pronouncing the name as if she hawked it—and that their new patron's rates were reasonable, they made a profit. It did not concern them who their master was, so long as it was not Earl Much.

I asked why no one could tell me where this Mr Voster was now, or anything about him. It was as if he had vanished.

"Perhaps he has," she said, scathingly, "and all *this* is a figment of your imagination, too, *sir* —" sweeping her arms towards the teeming hell beyond, mockingly. "But what does it signify?" Her voice threatened to become shriller. "*He* ain't in here—if you could call such a Molly a man. *I am.*"

She would say nothing else, except that I should speak to the lawyers Mr Voster had once mentioned—that *scabbier criminals never lived, hedge-wigs, doing business for all the Molly houses in London: Relling and Squire.*

I knew that name. They had been my mother's lawyers, through whom, acting in my best interest (or so I had believed), Mrs Beddoes sold Hipp Street to its mysterious owner. I had trusted her concerning the lawyers' character. It seemed I had been mistaken.

But there was too little time left, so I changed tack.

"Ah, Violet," Mrs Salmon began, without any inflexion of guilt, and a slight sneer. "I wondered when we would start on that. She knocked at the door one day—we looked out of the window, and let her in. What else, when a pretty girl *asks* admittance? We did not wait for fresh oysters at coaching inns, if that is what you think, *sir.* You have looked at too many vulgar prints. Ours was not that cheap trade."

Poppy—*Persephone*—then drew herself up. Surely I had heard of Marylebone Park and the Simultaneous Sensation? Her house commanded more money with one girl, in one night, she said, than any of those places in a year—and none against their will.

I knew that she spoke truth, but let her go on, just to continue looking at her. Here was my half-sister, my only living flesh, who, if

I did nothing, would have a capital trial set in the morning, and certain death thereafter. She was a murderer! The word beat so hard against the walls of my head that it must explode.

But even through waves of nausea, it was clear that she said fair: Violet had gone to Hipp Street of her own accord. How came the poor dead girl to know of such a place?

Persephone reminded me of Parson Denyss's fondness for the services she offered. "Do you not think it probable," she observed, "that Violet might have found something in his keeping that drew her to us? An advertisement perhaps, something with our address? That she pried where she should not?

"She was no child, but a spirited young woman who longed for adventure. She lived in a *rectory*! Young women should not be kept so strait, forced to watch from behind a tatting frame, or the embroidery of a hassock, while brothers and cousins enjoy themselves. If they are not already imbeciles they quickly learn envy and subterfuge. Why not throw them in gaol at the outset and be done with it? The effect is the same."

I recollected Violet's forward behaviour towards me the first time I met her. Again Persephone's words were just.

"You, on the other hand, did you not go abroad and explore the world?" My sister went on accusingly, suddenly touching my wrist across the raw wood. With another shock I saw that it was my mother's hand, pinkish and square across the palm, short fingers. Not elegant, like her father's.

Albeit uneasy that she now questioned me, I was unwilling to stop what might be our last conversation.

"We are of an age, you and I," she assessed, with the self-serving inaccuracy of a courtesan, staring all the while with that merciless directness of man or whore. "I, too, went into the world. Not as you did—not having the means—but after my own fashion. No one can say that I have not lived, even if I must now die for it. Young women like Violet spend their lives dead."

I would have protested at this last, had it made any difference.

"Violet Denyss was happy while she was under my roof," Persephone continued, "for the first time in her life. She had dainty clothes, she went out. She lived before she died—unlike most.

"The accident with her father . . ." My sister shrugged. "No one would have wished such a thing to happen . . . if it really did. We are not heartless! Yes, *something* must have taken place. But then, even if it had; one man or another, what difference, in the end? It was not the fact that killed her, but her own shame at what might have happened. If she had not remembered anything, she would be alive now. Happily married, from what they say out there." She gestured again towards the other women.

"Some of these bruises came from them, because of what they have heard about me. Why judge me again when I have already been judged—and by those who understand?"

Still occupied with the revelation of Persephone's identity I was not listening very closely. *Violet's* death, while it had been a tragedy, was one that could no longer be averted. I put it aside to concentrate on memorising the living face of the woman in front of me, as a talisman, to ensure that I would see it again. She was still speaking. Something else, so dreadful I did not even want to think it, was welling up as Persephone went on talking about Violet and her father.

"Tell me, where did Violet get the shame that killed her? Who bred it into her? *Her father,* and men like him—a world of hypocrites, making women so afraid of their inclination that at last they are lost, following whomever leads, like bulls with rings. Her father killed her, not I! Or say that society killed her, if you like, what odds? She was betrayed, just as I have been. Tell me, *Lord Danceacre,* since we will never cast eyes on each other again, why do Violet and I swing, instead of Parson Denyss *or Earl Much*?

My heart jumped. There was no doubt that Persephone knew who her father was. She had been his mistress! She knew they bore the same mark. It was on his hand for all to see. But did he know what he had done to her? Had she hidden the mark from him?

And if she knew that . . . could she have guessed that we were brother and sister?

Persephone stood up, put her hands on the table and glanced at me, before casting her eyes down. "Good-bye" she said, flatly, addressing the table. "Remember me."

She knows.

Doctor, there can be no doubt of the outcome of either the Grand Jury or the trial. Violet's auction alone is enough to hang my sister, your ward; and if Persephone is right that Violet found out about Hipp Street all on her own, there is nothing left that might mitigate the sentence, no one to share the blame.

Sweet Heaven, sir! My sister! Is it not Urban Fine who should die in her place? Her father, is he not responsible? Did he not set her on the path that has brought her here, step by step, as he did her mother before her, and God knows how many other women besides? What Justice lets such an abomination go free, a man who can buy freedom as he buys favours and flesh, one as cheap as the other? Even if he cannot be tried, he must save her; he has the power to call off—to buy off—the trial. All his money belongs to her! Let him use it to save his child's life. What matters how he does it, whom he pays?

If he will not do this, he dies. I am going there now.

Frederick Danceacre

Translated from French

9 PM

September 21, 1784

Martha Hublon

Marylebone Park

To Monsieur Laforge,

2nd Floor, Warp Lane

Laforge,

Vieux canard,

Here is some news to amuse you, sitting there like a flabby old spider, making out your reports. Send this to your Maltese master; I believe there is matter in it that will greatly please him.

Ever since Urban Fine discovered that I wasn't the heiress that Mrs Fox had led him to believe, he has been acting up. Not that he doesn't want me—oh, he can't do without it, bad as you—worse!

But knowing makes him spiteful. He thinks he has been short-changed: like all rich bastards, his true love is a bargain. That, and he hasn't been well these past weeks. Dizzy, off-colour, losing his balance. Sometimes when he was with me, his breath went short and his heart raced. That made him angry, and he was getting in the habit of taking it out on me.

This morning, instead of going for a ride (which as you know is his custom), he ordered a light carriage. He was pale. Since he was going in a chariot, he took a book he is very attached to. *Curiosities,* it is called, with drawings that he tells me are *too scholarly for my appreciation.* Too scholarly my arse! Filth! As if I care about his dirty little book, there can't be nothing I haven't seen before. He can choke on it! I have never even touched it.

As there is always housekeeping to do here, the minute he was gone I had a new footman come up to help move an armoire. From his looks he seemed Huguenot, which proved the case. The result being that we fell from conversation of one kind into that of another as easy as you like and the armoire stayed put. Nicely turned, twenty: *happy to serve the young mistress.*

We were well and truly taken up with each other, let me tell you, when my Lord came back unexpected. He had felt faint and turned around. He wanted to know where madam was. Found madam and went into a blind rage. I have witnessed his rages, but at others, never at me. It is my custom to laugh at him, for which he would kill anyone else; but standing up to a tyrant is the only way to survive, as I know well—better than all those spineless women he has tortured over the years.

However, *this* anger was different, possessing him so thoroughly that I could see him shaking, clear across the room. Then he started to draw his sword, which meant certain death for one of us. Guillaume, the fool, with nothing to hand to save him other than my modesty (which has more holes in it than a pincushion) tried to hide his huge frame behind me—which would have been comical in other circumstances.

My Lord took several paces towards the bed. Seeing in his face that he meant business I began shouting in earnest, determined to show no fear. He was dangerously close, so I shut my eyes, not to see the flash of death. But he fell, slicing into the covers with his sword—near taking my foot off into the bargain. Why could he not have managed it better and nicked his own evil head off? At all events, he was out cold, with no blood spilled. Guillaume took the precaution of running away.

With the help of salts, my master came round to find himself in my arms (sword far from reach). He demanded to know where *that cur* the footman was. I told him without further goading that he had left for Salamander Row to fetch his box and be gone, and that if his Lordship had any sense he would leave matters there, since it was only the pleasant diversion of *curs* such as Guillaume that made *him* tolerable in these black moods.

At my insolence Much leapt up, roaring that I would hear from him later, and went off like a bullet.

You may be sure, Laforge, that I have no intention of listening to him later! But instead, to put as much distance as possible between me and Marylebone Park. My time is run here: I have a good amount in cash, not to mention the yellow diamond and a great many other jewels put away here and there. A reward for hard work, every penny earned.

Although I meant to travel light, there were three dresses worth something, what with gold-work and seeds, that seemed a gross pity to leave for some other less able bawd to huff about in. I was folding them as tidy as could be, when Lord Frederick Danceacre was announced.

To be so singularly honoured was a surprise, I assure you, but today seemed set fair for such astonishments.

I received him in my chemise. He is a man and has heard what sort of a woman I am. A sort he is very familiar with, that *runs in the blood,* from what they say. He seemed agitated, so I patted the bed and invited him to make himself comfortable. I have heard much talk of him. He is well favoured, a head taller than the Earl; what's more he is near half his age and near twice mine, which knowledge made me already feel *familiar.*

He demanded to know my lord's whereabouts *since he must speak with him urgently, on a most important matter.* Alas, he had missed my master by an hour, I said, nor advised waiting, for who could say what mood the Earl might be in when he returned?

Which I for one did not intend staying to discover, I added slowly, intending him to take note; but was going to France—*to Dieppe.*

"Dieppe?" Lord Danceacre recollected himself a little, for the first time noticing the disarray of the room. Yet still he appeared surprisingly indifferent to my undress, which insolence I sought to correct.

"Why are you leaving all this, Madam, for Dieppe?" he asked.

I pointed to the great rent in the bedclothes, that any fool could see had been done by a very sharp blade, and asked if he did not think that reason enough? He wanted to know why Earl Much would wish me harm.

Accustomed to being given orders rather than asked civil questions, which were pleasant when put by such a handsome face in such a way, I found myself inclined to dalliance.

In a fit of devilment I recounted how the Earl had discovered that

I was not the heiress he had been led to believe—although it was none of *my* counterfeit, I added hastily, casting down my eyes and looking meek (lessons learned from Mrs Fox); but that it was a deceit put on me by someone else, who had pretended I was her relation. I too had been sore misused, perhaps even more than Earl Much!—but like all men, *he* felt that he had been palmed off worse—which was insult to me—since none of it was my intention or wish, but the work of another.

At which, as I had meant him to, Danceacre asked further questions.

"Mrs Fox was the one!" I cried, at last letting him prise it from me, pretending that he had pushed me to it against my will, yet all the while concealing my laughter and looking at him covertly to see how he was taking it.

"Oh, I was but an innocent manty-maker, until she trained me," I sighed, "treating me no better than a prisoner, taking my clothes, beating me and feeding me bread and water.

"At first, all she said she wanted was for me to act as a front, so that they could run sweet tricks out of their rooms at Warp Lane. *That* I agreed to, since it involved only sewing, at which,"—fingering some embroidery straining over my breast—"I excel."

Danceacre was swallowing these lies greedily, following the dawdling pattern my fingers traced. I made myself look as sorrowful and hard-done by as possible.

"They *promised* that I should have nothing to do with that *other side of things,* but then, sensing bigger game, forced me into harlotry, presenting me as an heiress: *a sprat to catch a Mackerel,* to spin money out of Earl Much and make him a laughing stock. They threw me to him!" I declared, warming to the part, my breast surging in indignation. "Shameful prostitution of an unblemished girl, to serve their wickedness!"

Danceacre sat down on the bed the better to listen, to which end I poured him a glass of good brandy and then another. He was very attentive, asking me to repeat many details, particularly those concerning Mrs Fox. Seeing that they were the ones that held his attention on me the best, I embellished them, leaving no part of her doings unaccounted for, adding more after my own imagination, where I saw fit.

Telling about them training me and teaching me courtly manners, *as well as some other tricks* that I blushed relating, interested him the most of all, so I made the best of it, *acting out what was meant,* when the tale merited.

Last, I told of my having pretended not to read nor write, which I had done in order to have my own bit of fun, it being a downright lie, my father having been a teacher at the Huguenot school at Mile End and I his assistant until I was thirteen, when he died. And how they became unguarded in the matter of their letters, because of it.

That Mrs Fox enjoyed everything as a kind of sport was quickly understood, I said. There was someone she wrote to often, who took a particular interest in Earl Much. *Those letters would be a fascination to read.*

Danceacre demanded to know this man's name.

However, in my opinion he had had more than enough free, while I had got nothing to show in return. Which quandary I put to him in no uncertain terms, and he as swiftly and enthusiastically remedied, to our very great mutual satisfaction

Then he quit me with *utmost reluctance,* to hie to Salamander Row, with a most earnest farewell, hoping that perhaps we should enjoy each other's company again one day, *in Dieppe.*

I was sorry to see the back of him, having greatly enjoyed the front; especially since Much will surely kill him the very moment they meet—and if the Earl does not, Danceacre looked so violently when I spoke of Mrs Fox manipulating and playing with people for her own pleasure, that he will doubtless kill her instead.

Tell this to your master: that after all, he will have no need to kill

Mrs Fox, nor for you to do it either, since shortly others will do his work for him, on my instigation. You may lay money on it.

Be sure to remember me to him for a reward.

Martha Hublon

I AM
September 22, 1784
Frederick Danceacre
Salamander Row
To Joshua Coats
Conduit Street

Coats,

Earl Much is dead.

I am fleeing to Dieppe. I will write more from France—it is too dangerous to stop.

In brief: I went to find that syphilitic devil at Marylebone Park, to force him to buy off Mrs Salmon's case, before it comes to trial.

Poppy Salmon is not to blame for Violet's death. It is true that she is a whore, but no murderess—and she is the Earl's own daughter! There is more . . . but no time to tell it.

For God's sake you must act at once! Trust me, Coats. Once, Mrs Salmon was a sweet girl of good family, little different from Violet . . . and it may prove that she has been worse treated.

I had gone to Marylebone Park to find Much, bent on destroying him; I could think of nothing else. But when I arrived, his servants and new mistress were leaving all at once and the place was in uproar.

They told me he had gone to Salamander Row so I followed, arriving there at eleven. The house was in near-darkness. At that moment, a pair of flunkies came rushing out, perfectly white from fear.

Inside, the hall was patchily lit, the stinking orchids overwhelming. The floor was covered in spots of light that lit up great pools and splashes of blood, leading to the sprawling figure of a footman with a wound gaping clear across his chest, as if some thing inhuman had slashed him from side to side. His handsome face covered with sweat and tears, he looked as if he would die from terror sooner than from his injury. He threw an arm out (which I took to be a pathetic attempt at pointing towards the basement). A few yards away lay a dead maidservant, face down.

The dying footman's sign was hardly necessary, but his agonised expression warned me to take extra care.

Knowing who must surely be below, and that I might never climb the steps up to the light again, I took my time, coming out at last in one of several linked chambers formed by the vaults.

Hundreds of tapers blazed from every wall, lighting an army of stone limbs and heads into a sort of petrified carnage. Those mouldy objects filled me with the determination to be rid of a man to whom nothing has any more value than a trophy.

As I felt my way step by step in the eerie, flickering place, rehearsing how I would put Persephone's desperate case to Earl Much and plead for her life, I was certain that he would not lift a finger for his daughter. He knew who she was; he must have done so for years, yet had done nothing to help her. Instead he had used her as his mistress, hiring her out, available to all and sundry; letting her risk her life for her own father's pleasure. He felt no more about my dear sister Persephone than he had for our mother. He had never cared for any human being. He was that rare thing: an aberration, a monstrosity, daring the world to extinguish him, gambling that no one would have the nerve to stand up against his supernatural cruelty.

I found this tormentor at last, in a central room full of Egyptian and Assyrian sculptures whose cruel faces stared from black stone. He was standing with his back turned, on a sort of dais into which a large, white sarcophagus had been sunk. He appeared to be waiting. One hand rested on the lip of the tomb, translucent skin merging with translucent stone, except for that birthmark, glaring even at such a distance.

Against his side, light from the candles ran up and down his sword; the only trembling sign that the Earl breathed. He must know exactly how close I was, for in that place, every step rang; yet he did not move.

"For the love of God," I cried, "will you help her?" Already in anguish, knowing what his answer would be.

He remained motionless, as if he had not heard, or did not care to consider my plea; abominable arrogance that was too much to bear.

Goaded beyond endurance I was rushing towards him when, at the very last moment, he turned slowly to face me.

In that wracked movement, in the effort it cost him, I understood that he had been holding on to the stone for support. For he was paler than death, bleached lips pulled back from colourless gums in a snarl; nostrils dark tunnels in his sharp nose. He held a book clamped to his breast, which he must have been reading.

Insufferable nonchalance! Taking his ease with a novel, when a man and a maid lay dying above, their blood not yet dry on his sword.

The Earl made no attempt to loosen his weapon to defend himself, and swayed towards me, as—quite unable to stop, even had I wished it—I ran him clean through.

And left him where he fell, collapsed against the end of the tomb.

Save Mrs Salmon, Coats, if it is all you ever do.

Even though I may never see her again, *she is my sister!* She cannot be allowed to die for faults that I swear on my life are not hers. The woman you seek . . . ah, help me, it is impossible to write her name.

For God's sake, pity me—and help my sister.

Danceacre

2 AM
September 22, 1784
Nathan Black,
The Strand
To Joshua Coats
Conduit Street

Dear Coats,

BURN THIS AT ONCE.

Having heard from that disgusting apology for a parson and his woman, I turned about without pause for breath, only taking the precaution to clean my pistol.

On reaching London I went to Salamander Row in search of Mrs Fox. You know with what aim. The bill that the Dutch whore had given me was folded up small in my waistcoat. I planned to hold it up before her face, to see truth and fear reflected in her eyes, before showing her the only true Justice.

It was midnight. The house was dark, except for light escaping like threads of fire from the basement shutters. The great front door stood ajar, so I went in unchallenged. From small items scattered down the steps and nearby street—a snuff box, a coin, a glove—it was obvious that the place had been abandoned in haste.

Inside there were two dead servants, a man and a woman, whom I almost fell over before becoming accustomed to the gloom and the stinking flowers—monstrous leprotic things looming from every quarter. After kicking the footman to make certain of him, faint light coming from the door down to the basement showed that it was open.

The vaults are where Much keeps the heaviest and most prized things in his collection. I had heard of it—who has not? But never seen it. I ran down the steps. Priceless, Coats, priceless! Stolen from all parts of the globe, shouldn't wonder, America too. There was a tiny Mesopotamian figurine in a narrow niche, and a small agate cup; so thin, like glass, it was a puzzle how it had been done. I put them in my pockets, one either side. That reprobate killed for them, take my word. Had he appeared I would have taken a pot-shot in return—except that he was not the one I had come for.

Crammed top to bottom with statuary, the place blazed with tapers that had burned a good way, making it into an oven. I went through the vaulted chambers one by one, looking in amazement, since it might be my only opportunity.

It would have been impossible to have been taken by surprise down there, for every sound echoed on the stone, even the merest scratch of a nail. My pistol was primed and cocked—although there was no reason why Mrs Fox should be in the vaults, for even if she had recently been in the house, would she not have fled with the rest? But something told me to wait and see.

At last, at what must have been the centre of the house, I came to a plinth, a long oblong, with an open alabaster sarcophagus sunk into it. The figure of Earl Much was sitting leaning against one end, staring straight at me, his head level with the top of the tomb, his skin a dunnish colour, livid against his lavender silk, looking for all the world like one of those dressed lay figures that Gainsborough uses. Clearly dead as anything. Done for. A vile puppet.

In his lap lay an open book, just as if he was reading it; the pages moving gently to and fro in the candle-draught.

I was taken aback by this sight, but having got my breath was on the point of approaching to see what had killed him—it being impossible to tell at that distance—when a faint sound announced someone else making their way carefully into the vaults, just as I had. From the doubting, delicate footsteps, you would have wagered it a woman.

Beside me an overwrought Egyptian stand bore a life-size marble bust of Apollo that I slipped behind to wait.

Having reached the bottom, the footsteps carried on slowly, stopping and starting at every few paces. There were sounds of picking up and putting down, then a distinct rustling, as of something being placed very carefully into a silk pocket. After some minutes of the same, Mrs Fox appeared, casually swinging a naked Etruscan figure against her leg.

At the moment she came level, when the merest glance to the side would have given me away, her attention was caught by the sagging body of Earl Much, slumped ahead. She was so close that I heard her gasp at the horrible sight. But after only a slight hesitation, she marched up to the plinth and bent down to examine the corpse, just as I would have done, reaching to prise the book from the hooks of his fingers.

I stepped out and called her name so loud it rang. She straightened, her silk slippers between the cocked feet of the dead man and turned, a smile of delight that I was quite certain she could not feel stretching her lips.

"Why, Mr Black!

"Surely this scholarly creature," she gestured teasingly behind her, towards the foul corpse, "cannot be your handiwork"

As she went on, blandishments dripping softly from those lovely lips as smooth as blood from a fatal cut, I brought to my pistol up to shoot without delay, before she could charm me from my purpose—of which I knew full-well she was able.

Although her cheeks paled slightly at the sight of the barrel, the impression of joy never left her face. "You can have no reason to wish me harm. I have nothing to fear from you. Put away your weapon and let us leave this awful place together!"

Smile blazing, she was on the point of coming forwards. If she began to move in that sinuous way of hers, all would be lost.

Just as my will to fire had almost ebbed, Earl Much rose up behind Mrs Fox. With a dreadful scrabbling rush his spectral figure gripped her like a vice, clamping her arms hard against her sides. Her astonished expression (no doubt a reflection of mine) stayed fixed on me, not prepared to countenance an unwelcome interruption, while directly behind her shoulder, Much's face was green mottled with dark red, carved from Levanto marble.

"*He* sent you," he spat in her ear, his contorted voice carrying through the airless space, "*he* sent you to destroy me with this," at which he tapped her with the book. "*Curiosity* would be the end of me, he always said so; don't you want a taste of it?"

His words appeared to fill Mrs Fox with terror, for she began rocking, desperate to escape his grip. With one pinioning claw, that gleamed against her like a mildewed eagle, he dragged the book up her stomach and over her bosom, finally struggling to press it to her mouth, as though to suffocate her. Then, with a straining effort, he pressed his own mouth deep into her neck, either to kiss or tear a hole in it. At which Mrs Fox, shaking her head free of his restraint with an inhuman effort that caused the book to fly through the air, screamed louder than any Indian savage, ricocheting screeches that set my blood like granite.

I was unable to move.

Much turned and bent her with appalling strength, threatening to snap her over the side of the great white coffin, the lavender silk that strained across his narrow coat blooming suddenly in a welt of blood. Her own back surely on the point of breaking, Mrs Fox was squealing when my shot rang out.

The charge must have gone straight through both of them, I was certain of it. Her cries stopped abruptly and there was utter silence. Gently, welded together, they toppled into the sarcophagus, clamped for eternity in a repulsive embrace.

Coats, I ran, knocking over the Apollo in my haste to get out. Back in the hall, I rested the pistol in the fingers of the dead footman, barrel pointing towards the door to the vaults.

I shall stay in my studio, restoring the painting of the angel, until I hear from you that it is safe to come out.

Nathan Black

Part Six

September 22, 1784
Monsieur Laforge
Warp Lane
To The Chevalier D—
MALTA

Mon cher Chevalier,

Accept my compliments.

Le renard est mort.

My business on your behalf being done, my account is enclosed. Once you have settled it I will destroy all correspondence that ever existed between us relating to this matter.

You requested that, after I had made doubly sure of the identity of the lady calling herself Mrs Fox—given our good fortune in her choosing this very house to stay in, after the carter's ineptitude—I kept her in my sights until you demanded her death, using the sword you had given me for the purpose.

Sir, at the last moment there was no need of it; regrettably that pleasure went to another hand.

Yesterday, around midday, a man arrived to take the rooms at the top of the house. He was tall, with an old-fashioned hat and a capacious yet apparently not heavy bag; of numerous years though not elderly; a gentleman. (This information was produced by Mrs Sorrell, who made her report while serving me supper.)

There was nothing untoward about *Mr Albrecht Oeben,* she said. But I noted that he came from Holland—he claimed the *Hague*—and Mrs Fox was in frequent contact with a Dutch gentleman. One of

Betty the chambermaid's lamentable attempts at spying had revealed that Mrs Fox's chief correspondent came from Amsterdam, the place where Mr Martin met his untimely death.

Though I doubted the link of any consequence, I determined to pursue it. For in my line of work it is true that many seeming coincidences prove to be nothing of the sort, once probed deeper; that nothing may be discounted, however small, until the final reckoning, since details that appear to have no connection with each other can on rare occasion turn out twins.

According to what Oeben told Mrs Sorrell, he was a spice merchant looking to set up at Spitalfields market, or thereabouts, and was confident of finding many takers for his wares.

English cooks, the most inclined to novelty in all Europe and quite indifferent to the use of rotten meat, are very forward in their reckless application of pungent flavours—Mrs Sorrell being in the van of this gruesome habit. So determined was she to get cheap spices for her concoctions that she offered Oeben very good terms. He had in fact already possessed the rooms for some months, but it seems that he gave her to understand unexpected losses in the Indian Ocean had delayed his enjoyment of them.

Until his unannounced arrival, the landlady, perfectly content with an arrangement to her advantage, was in the habit of airing her *hams* there, or using the rooms *otherwise.* I knew further (having the key), that Betty also entertained in them, for which she paid me several times over when Mademoiselle Hublon betrayed her. *That* young woman could have had a fine diplomatic career, had greed not got the better of her.

I digress, sir.

Upon making it my business, then, I watched this Dutch gentleman.

Some days ago, Mrs Fox returned very abruptly from Salamander Row, having sent her maid ahead with plentiful baggage, as if intending to stay.

While Mrs Fox had been a guest of Earl Much, you may be sure that I made use of her absence to visit her quarters.

Yet, though she wrote and received a great many letters, there were no papers to be found. She must have kept them close by at all times. Victoire had always posted her mistress's notes, so those too proved impossible to intercept. However, Betty was put to look out for whatever came *into* the house, as that provided better opportunity for interception.

Despite her incontestable stupidity, Betty got to the mail before Victoire on two occasions, before the letters were plucked from her grasp by the incensed maid. For which sleight, the girl got first a cracked rib and the second time was kicked down five stairs, twisting an ankle. Being naturally shiftless, however, she was not hampered by temporary immobility and carried on her preferred work as before.

Betty only once caught sight of a foreign mark on a letter addressed to Mrs Fox. It was a long word, with what she traced out, having memorised the shapes, as an *A* and an *M*. This naturally increased my curiosity regarding Mr Oeben, and his claim of having come from the Hague.

Mrs Fox was out most of the day yesterday and so missed the arrival of Mr Oeben. Later in the evening, she took a sedan back to Salamander Row, leaving her maid behind, whom Betty overheard being told that she would be sent for, presumably later that night. But Victoire's mistress did not return, nor send a messenger—which lapse aroused my attention, it being out of character, since the lady was both impatient and exact, unlike all the other females in that house.

At three this morning, a woman's footsteps passed my room, creeping up to Oeben's. They could only belong to Mrs Fox's maid, for every attempt at secrecy carries its own distinguishing marks and those were steps I had never heard pass before, in a house where women's feet at unusual times were not uncommon. Her approaching him surprised me, I had believed them strangers. I watched Mrs Fox's rooms from the spyhole under my chair. I knew that the maid had kept within doors the entire day, as she often did, eating cold meats and a dish of sallet.

It was a puzzle to imagine what connection there could be between them. To my certain knowledge, that gentleman had not quit his apartment since arriving, either. Any communication must have been by a note passed under the door by Oeben, on his way to his rooms. And with considerable dexterity, since Mrs Sorrell had shown him up.

Not long after, the pair descended and entered Mrs Fox's chambers, where they stayed ten minutes in darkness, then left the house. From the window I could see that the bag Oeben carried was much heavier than when he first arrived. The maid had a bundle of her own, and wore a thick cloak.

After a brief pause I followed. There was no doubt then that they were well acquainted, moving with the familiarity of demeanour one might expect in old friends, rather than those just met. They entered a stables and shortly emerged at speed in a closed carriage, whose destination I demanded of the boy. As soon as a second vehicle could be harnessed I set off after them, to Salamander Row, taking care that they were unaware of any pursuit.

The great, double front door stood wide open, the empty carriage outside, its horse still panting.

Having paid off *their* conveyance as a standard precaution and primed mine to look sharp, I went carefully into the hall.

A dead footman lay hacked to ribbons in a wide pool of blood, quite near the body of a maid who lay face down with no immediate signs of violence about her, whom I did not disturb. A fired pistol had slipped from the footman's fingers. He was only recently dead; the edges of the blood had not begun to congeal.

Noises coming up from below, from a small door standing ajar, called me speedily into the vaults. As I reached the bottom of the stairs, an appalling screaming began: rending, agonised wails. The vaults were only lit by a few dying tapers, guttering in the draught from above. Making towards the lamentation as swiftly as prudence and near-darkness dictated, I came upon a sight which it gives me great pleasure to describe and whose recounting can never cease to bring you joy.

Despite the gloom—for although outside it was approaching dawn, the sun's rays hardly penetrated that hateful morgue, and the weak candle flames threw what light there was into danker shade—and despite need for concealment, it was yet possible to make out the form of a large stone coffin some way ahead. It appeared to glow with an inner light, luminous, causing me some unease. There was an unworldly, sickening quality about the queer gleam, as unnatural as all the flowers in that ungodly house.

Even from a considerable distance it was easy to identify the figure of Mrs Fox's maid, bent over the top of this monstrous tomb. Arms clasped across her bosom she was swaying to and fro, staring into the depths of the thing and shrieking *Dieu! O! Madame! Mon Dieu!* in a voice cracked with horror. Oeben was trying to pull her away. I could tell that his hands were dark with blood; Victoire's face and dress were also dabbed with it. The very sides of the coffin that, as I have said, were aglow, were liberally splashed and smeared with the same stain, black weals on the stone. Not far from Oeben's feet a discarded rapier caught the light and shone out.

From Victoire's cries, I was convinced that it was her mistress she lamented. As I moved a litte further forward, spellbound, my foot touched a small bound volume, which I put in my pocket, never taking my eyes from the couple at the tomb as I did so.

Alas, engrossed by that arresting sight, unconsciously straining for a better view, I stumbled over a large piece of broken marble, making Oeben start. He released Victoire and began casting wildly round him, uncertain of the direction of the noise in that echoing place, trying to make me out. Since he made the common mistake of amateurs, attempting to see his prey before pursuing it, rather than following the instinct that he should have known was correct, my escape was easy.

Once outside, Oeben had no method of following—save running through the streets blood-soaked—so had to content himself in watching my carriage disappear, none the wiser as to its occupant.

I regret not having had the opportunity to mutilate the Bitch's body as you wished, nor send you a token from it. I must admit to an inability to present absolute confirmation that she is dead. Such dereliction was unavoidable in the circumstances, given that you will agree that it was needful to escape without delay, or run the risk of failing to make this report. I will go back in the morning,

However, that she is dead, there can be no doubt. The woman whose evil nature robbed you of your love and forced you into exile will trouble you no longer.

Given my uncertainty as to whether Oeben will return here or if he is able to discover me through the stables, it is not prudent to stay longer than necessary. I will quit this house this night and send notice where you may find me, now that my task for you is done.

Your servant,
D. Laforge

The above letter never reached its destination.

The following letter is a forgery.

September 23, 1784
Monsieur Laforge
Warp Lane
To The Chevalier D—
MALTA

Sir,

My business on your behalf being done, my account is enclosed. Once you have settled it I will destroy all correspondence between us.

You requested that, after I had made doubly sure of the identity of the lady, given our good fortune in her choice of this very house, that she was kept in my sights until you demanded her death, using the sword you had given me for the purpose.

There was no need of it.

It was my honour to despatch Mrs Fox with a single pistol shot.

After tracking her to the vaults at Salamander Row and trapping her there like a cornered animal, I denounced her on your behalf, so that she knew that there would be no mercy. Her lascivious attempts to dissuade me from killing her met with derision. Then, looking into her terrified eyes as she shrank from me, calling hell down upon her in your name, I shot her through the heart at blank range.

Afterwards, it was child's play to create the illusion of a different chain of events, which the newspapers have seized on. I enclose several of these misguided accounts for your amusement.

As you will learn from them, Mrs Fox appears to have been murdered by a footman in the service of Earl Much. From various ecstatic accounts now reaching the public, she had caught the fancy of this new servant—a handsome young Huguenot who, according to my sources, had only recently entered the Earl's service. This hot-blooded young man was consumed with jealousy when Mrs Fox would not humour him, at which he rashly challenged Lord Much to a duel. Which, they say, fired up with the super-human power of love, he won—but only after being mortally wounded. Enraged, dying, he shot the woman for whose love he was now on the point of death (the mark of a true yokel).

The unrecognisable remains identified as those of Mrs Fox and Earl Much were discovered in an Egyptian sarcophagus that had been heaped with candles and set alight. In the fierce conflagration, the flames cracked the alabaster clean across, but did not manage to spread to the rest of the house.

The romantic footman could not be questioned since, having

committed his crimes, he crawled into the hall and died, the pistol still in his hand. It seems that no one else was harmed, for no other bodies were found.

That the footman and Much duelled is doubtless true; they were both dead when I arrived. All that remained for me was the pleasure of dragging Mrs Fox by her hair from where she was cringing on the floor in her chamber, breaking several of her bones on the staircase, and snuffing her worthless life out exactly as I have described.

I tossed her body into the coffin with that of the Earl and set fire to them myself, where they charred like a pair of sucking pigs, creating a horrible stench. Their flesh melded into a disgusting unbreakable lacquer, like bobbing apples at a fair, so that they looked like nothing so much as a mandrake root when they were scraped out. This particular part has enthralled the popular imagination; there have been drawings in some of the papers, and a print is already circulating called "The Scene at the Tomb."

Trusting that this tale brings you pleasure, here are the cuttings, all of them lingering on the character of Mrs Fox. The consensus is that it was a great loss to the proper enjoyment of the populace that she escaped being burned alive at the stake for a multitude of other wicked offences against society, that are only now coming to light.

Rest in peace, sir, she will trouble you no more.

My job being concluded and payment made, you will hear no more of me.

Your servant,
D. Laforge

October 3, 1784
Dadson Darley
To Joshua Coats

Can you believe, Coats, that it is half a year since we went to visit the pretty manty-maker, but made the acquaintance of Mrs Fox, instead?

That spirited lady's death still fills me with horror, it is impossible to believe. If Black hadn't gone running back to America, he would have made sense of everything. You may say I'm not the brightest button in the box and ought to leave things be, but parts of the whole business just didn't hang well, like the wrong coat and waistcoat. How can the footman have been to blame, galumphing French fellow, hardly off the boat?

Now that the scandal about Mrs Fox is dying down, there has been a fresh outrage at Warp Lane, that no one could have predicted.

I went there yesterday, to see if anyone knew aught of Martha, having learned that she had left Marylebone Park without notice, merely taking a few valuable clothes, on the very day that Mrs Fox and Earl Much died. A runner! No trace.

It seems she left well before anyone could have heard about Salamander Row, which is deuced coincidental, my opinion.

Thought there might be sporting odds that she would go back to what she knew, once her protector was out of the picture—girl has to make a living, after all. Rather fancied she might give me another go, put things on a more regular footing. Always had a soft spot.

Long before reaching the house I could hear that there was a tremendous hullabaloo going on. The Lane was full of people, rough sorts in the main, thickest around the door, constables running in all directions trying to keep a lively crowd back. Entire street full of ruffians drunk with affray, banging on the shutters and shouting to raise the dead.

Didn't like the look of it! No sir! Knocked a few of them for six with my stick and went in. Rabble, what, weak on gin; vile spectacle; riff-raff.

Since there was no one in the hall, but voices coming from above, I had just started up the stairs, when I was forced to give way to two constables coming down, with a half-covered body under a cloth.

Stink! Worse than a stillborn foal. Disgusting. I was immediately sick all over it. Zounds, sir, any one would have done as much!

As they passed, I took the opportunity to flip the cover aside with the tip of my cane, but couldn't recognise the fellow for the life of me. Middle-aged, dark hair, coarse beard, foriegn-looking. Frog, at a guess, but so blotched and gone off it was hard to say.

They had found him in a cupboard! Run through and through, with a paper speared to his stomach by a fancy-handled stiletto sticking out of his blown guts, that looked as if it had been cut from a book. You could scarcely read what had been on it, the ink had floated off, except for what might have been the word *Curiosity* . . . I was reading it upside down, mind you.

The constables said he was some sort of spy, up to no good. Room full of boring military tomes, probably in code. And that there was something else; a peculiar stink coming off the sodden paper, as if the damp had released it: they declared it was poison.

Nasty end. Must have merited it.

Mrs Sorrell, the landlady, had been renting this dead fellow a room above Martha's—then Mrs Fox's—for more than two years. According to her he was as quiet as you please, rarely went out, troubled no one, called for her services when he wanted them. The quiet ones are the worst . . . not a problem I suffer from.

She, Sorrell, is insisting that Monsieur Laforge—the corpse—had left a note that he was away on business, which was his custom. So she had thought nothing of it for days.

Until he started to rot.

The maid Betty noticed the smell this morning and a locksmith broke the cupboard open.

Here's the surprise: carpenter discovered a secret panel and a doorway, from inside the cupboard to the house next door, and then a closed staircase down to the alley! Deuced murky all round. That place is a bad one.

Since Sorrell cannot provide any answers to explain who Laforge was, or what he was up to, she has been arrested as an accomplice and probable spy. Some other officers were wrestling with her when I was there, she was bellowing at the top of her lungs: something about a gentleman from the Netherlands, and why didn't they go and find him, instead of bothering her?

But there is no trace of that imaginary gentleman.

I stayed a while to listen. Next, she was trying to blame Mrs Fox's maid—as if that charming creature could kill a soul! The maid ain't visible either; vanished.

If Mrs Sorrell can't come up with a better story, given the racket she has been running, as well as harbouring a Froggy spy—and given that she is there and the others ain't—she looks set fair to hang. Filthy old hag. Good riddance. Didn't peg her for a murderer . . . although her cooking was poisonous enough to kill anybody.

What ho.

DD

October 3, 1784
Joshua Coats
Conduit Street
To Lord Frederick Danceacre,
Dieppe

My dear Danceacre,

This brief note is to let you know that all charges against your sister have been dropped. I was able to convince the Grand Jury that she was not the principal in Violet's downfall. She has returned to Hipp Street.

There was a deal of dispute over the identity of the owner of your mother's old house—until pressure was brought to bear on the lawyers. It turned out to have been Mrs Fox, who had bought it incognito! Now she is dead, there will be a probate sale. Persephone intends buying it back with the funds released by your trustee.

Dear Frederick, stop skulking in Dieppe—unless someone is keeping you there. The vile deeds of Earl Much and Mrs Fox have been accounted for. Everyone is satisfied. May they burn in hell.

Come back and stand in for Parson Denyss at my marriage to Clio. Darley agrees.

Your friend,
Joshua Coats

October 20, 1784
Hubert van Essel, Amsterdam
To Frederick Danceacre,
Hipp Street
Mayfair

My dear Frederick,

I am glad to hear of your decision to set up house with your sister. Nothing could give a childless philosopher more pleasure than to see a family reunited, after such trials.

Thank you for your kind offer, to consider Hipp Street as my own home. It is most unlikely that I shall leave Amsterdam ever again—although it would please me to meet you; for it is as if you and the world you move in are familiar, and it would give me joy to set eyes on the children of the woman I once loved.

As you know, my life has been given over to a study of human nature, the endless variety of which no one can fathom. How others live and die provides insights and parallels into our own lives, if we are prepared to read and unravel them.

In a few months I will have the double pleasure of publishing the crowning achievement of my life, my long-awaited treatise, and of marrying the woman who inspired it—who, indeed, could almost be called the author of it. A woman as beautiful as she is dishonest; endlessly tantalising, the only creature in the world whose mind I cannot hope to master. In my life, Frederick, I have loved only two women: one destroyed at the hands of a devil whose destruction became my life's ambition; the other snatched from that same devil's clutches, from the gaping tomb itself, scarce living. Having won her at such cost, I shall not leave her side again.

It is an undoubted truth that more knowledge can be gained from examining the motives and actions that belong to real lives, than from shutting oneself up in perpetual study. My treatise takes the form of a series of letters between imaginary correspondents.

Once published, and so my scholarship concluded, my bride and I plan a brief trip, to Malta to conclude some old business after which we will run a foundation for the advancement of young women.

Before you ask to read my work—as I flatter myself you will—you must know that this work, that can surely only be of interest to scholars and those who choose a contemplative rather than an active life, will be published solely in Holland, in Dutch.

It is the further whim of an old man that it will not be translated during my lifetime, but kept safe, for the edification of future generations.

But then, dearest Frederick, your own life has been so full of experience! On my honour, there is nothing in my treatise that you do not already know, no character that you could not recognise.

God speed.
Doctor Hubert van Essel

Human Nature

A Treatise in Letters

First published in December 1784

Translated from the Original Dutch

BY

Mme STOCKLEY

2005

Glossary

PART ONE

Nutmeg: Costly and versatile. Close-pared into infusions with milk, sweet dishes and meat stews.

Pinchbeck: Alloy of copper and zinc invented by Christopher Pinchbeck, used for flashy shoe buckles for those without pockets to support their pretensions.

Spanish Fly: The luminous wing casings, ground to powder, were believed aphrodisiac.

Cuckold's Point: A big curve of riverbank from Limehouse to Stepney. The land had been granted to a peasant cuckolded by King John, the point itself marked by a pair of horns on a pole and celebrated on 18 October with a fair.

Place Royale: In Paris. Designed by Sully for Henry IV; later renamed Place des Vosges by Napoleon Bonaparte. A very grand address.

Captain Cook: In 1776 Cook lived at 88 Mile End Road, near Spitalfields, before being murdered on expedition in the South Seas.

Holland: Common term for Holland Cloth—cotton, or linen, of exceptional quality and value. Smuggled to the south coast of England as well as being legitimately traded. Holland was considered superior to (and cost twice as much as) Irish linen.

Redriff: Rotherhithe.

Wapping High Street: Famous for whores, inns and gaming, a favourite resort of cheap sluts and sailors.

Silk-weaving and finishing: The centre of fashionable European silk production swung from Italy in the seventeenth century to France (with its later Protestant Huguenot offshoot in London) in the eighteenth. Once-persecuted Huguenot refugees brought to England not only silk-weaving and dyeing skills, but sericulture, which had limited success due to the climate, and was at last given up as a failure, just as Henry IV had in Paris. Spinning a thread (to be woven) from imported raw silk, had been done in Spitalfields but was a dying trade, since importing ready-spun was cheaper. The decline of spinning threw many women into prostitution. The word spinster remains.

Mantua: Usual seventeenth-century term for a gown, which remained current in the eighteenth. It was either corrupted from Manteau or possibly from the eponymous town in Italy, just as Paduasoy was a fine silk cloth [soy-soie] from Padua. Mantua-maker was the normal term for a dressmaker.

Blackamoors: General term for blacks, who, while certainly sometimes Moorish in origin, could also be African, brought over as slaves.

Musselmen: Muslims.

Church Street, Princes Street, Browns Lane: Names at the time. Later renamed Fournier Street, Princelet Street and Hanbury Street.

Chairmen: Two men carrying a sedan chair by means of poles front and back. Accompanied at night by the link boy (a running boy with a light)—since very few streets except major throughfares were lit, most relying on candles in windows. Chairs often ran right into the hallway to pick up and put down their charges, for convenience and safety.

Hand-me-down: Second-hand clothes markets, such as Petticoat Lane, hung garments for sale high up, out of the reach of thieves. They were handed down by means of a pole for inspection.

Tinsel: Derogatory term for pure silver or gold braiding, or galloon. Fashionable on coats and waistcoats until around 1750. By the 1780s out of date, worn by old men clinging to the past. The silver tarnished black and could not be cleaned. Embroidery replaced it for fashionable excess: pre-embroidered panels were sold for waistcoats and coats. Plainer coats, cloth rather than silk, were increasingly in the *ton* (fashionable)—which backlash against conspicuous wealth was in line with the modish theories of Rousseau, (cf *Emile,* 1762) and the earlier ones of Locke.

Powder: A white-powdered head (or powdered wig) was a sign of gentility or indicated an aspiration to it; although among the utterly fashionable there was a movement towards more natural-looking hair, often using tinted powders.

Bells: The Whitechapel Bell Foundry, the most famous foundry in England. Off Whitechapel Road, it still makes bells.

Manty-maker: Mantua-maker; dressmaker.

Somerset House, Strand: The home of the Royal Academy, keenly supported by George III, whose president at the time was Joshua Reynolds.

Calais Packet: Passenger boat bound for Calais (and back).

Bouleversées: Chucked.

Queue: Plaited and ribboned section at the back of a periwig, already outmoded, but retained for servants, legal and military.

Magazine: In their infancy, fashion magazines were replacing dressed miniature dolls as a means of communicating style.

Fleet: The Fleet River, in London (sealed over in 1737); but also the Fleet Prison, and the dodgy practices associated with it, such as Fleet Marriages.

Cow-something: Kauffmann, Angelica (1741–1807). Painter.

Panorama: Referring to a perspective-defying public illusion on curved surfaces, the neologism is not recorded until 1793.

Redingote: The French, taken with the English riding coat, corrupted it to *redingote* (rather like *rosbif*). Snatched smartly back again in England, the word connoted a female riding outfit; sometimes worn to ride but equally a fashionable, closely tailored daytime suit that buttoned left-over-right and was dashing and saucy. To increase the sauciness, tailors, not dressmakers, made these outfits—knowledge of which must have added further piquancy, both at the fitting and to their effect on the male viewer.

Called after an ape: Gibbon's *Decline and Fall of the Roman Empire.*

Magdalen: Charitable foundation for the rehabilitation and social restitution of fallen women.

Metheglin: Old name for mead, an alcoholic drink distilled from honey, often infused with herbs. There were many recipes; most households had their own ingredients and methods.

Marylebone Park: Now Regent's Park.

Plate-glass: Shopping was big business and fashionable, with streets such as Oxford Street full of shops fronted with new, costly large panes of glass (rather than tiny ones), and brightly lit. They often stayed open until 10 PM.

Madame Combien: Mrs How Much.

The politician for whom the hustings are out: Charles James Fox, Whig politician, who was standing for election.

Pup . . . Sire: The Prince of Wales had immense debts that his champion, Charles James Fox, argued in favour of paying off (which would guarantee Fox political favour when the prince later became king). However, King George III (a Tory) detested Fox. The hustings Danceacre mentions were a six-week election being held in Covent Garden, which were just then coming to a close.

The port of Amsterdam: At this time Amsterdam had a fine harbour.

Vide-poche: Literally "empty-pocket"—a little table for keys, loose change etc.

Maestro Buttony: Pompeo Batoni, prolific Italian portrait painter based in Rome, favoured by English gentlemen on the Grand Tour. Batoni saw no reason why tartan could not be painted draped like a Roman toga. His inevitably flattering images produced the effect of ennobling the (generally already noble) sitter. They were vastly popular.

That Shandy man: Laurence Sterne (1713–1768), very popular author of *A Sentimental Journey*, 1768 (an account of European wanderings on a slender wardrobe); and of *Tristram Shandy.*

Nostril: André le Nôtre (1613–1700), King's Gardener to Louis XIV, he designed Versailles and may have advised Charles II on the redesign of St James's Park.

Whipping: Stitching term—way of finishing an edge. Unlike a buttonhole stitch, there is no locking mechanism within the structure of the stitch, so it is quick to do. The same stitch on flat cloth becomes satin stitch.

Clock: Triangular shape in a stocking where the foot section inserts into the leg.

Chapeau-bras: Literally, arm-hat. In everyday usage as English. Described a tricorn hat meant to be carried under the arm rather than worn.

Blue-stockings: Clever, literary women, who were able to mix in some societies, such as certain coffee houses, without adverse reflection on their character. Also to go on the Tour, although generally as part of a group. Artemisia Gentilleschi (1597–1651?), Angelica Kauffmann (1741–1807), Louise-Elisabeth Vigée-LeBrun (1755–1842), Maria Hadfield (1760–1838), author Fanny Burney; artist Mrs Delany, and traveller Sophie de la Roche all qualified. Montagu House provided their focal point.

Trees: Berkeley Square was planted with what are now 30 spectacular plane trees, probably in 1789; Joshua Coats takes the liberty of planning them five years earlier.

Old man . . . hoist on a pony: An equestrian statue of George III.

Galloon: Ribbon or braid.

Poupées: Miniature dolls dressed down to the smallest detail, that came regularly from Paris, from which skilled dressmakers copied styles. They had preceded fashion magazines.

Polard Besh-a-mel: Corruption of *Poulet Béchamel.* From Mary Smith's *The Complete Housekeeper,* 1772.

Madame La Vôtre: Mrs Yours.

The 'Change: The Royal Exchange (which still exists). The precursor to a department store, it had many small booths selling items of ready-made clothing and millinery. A mecca for shopping and sexual intrigue.

Hanging on the wall: Clothes such as dresses—even grand ones—were generally hung by the armholes on simple pegs in the wall. Paintings show clearly that other items, such as aprons and petticoats, were kept folded.

Several thousands of pounds: A vast amount, worth many hundreds of thousands today. A maid might earn twenty pounds a year if she was lucky.

A dirt-coloured felted cape: Like the famous travelling costume of Goethe (which was white), in which that man was painted.

An ell: 45 English inches, so a quarter ell is about 11 inches. Hubert is very tall.

PART TWO

Duchess of Devonshire: Georgiana was said to give kisses for votes in support of Charles James Fox at the hustings in April–May 1784. Very salacious and scurrilous illustrated handbills circulated in coffee houses at the time, hinting moreover that she had 'intimate conversations' (i.e. sex) with Fox.

Tenter ground: A ground used for stretching cloth, which was fixed at the edges with hooks (hence the expression "on tenter hooks"). There was such a ground in Spitalfields at this time.

Beating the Watch: An established sport, as shown in Hogarth's *A Rake's Progress* (1733–1734). In *The Orgy,* the rake has a watchman's lantern at his feet, the spoils of a fight with the Watch. Getting arrested was also a way to a free night's lodging in the Watch House. The Watch (a law-enforcement patrol run by each ward) operated between sundown and 11 PM in certain seasons. Its efficiency, given its openness to bribery and its quitting the streets at precisely the time of night when crime was just warming up, is as debatable now as it was then.

Nail: Measurement of length, that of a standard nail, about two and a quarter inches, or around a thumb's length.

Post-boy: Mail services were proliferating, from slow mail-coaches, which also carried passengers, to private competing agencies running swiftly on relays (for a price). The wealthy could also send their own letters, by servant. Post boys were often older than the name implies (rather like bell-boys).

Affydaffy: Affidavit.

Fancy two-seaters: Fast and flashy two-seat carriage. Light, sporty, expensive.

Strings: Leading strings, strips of cloth sewn to the shoulders of very young children's dresses (unisex) and used to lead them safely along by, like a harness.

Country customs: Mealtimes varied in town and country: In London, the second meal (dinner) could be as late as 4 PM, but was taken much earlier in the country.

Modern methods: Revolutionary systems of farming, such as rotation cropping, increased yield and profitability dramatically. Gainsborough's *Mr and Mrs Andrews* (1748), in which half the canvas is devoted to neat stooks and well-stocked pasture, is the quintessence of a modern family proud of its avant-garde attitude to its fruitful land.

Rhomboids and Rhebuses: Romulus and Remus.

Leather breeches: Making these working garments was a dying trade—it was very hard work, and cloth was superceding it.

Jenever: Gin, from the word for juniper (jenever) often mistaken as Geneva, from where gin was believed to come.

Macaroons: Mrs Sorrell means Macaronis, wildly overdressed upper-class young men of the late 1770s, who sported towering wigs and effeminate dress. Not necessarily stupid—Charles James Fox had been one, when thinner. They were derided by working women such as Mrs Sorrell. But to call Dadson and Coats Macaronis was laughable, the term was dead as a dodo by the 1780s.

Bully: Doormen, usually ex-service men. Bouncers, able to kill and inclined to violence.

Petticoat Lane: Second-hand clothes market in Spitalfields, which still exists, although much reduced.

Counter for Vox'll: The New Spring Garden at Vauxhall, where individually engraved metal counters were issued as season tickets.

German Riff-Raff: The family of George III.

Ton **[Fr., literally *tone*]:** Fashionable people and style; the beau monde. In current use as English.

Drury Lane: The Theatre Royal, Drury Lane, one of the two theatres royal, was redesigned by Greenwood and Capon in 1783, who replaced the existing elegant rococo Adam designs with their own in pea-green and chiaoscuro and pinkish red upholstery, adding the great novelty of "patent lamps" (formerly, the only lighting was provided by candles). A hotbed of vice, prostitutes worked the onstage boxes freely.

Low into his collars: Coachmen often wore greatcoats with several large cape-like collars, to protect against the weather.

The Belle's Stratagem: A comedy by Hannah Cowley, first performed at Covent Garden, in 1780. This clever, oft-performed comedy of mistaken identity and masquerade is here purloined and put on at Drury Lane.

Domino: Enveloping and concealing full-length cloak usually worn at masquerades—practical and charming for either sex, mainly worn in conjunction with a mask. Generally black, but sometimes white.

These officers have no more right to arrest them: Drury Lane theatre's lobby stood on the boundary of two wards, St Martin-in-the-Fields and St Paul's Covent Garden. On the streets, watchmen from one ward would not touch crime in another ward (for example, on the opposite pavement), even if it happened within full view and easy reach. In the unique case of Drury Lane, the line went right down the middle of the lobby. Watchmen from one ward ignored prostitutes and other criminals who had simply crossed over to the other side (the neighbouring ward) to evade arrest.

Livorno: Livorno hat, a fine straw hat with a very wide brim, also called Leghorn, worn with the informal new fashions that were sweeping Europe.

Vis-à-vis [Orig. Fr., *face-to-face*]: A very sporty, jaunty, light carriage in which the two occupants sit face to face. Term used as English.

Feather-cap: Running messenger. These runners often wore winged caps, a nod to the god Mercury—also used centuries later by the American postal service.

Bags: Bag-wigs, the standard wig of an ordinary lawyer (but not a judge), with a short queue at the back tied in a black silk "bag."

Night-men: Removed so-called night-soil from houses. One such successful company in London was run by a woman.

Newgate: Public hangings had formerly been conducted at Tyburn, but recently moved to Newgate Gaol.

Dance in rows: At Newgate mixed-sex groups were often hanged in a line together—hanging until dead, which took some time, while their prolongued and agonised throes gave the appearance of "dancing," to the relish of the packed spectators.

Levée [Fr., literally *rising*]: The daily morning dressing-gossiping-meeting session, held by fashionable men and women. It could be light-hearted, or highly political. Term used as English.

Ranelagh: Pleasure gardens, rival to Vauxhall and considered superior. There were a great many pleasure gardens, offering varying degrees of sophistication, throughout London. The Jew's Harp was one.

Spring Gardens: New Spring Gardens, later called Vauxhall Gardens.

Pantheon: Fashionable assembly rooms on Oxford Street, between Oxford Circus and Tottenham Court Road, popular for dancing and exhibitions, now houses Marks & Spencer.

Balloon: Ballooning began in the 1780s.

New Scotland: Nova Scotia.

Déshabillé [Orig. Fr., literally *undress*]: Rather than nakedness, an alluring peignoir or wrapping gown. Term used as English.

Gloucester: "So wise so young, they say, do never live long.": Shakespeare, *King Richard III*, of the two princes.

Bagnio: Brothel, also Turkish bath.

Rhinoceros: First shown as a curiosity in the mid-eighteenth century, famously recorded in a painting now in Venice.

PART FOUR

Phial of volatile: Sal volatile, solution of ammonium carbonate (smelling salts). A whiff of its potent odour calmed palpitations; too much could kill.

Buckingham House: Later renamed Buckingham Palace. King George III's library was octagonal.

Private conversations: Sexual intercourse.

Fleet: The Fleet prison; but also the filthy river tumbling through London, already being paved over to run underground. *(See also Part One.)*

Bonne-bouche [Fr., literally *good mouthful*]: Tasty morsel, usually sweet; bite-size confectionary.

Saltimbocca [It., literally *jump-in-mouth*]: Tasty morsel, usually savoury.

"A hit, sir, a very palpable hit!": *Hamlet, V ii.*

Wood-eyes: Ancient childish name for woodlice.

Bolt-hole: Slang for whorehouse.

Sort out my water: Water was supplied by different companies, rather as now. In Lincoln's Inn Fields, for example, it was the New River Company. Any complaints about service could be addressed in person at Peel's Coffee House on Tuesdays and Fridays between noon and one. (See *The Soanes at Home* by Susan Palmer.)

Slop-shop: Slang for whorehouse

Tintoretto's *Magdalene*: In the Frare, Venice. Black proves that being a romantic idiot does not preclude being cultivated.

Golden Square: Smart address for a bordello.

Grope Cunt Lane (Later Grub Street): Offered low-class tarts—as the name implies.

Kitty Fisher or Fischer: Daughter of a German staymaker who rose to prominence as one of London's highest-paid courtesans, charging around 100 guineas for her services—an astronomical sum: a footman might earn £2 a year.

The sorts of arts that could get her hanged: Not true—female homosexuality did not attract the death penalty, not being recognised as an activity, let alone a crime.

Ebeniste [Fr., literally *worker in ebony*]: Used for practically any marquetière (master inlayer).

PART FIVE

Abraham: The inappropriate comparison contains inadvertent guilt.

Fewshers: Fuchsias—very rare, very expensive. In 1780, sailor John Westcombe brought the first fuchsias and crysanthemums (from Japan) to a market garden at the Prospect of Whitby.

Stew: Brothel.

The Angel: A coaching inn where people gathered for security in numbers, before setting off together across the fields (now Islington) where highway attacks were frequent.

Faggots: At this time (until 1786) burning was still an occasional, and terrible, death sentence (an alternative to hanging), carried out in public.

Wherry: According to Daniel Defoe (see *Moll Flanders*), wherries, while usually smallish boats, could also be big craft capable of long sea crossings.

David Street: Later renamed Davies Street (W1).

Banyan: Exotically inspired dressing/morning-coat, usually ornate, sometimes frogged, generally of figured silk, worn by upper-class men in company or not at home, frequently with a cap.

Link: Link boy—runner (with torch) accompanying sedan chair.

Paste: Mrs Fox knows full well that Poppy wore real diamonds.

Bills of lad—: Bills of lading. The whore recovered most of Mrs Fox's pearls and valuables by impersonating her at the Customs House. Before passports, possessing the relevant document and sometimes the judicious addition of bribery was usually enough to get through Customs.

Grand Jury: See *Moll Flanders* by Daniel Defoe. A Grand Jury confirmed (or not) a Bill of Indictment by declaring it "found"—the case then went, often very speedily, to trial. The enquiry of the Grand Jury created an opportunity to challenge an indictment. (In Flanders's case, the trial was two days after the Grand Jury.)

A disposition: Favourable evidence presented to the Grand Jury.

Hedge-wigs: Itinerant lawyers practicing their trade at the roadside (often next to the protection of hedges). Used here as an insult.

Molly houses: Male homosexual houses of prostitution.

Vulgar prints: Such as Hogarth's *The Harlot's Progress,* engraved 1732.

Seeds: Seed pearls, freshwater pearls drilled and stitched as part of a complicated embroidery.

PART SIX

Le renard est mort: The fox is dead.

Sallet: Salad.